MAGICAL BEASTS

BOOK ONE

GUARDIAN

THE CHOICE

GEOFFREY SAIGN

Interior design by Lazar Kackarovski

Printed in the United States of America
ISBN: 978-1-077313-49-1

BOOKS BY GEOFFREY SAIGN

Magical Beasts

Guardian: The Choice

Guardian: The Quest

Guardian: The Sacrifice

Guardian: The Stand

Divided Dragons

Wyshea Shadows

Nonfiction

Smile More Stress Less:
A Playful Guide to End Anxiety, Be Calm,
& Achieve Happiness with Awareness

Green Essentials: What You Need to
Know About the Environment

African Cats

Great Apes

Fiction

Jack Steel Action Mystery Thrillers

Steel Trust

Steel Force

Steel Assassin

Steel Justice

Alex Sight Action Mystery Thrillers

Kill Sight

KiraKu

Dark Domain
Jewel
Northern
Seratuk's
Mountain
West Domain
Yakul
Tris
Central Domain
Marsh Domain
Lesser
Assassins
Humka
Southern
Island of
the Merpeople
Death
Pass
Brighthold
Prison

Mad Ones
Dinosaurs
Tarath
Butterfly Warriors
Jade Dragon
Domain
Summoner Farice
Reorielle
Queen Valera
Salete
Old Ones' Domains
Baumel
East Domain
Daesha
Domain
MOS

For Emma V, Theresa, Emma O,
Dennis, & Kathy....

ONE

A GUTTURAL ROAR SPLITS the evening air in the meadow, sending shivers along my bare arms.

I stand rigidly, listening, while I stare across the hundred-yard-wide circular pond at the distant Superior National Forest. Shadows hide everything in the thick woods. The roar was too loud for a bear, too wild and harsh for any animal in northern Minnesota.

My thoughts flash back to the fanged and clawed demon from my nightmares of the last two weeks. Coming to kill me as it does in my dreams. Can't be real. Can't be happening. I try to calm myself by breathing evenly.

Slowly I back up through the waist-high meadow grass, my legs stiff. I focus my gaze across the pond. Ski-tailed emerald dragonflies and red damselflies flit by, as do a few yellow jackets. Mink frogs *creak* from the shoreline. Everything seems normal, except for the roar.

I'm standing at the far eastern edge of Dad's property. I have the staff with me, still wrapped in burlap. *WhipEye*. An odd name. I don't know what it means, or how I know it.

Two specks of gold appear in the distant forest. They look like eyes. The rest of the body is hidden in shadows.

The demon in my nightmares has red eyes, but the gold still freaks me out because two weeks ago a gold tint appeared in my eyes, which are ocean-blue, and then in Jake's eyes. That's also when the staff began calling to me, and when the demon nightmares began. And I've been visiting this meadow more and more for some reason. After two weeks of all of it I feel buried in crazy.

I get out my phone and dial Jake. No signal. I check. No charge. My battery has been bad for a while and needs constant recharging.

Dad is short on money so I didn't want to pressure him about it. *Way to go, Sam! You saved some money, but died.*

The gold eyes move toward me through the trees, about eight feet off the ground. I turn and bolt like a jackrabbit.

The tall grass whips across my bare calves and lower thighs, my tennis shoes quiet on the soft earth. I run over the blackened rectangle of earth—all that's left of our cabin that Rose burned to the ground a year ago.

I'm quickly out of the meadow and into thick forest. It's a half hour sprint back to the house. I can't maintain that, but I have a gut sense that my life depends on it.

Another roar splits the air. Prehistoric. Something closer to a dinosaur. I also sense anger.

My back stiffens and I pump my slender legs harder. Underbrush scratches my exposed skin. The burlap-wrapped six-foot staff in my right hand is slowing me down, making it awkward. But I'll never let it go. It feels like my life depends on it too.

Another roar. Closer. I glance over my shoulder. Something is flying across the pond. Fragments of it appear through the tree trunks, but not enough for me to identify the creature—just bits and pieces of a dark, large shape. Maybe the demon has a twin with gold eyes. The idea that I'm hallucinating is hard to avoid.

My right foot hits a dead branch on the ground and I cry out and stumble forward, trying to prevent a fall. The thought of something landing on my back while I'm on the ground is a huge motivator to remain upright.

Whirling my arms, I manage to regain my balance and keep going. I want to scream for help. No one will hear. I'm too far away.

I'm in okay shape, but still breathing hard. Amped up on adrenaline. I glance over my shoulder again. The creature is flying through the trees, twenty feet off the ground, a hundred yards behind me. I still can't make out the body, but the gold tinted eyes are clear. *Damn*. This can't be happening to me.

Rounding a boulder, I look back—and almost stop. Whatever was chasing me is gone. Where is it?

I run, my heart pounding hard.

Glancing to the sides, red and jack pine block my view—their scent fills the air. I look over my shoulder. Zip. Where is it? I aim myself at a hiding place—I know every inch of Dad's land.

A snarl splits the quiet of the forest. Startled, I look up. Above me a dark shape is flying over the treetops. Again I catch only glimpses through the canopy. How did it appear so suddenly? It's faster than a bird.

Once more I flash back to the demon of my nightmares.

I finally give in to panic and shout as loud as I can, "Jake!"

It's close to dinner. He's cooking lasagna, my favorite. It's August, so the house windows are open. Dad and Cynthia would be in the dining room. One of them has to hear me. Please hear me.

When I look up a second time, the creature has vanished.

A deep snort. Breaking branches behind me.

I veer around a tree trunk and look back. A small birch tree in the distance is knocked over. Another larger pine tree gets bumped and its branches shake. I don't hear the creature's pounding feet. A dark shape hidden in shadows. Freaky.

Circling around a fifteen-foot-high pile of boulders, I hear a loud *thump!* on the other side of it—the beast had to have jumped a hundred feet. Not slowing, I duck into a small opening at ground level in the stone pile.

Dropping to my butt, I scoot back into the side corner of a three-by-three-foot hole. Dragging in the staff, angling it into the opening, I shove it up into a crack between two boulders. Then I pull my knees up to my chest and wrap my arms around them. My long brown hair covers my face. I can't see outside and hope that whatever is chasing me can't see inside.

Something scratches its way across the rocks above me. Claws on stone. A snarl erupts. I sense fury.

Like a little girl hiding from the bogeyman, I close my eyes and quiet my breathing. More scratching across rocks. Then quiet.

I sit still. Sweat covers my skin. My hands are trembling.

Silence.

Not trusting that, I wait five minutes. Then ten. Fifteen. The thing is fast enough to have caught me already. It has to be toying with me—like a cat with a mouse. I could wait it out. I'm only wearing frayed jean shorts and a black tank top—with a Native American design of a dolphin on it—but the nights are warm. I wouldn't get hypothermia.

"Sammy!"

Jake. His voice is unusually high-pitched and he never calls me *Sammy* so he's playing around. He mustn't see the creature. It has to be hiding behind the boulders. Jake is running into a trap.

"Saaamyyy!" Jake follows that with a whistle that sounds like an elk bugle call. For fun he sometimes tries to imitate animal calls.

Slowly leaning forward, I spot him in the distance. Not sprinting, just casually running.

I finger the small jade dolphin on my silver wrist bracelet. Jake gave it to me a year ago on my sixteenth birthday and I never take it off.

Trying to pump myself up, I whisper, "Just do it, Sam," and quickly crawl out, the staff in my hands. My back is crawling with spiders of fear. I expect something to rip my head off from above.

Quickly out on my knees, I stand up fast and whirl. The rock pile is bare, but I can't see behind it. I turn and run.

Jake is still running and he flashes his goofy grin at me, which I fell for long ago. "Why are you hiding?" he calls.

In seconds I'm panting hard, running toward him, waving my hand to go back and mouthing in silence, "Run!"

His smile fades fast. He stops fifty feet away, waiting, his brown eyes glinting gold—another eerie reminder that something is wrong. Our parents brought us to doctors to get tested. But supposedly we're healthy. No one can figure it out.

"What's wrong, Sam?" he asks, his voice quieter.

Keeping my voice soft too, my jaw tight, I gasp, "Run!"

His face scrunches up—which happens when he's worried. I think it's about me, which is comforting.

He's wearing khaki cargo shorts and a banana-yellow tee. His skin tone is a deep brown and his straight hair is jet black. His facial features are defined and balanced in a way which make him look friendly, and handsome. He says he's an American mutt, with a blend of eight ethnicities, including German, Native American, Spanish, and Guatemalan.

He turns before I arrive and easily keeps pace with me. He's a fluid runner. We sprint beside each other and I feel a tiny bit safer. At six feet, he has five inches on me and his arms are strong.

"What's the hurry, partner?" he whispers.

"Did you see anything on the boulders or in the trees when you were running toward me?" I look over my shoulder, to the sides, and above us.

"Nothing, babe. What's wrong?"

He uses terms of endearment with me sometimes. I don't mind. I've had a crush on him for as long as I've known him. He's my best friend and I can't imagine my life without him.

"Something's chasing me." Jittery from head to toe, I keep my gaze roving.

"Are you sure?"

"I'm not making this up, Jake."

He frowns and glances over his shoulders and around in the forest. He's good at picking out details, but I don't feel any better when he says, "Just a squirrel to the east. You know all the wildlife in this region. What do you think it was?"

"I don't know." How could something that large just disappear? It would have to be very very fast. Fast enough to catch us without effort.

"A bear or cougar?" he offers.

"Much bigger. And flying." I expect him to look at me like I'm crazy, but instead he bites his lip and continues to glance around us as we run.

"We should talk, Sam."

"Absolutely."

Another roar erupts in the forest.

"That's a freaking monster!" Jake's eyes widen and he picks up the pace, forcing me to run all out to keep up.

I don't think we're going to have time to talk.

TWO

THE ROARS CHASE US all the way to Dad's ten fenced acres holding *Green's Wildlife and Sanctuary Shelter* for injured animals.

My arms are still shaking as I shut the gate behind us and peer through the ten-foot-tall chain-link fence. Nothing in the trees or sky. Yet I feel like I'm being watched. I also feel a little less crazy because Jake can hear the creature too. The roars are getting closer. It's coming. Whatever the creature was holding out for, I think it's done waiting.

The female Canadian lynx and male bobcat are standing up in their large pens on either side of me, hissing as they stare at the forest behind the fencing.

"Come on, Sam!"

I whirl and sprint after Jake across the back acre, past the old greenhouse. The other animals are all standing alert in their pens along the fence, and some of the hawks are screeching.

Jake stops abruptly, putting his arm in front of me as three white-tailed deer bolt by in front of us. We keep running as the deer bound to the northwest fence corner and huddle wide-eyed with the others, their ears and tails straight up.

Our houses are on a dead-end dirt road. With only a few neighbors it's secluded and quiet for the animals, but it also means we don't have anyone else to go to for help.

Running up the porch steps, I give one more glance at the forest and sky.

Jake looks too, and whispers, "I'm freaking out, Sam."

"You and I need to talk before we say anything weird to Dad and Cynthia," I whisper.

Jake stares at me, and then nods. "Alright."

Entering the back door, I hustle down the extra-wide hallway running from the back door to the front. Halfway down, I set the staff against the wall just outside the dining room entrance. I don't want to answer questions about WhipEye, at least not yet. Dad thinks our elderly renter, Rose, gave me the staff, but I don't remember that either.

When I enter the dining room, Dad and Cynthia are staring out the north window. Soft music is playing and the table is set with place settings and food.

Dad turns, frowning. A mop of sandy hair, jeans, and a T-shirt cover his lean body. "Did you see what's roaring out there, Sam?"

"You heard it too?" I feel better just knowing that he heard it.

"Of course we did. Did you see it, Sam?"

I shake my head and grip the back of a chair with both hands.

Dad looks at all of us. "It could be a sick bear. They can amp up their roars so much they don't even sound like bears anymore."

"It's not a bear, Dad!" I blurt. "Way bigger. Megafauna. Something larger than anything we have around here. I also saw it flying. It's huge."

I decide then and there that I have to tell everyone about the demon nightmares and the staff calling to me. It sounds desperate and heavy, and we're supposed to be celebrating Jake's seventeenth birthday and Dad and Cynthia's engagement. I also kind of wanted to figure out the nightmares and staff on my own, but the appearance of the creature doesn't give me any choice now.

"Sam, you know every animal on the planet, so what's your best guess?" Cynthia brushes back her black bangs, her brown eyes steady. Tall and slender, her sharp-featured face is calm, her skin a light brown.

"It stayed far enough above the trees or behind me so I never could make it out clearly. But whatever was chasing me had gold-tinted eyes, like Jake and me." I look at her and Dad, working out what to say.

Dad stares at me. He knows I don't make things up.

“I’m calling work, then the police.” Cynthia is already dialing her phone.

Relieved, I wait.

A US Fish and Wildlife agent, Cynthia specializes in illegally trafficked exotic animals. She came straight from work and is wearing a white blouse, slacks, and a blue blazer that conceals her gun.

In moments she pulls her phone down. “I can’t get a signal.”

Dad tries his phone next. He shakes his head, frowning. “No signal.”

I stiffen. “Mine’s dead. No charge.”

Jake quickly has his phone in hand. In seconds he says, “Me neither!” He motions toward the front of the house. “Let’s take Mom’s SUV and get out of here!”

A loud *crunch!* splits the air. It came from outside and we all stare toward the front of the house. A second crash occurs before we scramble to the front big bay window.

In the driveway the roofs of Cynthia’s SUV and Dad’s pickup truck are both smashed down to the door handles, as if someone dropped a wrecking ball on top of each of them. Undriveable.

"What the heck?" exclaims Dad.

Cynthia gasps.

“That’s impossible,” murmurs Jake.

“The creature knew we might try to drive away.” I look at everyone. “This thing is intelligent.” It makes the demon theory even more plausible, and scary.

“Should we run for town?” Jake backs up from the window.

We all turn to him and exclaim together, “No!”

Jake raises both hands. “All right, bad idea. Glad you all agree.”

The front bay window darkens, taking all of our attention. Another roar sends us backing up.

A loud *bang!* occurs and the west wall of the dining room pushes in slightly. We all stare wide-eyed at the wall.

Cynthia unbuttons her blazer and I can see her gun. She and Dad exchange glances.

"Let's stay calm." Dad talks quickly. "We'll shut and lock doors and windows. Cynthia and I will take the lower level, Sam and Jake you take the second floor. Stay out of view. Predators usually react to movement."

"Windows won't stop this thing." Jake looks pale. "Neither will doors."

Dad nods. "True. But predators sometimes don't want to go through glass or closed openings."

The west wall is banged again, and Dad and Cynthia whirl to face it. Cynthia pulls her gun, holding it alongside her thigh.

Dad turns to us. "Go!"

"Got it, Dad!" I run out of the room with Jake, grabbing WhipEye as I do. As I leave, I trip on a hall rug and nearly fall. "Klutz," I mutter.

I hurry across the hallway and bound up the wide staircase. Our house is old and everything is mansion-spacious, including the rooms. My arms are stiff as I pull on the rickety railing.

We hustle into Dad's bedroom first. It's a large room, and his balcony doors are wide open. Cautiously we sidle along the walls up to the doors on both sides, and peek out. Nothing. Quickly we swing the doors shut and lock them.

We run into my bedroom next. A mosaic of thousands of photos of wild animals and massive trees like sequoia, redwood, and Douglas fir cover my bedroom walls. Mom helped me create it over the years. She loved big trees and she had a gift with wild animals.

I set the staff against my bed and crouch behind my painting easel to peek out the window. Seeing nothing, I close the east window, while Jake takes the south. Finished, I see Jake slowly backing up, staring at a shadow outside his window.

I stop near my bed, watching. Waiting. I glance at WhipEye. Some of the burlap has fallen away from the top of it.

The chestnut-colored staff is the most beautiful thing I've ever seen. Two inches thick, it has dozens of exquisitely carved, lifelike miniature animal heads along its outer surface. The animal faces seem familiar to me, beyond just recognizing the species of reptiles, birds of prey, and mammals. It's strange that I can't recall how I obtained something so stunning.

The shadow outside the window disappears, and Jake is quickly beside me.

He glances at me, keeping one eye on the windows. "Okay," he says softly. "You wanted to talk, let's talk. Fast. Why did you bring the staff into the forest?"

"I really don't know." I haven't brought it out of my closet for a year, but the staff has been calling to me for two weeks now—reaching into my marrow—as if to say *Hold me!* I've resisted doing that because something equally as strong inside said *Don't!* I finally gave in to it today.

"Do you ever feel it...like...you know...calling to you?" Jake's hands whirl.

I swallow on a dry mouth. "Okay, the staff has been driving me crazy for weeks."

He lifts an eyebrow. "Why didn't you tell me?"

"I didn't want to sound crazy. What was I supposed to say? Hey, Jake, guess what? A stupid staff is calling to me."

"You can always share anything with me, Sam. You know that. Even if it is crazy."

I realize something then. "So the staff has been calling you too? Why didn't *you* tell me?"

"Like you said, it sounded crazy."

"Dork."

I finally notice the new tattoo on his left forearm. He told me he was going to get one for his birthday. A black dragon. That bothers me for some reason.

Jake's forehead furrows. "My sleep has been twisted for weeks."

"Mine too."

He chews his lip. "I've tried talking to you for weeks."

"I haven't been the best listener." My jaw clenches.

"This is going to sound really spooky." He glances at both windows, and we can hear Cynthia and Dad downstairs, their voices soft. "I've had scary dreams during the daytime for two weeks." He stops to check out my expression. "That makes me sound like a little kid, right?"

"About five."

"I was hoping for ten to twelve."

His words bring back the image of the demon nightmare in full force. And the creature outside. The sense of danger is almost overpowering now, as if I'm standing on railroad tracks facing a racing locomotive and can't get out of the way. "Do the dreams feel like daydreams or visions?"

"I'm not sure." He gestures to nothing in particular. "But they're more than just dreams." His hands swirl wildly. "It was intense today. I had three! I think I'm hallucinating. And I'm not on any medication." He looks thoughtful. "Though I did have a lot of maple syrup at breakfast today. Buckwheat blueberry pancakes."

"Jake!"

His hands stop. "Did I say the dreams are creepy?"

"Can't be worse than mine," I mutter.

"Oh yeah? What—"

He's interrupted by a loud creak on the roof. Something massive just settled on top of the house. We both stare at the bedroom ceiling. Quiet.

Jake's face tightens and he points an index finger up and down several times at the ceiling. We back up toward the bedroom door.

I have to keep talking or I'm going to scream. "Okay, weird dreams during the day. And?"

Jake nods vigorously. "You and I are on top of a hill. It's dark and stormy and there are all kinds of huge creatures. Monsters. Dragons." He stops to face me. "It feels real. Isn't that weird?"

The hair on the back of my neck is standing on end. He's starting to freak me out even more because that's how the demon image felt when I woke up this morning. Real. "Okay, that is weird."

"I know, right? It gets worse. There's a monster two-headed cobra and a giant demon of some kind."

I gape at him. "Is the demon a woman with fangs, claws, red eyes, and a tattered black cloak?"

"That's it!" he exclaims.

We stare at each other.

"How can we both be dreaming about the same freaking demon for two weeks?" I'm relieved that I'm telling him, and even more relieved that I'm not the only one experiencing all the crazy stuff.

"You think we have a psychic heart link? Like we're connected at the soul level?" He looks earnestly at me.

"Doubtful, Romeo."

He eyes the ceiling. "How come you didn't tell me about the nightmares?"

I shrug. "I thought it sounded crazy."

"Loser." His hand cuts the air. "It makes no sense. Gold-tinted eyes, demon dreams, and the staff calling us—all in the last two weeks." His voice is a whisper. "Do you think the demon is outside? On the roof?"

"It crossed my mind."

"This is so freakin' insane." His voice lowers. "In my dreams it feels like we're going to die, Sam."

"Same here."

"Sam." Jake points out the east window, his eyes wide.

I see something flash by outside, but what I focus on is WhipEye. The sudden urge to hold the six-foot staff makes my hands sweat.

I step toward it, but stop as the sound of splintering wood and breaking glass fills my ears. A giant green foot with black claws tears through the side of the house, shredding the animal photographs on the wall. My dresser falls over, but my legs won't move. At least I was wrong. It's not a demon. I wish it was a dream though, because it's way too vivid. And huge.

THREE

"YOU'RE SEEING THIS, RIGHT, Sam?"

I blink. "Komodo dragon, a.k.a. *Varanus komodoensis*."

"No way! A dragon," whispers Jake, his eyes round. "A real live dragon."

I recognize the mottled, reddish-gray bumpy skin of the monitor lizard, but Komodo dragons rarely reach ten feet in length. This one's forty, and bulky, as if it's on steroids. He's the size of a small truck and must weigh eight tons. And has wings.

"No wonder the cars were flattened," I murmur. All my worry, tension, and fear sink into my stomach like a heavy rock. Facing something factual—even if it's surreal and can kill me—feels better than having my imagination run wild.

From five feet away the Komodo glares at me with its two large golden eyes. Slobber drools from its open toothy jaw. Slowly beating its wide leathery wings, the lizard flicks out its yellow forked tongue, nearly touching my chest. I can't move. At first I think it's fear, but then I realize I'm paralyzed somehow by its gaze. When I try, I can't budge my head even a millimeter left, right, up, or down.

However my right hand actually moves of its own accord from my side toward the bed. It's as if the staff is screaming my name now, telling me to grab it, and pulling my hand toward it. I want to hold WhipEye in the worst way, but I still can't move my feet.

The dragon floats a little closer and I can see its sixty teeth, serrated like a shark's, white and eight inches long. I think I'm going to pee my shorts.

"Run, Sam!" shouts Jake.

I can't move and he grabs my arm and pulls me back two steps, finally breaking the Komodo's spell.

The lizard pushes its oblong skull into the room, its breath reeking of decayed flesh. Sweeping its head left to right, the Komodo appears to be searching for something. Its gaze rests on the staff.

My mind is a frenzy of jumbled thoughts and panic, but I pull away from Jake, jump toward the bed, and reach for the staff.

"Leave it, Sam!" Jake backpedals toward the bedroom door.

There's no way I can do that. The burlap sack falls away and my hand curls like iron around WhipEye.

Hissing, the lizard uses its front feet to tear a bigger hole in the wall, forcing itself into my bedroom. In three clumsy steps I'm almost past the Komodo's wagging head, but it lunges at me. I'm not going to make it. I stare like a raccoon in headlights at a toothy mouth large enough to take me whole.

Jake grabs my arm and jerks me out of the lizard's reach. I hear its teeth snapping together and feel a rush of air hitting my back from its closing mouth. Then I'm running like a rabbit from a wolf, the hair on my neck on end.

The Komodo gives a low rumble as shouts erupt downstairs.

I fly through the door behind Jake. Our parents are running up the stairs side by side. Both have taut faces.

Jake waves at them. "Go back!"

"Run!" I yell, flapping my arm.

"Sam?" Dad keeps coming, his eyes searching for the crashing lizard he can't see.

Cynthia's eyes widen and she's holding her gun in both hands.

A snarl erupts from my bedroom.

Our parents freeze when my bedroom doorframe explodes outward as the Komodo plows its head and shoulders through, leaving the opening three times larger. Wings folded, the creature roars as its dagger-sized claws scrape across the landing, tearing deep grooves in the worn oak floor. Too wide for the hallway, the lizard's bulky torso smashes into the railing, sending splintering wood falling to the first floor.

"What the..." Dad doesn't finish.

Cynthia fires three times.

Bullets zing off the Komodo's hide. The lizard's eyes flare bright gold and it keeps coming.

"Come on!" Dad yanks Cynthia down the stairs. Following them, Jake and I jump down several steps at a time. I stumble at the bottom, but Jake grabs my arm before I fall. I'd hug him but I'm too worried about dying.

Dad rounds the stairway wall into the hallway and yanks open a closet door. "Sam, the storage cellar!"

"Got it, Dad!" I run past him with Jake, my tennis shoes pounding the wood floor. At the back door I stop abruptly. I lost Mom two years ago and it took me a year to recover. I can't lose Dad too. And Jake already lost his father so he'll never walk away from his mother. He stops beside me.

The Komodo growls, but he's not visible. WhipEye is practically burning my hand. A name floats into my awareness but I can't focus.

Cynthia takes a wide stance in the hallway, holding her gun in both hands. Pulling a shotgun and a box of shells from the closet, Dad stands next to her, jamming slugs into the gun. He owns the gun to warn off bears, but I've never seen him hurt anything.

The bottom of the stairway wall bulges out, and the Komodo smashes through headfirst, falling into the hallway onto its side. The lizard fills the hallway to eight feet high. Plasterboard dust drifts into the air. The Komodo's head is inches from Cynthia's gun and its long tail thrashes near the front door. Stuck, the lizard goes still for a moment.

Cynthia fires once. Unharmed, the Komodo hisses and wiggles, pulling itself sideways through the hallway with its claws tearing into the opposite wall. Dad yanks Cynthia back from falling ceiling lumber.

"Run, Dad!" I shout.

"Come on, Mom!" Jake motions frantically.

Dad steps in front of Cynthia. The lizard closes its eyes as my father fires the shotgun. The blast is deafening, but the pellets don't even mark the dragon's face.

Our parents turn and run.

I whirl, shove open the screen door, and bolt through it. Jake is right behind me. My legs are shaky as I race across the wooden porch and down the steps. Forest runs up to the backyard fence on three sides of the shelter acres, and the cellar is to the far right. I run across the lawn, but stop when I hear a hiss.

The back door explodes outward, a big chunk of the adjoining wall coming with it. We all duck flying debris, and the startled deer on the other side of the yard bunch together, their eyes wide. Lowering its head, the Komodo leaps across the porch and down to the grass, landing in silence. Impossible.

The bobcat and lynx yowl from their pens at the back of the yard.

My heart is beating wildly. There's nowhere to hide. Sweat streams down my face. My right hand holds the hot staff and it feels like it's on fire now.

Their guns raised, Cynthia and Dad stand in front of Jake and me. We all keep backing up as the lizard plods toward us.

The Komodo halts abruptly, eyeing me, its head above Dad's. "The staff, guardian, or your elders die." The lizard's voice is male and guttural.

Cynthia and Dad gape at the dragon. I do too. A talking beefy Komodo. And why is it calling me *guardian*?

"Give it to him, Sam!" Jake gives an emphatic wave.

Our parents stare wide-eyed at me.

Jake chops the air with his hand. "Now, Sam!"

"Sam?" Dad keeps an eye on the Komodo while glancing at me.

I want to give the staff to the Komodo, but hesitate. Fear for Dad and Cynthia churns through me, along with the overwhelming desire to keep the staff. All of my emotions are mixed up. Panic. Confusion. My hand clenches reflexively around WhipEye. Heat sears my skin.

I *have* to save Dad so I whisper, "Just do it, Sam."

Mom always said those words to help me face scary things. But instead of loosening, my fingers tighten so hard on the wood that it hurts. I *can't* do it. WhipEye won't allow it. That terrifies me.

My eyes are drawn to the carved face of a caracal on the staff. One of the ten African species of wild cats. The name that came to me in the house repeats like a shout in my brain; *Tarath!* WhipEye is thrumming deep inside my bones. I've fallen into its spell as I lift it and slam it into the ground. *Boom!*

The surprisingly loud echo carries far into the distance. Having no clue what will happen, I shout, "Tarath!"

My grasp loosens on the staff and WhipEye spins once, stopping when the caracal's head is in front of me. The African cat's face glows brightly and her jaws and eyes open like a real animal as she hisses loud enough to make my ears ring.

"What the?" I'm gaping as energy pours from the staff into my hand and WhipEye rotates again.

A golden stream of light streaks from the chestnut rod, past the Komodo's snapping jaws, stopping above the patio. A reddish cat materializes there, ten feet high at the shoulder, lithe and muscular, her long, black triangular ears topped with black tufts of fur. Entranced over the caracal's beauty, I also want to cheer for the giant cat.

Dad and Cynthia stare at the caracal with wide eyes and mouths.

"Tarath," murmurs Jake. He pumps a fist. "Yeah!"

I know why he's excited, because I'm experiencing what he is—I think. I know who Tarath is—at least I recognize her and her name. Another word floats into my memory...*KiraKu*. I can't focus on that though as the caracal snarls and leaps unnaturally fast onto the back of the Komodo, slashing the lizard's hide with her claws.

The Komodo flicks its tail at her, but Tarath jumps twenty feet to the other side of the beast. The lizard's red wounds are already healing as the big cat lands on all fours, lowers her head, and stalks the dragon. The speed of both animals is beyond what should be possible, especially for their size.

The Komodo eyes our parents.

I remember the lizard's threat and shout, "Get back, Dad!"

"Move, Mom!" yells Jake.

The Komodo turns toward Tarath, its left foot sweeping forward in a blur before our parents can blink.

I can't see the blow, but Dad's and Cynthia's arms drop, their guns falling from their limp hands. They both collapse like ragdolls into the grass.

I stare at Dad, my lips going numb, and then give a wild yell and run forward.

"Mom!" Jake rushes toward her, his legs pumping beside me.

Holding WhipEye waist-high like a pole-vaulter, I pass Dad and ram it into the Komodo's side. It's like hitting a concrete wall, but golden energy shoots along the staff, crackling against the lizard's body. The monster jumps several yards away from me. I'm not sure if WhipEye shoved the Komodo or if he moved under his own power.

Roaring, the Komodo whirls to face me. Tarath charges.

The lizard snaps his tail at the cat. Leaping over the beast, Tarath rakes her extended rear claws over the Komodo's torso, again leaving red gouges in its hide. The wounds immediately begin to heal.

Tarath lands on the other side of the dragon. "Leave, Lesser, or you'll feel more than my claws." Her voice is velvety, but powerful.

"I don't fear you, Great One." The Komodo stares at me, slobber dripping from its mouth.

"Great One," I whisper. I think all the faces carved into WhipEye are Great Ones, and that I've called them before. But I'm not sure. My whole world feels upside down, as if I'm waking from a dream into another world that I don't recognize.

Keeping an eye on the Komodo, Jake drops to his knees beside his mother and checks her pulse.

Sirens blare in the distance, but I keep my gaze on the lizard. The Komodo lifts his head in the direction of the sirens, as if gauging them. Snarling, he lunges at me, his wings unfolding while he opens his jaws and lowers his head.

"Watch out, Sam!" yells Jake.

I fling myself sideways onto the grass, pulling WhipEye out of reach of the lizard's snapping jaws. The beast keeps going, leaping up.

Tarath springs vertically after it, but the Komodo's flapping wings lift it fifty feet in one beat, inches beyond the caracal's swinging claws. Tarath falls back to the ground, landing silently on the grass. She snarls up at the Komodo.

Hissing, the lizard hovers above us. His eyes bore into mine. "If you want to save your elders, bring the staff to Gorgon. Today. Alone. Or they die." Shifting his gaze to Tarath, he says, "We'll meet again, Great One."

Tarath yowls while the Komodo quickly flies away, giving a faint roar before it fades in the distance.

"Mom." Jake rests his hand on his mother's shoulder. She appears unconscious.

Scrambling over the lawn to Dad, I press trembling fingers against his neck. He has a pulse. Jagged cuts on his thighs have darkened his jeans with blood. The same ugly slashes mark Cynthia's legs. The wounds appear serious enough for stitches, but not life–threatening. In fact when I examine Dad's cuts closer, they've already stopped bleeding. Komodo bites can be deadly due to venom, but I'm not sure about claw wounds.

Jake looks bewildered. "Why didn't you give the staff to the Komodo, Sam?"

My throat thickens. "I couldn't." It sounds lame, even to me. With one decision everything in my life is in shambles. And I have no one to blame but myself.

Tarath surprises me when she shrinks to five feet tall while padding toward us. Lowering her head between our parents, she sniffs the air. "Poison," she spits.

FOUR

JAKE LOOKS UP AT Tarath. "Can you heal Mom?"

My stomach tightens, my voice desperate. "Please, help us." I have no idea what the cat is capable of, but I remember how fast the Komodo healed when he was cut by her claws.

"It's an ancient poison," she says. "If I try to heal them, it might make things worse."

My throat feels like chalk. "The Komodo said to bring WhipEye to Gorgon today. Who's Gorgon?" The escalating mysteries ramp up the tension in my neck.

"A Lesser." Tarath eyes us intently, the light breeze ruffling her coat. "There's a war coming, Samantha and Jake, and everyone on both sides will be coming for WhipEye now."

"War?" The caracal is making it sound like we're in the middle of it. That adds to the tension in my neck. "Why do they want WhipEye?"

"What's a Lesser?" Jake's face is strained. "How do you know us?"

"Answers will have to wait." Tarath turns her head toward the house.

The sirens go quiet and I can hear vehicles skidding to a stop in front of our home. We live in a small town in northern Minnesota so I'm not surprised the police got here this fast. I'm relieved. They can help our parents.

Jake turns back to Cynthia with tears on his face as he whispers, "I'll save you, Mom. I promise. No matter what."

I've never seen him cry and it turns my arms to jelly. My eyes mist over Dad too. I hear voices in the house, but ignore them as I look up at the silent caracal. The Komodo called her a Great One so she has to know a way to save our parents. "What can we do, Tarath?"

She doesn't answer, but her caracal body melts away as she morphs into a woman with long red hair. Shocked over her transformation, I gape at her. She's beautiful, soft-featured. About thirty. Barefoot, she's wearing jeans and a jean jacket over a white blouse—I can't tell where her skin ends and her clothing begins.

She steps closer, her voice still velvety and smooth. "Do you have an aunt, Samantha?"

Dumbfounded, I nod. "Aunt Sue, Dad's sister in Florida."

Tarath speaks gently. "I'll pretend to be her. I can't stay long, but I'll try to help you."

"Thanks." It calms my panic that she'll stay with us a little longer. Since she fought the Komodo I trust her, and feel as if I should know more about her. "Have we met before?"

Jake stands, his hands trembling at his sides. "Will Mom die?"

Again Tarath doesn't answer either of us, but instead she wraps her arms around Jake.

I grip WhipEye and pull myself to my feet, slumping a little. I think using the staff tired me out.

Men and women dressed in camouflage uniforms, berets, and boots run through what's left of the back door and through the gate at the side of the house, carrying what look like Taser rifles and flamethrowers. I'm surprised they don't have guns.

My thoughts swirl. I expected police and EMTs, not the army. There's no military base nearby, but maybe they spotted the Komodo dragon on radar and followed it.

"Over here!" I wave to them. "Our parents are hurt."

"Hurry up!" Jake motions rapidly too.

The soldiers ignore us and spread out across the back acres, facing the forest in combat poses with their weapons raised.

A man carrying a holstered Taser pistol arrives on the porch, his blunt face hard. Built like a tank, he has short gray hair and gray eyes. He walks down the steps, speaking with the authority of an officer. "Stay alert, soldiers."

Two soldiers follow him, carrying a black, seven-foot-long slender metal box. Beside them walks a tall man with glasses and civilian clothing.

Setting the long box on the grass in front of me, the soldiers open it. Lined with thick steel, the shape of the empty padded depression inside tightens my stomach. I step back.

"Help our parents," I plead.

The soldiers continue to ignore me.

"Hey, are you deaf?" Jake's hands whirl.

"I'm Colonel Macy." The officer eyes me. "We'll help your parents as soon as you surrender the weapon, Samantha Green."

My hand tightens on WhipEye. "How do you know my name? And I don't have a weapon."

Six soldiers point their Tasers at Tarath, while another soldier steps toward me, reaching for WhipEye. I yank it back. Someone grips my shoulders from behind and I try to pull away.

"Leave her alone." Jake charges the soldier behind me, but another soldier fires a Taser pistol at his back and he goes down, trembling.

"Jake!" Seeing him take a Taser for me sends adrenaline into my limbs and I elbow the soldier behind me. But two more soldiers push me to the ground onto my back. I'm not that strong, but it takes a third man to pry my fingers off WhipEye one at a time. My heart pounds when they finally pull the staff from my hands. Blood rushes to my ears.

"No," I gasp. "You can't."

When they place WhipEye in the open metal box and close it, I go limp. I want to yell at them. I can still feel the staff calling to me, burrowing into my mind and heart with the desire to hold it.

The civilian man kneels and locks the case with a key hanging from a thin black chain around his neck. "Amazing." He stands, looking at all of us with curiosity.

The soldiers zip tie Jake's wrists behind his back and pull him to his feet, while the soldiers holding me roll me onto my stomach and zip tie my wrists behind me too. Breathing hard, my face in the grass, I'm suddenly exhausted. I stare at the box holding the staff.

Tarath's brow wrinkles. "It's all right, Samantha."

Colonel Macy motions to Tarath. "You're a threat to this country and we'll Taser you if you show any resistance." He pauses. "Our rifle Tasers have a thousand times the power of standard pistol Tasers. They're lethal. Even to you."

"I'm a threat?" Tarath appears calm.

"She's my aunt from Florida." I struggle to sit up and soldiers pull me to my feet.

"That's a lie, Samantha." Colonel Macy gives me a grim stare. "We have photographs of your aunt."

I'm too stunned to reply.

Jake glares at the colonel. "She was helping us."

"Then, young man, you've picked dangerous company to keep. We've had this house under surveillance for a week with cameras inside and out." Colonel Macy wags a finger at Tarath. "You're a monster. We just filmed you changing." He points at the sky. "And that lizard is being tracked."

Three Army helicopters appear to the north, heading southeast in the direction the Komodo flew.

"I see," Tarath says coolly.

The tall man steps in front of Tarath. "My name is Dr. Spiel. We're excited to talk to you. I hope we can be friends."

Tarath eyes him. "Friends don't threaten each other."

"Yes, I'm sorry about that." Spiel sounds like he actually means it.

Colonel Macy lifts his chin to his men. "Take her away."

Four soldiers escort Tarath through the gate at the side of the house, their weapons aimed at her back. Dr. Spiel follows.

"She hasn't done anything wrong." Jake watches her leave.

I expect Tarath to change into a Great One and fight, but instead she walks away, her head erect. Maybe high-powered Tasers are more dangerous than bullets for Great Ones.

Whirling to Colonel Macy, I say, "You're making a mistake."

"I never make mistakes," snaps Macy.

Medics arrive. I tense as they check our parents' vital signs, place field bandages on their wounds, and transfer them onto stretchers.

When they carry them around the house, no one stops me from shuffling beside Dad. Jake walks next to Cynthia.

Dad's face is pale. The word *poison* crowds out everything else in my head. The side of the house looks like a wrecking ball hit it, but my attention is focused on my father. In front of the garage Colonel Macy clamps a heavy hand on my shoulder. "That's far enough, Samantha."

Jake is next to me, his face scrunched up as he watches them load Cynthia into an ambulance.

I turn to Macy, numb inside. "Where are you taking our parents?"

"The hospital. I'm not irresponsible." He taps his thigh. "And you're both coming with us."

I watch as they carry Dad down the driveway to a second ambulance. Mom's tall lilac bushes partially hide Tarath. She's standing in the street, her hands cuffed behind her and her feet shackled. My spirits plummet. Glancing at me calmly, she gives the tiniest of nods, and then takes small steps up a ramp into the back of a large armored truck. I swallow. I called her here so I feel responsible for whatever happens to her.

The ambulances take off, sirens blaring.

Colonel Macy gestures to his soldiers. "Keep Jake under restraint. You can release Samantha." He eyes us. "Both of you pack some things for an overnight."

Jake glares at Macy, but I know he wants to see Cynthia as badly as I want to see Dad. He glances at me, and then four male soldiers escort him across the street to his house.

Two of Macy's female soldiers escort me through the front door. I pick my way through the debris up to my bedroom, where one of the soldiers cuts off my zip tie.

My room reminds me of my destroyed happiness. Books, my painting, and the smashed dresser lie scattered across the wood floor, which has deep gouges in it. The distant forest is visible through the large, jagged hole in the wall.

One of the soldiers says curtly, "You have two minutes, miss."

I find a small duffel bag in the closet and stuff it with a change of clothes. While searching through the floor debris for my waterproof watch, I spot a plain gold ring. I've had it a long time. Somehow I know the ring is important. I palm it to hide it from the soldiers and pick up a family photo that's nearly torn in two.

In the picture Mom is smiling at me. When I was much younger, she used to play a game with me by naming an animal followed by a.k.a. Then I'd give the scientific name or some fun facts. Eventually we became more creative with it. Now it's a way to remember her. I play the game with Jake sometimes and like that we're close that way. I hope we still are.

I place the photo in my bag and strap on my watch. I'm about to leave when I spy my compass partly buried beneath scattered animal books.

Mom gave me the compass two years ago on my fifteenth birthday, the day she died saving my life from a hit-and-run SUV driver. Set in a gold ring, it's palm-sized with a gold needle set over a black face beneath the glass. All the numbers and directional marks are in gold letters. The outer crystal rim sparkles and four words are inscribed in gold cursive lettering on the edge of the inner black face: *Trust* at east and west, *Love* at north, and *Mom* at south. *Trust Love. Trust Mom.*

I haven't touched the compass in a long while, but I feel a strong urge to take it with me. I sling the leather string over my head so the compass rests against my chest. I'm immediately comforted. Wherever Mom is, she loves me. I hang on to that idea.

The soldiers hustle me downstairs. Then I'm escorted to an armored car that has a large Taser turret mounted on top of it. They gesture me in and I take a seat.

In minutes Jake enters. A zip tie still binds his wrists behind his back. Slumping onto the bench across from me, he lifts his chin to me in acknowledgment. He looks as if he can't decide if he should hit someone or cry. It unsettles me to see him in pain.

Colonel Macy enters, sitting beside me. Two more soldiers join us, one facing Jake, one facing me, both with pistol Tasers aimed at us.

Our vehicle is wedged between two other armored cars, and they all follow the truck holding Tarath. My thoughts turn dark. I'll never be able to live with myself if my refusal to give the staff to the Komodo costs my father his life.

Jake's eyebrows hunch. "Why is the Army here?"

Colonel Macy's voice is crisp. "We want you to tell us everything, Jake." He leans forward. "You can trust us. We want to help. We'll do everything possible to make sure your parents recover."

I don't believe anything he says. "Why were you spying on my house?"

"Not just yours, Samantha." He sits back. "We've been watching both of you. We're a special military branch. A tactical squad called VIPER. Versatile Intel to Protect, Engage, and Respond. Today we gathered the evidence we've been waiting for."

"It's not legal to spy on civilians." Jake glares at Macy.

"You jammed our cell phone signals." My voice has an edge. "We could have gotten help."

Colonel Macy's voice hardens. "Police and any other agencies have no jurisdiction here. We've been given special authority to respond to imminent threats to our country."

Jake frowns. "We haven't done anything wrong."

"Like we're a national threat." I suddenly worry Macy will search me and take the ring and my compass. "You're saying two teenagers are a danger to the country?"

The colonel stares at us coldly. "There was an incident last year at Sequoia National Park." He leans forward again, his voice quiet but razor sharp. "The creatures involved there were huge. Monsters. United States' soldiers died there. Helicopter pilots. Heroes. Someone is going to pay. Bullets and small missiles can't hurt these creatures, so we need to find out where they come from and stop them before they pose a greater threat."

I don't recall the incident, nor remember seeing it on the news. I turn to Jake, but he shrugs at me, his lips turned down. He has no more clue than I do. I frown at Macy. "What does this have to do with us?"

The colonel continues. "Our enemies have gold in their eyes. We kept searching databases for anyone else with that peculiar condition, and your doctor visit two weeks ago showed up on our radar." He stares at us. "Maybe you're going to change into monsters too."

I'm unable to respond for a few seconds. I can't believe he actually thinks we had anything to do with killing soldiers. "We haven't hurt anyone."

Jake straightens. "What do you want?"

The colonel keeps talking. "A giant Komodo dragon just tried to kill your parents. Where did it come from? The same place as the caracal? How do we get there?"

"I don't know." I stare at my hands in my lap.

Jake adds, "No idea."

Colonel Macy grimaces. "If you love your country, you'll help us." His voice lowers. "You're our prisoners until you do."

Drumming his fingers on his knee, Macy sits back. "If you want your freedom, you'll have to earn it by cooperating. For starters, what can you tell me about the weapon we confiscated, Samantha? What else can it do? How does it work?"

I lick my lips. "No clue."

"You're lying." Colonel Macy looks at Jake. "Are you going to lie too?"

Jake's voice is calm. "I want to speak to a lawyer."

"No lawyers." Macy speaks softly. "You two will start talking if you ever want to see your parents again."

No one says a word as the wheels hum beneath us.

In five minutes we're at the back of the hospital. Macy exits the vehicle, barking orders. Army personnel motion us out of the armored car.

Soldiers surround us and escort us up steps and through a door adjacent to the loading dock. We're led along hallways until we're ushered into a small, bare room with four chairs. A laptop computer and large monitor are set up on a small table against the wall. It smells of antiseptic. Everyone leaves. Except Colonel Macy.

I look at him hopefully. "We want to see our parents."

He glares at me. "Sit."

I do, my hands sweating. Jake bites his lip and takes a chair too.

Macy's voice is calm. "You're both bright. So why are you protecting monsters that attacked your country's military and tried to kill your parents?"

"Haven't you been listening, Mr. VIPER?" scoffs Jake. "We don't know what's going on any more than you do."

Colonel Macy goes to the computer, turns on the monitor, hits a key, and steps back. "This is helicopter video from the Sequoia National Park incident."

Frowning, I lean forward with Jake as the screen comes alive with images. It's an aerial view, looking down through giant sequoia trees at massive animals in the far distance that appear to be attacking something. One of the large animals might be Tarath. Great Ones. They're moving with so much speed it's hard to track them with my eyes. The animals are leaping, clawing, and jumping onto multiple targets—whatever they're attacking is big—but the camera wasn't able to capture the images. Invisible enemies.

Barely visible through the trees, a human figure is standing even farther back in the forest, dressed in black. There's something on his shoulder. Maybe a bird.

I hold my breath when I see two people running behind the giant animals toward the individual in black. The smaller figures have their backs to the camera and trees block much of the view. Still I get glimpses that show that the color and length of their hair is right for Jake and me. And if it is Jake, he's wearing something brightly colored on his torso. What seals the deal for me is that the other person running has long hair and is holding a staff. I lean forward, but something dark and black blocks the camera and the video ends.

I grip the arms of my chair and turn to Jake. He stares at the monitor.

"Maybe you used CGI," mutters Jake.

"And why would the government spend money to do that?" snaps Macy.

Jake continues to stare at the monitor. "The government wastes money on stupid things all the time."

Colonel Macy snorts in derision. "We can't prove you were there, but I think the height, hair, and skin color are convincing, as is the staff the girl is holding. The gold in your eyes is damning. So again, why are you withholding information? I have to assume the Komodo dragon isn't the only threat." He opens the door and pauses. "I'll find out if your parents are still alive. When I come back, you better be ready to talk."

He leaves, and I wonder if Dad is already dead.

FIVE

WE'RE BOTH QUIET FOR a few moments. My mind is racing with questions. I glance at Jake. He's still staring at the blank computer screen.

"I'm sorry, Jake." He doesn't reply. I don't blame him. I didn't give up the staff, for whatever reason, and his mother is dying. If our positions were reversed, I'm not sure I'd want to be his friend anymore either. It adds another layer of gloom to my thoughts. "Thanks for trying to help me at the house."

He shakes his head. "Getting Tasered didn't make it a fun birthday."

"I wanted to smack them for that."

"It really bothered me to see them hurt you too, Sam."

That makes me all gushy inside. I clear my throat. "Sorry your dad was a no-show for your birthday."

"It's been four years. I'm used to it."

"I'm still sorry, Jake." It has to hurt, even if it has been a while.

"Me too."

I say, "I'm remembering a few bits and pieces. Feelings more than facts."

He heaves a breath. "Some of the creatures in the video are like those in my daytime dreams. So maybe they're memories? Or visions?"

"The demon and two-headed cobra might be real." That doesn't cheer me up.

He glances at me. "I don't trust anyone at this point. Tarath or Colonel Macy."

"The video that Macy showed us. It seems like it could be us."

Jake bites his lip. "Which would mean someone erased our memories. The question is who and why." He jerks his head to the door. "Crack open the door. See if Macy's goons are there."

I walk to the door and quietly edge it open. After peeking out, I close it and return to the chair, grimacing. "Four. We need help."

"They took my phone at the house." His eyes glaze over.

It unnerves me, and after a minute I jostle his shoulder. "Jake?"

His eyes slowly become alert again, tinged with sadness. "I saw us holding our parents' hands when they die, Sam." He glances at me. "So maybe all my daytime dreams are visions of the future."

Unable to speak, I finger the jade dolphin on my bracelet. That can't be the future. I can't accept it. I won't. But it scares me just the same.

The door opens and Colonel Macy enters with our family physician, Dr. Paul. In his forties, Dr. Paul wears blue scrubs, has dark hair, and is slender. I've always liked him. He sits in front of us, his narrow face showing concern.

I sit on the edge of my chair, as does Jake, my gaze glued on Dr. Paul.

The doctor gestures to Jake's bound wrists. "Is this really necessary? These two are exemplary young adults."

Colonel Macy ignores him and remains standing. "The doctor is here to update you on your parents." He pauses. "But first, doctor, what can you tell me about the scars they have?"

The colonel points in the direction of the white star-shaped scar on my right palm, and the white scar bands circling Jake's wrists.

Dr. Paul frowns and looks at Macy. "They were burns from a cooking accident that happened a year ago."

Macy barely nods. "A year ago? Interesting."

I can't remember how I burned my palm, and in the past when I asked Jake, he couldn't remember how he burned his wrists either. Dad and Cynthia also had no memories of the accident. With all the cooking Jake does, kitchen burns seemed like the most reasonable explanation.

Dr. Paul turns back to us and speaks gently. "Samantha and Jake, your parents' wounds aren't serious, but they're both in comas. Can you tell me anything that might help us?"

Comas. I panic inside, my throat dry.

The colonel clears his throat. "We'll get back to you on that question, doctor. Anything else they need to know?"

"The lizard poisoned them." Jake's eyes flash gold at the doctor. "Did you test for that?"

"Lizard?" Dr. Paul's eyebrows arch and he glances at Macy.

Colonel Macy shakes his head slightly at Jake and me. "We're finished here, doctor." His voice is hard.

Dr. Paul ignores the colonel and leans forward. "Sam, you're an animal expert. What was it?"

"A very large Komodo dragon," I blurt. "But it didn't bite them, it clawed them."

Colonel Macy glares at me.

Dr. Paul asks, "Where's the lizard now, Sam?"

"It's been destroyed," Macy says curtly. "Time to leave, doctor."

Jake gives the colonel a sharp look, his shoulders hunching.

I doubt that Colonel Macy's soldiers already caught and killed the Komodo. But if that's true, it might ruin our chances of getting an antidote from Gorgon—whoever he is.

"That should be enough for now." Dr. Paul stands and gives the colonel a steely look, and then turns to us. "Are you two all right?"

Jake lifts his chin. "I want to see Mom."

My voice catches. "I want to see Dad."

Dr. Paul nods. "It's fine for you to visit them." He swings to Colonel Macy. "You have no right to keep them from their parents. What's this all about?"

"Classified." Macy opens the door. "Doctor, this is privileged, if you don't mind."

Dr. Paul stares hard at the colonel. Then he extends his hand and grasps mine firmly. "I'll do everything I can to help your parents."

"Thanks, Dr. Paul." I believe him, but I also doubt that he'll be able to heal them.

Jake says, “Please save them.”

“I’ll do my best.” After glaring at Macy, Dr. Paul leaves.

Colonel Macy shuts the door and leans against it. “Next time, Samantha and Jake, you don’t share information unless I give you permission.”

Get lost, creep. I swallow. “You said you would help our parents, but you didn’t tell Dr. Paul that a Komodo dragon attacked them.”

“I always keep my word.” Macy pats his thigh. “But a Komodo didn’t attack your parents. That thing was a monster, and *that* information is classified. I also think you earned your scars in the battle I showed you in the video. Are you going to deny that too?”

We’re both silent. Neither of us can answer his question.

Colonel Macy shakes his head, looking disgusted. “Let’s move on. Who’s ready to earn a visit?”

Jake raises his chin. “The staff, the weapon, connects us to a different world.”

I’m annoyed that he’s cooperating with Macy. But we know Tarath isn’t from our world, so it’s a logical assumption even Macy can make. Jake really didn’t give anything away. Smart.

“Good, young man.” Macy’s eyes glint. “That’s how it will be. You tell us something, you earn time with your parents. You just earned five minutes, Jake. Samantha, are you coming or are you going to sit this one out?”

Gazing at my shoes, I’m desperate for anything I can trade without betraying Tarath. Even if I’m not a hundred percent sure of her, until I know what’s going on I’m hesitant to tell Macy anything important. I glance up at the colonel. “The animals carved into the staff are Great Ones.”

“So what? A title tells me nothing.” Macy remains stone-faced, his hand tapping his thigh.

I whisper, “They can all be called through the staff.”

Jake arches an eyebrow at me.

“All of them?” asks Macy.

I nod. I’m guessing, but it feels right. And without knowing how to use the staff that information won’t help Macy.

Macy becomes still. "If either of you ever lie to me, you'll rot in prison for the rest of your lives. We'll hold you responsible for the helicopter pilots and soldiers that died in Sequoia National Park. You'll be considered murderers of United States citizens." He leans forward. "I'll give you one chance to correct your statement without penalty, Samantha. Do you stand by what you said?"

"Yes." I'm ready to beg.

Macy nods. "Interesting. It seems unbelievable, but a year ago I didn't believe in monsters either, so I guess a staff that can call all these monsters isn't any wilder. It's a good start. You both earned five minutes."

SIX

I SIT IN A chair and hold Dad's hand, while Jake sits next to Cynthia. Our parents' beds occupy half the small room. Monitors between the beds take up the other half.

Dad rests as if he's sleeping, his face pale—like Cynthia's. Tubes lead from bags of solution to IVs in their arms and each of them has a machine helping them breathe. I'm terrified that this is Jake's vision. The moment our parents will die.

I look at Dr. Paul. "Why can't they breathe on their own?"

He rests a hand on my shoulder. "They're weak and getting weaker, Samantha." He lifts the sheet over Dad's leg, revealing purple lines running like a web away from the stitched wound. "These lines are spreading. It has to be the poison, but it doesn't match Komodo dragon venom bite wounds I've researched online. We've never seen anything like it. I'm contacting the CDC and checking online databases."

The sight makes my mouth dry.

Jake turns to Colonel Macy. "Can we have a few minutes alone? Sam and I want to talk about helping you." He turns slightly and raises his wrists behind his back. "And can I get these off so I can hold my mother's hand?"

I'm not sure what Jake is up to, but I say, "We just need a few minutes, Colonel Macy. We want to help you."

Macy eyes Jake and me, and then gestures to one of the soldiers who draws a knife and cuts the zip tie on Jake's wrists.

The colonel steps to the door with his soldiers. "I'll trust you this once, Samantha and Jake. Don't make me regret it." He turns to Dr. Paul. "Doctor."

Dr. Paul walks stiffly past Macy, who wheels and leaves. Soldiers stand guard outside the glass door, and I hear Dr. Paul's angry voice from the corridor as he and Macy walk away.

Jake discreetly thumbs toward an upper corner of the room. I peek at it. There's a small security camera pointed at the beds. The room must be wired for sound too.

"Good eyes, Jake. What's the plan?" I talk softly, hopeful that he has one.

He steps in front of me and whispers, "Block the camera."

I look up and his dark eyes meet mine. I want to hold him, to remind him that we're in this together. But that moment is gone as he pulls a thin steel flask from a hip pocket of his shorts. We left our bags in the other room so he must have planned this while soldiers packed his bag at his house. I wonder what's in the flask.

When he turns, I move beside him to help hide his hands. He opens the bottle and immediately I smell whatever is inside. Bright. Sweet. Alive. I want to taste it. Jake dribbles a little of the clear liquid past Cynthia's lips. Her skin color improves almost immediately.

Shocked, I hold back an exclamation, but whisper, "You're my hero."

Cynthia doesn't wake up, but hope surges through me. Jake's eyes brighten. Keeping the flask hidden alongside his leg, he turns and steps closer to Dad's bed. I remain next to him, trying to hide him from the camera, but it's a harder angle to block. He pours the last ounces of the container past my father's lips. I'm relieved and excited when the color of Dad's face improves too.

"We have to get out of here," murmurs Jake. "And get more of this stuff."

"Where did you get the medicine?" I'm ecstatic that we have a cure.

"I... I don't know," he murmurs. "I had it stashed in my bedroom over the last year, like you had the staff. I was sick once and took a sip." He shakes his head. "It was like instant health. I thought I was crazy."

Frowning, I search his eyes. "You never mentioned it."

"I just knew it would help them." His lips twist. "What's wrong with us, Sam? Why don't we remember anything?"

The door slams open and Macy strides in, his face red. Three soldiers follow him. He grabs Jake's arm and yanks the flask from his hand, giving it to one of the soldiers. "Have the contents analyzed."

"Yes, sir." The soldier hurries away.

Macy grabs Jake's T-shirt and tugs him closer until their faces are inches apart. "You just made yourself an enemy of this country."

"Get lost." Jake's hands form fists.

Both soldiers pull their Taser pistols and aim them at Jake.

All my fears and worries jumble in my head and my eyes blur. "Leave him alone!" I move around the end of the bed, faster than I should be able to, and shove Macy's shoulder, forcing him to take a step back.

Blocking off Macy's arm, Jake palms him in the chest with both hands, sending him into a wall. I'm amazed when Jake twists to avoid a Taser shot, which hits the wall, and then pushes the soldier who fired it across the room.

The other soldier aims his Taser at me, and I whirl and shove his extended arm to the side so his shot misses. I turn to flee, but the soldier grabs me from behind. A surprising surge of strength fills my limbs and I yank free, turn, and push the soldier into the wall. Jake and I run toward the door, but two more of Macy's goons step into the doorway, both holding Taser pistols.

We stop, rigid, and put up our hands. I take a deep breath, wondering how I managed to fight like that. Adrenaline. Has to be. Jake has a black belt in kung fu, but even he seemed to move faster than normal.

Colonel Macy steps forward, glaring. All of his soldiers aim their weapons at us.

Another soldier bursts into the room. "Sir, the prisoner wants to talk to you. Dr. Spiel said it looks like she's dying and has only minutes to live. She'll trade information for the teenagers' safety, but she wants to verify they're unharmed."

Macy must have hurt Tarath in some way. The thought of the caracal dying makes my heart race.

"You have to let her go." Urgency fills my voice. "She hasn't done anything."

Jake says emphatically, "You saw her help us."

Colonel Macy ignores us. "The prisoner is still under restraint?"

The soldier nods. "Yes, sir. She's getting weaker, sir. She can't escape. She's in bad shape."

"Bring them." Colonel Macy gestures to us.

We drop our arms and Macy leads the way, while the soldiers follow us, their weapons aimed at our backs.

The colonel walks us through the hospital, past nurses, doctors, and Dr. Paul. Everyone gives us sympathetic looks, but they glare at the colonel. Jake glances at me once, his lips pursed. We're taken to the loading dock and down to the parking lot.

The large armored truck holding Tarath is parked twenty feet away. Lined up in a row behind it are the three armored cars. All the vehicles are surrounded by armed soldiers with Taser rifles.

Chattering house sparrows, dozens of them, flit under the eaves of the hospital building. Sadness builds in me and somehow that emotion flows toward the birds until I know they feel it too. Chirping louder, the sparrows flutter with more urgency, as if waiting for something. Surprised, I just stare at them, unsure what to do. But I feel I should know...

The back doors of the truck open and a narrow hydraulic ramp lowers with a whine. Colonel Macy pushes Jake up the ramp, while another soldier shoves me from behind. The rest of the soldiers remain outside.

Two long fluorescent bulbs on the ceiling light up the interior of the truck. Along the left side, four soldiers sit on a bench with rifle Tasers resting on their laps. The soldiers remain focused on Tarath as we enter. Dr. Spiel sits on the same bench, gazing at Tarath; he also ignores our entrance.

Halfway in, a metal chair is bolted to the floor. Tarath is sitting on it with chains wrapped around her torso and legs, fastening her to it. Her jean jacket is tattered and the skin on her face and hands is peeling. Her head droops in front of her chest. On the other side of her rests the long metal box holding WhipEye. Just seeing it makes my pulse race.

Tarath's appearance bothers me deeply and I cry, "Tarath!" Emotion that surprises me brings moisture to my eyes. I hurry forward and drop to the floor, resting my head in her lap, my arms around her waist. "I'm sorry, Tarath," I whisper.

"It's all right, Samantha," murmurs Tarath. Her eyes barely crack open.

Jake whirls on Colonel Macy, his voice heated. "What did you do to her?"

"Step back." The standing soldier aims his Taser pistol at Jake until he moves away from the colonel.

"Interesting." Macy turns to the guards outside. "Close and lock this door and don't open it unless I give the command."

The ramp rises and the rear doors close and lock.

Tarath lifts her head, her eyes suddenly wide and steely.

Colonel Macy's head snaps back, his eyebrows arching. "You don't scare me. What information do you have to trade?" He turns to the doctor. "What's your assessment, Dr. Spiel?"

Dr. Spiel remains silent and continues to stare at Tarath.

Tarath fixes her gaze on the soldier aiming the Taser at Jake. Her human head melts away, shifting into a caracal's. I'm gaping like everyone else. I wait for the rest of her to change, but it's just the head.

Taking a small step back, the soldier gasps and swings his Taser toward Tarath.

Macy gestures sharply to the sitting soldiers. "Fire on my command."

Gold flashes in Tarath's eyes as she gazes at the standing soldier; the man closes his eyes.

"Sleep." Tarath's voice is strong and commanding and the soldier collapses to the floor, unconscious.

Colonel Macy shouts to the soldiers on the bench, "Fire!

"No!" cries Jake.

"Don't!" I jump up between Tarath and the guards, putting up my hands.

The soldiers stare blankly at me, their Tasers still on their laps. Dr. Spiel doesn't say a word. I get it. So does Macy. He reaches for his weapon.

Jake palms the colonel in the stomach, sending him crashing into the truck wall. Leaping forward, I grab his arm. Macy gasps, but manages to pull his Taser. I hang onto his wrist, leaning into it with my weight to keep his weapon pointed at the floor. Jake grabs his other arm to keep him from using it.

"Let go!" mutters Macy.

Tarath's eyes flash gold again. "Sleep, Colonel Macy."

The colonel's eyes roll up into his head. As he slides down the wall to the floor, Jake and I let go of him. I have a strong urge to kick him.

"Samantha!" Tarath's voice is sharp.

I whirl, but a caracal's head on a woman's body keeps me motionless. "Are you going to stay like that?"

"That's some party trick." Jake steps closer to look at her.

The Great One hisses, sounding annoyed. "The box, Samantha, quickly."

I hustle over to Spiel and take the key chain off his neck, then dart to the box, my heart pounding. Kneeling, I unlock and open it. My fingers tremble when I stroke the animal faces carved into the chestnut-colored wood. It's as if I've been reunited with long lost friends and a small cry escapes my lips. WhipEye is mine and I'll never let anyone take it again. I grab it and stand.

Jake is staring at me like I've lost it.

"You're acting like a raving idiot, Sam." His hands fly up. "What's wrong with you?"

I lower my gaze. "That's a good question." Whatever control WhipEye has over me, it might cost us the lives of our parents.

Tarath growls. "Enough. There's little time. The colonel and soldiers will soon have their own free will back. I don't want to use energy on the chains. Break me free."

"We'll find the key." I whirl to check Macy's pockets, and Jake moves to check Spiel.

Tarath hisses. "Use the staff, Samantha! Quickly."

"The staff?" I'm unsure what the caracal wants me to do.

She says with obvious impatience, "Slam it into the chains! Both of you."

"Okay, okay." I step closer to her, holding WhipEye vertical in both hands, and aim the bottom of the staff at the chains wrapped around her ankles. Jake stands opposite me and grips the staff too. Lifting it together, we jam it into the bindings. Golden energy crackles along the wood in jagged lines and into the chains, which snap apart. Jake and I stare at each other.

"How is it doing that?" I shake my head in wonder. Déjà vu. I feel like I've done this before.

"That's a pretty good party trick too." Jake helps me repeat this action twice more on the other bindings until Tarath is free. Jake's hands *slowly* slide off WhipEye. That annoys me for some reason.

Rubbing her wrists, Tarath stands, her skin and jacket tatters fading away until her skin appears smooth and healthy.

I touch her fingers and hand in wonder, and then meet her gaze. "You're okay?"

Jake's hand wobbles. "I thought you were finished."

Tarath's eyes lighten. "Great Ones don't die so easily. Don't you remember?"

"We don't remember anything." I wait for an explanation, needing one to take away the tension in my back and brain.

"You will soon enough, but not here." She steps away from the chair and the rest of her human form shifts into a four-foot-tall caracal. "Get on and hold tightly, guardians."

I don't move, not satisfied with her answer. "Why are you calling us guardians?"

"What's a freakin' guardian?" Jake hasn't moved either.

Tarath eyes both of us. "Guardians are the bearers of WhipEye, sworn to protect KiraKu and your world."

Just hearing that is overwhelming, but I remember the word *KiraKu* from earlier. "KiraKu is your world?"

"Yes," says Tarath.

All of my concern is focused on saving Dad so I ask impatiently, "Why should we care about KiraKu?"

Tarath's eyes flash gold. I think I've offended her, but she says softly, "Those who threaten KiraKu threaten your world too." She stamps a paw. "Other answers must wait. Now hurry or we won't be able to get out of here!"

"Alright." I've gone horseback riding and am actually quite good at it. But there's no stirrup to put my foot into and no saddle pommel to grab. Plus I'm holding WhipEye. I grab Tarath's fur, hoping it doesn't hurt her, and clumsily hoist my stomach over her back. Then I have to pull myself sideways like a beached seal before I'm finally sitting atop her.

She glances back at me, looking annoyed. "What are you doing?"

"Sorry," I mutter. "All done now." I give her an awkward smile, and she looks forward again. It's like sitting on a small horse, except that her body feels warmer and her thick fur is soft. The cat's strong muscles flex beneath me. I sense her power. She makes me feel safe, even with Macy's soldiers outside.

Jake still hasn't moved, but his hands are making doughnuts. "Where are we going to go, Sam? Macy's VIPER goons will just chase us. Or kill us. This is all psycho crazy."

I agree, but say, "We can't help Dad and Cynthia if Macy has us, Jake. We have to get the antidote."

"Jake." Tarath's voice is sharp. "I sense the butterfly scale in your pocket. Wear the armor."

"Armor?" Jake's eyebrows raise, but from a pocket he pulls out a small, flat, one-inch oval object. It has bright iridescent colors of yellow, orange, and red. Tapered at one end, its other end is flat with three short prongs. It looks like a butterfly scale.

I've seen microscopic images of them before, but this one had to come from a giant butterfly. Maybe with a six-foot wingspan.

Jake's eyebrows arch at me. "Don't ask. I found it with the flask and knew I should bring it."

Like my ring and compass, he had his own stash of forgotten items.

"What do I do with it? Swallow it? Stick it in my skin?" He tries to stretch it apart by holding it on both ends with his fingers. "Nope, won't stretch."

Tarath chuffs. "Press it against your chest and visualize what you want. Hurry, guardian!"

Jake glances at the cat, and then slowly raises the scale and presses it against his chest with his palm. Nothing happens. He closes his eyes. In moments the colors of the scale seep out past the edges of his hand, quickly expanding to cover his whole torso like form-fitting armor, stopping below his neck, just before his shoulders, and at his waist. It's beautiful. I gape in wonder.

Jake opens his eyes and stares at it too, running his hands over it. "Okay, this is the best party trick ever! Freaking amazing! Instant armor!"

"Huh. Why don't I have armor?" I'm in shock that a butterfly scale created his.

"Climb on, Jake!" Tarath's voice rises another notch.

Jake hesitates, but then jumps up behind me like he's done it a million times. Mr. Cowboy. I don't think he's ever ridden a horse either. My beached seal routine is even more embarrassing.

And I don't understand what Tarath plans to do. We're locked in an armored truck. Maybe we'll just wait for someone to open the door, but Colonel Macy, Dr. Spiel, and the other soldiers begin to stir.

"What about our parents?" The image of the purple lines spreading from their wounds terrifies me.

Tarath stamps a paw. "I waited to act, hoping the hospital could help them. They'll die unless you give them an antidote for the poison. I smelled healing water on you before you entered the hospital, Jake. Good job. Otherwise your parents would have died by tomorrow morning."

"Healing water?" Jake clears his throat. "Can we get more of it?"

I wonder that too, but I cringe over Tarath's words; *your parents would have died by tomorrow morning*. I grip my compass.

Colonel Macy groans.

Tarath turns her head slightly. "Healing water has done what it can, Jake. More won't matter now. This poison is rare, from a plant in KiraKu called dragon's breath. The Komodo must have had it beneath his claws. The remedy is almost impossible to obtain."

Her words unsettle me so much that I can't speak for a moment. The urgency for answers crowds my brain.

"How long will our parents live with the healing water?" Jake asks quietly.

Tarath hisses. "Your elders are young, healthy." She lowers her head, as if focusing. "Two days from when the Komodo poisoned them, at most."

Panic crowds out everything else in my brain. "That's not enough time."

Jake sounds scared. "Will more healing water help them live longer?"

"No." Tarath huffs. "I will do everything I can to save your elders."

I'm reminded again of Jake's vision of us holding our dying parents' hands. My watch says seven p.m. The Komodo attacked Dad and Cynthia an hour ago. We have until Sunday night, six p.m. Adrenaline shoots through my limbs.

Tarath crouches while slowly growing taller. "Ready yourselves."

I note the ceiling just above us and bend over. "Jake, you better hold me."

He wraps his arms loosely around my waist. I think he's too shy to really grab me. "Tighter, Jake."

His arms tighten a bit, but they're still too loose for what I think is coming.

"Don't you want to hold me?" I'm annoyed now.

"No, I, uh, of course, but I wasn't sure—"

"Do you need me to show you how to hold me tightly? Come on!"

"I didn't want to hurt you, Sam."

"You think I'm a paper doll or what?"

His grasp tightens significantly then and I get goosebumps from it. It's kind of romantic that we're making an escape from the VIPER goons atop a giant cat. But I still don't have a clue how we'll do it.

Tarath grows higher, and by the time her tufted ears brush the ceiling we're forced to lay flat on her back. Jake's armor is hard against my back then and his weight is crushing my lungs. So much for romance. "Jake!" I sputter. "I can't breathe!"

"Sorry!" He pushes against Tarath's back to take his weight off me, and then he must do something else because the armor isn't as hard against my back. I can actually fill my lungs.

"How's that?" he asks.

"Much better." I rub Tarath's neck to feel her soft fur. "They have Tasers, Tarath."

She twists her head back almost a hundred-eighty degrees. "Why are you rubbing my neck?"

My cheeks feel hot. "Ah, no reason, sorry."

"Ms. Touchy-feely couldn't resist," whispers Jake. "Sheesh."

"Shut up," I whisper.

Tarath faces forward and her muscles tense beneath us. I still worry about the Tasers. She didn't answer my question and I think better of asking it again. Maybe Tasers can't hurt her any more than bullets hurt the Komodo. I doubt even Macy's goons will fire lethal Tasers at unarmed teenagers.

Tarath amazes me again when she calls out in Macy's voice, "Open the back door."

Squeezing the cat with my thighs, I clutch her fur with one hand, WhipEye with the other. Jake tightens his arms around my waist a bit more—I think he finally realizes what's going to happen. I'm surprised his armor isn't hard against my back—it's almost soft. I hope it can protect him from Tasers.

His eyes still closed, Colonel Macy murmurs, "No, it's a trick. Don't do it." He lifts his Taser a few inches, but his hand flops back to the floor.

Jake presses the side of his face into my shoulder, which I like, and I nestle my head into Tarath's neck so I'm looking forward on the right side of her.

The truck doors swing open and the ramp begins to lower. Tarath leaps onto it, sending it banging into the pavement. She snarls at the soldiers facing us and they duck as she leaps over them onto the armored car parked behind the truck. Her size nearly doubles in midair and her weight lifts the opposite end of the vehicle off the ground.

"Ahhh!" I exclaim.

"Whoa!" gasps Jake.

But aside from the up and down motion, riding on Tarath is unbelievably smooth. She leaps over the stunned Taser operator to the next vehicle, and the next, each armored car smashing into the street when she springs from it. Soldiers run at us from all directions, sighting on us with their Taser rifles.

Abruptly I'm aware of the house sparrows again. Clear about what I want now, I send my emotion out to them and visualize them flying from the eaves in droves. When Tarath bounds off the last vehicle and onto the parking lot pavement, I twist to look back. Streams of sparrows are leaving the eaves.

Letting go of Tarath's fur with my right arm, I motion to the circling sparrows, my urgency for help calling to them. The birds dive at the soldiers, pecking and clawing at their faces as Tarath races away. But there are too many of Colonel Macy's goons and too few birds. The nearest armored car is quickly roaring past the birds and chasing us.

I'm going to shout a warning to Tarath, when a silent, large yellow blur flies up to the side of the VIPER vehicle. I don't recognize what it is until it slows down. It's a six-foot-tall woman with yellow dragonfly wings as wide as her height. Using the soles of her feet, she kicks the moving vehicle onto its side, sending it skidding across a hundred feet of pavement. Her feet are bare, but her long golden hair falls over a black blouse and black jeans—just like Tarath, her clothing nearly blends with her skin. Her body shines like a pale sun. She looks like a faerie.

"Insanely beautiful," I murmur. The world keeps getting stranger. Tarath said both sides will be coming for the staff—I wonder what side the faerie is on.

"What the heck?" gasps Jake. "Are you seeing that faerie too, Sam?"

"In living color."

Soldiers on the other armored cars take aim at the faerie, but two young men run up in blurs and push those vehicles over too. Both men wear white T-shirts and jeans, and run barefoot. Soldiers fire their Tasers, but the young men leap over the toppled vehicles, ducking for protection as they chase after us. Unlike the faerie, the men look human—but they can't be with that kind of strength and speed.

The faerie flits over the ground in zigzag patterns, using her feet and shoulders to knock down soldiers faster than they can point their weapons at her. Then she flies after us, the two young men running impossibly fast behind her.

Soldiers climb out of the tipped vehicles, and I was wrong. They fire their Taser rifles at us. Colonel Macy lies in the open truck doorway, staring at us.

Tarath swerves sharply, taking thirty-foot flashing strides around the corner of a building and into a side street.

SEVEN

TARATH RACES THROUGH THE city park to the dirt road leading to our homes, where she streaks off the street, across a grass field, and into the woods. She runs inside the tree line, heading south behind the few houses along our block.

I can hardly feel the caracal moving. Her stride is perfect and I can't deny my excitement over riding her. My hair flies back and my eyes water as the trees blur. Jake's armor presses against my back—still weirdly comfortable.

Images of soldiers shooting at us, along with toppled vehicles, rattle my nerves. Colonel Macy will come after us. I wonder if it means we'll be running and hiding from our country's military for the rest of our lives. Ugh.

The faerie and the two young men follow us. Only the faerie's small-featured face and long blond hair are clearly visible as she flies behind us, her wings a blur, her arms at her sides. The legs of the young men are also a blur.

"We've got crazy company." Jake looks back at our followers.

Tarath throws over her shoulder, "They're friends."

She doesn't sound enthused and I wonder why. "Where are we going?" I ask.

"You have to get the antidote from Gorgon." Tarath sounds even less enthused saying that, but I don't think she's upset with us.

The idea of leaving triggers another concern. "The animals. If we're going, we have to give them food and water."

"No way!" Jake taps my shoulder. "Macy will see us on the cameras."

My voice rises. "I'm not going anywhere without giving them food and water."

"Stupid," he mutters.

"My middle name."

Jake doesn't argue further. He cares about the animals as much as I do. It's a risk, but I won't let the animals starve. They're Dad's life, and I doubt Macy and his soldiers care about what happens to them.

Suddenly, without my being aware of her slowing, Tarath is standing quietly among tall jack and red pine trees, their scent filling the air. Blue jays and gray catbirds sing. The back fence to my house is fifty yards away, barely visible through the trees.

I try to sit up but I can't budge since Jake's weight is against my back. "Jake, I can't move. You're squishing me."

"Right, sorry." He releases his grip on my waist and sits up, so I can do the same.

Tarath shrinks to pony size and Jake dismounts like a pro, swinging one leg off behind him and jumping to the ground. I have to go to my stomach to slide off, and Tarath again turns to gaze at me. I think she's scowling.

"That was better, right?" I give her a quick smile and turn away.

I stare as the six-foot faerie flies up in a rush and lands in front of us, her wings folding and melting into her back. Staring at her in wonder, I'm speechless. She shrinks to a slender, petite woman in her mid-twenties. Golden hair frames her small-featured face and her green eyes shine.

"Guardians." Her soft voice is filled with kindness.

For some reason my heart flutters over seeing her. And I'm fascinated.

She hugs Jake first, beaming at him. Jake hugs her awkwardly, barely holding her. I don't think he remembers her any more than I do.

When she pulls back, he says, "Thanks for giving Macy's goons a nice welcome, uh, Ms. Faerie Lady."

"My pleasure. My name is Lewella." She smiles at him, and then turns to me.

Her name strikes a chord in me, but I just stare stupidly at her. She opens her arms and I grasp her, a surge of emotion in my chest. I like that she grips me firmly. "Perfect timing," I murmur.

When she pulls back, her green eyes shine. "I've missed both of you."

I don't know what to say to that, and turn to her friends. Neither of the young men show signs of sweating, making me wonder *what* they are. They both look about twenty. The stocky one with a dark crew cut steps up and claps our shoulders.

"Always fun with you two." He winks. "Name's Brandon. Good to see the guardians again."

I like him immediately and touch his thick forearm. "How do you know us?"

He just keeps smiling.

Tall and lanky, the other man stands aloof to the side, eyeing Tarath, his arms crossed. Seven gold studs ring his right ear, his red hair still perfectly spiked after the run.

"We appreciate the muscle." I gesture to him, but he looks away.

"My brother Tom isn't the talkative type." Brandon smiles. "In fact he keeps his sentences shorter than most."

"Don't care to talk like humans," grumbles Tom.

I see the resemblance in their chins, cheekbones, and eyes.

Hissing, Tarath swings her gaze from the young men to Lewella. "You bring more attention than we needed."

"Want your guardians shot in the back then?" asks Tom.

Tarath's eyes darken. "This Great One needed no help."

Tom's eyes flash gold, his gaze moving to WhipEye. I clench the staff, abruptly feeling protective of it.

"Hardly a fight with the soldiers." Brandon flexes his arms. "Just a little play. Nice move with the sparrows, Sam."

"I hope none of them were hurt." I never want to hurt any animal.

"We heard the staff and came to help the guardians, Tarath." Moving gracefully, Lewella walks up to the caracal and strokes her lowered neck. "Of course you didn't need us, old friend."

I don't say anything, but I can see from Jake's eyes that regardless of our absent memories, he's as glad as I am that Lewella and the brothers are here. The more help the better. But the lack of answers is making me crazy. Also Tarath doesn't seem to mind Lewella being touchy-feely with her. They must know each other better—which the caracal quickly verifies.

Tarath's eyes lose some of their intensity. "Always a friend, Lewella."

"Suicide to stop." Tom studies his nails.

"But more fun." Brandon ignores Tom's glare.

Putting my hands on my hips and trying to look tough, I regard everyone with a steely gaze. "How do all of you know us? And why can't we remember you?"

Jake crosses his arms. "Yeah, where have we met before? I haven't seen you around town or at the local alien zoo."

Brandon just keeps smiling, but Tom shakes his head, looking disgusted.

Lewella bows slightly. "Our families have sworn to protect and assist the guardians for generations, and we vow to do the same for you, Samantha and Jake. You did us a great service when you defeated the evil guardian and freed the methuselah energy from the shadow monsters. Their released energy helped all of us."

"We don't remember being heroes." However her words suggest that it *was* Jake and me on Colonel Macy's video tape. I also think the invisible targets on the tape had to be the shadow monsters she mentioned. "Were you at the battle in Sequoia National Park?"

Jake steps closer to Lewella. "What's a methuselah? And are shadow monsters invisible?"

Tarath hisses at Lewella. "There's no time for this now."

The faerie nods as if in deference to the caracal and doesn't answer either of our questions.

"Doubt you are the true guardians." Tom scowls. "Can't remember the staff. Maybe it doesn't want you to remember."

"Then tell us!" I exclaim. "Our parents are dying!"

The caracal lifts her head, looking northwest. "Hurry, Samantha. Soldiers are coming. Fast. You'll have minutes."

"I don't hear them." But I believe her. Wanting to yell at all of them, I turn and run with WhipEye. The ground is soft with pine needles.

I'm glad when Jake lopes fluidly beside me. I glance at him, noting the fading sunlight shining on his black hair. "Thanks for helping."

He waves it off. "Of course. Two's faster than one, Sam." He bites off his next words. "We don't have time to waste." His voice softens. "That was amazing with the sparrows."

"I know, right?" Glad for his praise, I reach out and flick my fingers against his armor—it feels hard and rings softly. "Your armor felt like a pillow. Where did you get it?"

"No clue. The butterfly scale was in my bedroom with the flask and I grabbed them. Somehow I knew the scale was important. And how the heck did I know it was a butterfly scale before Tarath said anything? You're the animal wizard, not me."

"It's huge. It's not from any butterfly in our world. Maybe it came from KiraKu."

"I asked the armor to form to your back." He says the last as if it's no big deal. "I just visualized what I wanted it to do."

"Huh. Good going, genius." I wonder what else he can do with it, and if it calls to him like WhipEye calls to me.

"We can't trust them," he whispers, glancing over his shoulder. "No matter how we may feel about them. Maybe they're manipulating our emotions somehow too."

"We've been brainwashed or something." I touch his forearm. "How could we have forgotten a six-foot faerie or a ten-foot caracal? And why haven't we ever talked about Tarath or any of them? Or the big battle?"

Jake shakes his head. "We don't know what they really want from us or what's going on."

I consider that and think he's right. "We need their help though."

"Ah, look, Sam, I know you love animals—"

"I know! Isn't Tarath amazing? Riding her was like sitting on a magic carpet! Smooth! And Lewella! A real live faerie!"

Jake frowns. "Tarath's not an animal, Sam. You can't be Ms. Touchy-feely with them like you are with your Dad's sanctuary animals."

"You can blame Mom for that." Mom had a magical gift with wild animals and was often able to get close enough to touch them. Jake is right, but I find the giant cat and faerie stunning and it's hard not to fall in love with them. "They're unbelievable though, right?"

"You're already treating Tarath like she's one of your deer. Rubbing her neck. Even she thought it was weird."

"Hey, it's not like I ride a ten-foot-tall caracal every day."

"She could have us for breakfast!"

"That's a nice image." At the rear gate I pause. "Give the animals enough for several days. We have no idea how long we'll be gone."

"Duh." He isn't smiling, but he doesn't sound angry. "It can't be more than two days."

"Right." I swallow. Two days to save our parents. My fault.

In the rear cages the lynx and bobcat are pacing. They're probably still spooked from seeing the Komodo, but they pause to watch us.

"Hey, guys," I whisper. "It's okay. You're safe."

Their tails flick and their eyes seem to soften with my words.

The back acres of grass are empty of soldiers so we dash in, heading for the food bins and water hose beneath the awning over the back patio. The hole in the rear of the house reveals shattered timber, reminding me of our parents. Dad and Cynthia are dying because of me. That thought won't go away, even when I try to push it aside.

Setting WhipEye against the wall, I fill pails with food and water for the cats, coyote, and gray fox. Jake takes care of the bald eagle, red-tailed hawk, flightless crow, and other birds. Several times we run past each other, carrying water and food in buckets to the pens. I stumble once and almost do a header into the grass.

I slide the food dishes into cages while talking to the animals to try to calm them. They all seem jittery. My stomach knots every time I leave the staff. Especially when Jake returns to the patio before me. Why am I so crazy about the stupid staff?

The August heat leaves a film of sweat on my skin and I wipe it out of my eyes. Near the northern corner of the fenced acres the deer huddle together, still skittish from the Komodo's attack. After I leave food and water for them beneath a shade tree, I gently stroke the soft fur of their necks, whispering words to comfort them. It seems to help, but I wish I had more time to calm them.

Finished, I end up at the patio the same time as Jake. We both stare at WhipEye, its carved animal faces shining. It's awkward.

I step forward and grab the staff, the chestnut-colored wood calming my thoughts immediately. Jake shakes his head, but I don't care. I glance at the spooked deer, debating on whether I should free them in case we're not back soon. But they all have injuries, making them easy targets for predators.

"Gotta go, Sam." Jake flicks my shoulder and runs.

"Coming." I follow him, telling myself the animals will be all right. We'll be back soon. We have to be.

The whine of engines comes from the front of the house. There's no way the soldiers could have righted the armored cars already. Colonel Macy must have backup close by or he called the police.

When we run through the back gate, the lynx and bobcat hiss, facing the house. After sprinting into the woods, I glance back through the trees, peering at the hole in the house's rear wall. Soldiers are barging through the front door. I run faster. Tarath is waiting for us, her canines bared as she faces the house.

"Should we play some more?" Brandon grins and flexes his thick arms.

"Crazy." Tom gestures in exasperation.

Brandon winks at me, but I can't believe he's talking like this. Tom seems more sensible.

Jake glances at me and the others. "Hey, maybe we're not looking at this right. Maybe Macy's VIPER goons could help us with this creep Gorgon. I mean, more muscle can't be a bad thing, right?"

As much as I don't like Macy, I'm instantly in love with the idea of soldiers helping us. I gesture to Lewella and the brothers, "Gorgon poisoned our parents and we have to bring him WhipEye to get the antidote."

Lewella frowns. "Gorgon will never allow soldiers to get close to him. If you bring them, you won't find him and your parents will die."

Jake looks as disappointed as I feel. Fidgeting, he stares at the house. "Then we should get out of here, like now."

"I second the motion." I don't want to fight soldiers again, nor face Tasers or worse.

Lewella's green eyes flash gold. "We could delay them."

I'm glad when Tarath hisses and says, "No. We flee. Guardians." The caracal crouches so she's even lower.

I only have to squirm for a few seconds to get atop her. She barely glances at me this time. Jake still climbs on like he's a rodeo rider, which annoys me. His arms circle my waist again, this time tightly. I like that.

"Where to?" I ask.

Lewella steps closer, her voice soft. "Gorgon is in the central Amazon jungle, and Mentore is leading the Lessers that oppose him. Mentore will help us."

"Amazon?" Jake flicks his hand. "Are you kidding? How are we going to get there? Hitch a ride on dragons?"

"WhipEye." I look at all of them. "I'm right, aren't I?"

"And again, what's a Lesser?" asks Jake.

Tarath chuffs. "We need to talk, guardians, but not here. Use the compass, Samantha." She gives a low growl. "Hurry."

Not understanding why she wants me to use the compass, I grab it and hold it level. The needle does an odd thing and moves off north, pointing east toward *Trust*, which echoes my gut. It quickly bounces back to north. Strange. But strange seems to be the norm now.

"Is that thing alive?" Jake shakes his head.

"Rose's cabin," I say. "Due east."

Growing in size, the caracal leaps forward, the woods flashing by in a mosaic of colors. Remaining in human form this time, Lewella runs fluidly over and around tree trunks and brush, her hair flying past her shoulders. Brandon barrels through lighter obstacles like a bulldozer, but jumps fallen trees, and Tom swings and pulls himself around obstructions like a flying chimpanzee, graceful as a ballet dancer.

"Cirque du Soleil in the forest," I whisper.

"Mind-bending," Jake whispers near my neck. "Kind of a weird birthday though." His voice is tinged with sadness. I feel it too.

Helicopter blades whir in the distance. Colonel Macy. Has to be.

EIGHT

THE CARACAL ACCELERATES UNTIL trees, brush, berry bushes, and saplings become blurs. Bird songs don't register, and Lewella, Brandon, and Tom fade away. I close my eyes and lean into the cat's strong neck, her fur soft on my cheek and the wind tangling my hair. Jake is comfortable against my back and I like having him there.

When we stop it's without warning again, the air no longer blowing against my face. There's tall grass beneath us, and we sit up. I'm aware of how fast Jake's hands fall off me, unsure if it's because he's uncomfortable with holding me or wondering about our friendship. I hope it's the former.

The caracal is standing in the middle of the meadow that borders the pond. In front of us lies the rectangle of black soil, where Rose's cabin used to stand. Rose rented the cabin from Dad and we think she took off when it burned down. Maybe she was afraid Dad would try to get money from her. He wouldn't. He has too big of a heart for that.

Tarath shrinks and we slide off—I'm getting better at not making a marathon out of it, but the staff doesn't make it easy. The cat walks back to the edge of the meadow, staring into the woods. The waning sunlight creates shadows in the forest.

"The soldiers will be here in minutes," says Tarath. "Helicopters are bringing them."

I'm discouraged we can't get rid of our hounds. "How could Macy's goons track us?"

Tarath doesn't move. "I don't know, Samantha."

"Where are Lewella, Brandon, and Tom?" Jake brushes back his hair, sounding disappointed. "Did the circus decide to bail?"

"Our parents are dying, Tarath." I feel empty saying it.

Jake faces the caracal. "It's time for answers, Oh Great One." His voice has a tinge of sarcasm—I understand his frustration.

"Let's start with Gorgon." I grasp my arms. The air is warm but I'm not feeling it.

Tarath walks over, her shoulder muscles rippling. "Gorgon is a powerful Lesser. He'll do anything to get WhipEye, including kill your parents and you, if he has to. He wants to take the Jewel of Origin from KiraKu. It would make him very powerful, and WhipEye is the only way he can return to KiraKu to get it."

Fear for Dad runs through me.

Jake slashes the air. "Okay, for the last time, what's a freakin' Lesser?"

Tarath continues calmly. "Great Ones that left KiraKu to come to your world are called Lessers. Like Lewella and the Komodo dragon. They can't go back to KiraKu. The ruling crocodile in KiraKu won't allow it."

I wonder how Lessers have remained secret for so long in our world. But when I think of all the monsters in human mythologies, maybe they haven't. I study WhipEye and find the face of a crocodile carved into the staff. I look up at Tarath questioningly.

She hisses. "Yes, that's the crocodile."

From the sound of her voice they're not friends. "So he's somehow bonded to the staff and will answer the call?" My gut doesn't give me a good feeling about the croc.

Tarath chuffs. "There is an ancient prophecy in KiraKu that the true guardians will use WhipEye to unite KiraKu in time to face a great evil. The crocodile doesn't believe it's you two."

"Hey, I've got news for you, kitty-cat." Jake throws a hand wide. "We just want to save our parents."

I agree with Jake. For a moment I wish that I had given the staff to the Komodo—but I could never do that even if I could replay the event.

Tarath says, "It was foretold that one of the true guardians would have a star on her palm, and her protector would have bands around his wrists."

I stare at the star scar on my palm, and Jake slowly raises his hands to look at the scar bands circling his wrists. We exchange glances, but he looks as unenthused as I feel.

"I'm not going to try to fulfill some crazy prophecy based on burns on my wrists." Jake shakes his head. "That's as nuts as everything else."

"How did I get WhipEye?" I ask.

Tarath eyes me. "Rose passed the staff on to you, Samantha, by bonding you to it. And you bonded Jake to it."

"Old lady Rose who rented Bryon's cabin was a guardian?" Jake stares at Tarath in disbelief. "You could blow her over with a puff of air."

Tarath huffs. "Rose was the first guardian, but she was only a temporary keeper of the staff. Some also doubt that you are the true guardians."

"You're looking at two big-time doubters." Jake gestures to include me.

I frown. "Okay, let's pretend what you're saying is true. Why did Rose pick me? I'm a nobody."

Tarath hisses. "Rose did not make a mistake. You care deeply about all living creatures, Samantha."

That's true, but it still feels too random. "Where is Rose now?"

Tarath turns to the forest. "Gorgon is holding her prisoner."

Jake faces me. "Sam, we need more answers. We can't just run down to the Amazon. What if Gorgon lied about having the antidote?"

Tarath paws the ground. "Like me, all Lessers and Great Ones are honor-bound to keep their word. Gorgon has the antidote."

Jake steps closer to her. "Colonel Macy showed us a video of Great Ones fighting invisible creatures in Sequoia National Park. You were there."

Tarath growls. "I was proud to be there with you."

"The invisible enemies were shadow monsters?" I grasp a stem of grass.

"Shadow monsters can't be seen by humans or cameras," says Tarath. "But the gold in your eyes will allow you to see them now."

Jake points a finger at his eyes. "And the gold in our eyes came from?"

Tarath stamps the ground. "KiraKu's energy and Great Ones."

"Of course it did. Why didn't I think of that?" Jake sounds exasperated.

The faint sound of helicopters tenses my back. Maybe they're doing a search pattern. I turn to Tarath. "What about our memories?"

Tarath eyes both of us before answering. "Six months ago the ruling crocodile in KiraKu wanted to take WhipEye from you, Samantha. The staff had remained silent for half a year, and he worried that you were not the true guardians. And since WhipEye is the only way for humans to get into KiraKu, he wanted that doorway closed. He has always wanted to protect KiraKu at all costs. The crocodile said you could keep the staff only if we erased all of your memories tied to KiraKu. If you were the true guardians, he felt WhipEye would call to you again."

I'm shocked that Tarath did this to us. And I'm immediately distrustful of her. Yet she's helping us now. I chew my lip.

Jake sputters, his hands flying. "You mean ...you just...you erased our memories?"

Tarath continues. "When I came to you six months ago you both were having nightmares. I gave you the choice. You could retain your memories, but lose WhipEye and the butterfly scale, or you could lose your memories and keep WhipEye and the scale. You chose to have your memories erased. I would have never done it without your permission."

She pauses. "The staff called to you, and it will have awakened some feelings and memory fragments. But I can restore your memories fully. If that's your choice."

I shield my eyes from the setting sun. "It's believable, Jake. I never would have given up WhipEye, and you would have been fine with losing your nightmares."

Jake looks like he might prefer swallowing a handful of beetles to restoring his memories. "I don't want to fight monsters or have to fulfill some crazy prophecy." His voice lowers. "I just want to save Mom."

Tarath raises her head. "There are no expectations for you to fulfill, Jake. Saving your mother is enough."

Shivers run over my skin. I agree with Jake. I don't want to enter into a war we know nothing about, for a world we can't remember. I just want to save Dad. "Will it help save our parents if we get our memories back?"

"Possibly." Tarath morphs into the red-haired woman and steps closer so she can place a hand on each of my shoulders. "What's missing are your memories of all things related to KiraKu—Great Ones, Lessers, Originals, battles, fears, the evil guardian, and his nine shadow monsters. It occurred over one day, on your sixteenth birthday, Samantha. I can restore everything."

I swallow hard, staring into her eyes, my voice uncertain. "You're our friend, right? You're trying to help us?"

"Sam!" Jake steps closer. "We don't know what she's going to do! Messing with our brains for all we know."

Tarath's eyes hold mine. "I would give my life for you if it came down to it, Samantha Green."

Her words touch my heart, and the staff is suddenly warm in my hand, its energy flowing up my arm and into my chest. I'm strangely calm, but it also feels a little like I'm going to jump off a cliff—and heights terrify me.

"Sam." Jake's eyes are pleading. "It's dangerous. We don't even know her."

I glance at him. "You're right. Maybe it's a huge risk. But I want to save Dad, Jake. Whatever it takes."

"You're too trusting," he mutters.

"Maybe." My chest heaves. "Do it, Tarath."

"Close your eyes, Samantha."

I do, and Tarath presses her hands softly against both sides of my face. Heat from her palms warms my skin and head. I swoon but she keeps me upright. In minutes or a few moments, I'm not sure which it is, she removes her hands.

I blink my eyes open, feeling a bit faint as Tarath drops her hands to my shoulders to steady me. No big flood of memories. No huge understanding. I'm disappointed.

"That's it?" I stare at Tarath, and then Jake. "Nothing happened."

"Your memories will return slowly. It will take days, but things will begin to feel familiar to you." Tarath steps back, looking at Jake. "You don't have to remember, Jake. It's your choice, just as it was your choice to have your memories erased."

He looks at me, his forehead lined. "Oh, what the heck! I mean I'm wearing butterfly armor so I'm already probably under some kind of spell anyway." He steps up to Tarath. "Okay, just in case you're upset that I called you kitty-cat, I'm sorry. I don't want you to mess up my brain. This is safe, right? No chance of brain damage?"

Tarath nods. "I would not hurt you, Jake Morris."

"You're honor-bound to that, right?"

"I am."

He closes his eyes, his face scrunched up. "Ready when you are."

Tarath smiles and places her palms on Jake's face. It only takes seconds.

Jake opens his eyes afterward, looking nonplussed. "That's it? You're right, Sam. No biggie."

Tarath morphs back into the caracal, her voice gentle as she stares down at us. "Both of you will have to decide what you will do for love."

"I know what I'm going to do." Jake looks determined. "Save Mom."

"What about the other Great Ones on the staff? Will any of them answer my call?" I hope the answer is yes. We need all the help we can get.

Tarath hisses. "The other Great Ones bonded to WhipEye won't answer the staff again until you've proven you're the true guardians."

"How do we prove that?" More disappointment, and I don't think I want to be a guardian anyway.

Tarath scratches the ground with a paw. "You will know."

"We just can't catch a break, can we?" Jake shakes his head.

Tarath leans closer to me. "I will come whenever you call, Samantha."

"You're leaving?" That tanks my mood. "Why would you leave us now?"

She stamps the ground. "Great Ones are despised by Gorgon's Lessers. If I go with you to Gorgon, it will mean certain battle and death for me. If I go to KiraKu, I can at least look for a cure for the poison." She pauses. "There are creatures there who can heal this poison, but they are independent. I will see if there is another way."

Jake steps closer, his shoulders bunched. "Can we go with you to KiraKu to help look for the cure?"

"Great idea!" I look hopefully at Tarath.

The caracal swings her head to Jake. "The ruling crocodile would try to kill both of you and take WhipEye."

Jake looks dismayed. "More wonderful news."

Tarath chuffs. "Go to Mentore. The staff will take you there. Even if you don't remember everything, it will guide you. WhipEye is the most powerful weapon of KiraKu. It's made from the root of the WhipEye tree, the strongest wood in KiraKu."

"A carved stick." Jake looks at the staff. "We're screwed."

I can't disagree.

Tarath hisses. "Remember, you need each other. No matter what happens, never forget that."

Jake glances at me. I hope he heard her. He shocks me when he steps up and wraps his arms around Tarath's lowered neck, his voice betraying vulnerability. "Do you have to leave, Tarath?"

The cat growls. "If I find someone willing to help, I'll return to you, wherever you are, Jake."

His arms slide off Tarath and she swings her head to me. I hug her too. For better or worse, there's something about her I trust deeply.

Her mouth is near my ear and I barely hear her soft words: "Outside of Lewella and the brothers, trust no one, Samantha."

The warning sends shivers down my spine.

Backing up from me, the Great One melts into a golden ray of light and streaks into the staff, and I guess back to KiraKu. Everything is bleaker with her gone. Her presence gave me strength.

I look at Jake with one eyebrow raised.

He makes a weird face. "What are you looking at?"

I nod slowly. "It was nice to see you all touchy-feely with the kitty-cat."

He fidgets. "What? Maybe she planted memories of warm feelings toward her in my brain."

"It almost brought tears to my eyes."

"Shut up."

The helicopters sound closer.

NINE

"VIPER GOONS." JAKE STARES west, his brow knit, his hands fists.

Fifty VIPER soldiers holding Taser rifles appear running through the trees. Macy runs with his soldiers. Maybe the helicopters dropped them off. Angry words fill my throat. I'd like to scream at Colonel Macy, at our situation, at everything, but thoughts of failing Dad override that temptation.

A helicopter finally clears the trees, the chop of its blades deafening.

I look at Jake. "We have to book."

He spreads his hands. "How can a piece of carved wood move us to the Amazon?"

"It brought Tarath here."

"True."

I lift my chin. "We either stay here and let Colonel Macy catch us again, or we try to go. What's it going to be, Jake?"

His voice becomes very soft. "I don't want to leave Mom. I feel like I'm abandoning her."

I nearly choke on my next words. "I don't want to leave Dad. But there's no other way to save them."

His hands whir. "What if we don't come back? What if we die? These are giant animals with power. This Gorgon could be a monster. End of the world type guy." He pauses. "Right out of my comic books."

"At least you have kung fu and you're strong, fast, and have armor! What do I have?"

He nods to WhipEye. "A stick."

"Great. I can jab it at animals." I heave a sigh. "I'm going, and I can't do this without you. Please, Jake."

He fidgets on his feet, thinking about it. "I'm the stupid protector, right? So that means I take the bullet for you. I already took a Taser. Superheroes often have a sidekick fall guy." He shrugs. "I can't let you go alone any more than I want to leave Mom." He looks like he wants to shout at someone.

I'm relieved when he finally steps to my side.

Biting his lip, he grips the staff beneath my hands. "Okay, Sherlock. Got it figured out?"

I feel warmth in my hands and a vague memory returns. "I hope so."

His eyes widen. "You hope so? I don't want to end up in Africa or on top of a skyscraper! What if we end up inside a rock? I mean we're turning into what? Beams of light? Maybe we'll end up off the planet. What if they're aliens? I mean they are anyway, right?" He's quiet for a few moments. "Weird, I think I remember this too."

The soldiers stop at the edge of the meadow, aiming their weapons at us, while Macy's voice booms at us. "Drop the staff now, Samantha and Jake."

"Forget you, Macy." Jake pushes me around so his armored back blocks me from Macy's VIPERS. "Hurry it up. They can still Taser my legs. And I have to tell you, it was not fun the first time."

"Thanks for taking one for the team, Jake."

He squints at me. "I just don't want to take another one for the team. What kind of team are we anyway? Batman and Robin? They both get beat up a lot."

"How about Ant-Man and the Wasp?"

"That's a little better." His eyes light up. "They were romantic, you know."

I roll my eyes. "Don't push it."

We lift WhipEye off the ground, but Taser darts bite the dirt on either side of us and we freeze.

"Don't move!" yells Colonel Macy.

"Now what do we do?" mutters Jake.

Macy's soldiers twist around when a yellow streak flies up from the trees behind them in a zigzag pattern. My heart beats faster upon seeing Lewella. But she's eight feet tall now. Apparently she's able to shift to whatever height she wants, like Tarath. That makes me wonder how big either of them can get.

"Shoot that monster!" yells Colonel Macy.

Some soldiers fire at the faerie, but her erratic flight is too fast for any of them to hit her.

Gripping the landing skid of the helicopter, Lewella flies hard and rotates the aircraft in a circle until it's upside down, shielding her from the soldiers. The strength to do that is stunning and I want to cheer her on.

"Now that's a faerie!" Jake watches Lewella with wide eyes.

I look for the other helicopters, surprised they haven't arrived yet. I can still hear them.

Without showing much strain, Lewella pushes the helicopter away from the clearing and over the trees. The soldiers watch, wide-eyed like us.

"Keep alert, soldiers! Every other man, eyes on the fugitives." Colonel Macy glares at us. "Drop the staff or we fire!"

Jake whispers, "Follow my lead." He takes one hand off the staff and shouts, "Okay, don't shoot! Don't hurt us! We give up!"

"Good plan," I murmur. I raise one hand too, and shout, "We'll do whatever you want! Please don't fire!" WhipEye's warmth seeps into my hand, working its way through my limbs and into my heart. I'll never let it go.

Half of Colonel Macy's goons aim their Tasers at us, striding toward us while glancing all around. They have to be looking for Tom and Brandon. Where are they?

"Last warning, Samantha and Jake," yells Macy. "I'm counting to three! Drop the staff or we're firing."

"What a dork. He already warned us once." Jake glances over his shoulder. "Any birds around, Sam?"

"Great idea." I peer into the trees for any help, but notice only a few sparrows. Not enough to stop a line of soldiers. But I sense something better, not with my ears or eyes, but with something deeper I don't understand. In a burrow in the ground. I send my plea for help—and I know they hear it.

In seconds a buzz fills the air as a line of yellow jackets flies out of the forest and descends upon the soldiers, who shout and swat at the stinging insects. The yellow and black wasps can't distract all of Macy's goons, but hopefully enough of them to allow our escape.

Jake glances over his shoulder. "Now we're talking! You took the Wasp thing literally."

I watch in satisfaction. "I hope they sting Macy in the butt."

"More than once, the way it looks from here."

The way Macy is jumping around, I think Jake is right.

Brandon explodes from the undergrowth to the south, running along one end of the line of yelling soldiers. Moving too fast for them to react, he pulls Tasers from their hands and gives the soldiers hard pushes and bumps while flinging their weapons into the woods.

While ducking wasps, Macy shouts unintelligible orders through the speaker.

From the other end of the line, Tom moves just as fast in acrobatic fashion, his eyes flashing gold. He's like a souped-up Olympic gymnast, spinning, twirling, leaping, and flipping.

Soldiers whirl around, but they can't fire at the speedy young men without risking hitting their own people.

I swallow, not wanting Tom or Brandon hurt or caught. They're taking a huge risk for us.

The helicopter's blades strike branches and trunks with loud shudders until the engine halts. Lewella jams the wreckage into the trees so it won't fall. I'm glad she didn't kill anyone. Brandon and Tom don't seem to be using lethal force either.

Macy's soldiers are quickly disarmed or occupied, so Jake and I grab WhipEye again with both hands and move the lower end of it in three sideways figure eights, a.k.a. the mathematical infinity symbol. I experience *déjà vu* while doing this. No. I remember.

I don't want to leave Lewella, Tom, and Brandon to fight Macy, and shout, "Lewella! Tom! Brandon!" I'm relieved when they streak toward us from the ground and air.

Some of the soldiers jump to their feet, running for their Tasers. My back tenses. Where are the other helicopters? It bothers me that

I still can't see them. Macy has to have radio contact with them. The helicopter Lewella wrecked has to have it too.

Stepping through his rising soldiers, Macy aims a rifle Taser at us, his broad face twisted. "Stop them!"

Soldiers scurry to walk in line with him, raising weapons.

Three times Jake and I hurriedly call out, "Mentore!" Then we lift WhipEye and slam it into the ground, sending a loud *boom!* into the distance. The force of that amazes me again. Even the advancing soldiers pause. We repeat it a second time. *Boom!*

"I really hope we don't end up inside a tree or a rock," mutters Jake.

I frown. "Don't jinx us. Maybe any words you speak guide the staff."

"You think so?" Jake looks horrified and says quickly, "Sunshine, grass field, no trees."

By the time we bang the staff a third time, Tom reaches and grips my shoulder, while Lewella lands and grabs Jake's arm—her wings folding into her shrinking body until she's a petite young woman again. Brandon holds my other shoulder, grinning as if he's arriving at a party.

Taser darts fly all around us as everything fades.

TEN

I CLOSE MY EYES and lean on the staff. Holding WhipEye while moving everyone tired me. The air is warm, and when I look, dusk casts deep shadows among the trees and surrounding vegetation. The scent of greenery fills my nostrils. Jungle. I guess it could be the Amazon.

Relief hits me that we escaped Macy and his VIPER goons.

Jake is sagging a little too. He looks at his feet. "At least we're on the ground, safe and sound. Well, we don't know about safe yet."

"You can let go," I say lightly.

He looks surprised, and maybe a little hurt, but his hands slide off WhipEye. A flare of resentment shoots through me that he was still holding the chestnut rod. *My staff.*

Jake shoves his hands in his pockets, looking away.

My cheeks are hot. I'm embarrassed by my reaction. WhipEye is gaining control over me. And I can't—and don't want to—resist it. "I was being stupid."

He waves it off. "It's okay. We're both going a little crazy."

I turn to find the others, surprised they moved away so fast. My mouth is suddenly dry. "Oh no."

Jake stares, biting his lip. "That VIPER cretin, Macy."

A few yards away in a clump of ferns, Lewella and Tom kneel beside Brandon, who lies facedown. Three Taser darts are stuck in Brandon's back. Worse, he's not moving. Guilt sweeps me. Not giving WhipEye to the Komodo might cause the death of Cynthia, Dad, and now Brandon.

"Not worth it." Tom glares at me. "Costs Lewella energy to heal us."

I'm unable to argue with him and don't know what to say.

"I don't think it will cost me anything, Tom." Lewella pulls out the Taser pins and tosses them aside. Then she extends both palms over the wounds. A gold film surrounds her hands, which glow brighter and brighter until Jake and I have to shield our eyes with our arms.

The brightness dims and I look again. Lewella's hands have stopped glowing and she's rubbing Brandon's back. Brandon moans and Tom carefully rolls his brother over.

Brandon's eyes blink open and he smiles weakly. "That was fun."

"Stupid." Tom's voice has no anger as he gently helps his brother sit up.

Brandon grasps Lewella's arm. "Thank you."

"Of course." Lewella looks at him fondly and caresses his face. Rising, she approaches Jake and me. "He'll be fine after a short rest."

"Brandon and Tom aren't Lessers like you?" Jake squints at them.

Lewella shakes her head. "They're Originals—First Humans—that came from KiraKu and entered your world. They are also immortals—like all Great Ones and Lessers—but like all of us they need KiraKu's water and air for survival. Without it, over many centuries they weaken and eventually die."

"Huh." I let that sink in. Tarath and the Great Ones are immortals. That feels right. I look at Tom's and Brandon's youthful features. It's hard to believe they're ancient. "Why would any Great One ever leave KiraKu to come to our world?" I note Tom scowling when I ask that.

Lewella's eyes sadden. "When humans in your world moved toward technology, the ruling crocodile feared Originals would too. KiraKu is pristine and he saw your technology poisoning your air, land, and water. Thus he forced all the Originals out of KiraKu and into your world."

She pauses. "Some Great Ones, like myself, left with the Originals so we could help them and protect them here. The crocodile labeled us as Lessers and won't allow us to return to KiraKu. He says we'll contaminate it, but I think it's to punish us."

Jake whirls a hand. "Sounds like a racist dictator."

Lewella adds, "We weren't sure how long any of us would last away from KiraKu's air and healing water, but it was the right thing to do." She regards me. "The yellow jackets made our escape easier, Samantha. Your power is growing, but be careful when you ask animals for help so they don't get hurt."

"Yellow jackets don't die when they sting." I don't want birds, even wasps, dying to save me if I ask them for help. The other thing is that I remember gaining this ability after visiting KiraKu the first time. KiraKu's energy changed something in me.

Jake moves closer. "Why are you really here, Lewella? Why are you helping us?"

"Over millennia in your world I've seen enough misery and wars. I don't want Lessers fighting each other, and I don't want Gorgon to destroy KiraKu." She rests a hand on his shoulder for a moment. "And I want your parents to live, Jake."

Jake stares at her, looking uncertain. But he says, "You helped us at Sequoia National Park so I believe you."

I remember her help there too, with Tom and Brandon, but again in fragmented images, not whole memories.

Lewella bows and rejoins the brothers.

Jake looks around us. "Well, Einstein, are we in the Amazon? Looks like jungle, smells like jungle, must be jungle."

"That's very scientific." I feel some excitement over being here. "I've always wanted to travel to the Amazon." I heave a sigh and study our surroundings. The canopy is two hundred feet above us. Cicadas are buzzing, Amazon parrots chatter, squirrel monkeys squeak, and other insect sounds patter like raindrops. The spongy leaf litter beneath my feet smells like healthy compost.

According to Lewella we're in the central Amazon rainforest, and thus close to the U.S. Eastern time zone. My watch reads seven-forty-five p.m.; I set it to eight-forty-five.

My thoughts churn. What if something happens and we don't reach our parents in time? What if we never return? What if we can't get the antidote and we spend the last days of our parents' lives away from them? The finality of what I've done hits me, making my knees wobble.

Jake touches my arm. "You haven't done anything wrong, Sam."

"How do you know I'm blaming myself? Are you psychic now too?"

"The corner of your mouth does a little tick when you're worried." He demonstrates the tick.

"Huh." I take a breath. "If I haven't done anything wrong, then why do I feel so crappy?"

He drums his fingers on his armor. "Look, I was a little upset with you for not giving the Komodo the staff. Well, a lot upset actually. But I've thought about it. It's not on you. The Komodo, Gorgon, and WhipEye are to blame."

I reach out, waiting, and he wraps his arms around me. My chest heaves. It feels good to be in his arms. We've given each other hugs a few times, but they always felt a little awkward, and Jake's arms were always loose around me. This feels different.

I say softly, "You're getting better at holding me tightly."

"I had practice on a big kitty-cat," he whispers. "Partner."

"Five-stars." I could almost kiss him, but instead pull back. I wonder if he's completely over what I did. How could he be? I'm not.

"Where's Mentore?" Jake sounds impatient. "We're supposed to get the staff to murderer Gorgon today. We're running out of time."

Lewella turns to him. "Lessers and Great Ones have the ability to deflect WhipEye with their energy, otherwise you would land on them. He's nearby, Jake."

Brandon lifts his chin. "I'll be ready to go in minutes."

Jake lifts a hand to him. "No worries."

While we're waiting for Brandon to recover, Jake sits on the ground and stretches his legs.

I study WhipEye. Tarath said it's the most powerful weapon of KiraKu so I wonder what else it can do. Thinking about how Jake molds his armor, I hold the staff vertically and visualize energy coming out the top end of it. Nothing. I try the same thing with my eyes closed. Still nothing.

I try moving the bottom of the staff in a figure eight. Nothing. I repeat that while visualizing a figure eight too. Nothing. But this feels familiar.

"What the heck are you doing, Sam? Stirring a potion?" Jake eyes me from the ground.

"Nothing, I guess." Frustrated, I allow the staff to slide through my fingers until the bottom hits the ground. *Boom!* The echo is loud and startles everyone, including Jake.

Lewella shakes her head at me, putting a finger over her lips. I get it. I just announced our arrival to anyone within three miles, give or take. Stupid me.

I see something slithering near my feet and awkwardly stumble back. I peer closer. It's just a vine. But it forms a figure eight on the ground. Huh. That fills in one question, but I doubt that was worth giving our position away.

Jake stands and looks down at the vine too. "That's a very powerful weapon. The enemy will be shaking when they see what it can do."

"Dork."

Brandon finally gets to his feet, flexing his arms. I'm astonished over how quickly he recovered from a near death experience. He smiles at me as if to signal he's alright, and I nod to him.

Without waiting, Lewella leads us away, lightly stepping through the underbrush, graceful as a ballerina. She twirls once without breaking her stride. Smiling, she says, "We go to friends."

"No arguments here." While walking I spot a giant spider sitting in front of a hole. I think it actually cringes as I look at it. Maybe it senses my fear. I step wide of it, as does Jake.

"What is it?" whispers Jake.

I make a face. "Giant bird eating tarantula, a.k.a. *Theraphosa blondi*. Aggressive and fast. They don't eat birds often, just a lot of little animals. Mice, snakes, toads."

"They sound lovely, Sam. I can't wait to sleep on the ground tonight."

Looking at the spider, I desperately hope we're not sleeping on the ground. "Their bite is like a bee sting."

"Wonderful."

As much as I love animals, spiders always make me uneasy. It's because they don't have a face—at least one I can relate to. I can't imagine going barefoot like the brothers and Lewella.

"What's our plan, Lewella?" I ask.

Without turning, she says, "Mentore controls this area and he won't allow us to look for Gorgon unless we talk to him first. Hopefully he'll help us. Then we rescue Rose, get the antidote, and save your parents."

It sounds easy the way she says it, but deep down I doubt it will be.

After a half–hour Lewella stops. Her head whips around to face east, behind us. She's a blur as she moves twenty feet past us where she stops again to peer east into the jungle. I whirl but don't see anything. I grip WhipEye. The jungle is darkening fast.

"What is it?" I whisper.

Brandon and Tom bracket Jake and me, and follow Lewella's gaze. Tom picks up a thick branch lying on the ground and holds it like a club.

Brandon glances at us. "We've got company."

"Not friendly," says Tom.

I still don't see or hear anything.

"Protect the guardians!" Lewella says sharply.

"I'll protect you, Sam." Jake fidgets at my side, glancing everywhere.

A blood-curdling screech erupts. I'm immediately thinking of the demon again.

"That doesn't sound like a friend." Jake pulls me back a few steps and whispers, "Get ready to run."

A large figure the size of a small elephant silently charges out of the darkness, its body a blur. It's running as fast as I've seen Lewella move. Before she can morph into her faerie form the charging creature backhands her in the side with a clawed paw, sending her flying.

"Lewella!" Tom charges and swings his club at the beast's lowered head, while Brandon crashes into the creature's side with his shoulder. The beast jerks its head back, out of reach from Tom's weapon, and bats him aside, and somehow absorbs Brandon's blow and swipes him away too.

Then the animal is upon us.

Jake jumps in front of me. I'm instantly thinking how brave he is, just before the creature hits his armor, sending him flying.

"Ahh!" he yells.

"Jake!" I cry.

I recognize the fifteen-foot-tall mammal. Its large head and neck make it obvious. Tasmanian devil. Pound for pound it has the strongest bite among mammalian predators.

I jab WhipEye at its head, but it rears back fast and clamps its teeth on the end of the staff. My fingers tighten reflexively like vises on the chestnut wood. The devil jerks its head and twists me sideways. I stubbornly cling to the staff and wonder if the devil will crush the staff in its jaws.

A paw flashes at me and my back erupts with pain. I cry out and drop to my knees, numb all over, gasping. The only thing keeping me upright is the Tasmanian devil hanging onto WhipEye. I'm amazed I'm still hanging onto the staff—my hands won't let go. I expect the beast to drag me through the jungle and struggle to keep my eyes open as agony engulfs me.

I'm barely aware of an eight-foot airborne Lewella as she rams the devil from the side with the soles of her feet, while the brothers hit it from the other side. More roars and screeches surround us from other creatures hidden in the jungle. We don't have a chance if there's that many attackers.

The screaming Tasmanian devil finally releases the staff and I fall face forward onto my belly, atop WhipEye. My back burns and a deep ache reaches into my torso. My view is ground level. Lewella must hit the devil again, because I watch the beast roll along the ground until it bangs hard into a tree. Righting itself, it scrambles away into the darkness, sending a final screech of defiance into the night. The other roars around us subside and no new attackers appear.

Shock overtakes my senses as I stare at leaf litter. I shudder and my stomach convulses. I think I'm going to puke.

"Sam! Sam!" Jake's voice sounds faint and far away.

I'm unable to speak, but am vaguely aware of him gently pulling my hair off my face and stroking my head. The brothers are murmuring nearby. Something trickles down my waist. My back is numb. Groaning, I can't muster the strength to move my hands or feet and my eyes fill with tears.

"Can you save her? Please!" Jake sounds horrified. "Oh my...can you even heal that? I can see her..."

His words fade as I grow sleepy. But I do wonder if he can see my rib bones, or something even worse.

Golden hair falls in front of my eyes. Lewella's. In moments first warmth, then burning heat spreads across my back. I cry out softly and close my eyes. Everything fades.

When I come to, Jake is gripping my wrist. "Hang on, Sam."

"Don't let go," I murmur.

"I won't, Sam. You're safe now. I've got you."

Another shudder sweeps my limbs and my pain begins to ease. At least the worst of it. I feel like a limp noodle though.

"Wow. That's unbelievable." Jake's voice is soft. "Sam, you're going to be okay."

Multiple hands gently turn me over. My own hands are still glued to WhipEye. My fingers won't let go. I crack my eyes open. Jake is staring down at me, his forehead lined.

"We have to leave," whispers Lewella. She's standing nearby, eyeing the jungle. That worries me.

"You're safe, guardian." Brandon picks me up in his arms, which feel like iron, his face serious. And then he's running. Fast. The jungle canopy flies by as I stare up at it. My back is sore against Brandon's arms, but the pain is bearable. I'm aware of Jake running nearby. The staff is vertical along my body while I still hold it. That seems insane. I close my eyes and I'm immediately asleep.

I'm walking across the intersection with Mom, both of us happy-go-lucky. Sunshine and laughter. Mom hums her favorite song. An engine roars. Squealing tires. Startled, I turn, but I'm pushed strongly from behind. My body twists as I fall, and just before I hit the pavement, I see Mom slammed by a black SUV. She flips in the air, landing hard. Her eyes go blank. I shout, "Mom!" The SUV slowly transforms into a demonic-looking creature with claws, fangs, and a black tattered cloak. Fire dances in its red eyes as it floats toward me. The stench is unbearable. I try to run, but my feet sink into the pavement. Jake is shouting. All I can do is scream...

ELEVEN

I WAKE UP GASPING. It's completely dark and I'm lying on soft ground on my back. My hands are still wrapped around the staff. At least my back isn't burning. I haven't had the SUV nightmare for a long time. Stupid demon.

"You're safe, Sam." Jake gently cradles my head, softly rubbing my forehead with his fingers.

It feels nice and I just want to lay here for a while.

Lewella is kneeling beside me too. Her outline is covered by a gold sheen, her eyes bright green. Jake's eyes glow. Mine must have shifted to gold too, because the surrounding jungle has a faint sheen. Trees, vines, ferns, and leaves all shimmer.

"Thank you, Lewella," I whisper.

She strokes my arm, her voice betraying sadness. "I'm sorry I allowed that to happen, Samantha."

"I gave our position away messing with the staff."

"Lessers and Great Ones can sense WhipEye's energy arriving," she says. "They knew we had arrived before you struck the ground with the staff."

"Huh." I don't feel so guilty then.

"Why did the Tasmanian devil attack her?" asks Jake.

Lewella shakes her head. "Some Lessers fear what Gorgon can do with WhipEye."

"So let's not talk like adults, let's just attack and chomp." Jake sounds disgusted.

I try to digest Lewella's words. "Why did we stop here?"

"This is as far as we could go without an invitation." She turns away to peer into the jungle.

Her caution makes me worry about another attack. Jake is bending over me, his eyes worried. His hand is on my arm and I like it there. "Are you in pain, Sam?"

"Amazingly, no." My fingers finally loosen on WhipEye. They ache from holding the wood so tightly for so long. Grasping the staff loosely in one hand, I allow it to fall to the side. "Help me sit up."

Jake does, and I see Tom and Brandon standing near my feet, staring into the jungle too. I cautiously move my other arm. I'm glad it still works. I feel behind my back to see if my bra is in one piece. All okay. But the area of skin where I was slashed is rougher. I wonder if I'll have another scar there.

"I was going out of my mind, Sam." Jake's voice lowers. "Your back, it was really bad. I could see bones, there was so much blood—"

"I get the picture," I say hurriedly. It sounds gross. Great. I'll be called the scarred guardian. If this is what a guardian does, I have another reason to turn down the job.

Jake keeps his hand on my back. "I...I jumped in front of you."

"That was brave. I was worried when you got slapped like a banana peel."

"Yeah, me too! But this armor is cushioned inside somehow." He frowns. "Why didn't you let go of the staff, Sam? You could have been killed! You were flying around like a puppet!"

That sounds stupid even to me, and dangerous. "The Tasmanian devil didn't say please."

"Crazy." He sighs. "I don't know what I would do if...if..."

His concern melts my heart. I place a weak hand on his chest. "I'm okay, Jake." I wouldn't mind being alone in his arms a while longer. Maybe it's my imagination or I'm still in shock, but he looks like he wants to kiss me. But he doesn't budge.

"I wonder if Lewella could heal our parents?" I ask.

Jake shakes his head. "I asked. She said if Tarath couldn't, there's no way she can."

I forget about that as soft words seep out of the forest. The number of voices quickly increases.

"We must be ready." Lewella squats beside me.

She and Jake each grab one of my armpits and lift me to my feet. Amazingly it doesn't hurt. I wobble, but Jake wraps his arm around my waist to steady me. At least I can wiggle my toes.

"You're sure you're okay?" he whispers. He holds me firmly. "There was a lot of blood."

"Okay, enough with the blood reminders. Actually I feel good for just escaping death." I hesitate, not wanting to ask this. "Can you check if I have scars?"

He ducks his head to study my back for a few seconds. He's gone kind of a long time.

I finally say, "Everything okay back there?"

When he reappears, he says, "You just have one!" He says it like I should be thrilled. "Just one massive one along your spine. I was trying to measure if it was six or eight inches long and one or two inches wide."

"Really?" I can't keep the disappointment out of my voice.

He squeezes me with his arm and winks.

"Loser." I say it with fondness. "Okay, what do I have?"

"A curved one. Thin. It looks like an arty tattoo."

"Huh." The area of the wound is stiff, like cardboard. And I can feel air against my back—my favorite tank top must be shredded. I can feel Jake's forearm press against my skin so it's not all bad.

"Should we run again?" Jake squints at the woods.

"I don't think I'm up for a sprint, Jake. Maybe a slow walk or a crawl."

"Lessers are all around us." Brandon's hands are fists, his arms tense.

"Don't like it." Tom backs up, appearing ready to bolt.

Lewella puts her hands on her hips and speaks loudly. "Friends, we come in peace."

Words fill the air, but most are too quiet to understand. I can only make out a few fragments; "...the guardians...it's them."

Large shapes move toward us through the forest and dozens of golden eyes blink at us from fifty feet away, some at eye level and others higher in the trees. All of them are still partially hidden by jungle growth.

Lewella remains relaxed, which helps calm my nerves.

The whispering increases as the dark shapes move closer. The height of their eyes gives me a good idea of how large the creatures are, and they all have oddities. Maybe all Lessers do.

A fifteen-foot-tall red kangaroo with big ears appears between two trees, tufts of thick hair covering its hide. I've always wanted to see kangaroos in the wild and stare in wonder. Beside it stands a massive beaver with tusks and clawed feet. Stepping into view, a monstrous tiger salamander has clumps of stiff bristles growing from its back and legs.

One pair of bright eyes appears fifty feet above the ground, rapidly lowering toward my head. Chills sweep over my arms when I recognize the approaching animal. Bright green with white bands.

"I *hate* snakes," murmurs Jake.

"You're gonna love this one." Jake was bitten by a baby boa when he was younger, so I can understand his concern over the snake coming at us. His visions of a giant two-headed cobra probably don't help either.

"Emerald tree boa, a.k.a. *Corallus caninus*," I say. "Nonvenomous. Grow to ten feet. Very long front teeth. White lightning bolt designs on emerald background. Gorgeous. This one looks over sixty feet long, its body five feet thick. Large enough to swallow us as tidbits."

"That was a wonderful description, Dr. Sam. I'm sure I'll sleep well tonight."

"Anytime."

Just behind the boa's jaws, and running along its midsection on both sides, a thin six-inch-wide green fin undulates along the length of its body into the darkness beyond. It must be a Lesser oddity, because emerald boas don't have side fins—at least not in our world. The fins beat slower when the serpent stops a few feet in front of me.

The boa's enormous head causes me to lean back. I love snakes, but this one is a little too close to me after just being ripped open by a Tasmanian devil. My fingers curl so hard on the staff my knuckles hurt.

Jake stands rigidly beside me, his eyes wide.

"These are the guardians, Lewella?" The snake moves its head closer to me, its soft voice obviously female and excited.

"Yes, Canaste." Lewella walks beneath the boa's head, stroking her lower jaw. "Samantha and Jake."

Canaste's eyes find mine. "Thank you, Samantha and Jake. We owe you much for the methuselah energy you released."

I relax a little and straighten. "Hey, don't mention it."

Jake mutters, "Sure. You know, we always want to help giant snakes."

Voices with many different tones chime in. "Yes. Yes. Thank you, Samantha. Thank you, Jake. We owe you. We honor you."

Canaste lowers her head nearly to my feet, then to Jake's, as if she's bowing to us. Next she raises her snout until her eyes are level with mine. "You have nothing to fear from me, Samantha. Never."

Her words help. "That's nice to know."

The boa regards Jake. "You too, Jake. You'll always be safe with me."

"That's uh, really really kind of you." Jake doesn't sound confident.

Canaste bends down to inspect the scar on my right palm, and then Jake's wrists scars. Jake's hands are trembling.

Canaste hisses softly. "You have the markings of the true guardians in the prophecy. You suffered for us."

"We still are." I almost blurt out that I could care less about the prophecy, but I hold my tongue.

The boa sways her head toward WhipEye until her nose nearly touches it. Her tongue flicks out, curling around the chestnut-colored wood several times as if tasting it, before sliding off. All a little weird.

"Our doom." The boa hisses louder at the staff, and then shifts her attention to me again, her head rising. "You must destroy it."

I stiffen, ready to fight again.

TWELVE

"FORGET IT," I SNAP. Gazing into Canaste's eyes, I expect to see anger, but I sense only sadness.

I take a step back from her. Without WhipEye we have nothing to bargain with for the antidote to save our parents. And the staff is our quick ticket home. A deeper part of me argues that no one, not even Gorgon, is taking the staff from me.

Silence surrounds us and I sense the mood changing. Jake removes his hand from my back and grips WhipEye too, his hands touching mine. I don't seem to mind him holding the staff this time. I think because it feels as if we're a team—memories hint at that.

Faint voices float from the forest: "Yes, destroy the staff." "Destroy it." "Must destroy."

"You can't have it," I snarl. The words jump from my mouth. I don't mean for them to come out so forcefully, especially when facing Lessers.

Everyone stares at me. Even Lewella frowns.

Jake nudges me. "Steady, Sam. There's more of them than us."

I take a deep breath.

More voices join in, growing in volume. My arms tense and Lewella's eyes shift to gold as she steps behind Jake and me.

Dark shapes surround us, cutting off any avenue of escape. Brandon and Tom step in front of us.

Men and women appear among the Lessers, barefoot and wearing jeans, shorts, assorted T-shirts, and muscle shirts. Originals, I assume. All appear young, like Tom and Brandon.

A whispered chant rises among the Lessers; "Destroy destroy destroy."

"Where's the love?" Jake steps partly in front of me, his armor acting as a shield. "First they thank us, then they hate us. You'd think they could at least make up their minds."

"Very disappointing." I hope we're not going to face another attack. Images of the Tasmanian devil swirl through me, tightening my jaw. I look but don't see it.

When a few shouts erupt in the jungle, Canaste turns her head to look at the approaching Lessers. Moving fast, she whips around all of us. I gasp and Jake steps back and raises a hand for protection. Tom and Brandon crouch, while Lewella sprouts small wings. Before I can even turn my head the boa circles all of us in a loose coil.

"No!" Canaste hisses at the approaching Lessers and Originals. "It's their choice."

All movement stops. The glow around Lewella's body increases and her arms slide up under ours, her long hair falling on our shoulders as she gently lifts us two feet off the ground.

A flapping sound raises the hair on my arms. I look up. A large animal with two golden eyes is hovering above us. The mammal has two short, curved horns sticking out of its head, a flat nose, small ears, and a short tail. I shiver.

"What is it?" whispers Jake. He's looking straight up.

"*Desmodus rotundus*, a.k.a. the common vampire bat."

"Gross." Jake's hand does a nervous shake. "A.k.a. bloodsucker. Let's skip the description this time."

I swallow. "I can do that."

Shrieking and barely beating its wings, the bat spreads its two claws wide, its canines glistening.

The chants of the Lessers and Originals continue. Canaste rises, her head swaying back and forth in front of us.

"We have to get out of here, Lewella," I say.

"What are we waiting for?" Jake asks sharply.

"Gorgon is somewhere nearby, which makes it dangerous to leave, and we have to talk to Mentore." She adds, "We have no choice."

"We have to get the staff to Gorgon today and we're running out of time." I look up and see Lewella's green eyes on mine.

"We'll have time, Samantha. I promise."

Jake looks at me and shrugs. I trust Lewella—she saved my life. And I think Jake is resigned like me to the fact that we need her help. Going alone into a jungle filled with angry giant Lessers isn't going to work.

Claws extend on some of the creatures, while others show us dagger-sized teeth. Giant feet tipped with sharp nails advance toward us.

Canaste swiftly winds around us twice more on top of her first coil so fifteen feet of snake hides us. She appears ready to die for us.

"Destroy destroy destroy." The chant for WhipEye's destruction reaches a crescendo.

Lewella expands her body to six feet, her wings growing too. Lifting us higher, she floats us to the top of the boa's coils so we can see our attackers. Climbing Canaste's body as easily as if they're walking, Brandon and Tom rise with Lewella.

Above us the bat lowers further to cut off any escape. I'm unsure if Lewella could dart past the mammal.

Many massive, exotic animals approach Canaste, among them a hedgehog with a long tail, a sun bear with three eyes, and a tapir with large canines.

I sense their anger. *We're so dead.*

"Enough." A deep voice booms from above, cutting through all the surrounding cries.

Silence. All eyes shift upward.

"Is this how you show gratitude? How you treat guests?" The voice from above is weary, not upset.

Mouths close, claws retract, and the Lessers and Originals retreat, their golden eyes moving back into the jungle until only darkness remains. The bat glides away.

From above, the voice commands, "Climb the tree, please."

Lewella flies us over the snake's coils and down to the ground, where she releases us. I'm glad to have dirt beneath my feet again.

The brothers jump from the top of Canaste to the ground, landing in silence.

Shrinking in size, Lewella folds her wings into her back. Facing the boa, she bows. “I won’t forget your help, Canaste.”

“I’m your friend, Lewella.” The boa uncoils, her body sliding away while her head remains close. “Sorry, Samantha and Jake.” Pausing, she moves close to my ear, her giant head beside mine, wider than I am tall. Her bright emerald skin is only inches away.

I freeze, unsure what she will do. But then I reach out to touch her skin. It’s warm and dry, and the scales actually feel like armor.

Canaste’s words are very faint. “You must destroy WhipEye.” She rears back quietly into the night, disappearing into the trees.

I’m tired of threats and orders.

Jake stares at the jungle where Canaste disappeared. Then he nudges me. “Ms. Touchy-feely couldn’t help herself.”

I smile. “Well, she didn’t seem to mind.”

Jake tilts his head. “One of these times you’re going to get your hand bit off.”

“I wonder how good Lewella is at reattaching body parts.”

“This way.” Lewella motions for us to follow.

I hurry to stay close to her, my legs slowly recovering their strength. Rustling accompanies us as large shapes shift and move at the edge of my vision, murmuring words I can’t quite hear. Occasionally a flash of gold betrays a distant eye in the jungle.

After a few minutes we arrive at the base of an enormous tree. Massive white fungi several feet wide spiral up around the trunk in a counterclockwise footpath. Lewella immediately walks up the fungi steps.

I lick my lips, watching her, not trusting my feet or balance on mushrooms of any size. The tree towers above us and I imagine falling. I wish Lewella would carry me but I’m embarrassed to ask.

Tom, Brandon, and Jake wait for me, but I don’t move.

“I could stay here. Stand as a lookout.” I shrug. “You probably don’t need me, right?”

Jake rolls his eyes. “She’s scared of heights.”

I fidget. "It's healthy to be scared of some things."

Jake gestures to Lewella. "Can you carry her?"

From the fourth step up, Lewella stares down at me, her voice kind. "Even I must do as asked. The steps will hold your weight, Samantha."

"Keep you safe," Tom says gruffly from behind me.

His expression isn't happy or encouraging, but his eyes reveal sincerity. He runs a hand through his spiked red hair.

I gesture to one of the steps. "Maybe we can eat one later. Jake can cook it."

Jake hurriedly steps in front of Tom. "I'm the protector so I should help her."

I'm surprised, but I think he doesn't want Tom to have his hands on me. I raise my eyebrows as Jake flicks fingers at me. "You can do it, Sam. I'll be right behind you." He looks back. "And Tom will be right behind me, right?"

Tom nods to him, looking slightly amused.

My legs stiff, I climb. A little mushy under my feet, the fungi at least slant into the tree. Holding WhipEye close to my body with my right hand, I trail my left fingers along the rough bark of the massive trunk, thus keeping my shoulder close to it. It gives me some security. The steps circle the tree, taking me higher. I see Jake tracing the tree with his palm too, but his steps appear smooth and confident.

Eyes shine at us from deep in the forest. Hundreds. Maybe thousands. Certainly more than those surrounding Canaste a few minutes ago.

I make the mistake of glancing down once. The ground already seems far away, the sight making me wobble. Hurriedly I lean back into the tree.

Lewella's glow leads me continually around the trunk. I keep my gaze on her back. Higher and higher we climb until I'm practically hugging the tree. Sweat covers my skin and my thighs and calves are burning from fatigue.

Not far away I spy large golden eyes level with mine. It must be a huge Lesser, but the foliage hides it. I lean forward a few inches to try and see it, and miss my footing. My arms flail and a scream sticks in my throat as I teeter over emptiness.

Jake grabs my arm and pulls me back until my shoulder is against his chest, my cheek near his. I note the strength of his grip and it's reassuring. My weight pushes him back a little, and Tom braces his back with a palm.

"Did you plan that, honey?" Jake eyes me. "You could just ask for a hug if you need one."

I brush hair from my face and glance at him. "I was just enjoying the view."

He winks at me. "Whatever you say, blue eyes."

Huh. Maybe he does like my ocean-blue eyes.

While Tom steadies Jake, Jake helps me regain my footing. When I look into the jungle again, the eyes are gone. I keep trudging. Every step feels like I'm walking the plank.

The path winds above and below branches, some as thick as tree trunks, with only emptiness between the fungi.

When Lewella finally steps through a hole in the crown of the tree, I want to push her aside to get past her. I hold back, and end up standing beside her. The tight weave of branches beneath my feet is spongy, but solid. I'm near the middle of the crown of the gigantic tree.

Inhaling deeply, I view the rolling canopy of the Amazon jungle. The stars sparkle in the sky and a slight sheen covers the treetops. It feels like I'm standing on top of the world.

Jake arrives beside me and gazes out over it too. "Now that wasn't so bad, was it?"

"Definitely worth a near-death experience." I dread going back down.

"Well, if it isn't the young man and woman who saved the planet."

I whirl, peering across the tree's crown at the speaker.

Lewella steps forward. "Sam and Jake, I'd like to introduce you to Mentore."

THIRTEEN

"KING KONG," MURMURS JAKE. "He could play in the movie."

"Be nice." I thump his thigh with a soft fist. "The last thing we need is to offend the leader of the angry Lessers below."

"Please don't pet him, Sam," whispers Jake. "No touchy-feely."

"Maybe just a little one on his foot."

The Western lowland gorilla is relaxing more like a human than a great ape. Gorillas spend most of their time on the ground, but this ape seems at home up here.

Lying on his side, his head rests on his raised palm as he stares at us. Over twenty feet long, he has a crop of red hair and his eyes are thoughtful. Short gray hair covers the rest of his body, and his thighs and back are silver like a typical silverback. His lithe limbs aren't as stocky as a mountain gorilla, but he appears every bit as strong.

Mentore waves us forward, a long tail flicking behind him. It's furry with a tuft at the end of it. Kind of like a lion's tail. Great apes don't have tails so it must be his Lesser oddity.

To the far right a male and two female gorillas are also lounging on the tree's crown, along with three women—Originals. All of them stare at us, their eyes revealing curiosity—I don't detect anger.

Jake and I hesitantly walk across the crown, while Lewella, Tom, and Brandon remain near the fungi stairway. The animal lover in me is amazed and curious at seeing the gorilla, but after our reception below I'm wary of what he wants. Hopefully he can help us.

Mentore signals one of the Originals and she approaches him. The ape leans over to whisper to her. The Original nods and walks toward the stairway, flashing Jake a smile as she passes us, which I find annoying—mainly because she ignores me. She pauses in front of our friends, whispering, and then quickly disappears down the fungi steps.

We stop in front of the gorilla, and I say, "Thanks for keeping the bullies in line."

Mentore's voice is deep and serene. "I don't control them. I just offer suggestions." He regards me. "I'm truly sorry for the attack by the Tasmanian devil. He is an outcast, not of this camp."

I believe him, but say, "That's good to hear since he almost killed me."

"Okay, explain the crazy," says Jake. "One moment they love us, the next they hate us."

The ape holds his chin. "When you released the methuselah energy from the shadow monsters in Sequoia National Park, it flew to the four corners of the planet. All Lessers and Originals absorbed it to replenish themselves."

Mentore's words are another confirmation that Jake and I were in Colonel Macy's video.

The gorilla continues. "A year ago I stood half this size, bent over, weak, and losing my hair. Slowly dying over thousands of centuries. The Great Ones have no idea how powerful the methuselah energy has made Lessers now. Perhaps immortal in this world, like Great Ones in KiraKu. So we are thankful to you."

I turn to Lewella. She gives a slight nod. So she also benefitted from the released energy. Perhaps that's why it didn't cost her anything to heal Brandon.

My free hand fingers my compass. "Then why are the Lessers upset?"

Jake waves to the jungle. "Yeah, why the hate for WhipEye?"

Mentore's voice becomes softer. "Our spy in Gorgon's camp tells us that if Gorgon gets WhipEye he plans to reenter KiraKu, take the Jewel of Origin, and return here with enough power to control all Lessers and humans."

"How can he control everyone?" It sounds like a stretch to me, even for a Lesser.

Jake flings a hand. "Yeah, is he like a god or something?"

"Gorgon's mind is very powerful in many ways, and with the Jewel's energy he would find it easy to control humans, and even Lessers. Many Lessers would rather destroy the only way into KiraKu, closing it off forever, than risk being ruled by Gorgon. Thus we're gathering here to fight him."

"Great," I mutter. It's the coming war Tarath mentioned. I remember Jake's visions of us standing with a lot of giant creatures. I wish I had listened to him, and asked more questions.

Jake tosses a hand to the side. "Whose army is bigger?"

"That remains to be seen." Mentore continues. "Stealing the Jewel of Origin will destroy KiraKu. We are not allowed to go back, but KiraKu is our first home. We're here to ensure that Gorgon and his followers fail. And even though this world isn't where we wish to live, we'll protect it if we have to."

"Are you friends with the Great Ones?" I'm curious if he's on Tarath's side.

"It was our choice to leave KiraKu to help the Originals when they were forced to leave. Some hold it against Great Ones that Lessers are outcasts. And some of us wonder how the Great Ones would react if they were aware of our strength now, and knew we were using it to protect KiraKu."

He sounds wistful and sad. Like Jake and me, Mentore lost something precious and he wants it back.

"Where is Gorgon now?" I ask.

The ape's eyes narrow. "We're hoping you can find him."

"Do we look like magicians?" Jake rolls his eyes. "We don't even know what the creep looks like."

Mentore leisurely points to the jungle. "It's easy. You'll leave our camp and he'll find you. He will have sensed the staff's arrival, and certainly heard it. When he approaches you, we'll capture him and end this before it goes any further."

"We'll end up at the bottom of a doggie pile of Lessers jumping on him." Jake raises his eyebrows. "We'll be pancakes."

Mentore huffs. "We'll keep you safe. You have my word."

My main focus is the antidote, but I want to help Rose too. I sense that she's a friend. And according to Tarath she bonded me to WhipEye. I study Mentore. "Then you'll help us free Rose too?"

Moving fluidly, the big gorilla rises and crosses his legs like a yogi, his massive palms resting on his thighs, his tail curling into his lap. Looking down at us, he says calmly, "As one of the first guardians, Rose is highly regarded by all Lessers. Gorgon earns no respect by keeping her captive."

He points to both of us. "Raise your hands. I would like to see the markings of the prophecy that Canaste mentioned."

Jake raises both of his hands, and I raise my right palm.

Mentore leans forward, huffs, and sits upright. "Perhaps you are the true guardians and you will unite KiraKu and bring back all the lost. We shall see."

Jake shakes his head but remains silent.

I could care less about all that too. "What about the antidote for our parents?"

Mentore says confidently, "Once Gorgon has been captured, we'll find the antidote." He swings his gaze to Jake. "Tell me, Jake, why do you carry the markings of Gorgon's followers on your arm?"

Biting his lip, Jake stares at the dragon tattoo on his forearm. Mentore caught him by surprise. I know the answer; dragons haunt his recent visions.

"A birthday present." He shrugs. "I was deciding between this and a mouse."

"Nothing happens by chance." Mentore regards him thoughtfully, and then he looks at me. "And Samantha, you wear the markings of a water creature."

"It's just a dolphin on a bracelet from Jake and a shirt from...." I see Jake's face tighten. Since Cynthia gave me the shirt it's reminding him of her. "I love water and dolphins. Why do you care?"

Mentore leans forward. "Gorgon loves water."

"So do millions of animals and humans. Are you superstitious?" I'm annoyed that he thinks a T-shirt and bracelet ties me to the murderer who poisoned our parents.

Mentore's eyes narrow.

Jake says quickly, "What the heck, you seem like a nice guy. We'll help you."

I'm surprised by Jake's response, but I'm not convinced about Mentore. "Any conditions?"

"WhipEye remains in my camp." Mentore's voice is firm. "I can't risk Gorgon getting his hands on it, no matter how careful you are."

"Forget it. The Lessers might destroy the staff while we're gone." My fist won't let go of the chestnut wood. I consider running down the fungi steps, but imagine falling. I quickly rule that out.

"If the staff isn't in your possession, you can demand that Gorgon free Rose as a gesture of goodwill." Mentore sits back, his brown eyes confident. "Then you only need the antidote."

"No way." My throat thickens. I don't want anyone else to have the staff. And I suddenly don't trust Mentore—his priority will be Gorgon, not saving our parents or Rose.

Jake's hands do arcs. "Gorgon won't give us the antidote if we don't have WhipEye."

Mentore growls. "Tell him you left it hidden in our camp. He'll respect that precaution."

"You make a good case. That's sounds fair." Jake gestures to me. "Can Sam and I get some food and rest, and hunt Gorgon in the morning?"

"Of course." Mentore looks at me.

I'm caught off guard by Jake's acceptance, but then I get it. Jake understands we have to reach Gorgon tonight. He has no intention of working with Mentore. "Sounds like a plan."

Mentore calmly extends a large palm toward me. "WhipEye."

My hand screws tight around the wood and I try to find any excuse to refuse him.

Mentore's voice softens. "It will be safe. I give you my honor-bound word."

"I've heard that before." I don't move and murmur, "Just do it, Sam."

"The staff." Mentore's voice is harsh. "Must I take it from you, guardian?"

"I wouldn't try." I clench my jaw. The big ape could break me in half with two fingers, but I won't release WhipEye.

Jake bites his lip as he stares at me. "She's kind of attached to it."

Mentore's face darkens and he uses his free palm to slide closer over the tree crown, his eyes slits. I step back.

Sliding into a martial arts stance, Jake says, "I'm warning you, I'm a black belt."

Mentore seems to chuckle over that for a few seconds. Then his eyes narrow again.

The other three gorillas rise to all fours and Mentore's Originals are on their feet.

I say curtly, "You said you were a friend, or are you just another Gorgon, wanting WhipEye for power?"

The gorilla's lips part and he silently displays his large white canines. Beating his chest with knuckled fists, he sends a loud drumming into the forest. I cringe. I sense Lewella, Tom, and Brandon stepping closer. Lewella faces the other gorillas and Originals. There's no way we win a fight here.

Mentore lifts a massive hand to Lewella and the two Originals, and to his companions. Everyone remains where they are. Regaining his composure, he sits back. "You dare question my integrity, guardian?"

I lift my chin. "Prove it."

Mentore's lips press tight. He looks as if he's ready to smack me. "Who would you trust with the staff?"

I don't hesitate. "Lewella."

Mentore shakes his head. "She's a friend, but not a member of this camp."

I consider that. "Then let me give it to Canaste in the morning. She said the staff is mine and she won't let anyone destroy it."

Mentore considers this, and then nods. "I'll have Canaste watch you tonight, but in the morning we hunt Gorgon. I hope this shows good will on my part, because I could take the staff if I wanted to."

I want to say *Get lost*, but instead tighten my jaw and manage, "Thank you for your hospitality."

"We appreciate it. That's the nicest offer we've had since arriving." Jake gives a limp gesture.

Mentore eyes us carefully. "We'll show no hesitation to use force to stop anyone who tries to give WhipEye to Gorgon." He gives a dismissive wave. "My friends will escort you to where you will sleep."

We turn to leave, but a tremor in the web of branches beneath our feet signals the gorilla is approaching us.

"Don't move." Mentore's voice is harsh.

I stop, the ape's warm breath on my neck. My arms go rigid when he plucks something from the back of my tank top. Lewella, Tom, and Brandon move closer. When they halt, I think Mentore scares them. But Brandon's face is relaxed.

Jake's shoulders bunch when Mentore picks something from the back of his T-shirt too. We both slowly turn.

Mentore is staring at his palm. On it lie two tiny plastic disks, a half-inch in diameter and clear except for a tiny microchip embedded in each.

"Human technology. You betrayed us." He slams his empty palm into the platform, sending a shower of debris into the air.

My voice cracks as I step back. "We're not spies. Where would we get stuff like that? I don't even have a paying job."

Jake stares at the disks. "We were imprisoned by Colonel Macy and his VIPER goons. He's the guy who bugged us."

Mentore huffs twice, and then sits back.

I remember when Colonel Macy and the other soldier shoved Jake and me into the truck holding Tarath. They must have planted the bugs on us then as a precaution in case we escaped. But I also remember Macy saying he never makes mistakes, so more likely he planned for our escape all along so he could find the rest of the Lessers and Great Ones.

I look at Jake. "That was how Macy tracked us in the woods on the way to Rose's cabin, and why the other helicopters never appeared. The colonel never intended to capture us there." But Brandon took several Taser shots, which means Macy gave orders that everyone else was expendable. The jerk.

Jake's eyes narrow. "I hope Macy is in the hospital with multiple wasp stings on his butt."

"They'll be here by morning." Mentore's fingers form a fist around the bugs. "No matter. I'll have a Lesser take these far to the north tonight, and we'll leave at first light. If the soldiers come south, they'll find nothing but jungle here. Tomorrow we'll capture Gorgon and end this."

His dark eyes bore into mine, showing no mercy.

FOURTEEN

I WALK TOWARD LEWELLA, thinking that as soon as we're off the canopy I'll ask her to fly us out of Mentore's camp. Tom and Brandon can find us later. Jake barely lifts his chin to me—I know he's thinking the same thing. But I wonder if Lewella's loyalty is with us or Mentore.

My question is moot because the three gorillas on the treetop move closer to Tom and Brandon, towering over them. Worse, the vampire bat, a massive harpy eagle, and a half-dozen other bats appear hovering over us. Mentore is making it obvious that we're his prisoners until dawn.

Jake's eyes widen as he gazes at the vampire bat, but I'm focused on the harpy eagle. It's magnificent.

Brandon smiles at the gorillas, but Tom bites his lip.

Lewella remains calm and grows to eight feet, sprouting eight-foot golden wings. After gently sliding her arms around Jake and me, she flits across the treetop, cradling us in her strong grip. I feel like a child held by a giant.

As soon as we're over the canopy edge I look down. Dizziness floods me as warm air sweeps against my face. "This is insane!"

"What a rush!" Jake winks at me.

"Dork."

Lewella plummets, while Tom and Brandon swing from branch to branch, using terrifying gymnastics. The gorillas follow them, while the bats and eagle bracket Lewella.

I'm quickly dizzy and nauseous and close my eyes.

When my feet touch ground again, my chest heaves. Lewella releases me, already in her petite human form. I take a few awkward steps, happy to have earth beneath me again. "Safe and sound. I love dirt."

There are a dozen Originals, the gorillas, and three leopards waiting for us. One of the Originals waves us to follow him.

I frown at Jake—he's biting his lip. There's nothing we can do for now.

Distant howls and growls drift through the jungle.

Jake's eyes widen. "Okay, that doesn't sound good."

I brush back my hair. "Howler monkeys. Loudest land animal alive. They can be heard three miles away."

"Huh. Do you ever get stumped?"

"Not lately." My shoulder brushes his and for a moment I think he's going to hold my hand. I wouldn't mind that, but he moves slightly away from me. Huh. I let it go. My mind is racing, wondering how we'll get out of Mentore's camp.

A short distance from the base of the tree stands a hut that wasn't there earlier. It's made from long, woven plant leaves with supporting sticks. In the middle of the nearest wall is an open doorway. Our escorts stop there and the leading Original motions us in.

I follow the others into a space the size of a large living room, with a high, sloped ceiling. A thin woven floor covers the jungle litter.

In the middle of the hut are wooden bowls filled with acai berries, cashews, Brazil nuts, water, and unleavened bread covered with some kind of brown paste.

I glance at the door. The gorillas and Originals are sitting and standing outside. I assume the hut is surrounded. Dejected, I look at the food.

Jake stares hungrily at the bowls. "That's a nice spread. I hope it's not like a last meal kind of thing."

"Mentore ordered this for us." Lewella sounds thankful.

Hungry, I sit, drink water, and eat a handful of nuts and some of the berries. I'm starved so it all tastes good.

Jake tastes the bread, looking quizzical. "A bean spread. Basic but nice. Maybe a hint of vanilla and ginger. I like it."

Tom and Brandon eat heartily and slug water. Tom's face is strained, but Brandon smiles as if he's on a picnic. Lewella's expression is unreadable.

Another fuller memory flashes into my brain of Lewella and the brothers helping us defeat the shadow monsters. We already knew this, but the memory makes my warm feelings toward her stronger. Yet I wonder where her loyalties lie.

I gesture to Brandon. "I never thanked you for carrying me earlier, so thanks."

Brandon smiles and winks at me.

Even though I'm sure our guards are listening, I decide to take a risk. I look at Lewella. "How well do you know Mentore?"

Lewella nods. "If I were you, I would ask the same thing. Over millennia in your world many of us have maintained contact with each other. Even in KiraKu, Mentore was respected as a leader. When word spread about this conflict, I knew he would be here opposing Gorgon. I trust his motives."

Disappointment hits me. She sounds loyal to Mentore. And she gives no facial signals that would indicate otherwise. Jake gives her a quick glance, probably concluding the same thing. Quiet surrounds us. I remember the Komodo's statement that we have to bring the staff to Gorgon today. Panic rises in my chest, but I don't know what to do about it.

"How have Lessers remained secret in our world?" No memories of other Lessers have surfaced so I doubt I know much about them.

"Kind of hard for giant mutant animals to hide for countless centuries." Jake chews a Brazil nut.

Lewella nods. "Some of us haven't. When away from KiraKu's air and healing water over centuries, Lessers mutate—as I have. Thus many of us became the creatures of human mythologies and legends. Some of us, like myself, also chose to take on human form to blend in better. All Great Ones and most Lessers are capable of this."

Jake slaps his knee. "I knew some monsters had to be real! Do you know if UFOs are real too?"

Lewella just smiles.

I study her. "Were you a dragonfly in KiraKu?" Given her wings, it makes sense. She doesn't answer, so I ask, "Do you miss KiraKu?

She nibbles on bread. "Like Mentore, I'm sorry to be away from KiraKu for so long, but I would never choose to live there again."

"How can you say that? KiraKu. Home." Tom clasps his hands together, staring at the ground. "Breaks my heart to be away."

Brandon rests a hand on his brother's shoulder. "The price to live in KiraKu is obedience to the crocodile. Here we have freedom."

"And slowly die." Tom's eyes reveal his loss.

Lewella stares at me, seeing the question on my face. "Rose smuggled healing water out of KiraKu for thousands of years, against the crocodile's wishes, and gave it to us. She kept us alive and healthy. She was always more interested in doing what was right instead of blindly following rules."

"I'm glad Rose helped all of you." And I'm glad she bucked the authority of the crocodile. Somehow that feels good.

Lewella nods to me and sips water. "For some of us, the crocodile's decision to expel Originals was not honorable. It's part of the reason a number of us chose to leave. Perhaps Mentore has forgotten."

"KiraKu beautiful. No pollution." Tom stares at Jake and me. "Humans love pets. Cats. Dogs. But not all life on your planet."

I remember Tarath's words that Jake and I have to decide what we will do for love. Anything more than saving our parents feels overwhelming. I don't even know how we can get out of Mentore's camp. Every idea I come up with feels impossible. I want to talk to Jake in private.

"No war in KiraKu. Peaceful." Tom regards his brother. "Our parents would be alive. Not killed in a stupid human war."

Brandon gently squeezes his brother's shoulder. "We mustn't have regrets, brother. But if we do, we should acknowledge that our parents willingly helped others. They weren't forced."

Jake flicks fingers at Tom. "Why did your parents risk their lives for humans?"

Tom doesn't reply, but Brandon says, "They couldn't stand by and watch when Hitler was killing so many. They said love demanded they help your people."

Jake looks at Tom. "They were brave."

Tom nods in silence.

I wonder if I could ever be as brave as his parents. If I lose Dad the pain will overwhelm me. It must be a hundred times harder if you've lived with your parents for millennia.

"Are we Originals?" I regard Lewella and the brothers. "I mean, we have gold in our eyes..."

Jake looks excited. "I've been wondering that too."

"Not born in KiraKu," scoffs Tom.

Jake raises an eyebrow. "I guess we're not immortals, huh?"

Lewella and Brandon don't add anything, but I'm not sure what that means. I close my tired eyelids and find myself humming Mom's song to myself, the one from the nightmare. Mom said the song was passed down through generations of her family and she hoped I would keep the melody alive. She always said it would have great power to help me in times of need. I just like that it calms me now.

Lewella leans forward. "That's a lovely melody, Samantha. Who gave it to you?"

I blink my eyes open. "Mom."

Brandon's eyes light up. "Can you sing it?"

"Songs are always welcomed, Samantha. If you don't mind." Lewella looks eager.

"I'm not very good," I mumble.

Tom clasps his hands over his heart. "Please. Too long without songs."

Jake taps my knee. "You have a great voice, Sam. Remember? Hoarse gator?"

"Thanks for the confidence boost." He's heard me sing before.

Everyone is staring at me with hopeful expressions, especially Tom, so I feel guilty turning them down, especially since they've been our bodyguards. Even the Originals and gorillas near the door are peeking in.

I sing softly, which makes my flawed tone less obnoxious. More like a croaking frog. *"I'm waiting for my true love, the one who always knows, true friendship is the rock, that true love always sows, for love I'll make my stand, the only true power to command.*" It seems too short so I surprise myself and repeat it a second time.

When I finish everyone looks satisfied, and I even feel good about it.

"Love is always worth singing about." Lewella bows to me.

Jake winks at me. "You should cut a record, Sam."

I look into his dark eyes, glad for his humor, bravery, and friendship—I hope I don't lose it. In the back of my mind is the certainty that if Dad and Cynthia dies, Jake and I are finished. Gloom settles over me.

Lewella gestures to me. "We watched your mother sometimes, Samantha. She was very skilled with wildlife. And Rose felt for some time that you were special."

I love hearing anything about Mom, but again wonder why Rose would end up in northern Minnesota, and have any interest in me.

Leaf litter rustles near the open doorway, advertising Canaste's presence. A changing of the guard. The gorillas and Originals have left. The boa's membranous fins undulate along her neck and her emerald head is wider than the doorway. I'm sure the snake is wrapped completely around the hut.

Canaste eyes us. "I'm sorry I have to watch all of you. I trust you."

Lewella's green eyes shine. "Your presence is an honor, old friend."

"My honor." The boa stares at Jake, her long tongue flicking out. "You have the sight, don't you?"

Jake's eyes widen as he glances at her. "What do you mean? Eyesight?" He quickly looks away.

The others regard him with raised eyebrows.

"I won't tell anyone, Jake." The great snake settles her head on the ground outside, blocking the exit. "Sleep well, Samantha and Jake. And Lewella, Brandon, and Tom."

"And you, Canaste," says Lewella.

Brandon says cheerfully, "Sleep well, our friend."

"Sweet dreams," I say.

Tom retreats to a back corner, his face in shadows. Lewella and Brandon join him, talking quietly, most likely about us. Maybe they're deciding to dump us.

I tap Jake's thigh and tilt my head toward the opposite corner, as far from the doorway as possible. I get up and head there, and he follows.

We sit with our backs to Canaste. I rub the jade dolphin on my bracelet with two fingers, my voice a whisper. "So your visions are some type of clairvoyance."

He brushes crumbs off his shirt. "I wonder how Canaste could see that from just looking at me? She must have the sight too."

"How are we going to get out of here, Jake?"

"Tell me again about the staff." He looks at me intently. "You said you couldn't let go of it with the Komodo and with the Tasmanian devil."

I clutch my knees. "It wouldn't let me, Jake. Honest. I'm not making this up."

He tosses a hand. "It's controlling you somehow."

"You saw what happened when the Tasmanian devil attacked us."

He pushes hair off his brow. "I believe you, Sam, because every time I hold the staff I feel like I don't want to let go of it either. As if I'm married to the stupid stick." His brow wrinkles. "Give WhipEye to me. I'm not connected to it as strongly as you are and can probably handle it better."

He might be right, but I avoid his eyes. "It could end up doing the same thing to you."

"Let's find out, Sam. Experiment. I do it all the time with recipes. Even in kung fu."

His suggestion makes sense, but I still can't give it to him. WhipEye lies at my side, away from him, and I leave it there, unable to hand it over. Just the idea makes me queasy.

He shakes his head. "What if the staff is hurting you in some way that we don't understand? Or playing some kind of mind game on you?"

A small fear stirs inside me. What if Jake plans to give WhipEye to Gorgon in exchange for the antidote? He might do anything to save Cynthia. But then again, he needs the staff to get home, just as I do. I hate being paranoid about him. "Does your armor have any control over you?"

He shrugs. "A little, but not like WhipEye has over you."

"I hope you have a plan, Jake."

His hands form fists. "I'm going to do whatever it takes to save Mom."

I straighten. "Ditto for Dad." Anger wells up inside me. "Do you think I want to have my back cut open, fight monsters, or worry about saving the world?" I take a deep breath. "I don't care about fulfilling their stupid prophecy." My voice becomes very soft. "Mom died for me. I can't live with Dad dying because of me too."

He's quiet for a few moments, and then he murmurs, "I've had more memories about KiraKu and the evil guardian—which was all a little mind-blowing—but I have no interest in the guardian thing either. I mean, they're all mentioning this prophecy like it's a done deal that we have to fulfill. It's crazy."

His face scrunches up, but he says, "You know, the bean paste was pretty good."

"Yeah, it wasn't bad. You could do better."

He nods. "Maybe a little more vanilla. And some cinnamon. They have cinnamon down here you know."

"Jake."

He looks at me, hemming and hawing, and when he finally speaks his voice betrays sadness. "I...I still want to be friends, Sam."

"We are!" My throat fills with emotion. "You're my best friend, Jake!"

He looks at his lap, talking fast. "I'm afraid things are going to get bad, Sam. Dangerous. Life or death. Well, you already almost died once. Twice! And we haven't gotten to the worst part of it yet. Gorgon is sounding like pure evil."

"We can do this, Jake. You're my protector."

"I think you're right." He eyes me uncertainly. "I mean I did take a few for the team already."

I pull my hair back behind my ear, eager to talk to him. "We need a better plan than just running into the jungle."

"Guardians." Lewella's whisper comes from behind us. She's kneeling on one knee.

Embarrassed over what she might have heard, I wonder how long she's been there. Tom and Brandon squat on either side of her, shielding us from Canaste.

"What's your decision?" Lewella's green eyes bore into mine, her gentle face reassuring.

I finger my compass, not wanting to lie to her. She admires Mentore, but without her help escape will be impossible. "We don't trust Mentore."

Jake's eyes flash gold when he glances at me.

I look at him and shrug. "We have to trust them, Jake. We need their help."

He looks at Lewella. "Okay. We want to escape, find Gorgon, free Rose, and get the antidote without giving Gorgon the staff. Should be a breeze."

Tom's face shows caution, but Brandon's eyes shine.

Lewella speaks quickly. "I suspected as much and we've agreed to help."

Jake's eyes widen. "Why would you betray your friend, Mentore?"

Lewella places a hand on his shoulder. "I believe you'll do the right thing, Jake. I believe you are the true guardians the prophecy speaks of, and I don't fear WhipEye in Samantha's hands. Even though I trust Mentore, I agree he shouldn't have the staff, nor destroy it."

I drop my hand to WhipEye, glad Lewella has given me another reason to keep it to myself.

"That...that's super." Jake raises a hand in acceptance.

"Gorgon and his followers will be too powerful to defeat in his stronghold." Lewella looks at us.

"Then let's demand he bring Rose and the antidote to us in the jungle, and then we'll leave with WhipEye." Even as I say it, it sounds too easy to be true.

"At worst we can trade WhipEye for the antidote and Rose. We would have to find a fast way home." Jake watches me for a reaction, but I don't give him one.

I regard Lewella. "Will Gorgon be honor-bound to give us the antidote?"

Lewella nods. "He will have to or his followers will leave him."

Brandon rubs his hands together enthusiastically. "What's the escape plan?"

FIFTEEN

LEWELLA'S SMALL HANDS QUIETLY tear apart strands of the weave on the back wall. Canaste doesn't stir, but since snakes sleep with their eyes open it's difficult to know if the giant Lesser is really sleeping.

Lewella's nimble fingers flash so fast I can't follow them, undoing the woven leaves until there's a hole big enough for her to step through. I expect to see Canaste's body wrapped around the hut—I'm surprised when I don't.

"Wait." Lewella exits, and soon gestures for me to follow.

My foot catches on the lower strands as I step through—I nearly topple. Lewella grabs my arm to steady me.

"I'm a klutz," I murmur, staring into her green eyes.

"It's genetic," Jake whispers behind me.

"Funny."

Humid air clings to my clothing, the scent of humus and leaf litter thick in my nostrils. The night is warm. Cicadas chirp and other insects drone on, giving some cover for our movements.

When everyone is out, Lewella whispers, "Samantha, any idea of direction?"

"Mentore is sending Macy's tracking chips north so..." I lift the compass and the needle does its strange thing and moves off north to south, confirming my gut. Something about that seems too easy, but I say, "South."

"Stay close." Lewella's body gives off a golden glow, easy to follow, and she runs quietly, pacing herself to my best stride. At least when I'm running I'm not as awkward.

Lewella's long shining hair is a beacon to follow in the night, though her black blouse and jeans make the rest of her body nearly invisible. Jake runs behind me, with Tom and Brandon taking up the rear. Dad's image sneaks into my thoughts and I run harder, wincing over the crunch my tennis shoes make on every step. Jake isn't any quieter.

When we're a hundred yards from the hut, a shout pierces the night.

"Keep running," Lewella whispers over her shoulder.

Increasing her height to six feet, she spreads her wings wide. Circling around behind us, she flies between Jake and me, her arms sliding around our waists. Lewella smoothly lifts us off the ground, her wings a blur, and continues south, darting around trees as we flee.

Brandon and Tom run on either side of the faerie. Tom moves fluidly and silently around trees and brush, while Brandon barrels through the lighter stuff.

More voices stir behind us until a deep howl fills the jungle. Mentore. I hoped we would be long gone before he noticed. An image of the gorilla baring his canines at us sends shivers along my arms.

Glancing back, I see dozens of gold specks moving at different heights in different patterns through the jungle. Lessers and Originals. Chasing us. Fast. In silence.

After a mile Lewella swerves around a tree and stops, hovering, her wings beating so fast they're a blur. She peeks around the trunk, both of us snug in her arms.

Jake grimaces. "How far south are we going, Sam?"

I shrug. "Gorgon is probably watching us now."

"Really?" Jake's lips turn down and he glances around the jungle.

Not far away to the north a wide semicircle of eyes shines in the night, leaving us one direction. "They're herding us south," I say.

"Why?" whispers Jake.

"They're hoping Gorgon shows up," says Lewella.

"We have to lose our followers." Jake glances at her. "Can't you outfly them?'

Lewella peers into the jungle. "Yes, but Gorgon is somewhere nearby, so that won't help us find him."

An idea comes to me. "Put me down, Lewella."

Her eyebrows raise, but she shrinks in size and lowers us until we stand on soil again. She folds her wings behind her and her green eyes blaze gold. "Hurry, Samantha."

"Come on, Jake." I stride around the tree, facing a thousand distant eyes racing toward me. Imagining teeth and claws belonging to Lessers who hate the staff, I stand there, blinking.

Jake stands beside me. "Kind of in a hurry here."

"Ready or not," I mutter.

"You know what you're doing, right?"

I look at him. "Not sure. Thought I'd just try something for fun. Hold on."

"If you're trying to worry me, it's working." Jake grips WhipEye with me, his shoulder against mine.

I guide the staff, moving it back and forth in crisscrossing patterns, weaving the bottom of it in a mess of lines. While moving the staff I visualize what I want to have happen. I hope my experiment with the staff when we arrived wasn't just luck—I still don't have a memory of using WhipEye like this.

Hoisting the staff, we strike the ground hard. *Boom!* The echo carries far into the jungle and our pursuers pause.

Fatigue hits me. Jake leans heavily on the staff too. We're trying to do something much bigger than just moving people and I expected it to cost us.

Our pursuers come faster now, their eyes at all levels, their dark shapes blending with the jungle.

Slithering sounds like a thousand moving snakes break the night's silence as vines and branches of younger trees and saplings wrap around the limbs and torsos of the closest Lessers and Originals. Startled cries, shrieks, and animal calls fill my ears.

Jake waves a hand. "There's more coming!"

I peer into the jungle. "Crap."

Eluding the grasping vegetation, some Originals still run at us over the ground. Tom and Brandon split up to face them, while Lewella expands to eight feet and rises into the air to block massive primates swinging through the trees toward us. She won't be able to handle all of them, and birds and bats are flying toward us too.

Most of the Originals and Lessers are caught by vines wrapping around their ankles and legs. However some get through by taking long leaps over the ground, only to be met by snaking vines and small branches that wrap them up like mummies and drag them back.

Some primates in the trees also avoid traps. But eventually branches sway, curl, and bend to block them, even for an instant, and then they're immediately imprisoned by writhing vines and vegetation, as are the birds and bats.

One massive dark shape darts around entanglements and rushes us. Jake and I back up against the tree, unable to sidestep its charge. Lifting the staff like a spear, we hold it ready. I remember the Tasmanian devil and my arms stiffen.

When the animal is closer, vegetation wraps around its front legs, slowing it. The beast tears wildly at the vines with its jaws.

"Capybara, a.k.a. *Hydrochoerus hydrochaeris*," I say. "Weighs up to one-hundred-fifty pounds. Largest rodent in the world. South America. Kind of cute."

Jake grunts. "Looks like a monster guinea pig. What does it eat?"

"Grass and water plants usually."

"This one looks starved for meat."

The giant Lesser breaks free and bolts at us. I'm ready to hit it when green vines wrap around its torso, stopping it abruptly just a few yards from us. Towering over us with huge incisors, the capybara pushes its big snout forward until it's three feet from our faces. More vines wrap around its neck. We lean back as it struggles to come closer.

"Let's smack it," says Jake. "We should, right?"

I hold WhipEye stiffly, aiming it at the capybara's jaws. "Wait."

"It's going to bite us in half, Sam!"

"It will cost us energy to use the staff and we may need that energy soon with Gorgon."

"If we're guinea pig snacks, saving energy won't matter!"

"True."

The Lesser's bared teeth push to within a foot of my face. My jaw clenches. I'm thinking of the scar on my back and lean sideways.

It inches closer.

Jake nudges my shoulder, his eyes round. "How about now? Maybe just a little smack."

"Not yet." I stare into the capybara's big brown eyes. "You're supposed to be a vegetarian."

Another vine wraps around the mammal's snout, forcing it closed, and encircling branches quietly lift the Lesser off the ground and away from us into the darkness.

My clenched fingers relax on the staff. Eyes blink and our pursuers stop moving forward as they wrestle with the living blockade of green growth. Many of the Lessers will eventually get through, but it will slow all of them. I stare in awe at the staff.

Tom and Brandon are wide-eyed as they peer into the jungle. Lewella appears just as surprised. They never had to lift a finger.

"Okay, gotta say, that is powerful!" Jake shakes his head in wonder, looking at the staff, and then me. "Good work, Einstein."

"Good work, partner." I look into his dark eyes, wanting to throw my arms around him.

"Five-stars," he says softly. But he releases the staff and steps away.

"Let's go." Lewella lifts us once more, immediately carrying us south through the jungle. She flies no more than a hundred yards, when she stops and looks up.

A quarter mile ahead of us, a dark shape is diving at us from above. As the attacker draws closer, its outline, bright eyes, and two horns make it obvious. The vampire bat.

Lewella quickly rises fifty feet off the ground to face the creature, stopping with her back ten feet in front of a massive tree. The upward change in height makes me jittery.

"Can't they just leave us alone?" asks Jake. "Yell, chase, bite. Sheesh!"

I don't want to fight the bat either. "Lewella, you fly faster than a bat."

"It can track us." Her voice is calm. "Better to end it here."

"Yeah, no use just escaping," grumbles Jake.

Brandon and Tom climb trees like squirrels to either side of us, soon twenty yards off the ground, gripping the furrowed tree bark with their hands and feet. None of this slows the bat's flight or changes its line of attack.

Thirty feet across, the vampire bat seems to target me. I clutch the staff.

The brothers leap, landing on the mammal's dark wings. Teetering wildly, the bat passes to the right of us, and the brothers jump off the creature onto other trees.

"More Cirque du Soleil," I mutter. But Tom and Brandon's acrobatics are astonishing.

"Good job!" Jake gives a thumbs up to the brothers.

Tom's forehead wrinkles, but Brandon grins. Like flying squirrels, they quickly jump from tree to tree to get in front of us again.

The bat wheels around, but this time it veers wide of the Originals, its wings nearly vertical with the ground as it passes them. Lewella rotates to continue facing the creature, her wings moving slowly. If she was alone she could easily outmaneuver the bat, but maybe not with us in her arms.

Brandon and Tom anticipate the bat's plan, leaping and swinging to other trees to intercept the Lesser, but they won't be in time.

Flying at sharp angles to avoid the two Originals, the bat keeps its distance from them and aims straight for me. In nature a dragonfly is no match for a bat, but I've seen Lewella push over an armored car and giant Lessers so I know she's not afraid. I lift WhipEye with both hands as Lewella's wings beat faster.

A dark shadow in the night, the bat flaps toward us, claws spread wide.

"What's the plan, Lewella?" Jake has his hands up as if he's going to kung fu chop the bat.

I don't think he can hurt a Lesser with a thirty-foot wingspan, but he looks brave. I'm glad I have WhipEye to jab but doubt that will stop the bat either. "Lewella? Any thoughts?"

The faerie is intent on the bat and doesn't answer. Maybe she's planning a last-minute dart to the side and a swift kick. Or maybe she'll move at the last minute and the stupid bat will fly into the tree. That must be the plan. Has to be! The bat is so big it's blocking out my view of the jungle.

"It's pretty close," I say nervously.

"Do something!" yells Jake.

When it's ten feet away, claws reaching for me, I shout. "Move, Lewella!"

In a flash Lewella backs up a few feet, and the vampire bat abruptly tumbles straight down, its wings curling. Something hammered it from above. I feel a rush of air as the falling bat just misses me, one of its leathery wings sweeping inches from my right cheek.

I gulp. "Well that wasn't scary at all."

"Didn't even come close." Jake wipes sweat off his forehead.

We watch the bat tumble. Just before it hits the ground the Lesser manages to straighten its wings and glide away, giving a high-pitched shriek as it disappears.

Jake snorts. "Too bad it didn't take a header into the dirt."

I tense as another pair of eyes looms out of the darkness in front of us. "Canaste."

That's why Lewella never moved—she knew the snake was there and assumed it would help us. Maybe the giant boa is her secret partner.

Hanging from a high branch, the giant emerald boa holds her head level with Lewella's. Abruptly I'm nervous, unsure what the snake will do and why it attacked the bat. Jake's eyes are round—the snake wouldn't be his ally of choice. Brandon and Tom leap to nearby trees, watching the boa intently. But Lewella doesn't move and her beating wings seem calmer.

"This way." Canaste retreats into the foliage above us.

"Samantha?" asks Lewella.

I exhale through pursed lips. I'm actually relieved the boa is helping us, but I glance at Jake. He doesn't trust as easily as I do. Especially giant snakes. But he frowns and shrugs, so I say, "Yeah, why not? The more the merrier."

Slithering into the darkness above, Canaste leads Lewella, with Tom and Brandon climbing fast behind us. Lewella grips me firmly, but the height motivates me to cling to her arm anyway.

Once above the treetops, the snake waits until Tom and Brandon climb atop her back. Then she whispers, "We can avoid Mentore's attack by heading north. He won't expect it." She looks at me. "You want to find Gorgon, right?"

"We have to." She knows something that we don't. I'm a little shocked over her continued help. I hope there isn't another surprise coming—like a betrayal. But Canaste seems sincere, as she was when we first met.

"Alright." The boa's fins ripple along her body as she quietly takes us north, along the tops of the trees and toward our pursuers.

Lewella flits beside Canaste, with Jake and me firmly in her grasp.

Again the Amazon canopy spreads out before us in an undulating dark pattern. Stars shine and the air is warm and humid. I pretend we're near the ground, but breaks between the trees curl my toes. When I do have the courage to glance down once, golden specks betray our pursuers' eyes, barely visible through the branches as they pass beneath us.

In minutes Canaste stops, tasting the air with her long tongue. The boa curls back onto the top of a large tree, and Lewella hovers in front of her. Brandon and Tom remain on the snake.

"Thank you, Canaste." Lewella bows to her.

Her head level with me, the boa crawls closer, her large eyes finding mine. "If you go to Gorgon, you may destroy us all."

I don't want the weight of that responsibility, of risking a power-hungry lunatic gaining access to WhipEye or KiraKu, but I have to save Dad and Cynthia. "We don't have a choice."

The boa's voice is soft. "You always have a choice."

I swallow. "Not if we want to save our parents."

Jake flicks his hand. "And we're not going to destroy everyone. That's a bit over the top, don't you think?"

Canaste swings her gaze to Lewella. "Can they succeed?"

Still hovering, Lewella speaks calmly. "I believe in them, Canaste. They succeeded against the evil guardian when everyone thought they would fail."

Hearing that is odd, since only fragmented memories of that battle have returned. But it still gives me confidence and hope.

The boa's head floats back to me. "Gorgon will never quit until he has WhipEye."

"He can't have it. It's mine." The harsh words escape my mouth before I can stop them.

Everyone stares at me and Jake's jaw tightens.

Flicking out her tongue, the boa says, "The staff is dangerous to everyone."

Jake studies me, looking concerned. "The staff is driving you crazy, Sam."

"Maybe." I lower my eyes, my face hot. I *am* losing all control to the chestnut staff. Even while holding it I ache to have it in my hand.

I look up. "Do you know where Gorgon is?"

Canaste pulls back. "I can take you to his stronghold."

Jake's hands do circles. "You knew the location but didn't tell Mentore? Wow."

"If I do, he will attack." The boa's voice is sad. "Lessers fighting Lessers. War. Doing what humans have done forever. I couldn't bear it." She pauses. "Catching Gorgon might have ended this, but I sensed you wanted to leave and I didn't want you hurt."

"You heard us talking the whole time, didn't you?" I look at her. "Good ears for a snake."

The boa's eyes flash gold. "I didn't want to alert Mentore or fight you, so I waited and followed."

"We owe you, my friend," says Lewella.

Jake waves a hand at her. "You know, for a snake you've been pretty darn nice." When he says this, he looks like he's sucking on a piece of sour candy.

I frown at him. Another compliment like that won't help. "You took a big risk, Canaste. Is that why you weren't wrapped around the hut?"

The boa slides even closer. "You saved all Lessers, Samantha and Jake. Gave them life again, possibly forever. I couldn't imprison or hurt you. Ever."

"I'm glad we helped you, Canaste." Something stirs inside me. I'm suddenly very glad that we defeated the evil guardian. Proud even. It sounds like the biggest thing I've ever done in my life, even if I still can't fully remember it. Weird.

I study the boa. "Can you get us inside Gorgon's fortress?"

The boa gives a low hiss. "It's dangerous, but there is a way."

Jake frowns. "How dangerous? Are we talking lose a leg or arm dangerous?"

Brandon looks eager. "An adventure."

"Stupid." Tom runs a hand through his hair and then rubs the studs in his right ear.

Brandon keeps smiling and claps his brother on the back. Tom just shakes his head.

"Well I'm all for it." Jake pats his armor.

Everyone turns to me, waiting. I didn't realize I would have the final say. I don't want the boa or anyone else to risk their lives for us. But saving Dad and Cynthia consumes me. "Let's go steal the antidote."

"Hurry." Lewella rises into the air.

Canaste turns and glides across the treetops. After a few minutes she ducks below the canopy in a steep dive, heading west. Lewella follows.

"This is great, right, Sam?" Jake smiles as the wind blows his hair back.

"Ah huh. Twice in one night. Talk about torture. If I puke I'll make sure it's in your direction."

"Try to miss me," Lewella says lightly.

"Sure." My stomach churns and I close my eyes. I look once, but that's worse. Branches aren't supporting the boa as her body extends far between trees. I'm thankful I'm not riding her. Having Lewella carry me isn't much better. The Lesser flies beside the snake, her flight like a rollercoaster plunging into free-fall. Feeling faint, I close my eyes again and cling to her arm.

Soon the air isn't rushing into my face and I open my eyes. Lewella is flying level again, which calms my stomach. She's carrying us only a few feet above the ground beside Canaste, whose fins seem to float her over the soil.

We enter the bottom of a large, grassy gully with trees lining its upper edges. Far ahead, the gully dead-ends at a large hill. Canaste crawls toward it, tasting the air with her tongue.

I peer closer. The distant hill has a dark area at ground level. A tunnel opening large enough for a Lesser. The way into Gorgon's stronghold. I'm both excited and wary. Jake glances at me and gives me a thumbs up.

Slowing, the boa appears to sense something.

About halfway between us and the tunnel, a smooth voice filled with power calls out, "No farther, snake."

The boa stops, her head rising ten feet as she hisses and coils her body, her fins fluttering fast.

From behind a thick bush in the gully, a tall, muscular man steps into view. Instead of hair, writhing tentacles cover his head.

The kingly way in which he holds himself makes his identity easy to guess.

SIXTEEN

"WE COME IN PEACE, Gorgon." Lewella's usually gentle voice has a hard edge.

Tom and Brandon leap off Canaste and crouch in front of Lewella, while she rises in the air, still holding us in her arms.

The boa keeps her attention fixed on Gorgon. I wonder how well Lewella and Canaste know him, and if they were enemies in KiraKu.

Barefoot, Gorgon has chiseled features, broad shoulders, and stands six-four. He looks about thirty, but like all Lessers in our world he has to be ancient. Wearing black jeans and a long-sleeved, red silk shirt, his golden eyes flash brightly.

"I'm thinking Medusa." Jake squints. "Don't look at the slugs on his head, Sam."

But I don't take my eyes off the dozens of deep red tentacles on his head, tinted gold and looking like fat dreadlocks. I whisper, "I don't feel hypnotized so Medusa just seems like a name he earned along the way in our mythology."

"You sure?" Jake opens his eyes a bit more. "Yeah, just bad dreads I guess."

I run through ideas of what kind of animal Gorgon might have been in KiraKu. Not an octopus or squid, and nautilus doesn't seem right. Something else. I want to know.

Gorgon smiles. "Ah, Lewella of the Dragonfly Clan. I would not fight you, dear. Nor harm the guardians as Mentore threatened to do tonight."

"For someone who poisons people you sound like a peaceful guy." Jake's voice has an edge.

"So you were there when we met Mentore?" I remember the eyes I saw in the jungle when we climbed the mushroom steps of Mentore's tree. Either it was Gorgon in his Lesser form, and he's huge, or he climbed a nearby tree. How did he infiltrate Mentore's camp so easily?

Ignoring my question, Gorgon walks toward us, dreamlike in movement. "I expected the guardians to come to me. They want to save their elders. And of course, Canaste of the Boa Clan, I knew you would betray Mentore because of your good heart. You don't want the guardians hurt, do you?"

"Stop." Canaste's fins undulate slowly. "Close enough."

Gorgon gives off a vibe that sends chills down my spine. He emanates strength and power, but I don't know why. That's what scares me the most. He's an unknown, and our friends are wary of him. Mentore said Gorgon had mind powers. I regret not asking more about those.

Spreading his hands, Gorgon pauses twenty feet away, his face calm. "The guardians want the antidote for their elders. If they come with me, they'll have it."

My gut says Gorgon is telling the truth, at least about having an antidote, which means it's possible to save Dad and Cynthia. "We want it, but we don't want to go with you."

"Yeah, your Komodo assassin said to bring the staff, which we've done," says Jake. "Now it's your turn, Fish Bait. We'll wait here and you run along and bring the antidote to us."

I frown at Jake. Calling Gorgon Fish Bait isn't going to help our cause, especially if the guy has a temper. Though Jake is creative in his names, I'll give him that. I also know he's angry—as I am—this is the guy that ordered the hit on Cynthia and Dad.

Interestingly enough, Gorgon remains calm.

"Bring the antidote and we'll trade," I lie. "WhipEye for the antidote. Bring Rose too. You promised to free her."

Gorgon shows his empty palms. "The antidote is unusual and doesn't fit into a pocket. You'll have to come with me to get it."

I hesitate to call him a liar, but say, "That doesn't sound true."

"Oh, come on!" Jake sounds frustrated. "If it doesn't fit into a pocket, what is it?"

Gorgon smiles.

"You want WhipEye." Canaste's head moves back and forth. "But you can't have it."

I'm willing to give anything for the antidote, but Canaste is right. I never want Gorgon to have WhipEye.

Gorgon lifts his chin. "Mentore spreads lies, telling everyone I want the staff for personal power, but I want it for everyone."

I don't believe him. "You're refusing to bring the antidote to us?"

Gorgon spreads his hands. "You'll have to trust me. There is no other option."

"Then our friends come with us." I thumb at Lewella and Canaste. "As insurance."

"Canaste and I are willing to accompany the guardians." Lewella floats a little lower.

"Me too." Brandon flexes his arms. "I want to see this famous stronghold of yours."

Tom stares at his brother, cocking his head as if he hasn't heard him clearly.

"Why not?" In a flash Gorgon expands to ten feet tall, his body still appearing human. One of the sluglike tentacles on his head elongates just as fast and hits me in the stomach, while another tentacle wraps around WhipEye just above my hand. Shocked by how fast he moved, I'm gasping for air, which weakens my grip. He yanks the staff from my hand with a force that jars my shoulder.

"No!" All of our plans vanish and I stare stupidly at him, immediately wanting the staff back in my hands. I don't understand it, but it's as if he stole a piece of me.

Shrinking as fast as it expanded, Gorgon's tentacle resumes its former size. Gorgon remains ten feet tall though, and grips the staff with his hand, his eyes gleaming. "At last." He caresses the faces on the chestnut-colored wood. "Come, Samantha of the Green Clan and Jake of the Morris Clan. If you want the antidote, it's yours."

Jake gapes. "Okay, that did not just happen. That was mind-bending impossible."

I swallow. We're at Gorgon's mercy now.

"I won't allow you to take WhipEye." Canaste rears back farther, as if to strike.

"Nail him!" I blurt.

But Canaste hesitates and Lewella's face is taut. Tom and Brandon cautiously step forward. I don't see how Gorgon can fight all of them, but our friends don't look eager. Even Lewella seems cautious. There must be something about the guy we don't understand.

"There's nothing you can do." Gorgon appears calm. "Accept it."

"They don't have to." A large figure leaps into the ravine fifty yards behind Gorgon, landing with a thump.

Gorgon does an about-face. Mentore stands between him and the tunnel entrance, hunched over on his knuckles. The ape's face is shadowed, his limbs tense. I'm surprised but also relieved to see him.

"Go Mentore!" Jake raises a fist.

"Let's take him down now!" I add.

Mentore moves forward cautiously, his knuckles sliding over the leaf-littered ground, his tail flicking behind him. "I knew of this entrance long ago. But it would have been difficult to capture you among your followers, Gorgon. I needed WhipEye as bait to draw you out." He looks past Gorgon. "I knew you would help the guardians, Canaste. You have a good heart, even if your loyalty is misplaced."

Like Colonel Macy, Mentore planned for our escape. I'm guessing his angry outbursts on the treetop were all an act too. We're being moved around like pawns on a chessboard for everyone else's schemes. I want to yell at all of them.

Gorgon responds calmly. "Do you really think I came here alone, Mentore?"

Beyond the ape, two dark figures edge out from behind trees. Two Lessers. An eight-foot-tall gray wolf with short spikes sticking out from its legs, and a twelve-foot-tall frilled-neck lizard standing upright on its two hind legs. The wolf growls and the lizard unfurls the pleated skin flap around its head and hisses.

"*Chlamydosaurus kingii*, a.k.a. frilled lizard," I murmur. I've observed wild wolves in Minnesota, but not frilled lizards, which live in Australia. I whisper, "I'd love to see the reptile under different circumstances."

"Focus, Sam." Jake shakes his head. "Let's do the wildlife show another time."

"How are we going to fight giant animals, Jake?"

"You have a point."

Mentore glances back, but he doesn't appear worried. "I didn't come here alone either, Gorgon." He drums his chest. Dark shapes appear along both upper ridges of the gully. Lessers and Originals.

Gorgon motions to Mentore's followers. "And if you do capture me, I've left instructions to destroy the tunnel so there will be no way into my stronghold. Would you deny the guardians the antidote for their elders?"

"You lie," Mentore says with conviction. "About everything."

Gorgon spreads his hands. "If that was true, no Lesser would stand by my side."

Tension connects everyone like steel cables.

If Gorgon is telling the truth about the tunnel, our parents will die if he's captured. We can't risk going along with Mentore. I whisper, "We'll be safer if you put us down, Lewella."

Hovering backward fifty feet, she keeps her eyes on Gorgon while lowering us to the ground. "Stay here, guardians." She flits back to Canaste's side.

Jake whispers, "Good move. We don't have a choice."

"That's how I felt when I kept WhipEye." I ignore his surprised stare and try to steady my nerves. We have to go with Gorgon and somehow get the antidote and WhipEye. But how can we help Gorgon escape without a battle? Going alone with him terrifies me. I trust him even less than Mentore.

There's perhaps one way to avoid a fight. I level my compass for reassurance. The needle moves off north and points in the direction my gut says to take.

"We have to do something quick, Sam." Jake gestures ahead of us. "It's going to get ugly here fast."

"Come on," I whisper. I lead him in a walk behind Canaste, to her other side, opposite Lewella, Brandon, and Tom.

"Yeah, I figured we'd have to go to Fish Bait." Jake's eyes have a golden tinge and he looks disgusted. "This guy is A-1 creepy."

Guilt sweeps me that I'm betraying our friends, mixed with pain over missing the staff and worry over Dad. All jumbled together. I try to ignore it as we walk along the side of Canaste.

Mentore lifts his chin. "Surrender the staff and yourself, Gorgon, and we'll end this here."

Gorgon shakes his head. "And do what, Mentore? We were once Great Ones, able to go anywhere. Long ago in this world we did that, and many of us perished. Now we hide like outcasts, faint memories described in human mythologies and fairy tales. Should we continue to sit idly by while humans destroy this planet? Every day, humans burn this beautiful jungle, which you love, and pollute the oceans, which I adore. Yet you insist we do nothing. I lost KiraKu and I won't lose the beauty of this world too."

Mentore growls. "And your solution is to seek personal power to take over this world and KiraKu and control everyone. You behave like the humans you despise."

Mentore is right. Gorgon wants everyone to bow to him. His eyes and posture make it obvious, and I hear it in his voice. I hustle faster with Jake.

"I don't want to fight another Lesser." Mentore bares his teeth. "But I will if I have to."

Gorgon doesn't budge. "You overestimate yourself."

Gorgon sounds supremely confident, but I'm not sure why. Even though he's lightning fast with his head tentacles, he can't stop all of Mentore's followers.

Mentore bunches his shoulders, as if ready to launch himself. "You're greatly outnumbered, Gorgon."

When we hurry past Canaste's head, she turns to us, sadness in her eyes. Lewella sees us too, but her eyes show concern. I'm surprised neither of them tries to stop us. Jake slows down as he looks ahead at Gorgon.

I grab his hand. "Come on, Jake."

He looks like I'm asking him to jump off a cliff. "Ugh. Why not?"

We run for Gorgon, every step making me think this is suicide.

A roar comes from the south. I glance over my shoulder. The forty-foot Komodo dragon is flying through the trees, its two large eyes visible as it dives at the gully.

By the time we're beside Gorgon, Mentore is standing on two legs, thumping his chest with his teeth bared. I look up at Gorgon, feeling puny at his side. I'm only a half foot above his waist.

Gorgon glances down at us. "Good choice, guardians."

"Like we had one," I say.

"Great to see you up close." Jake gazes at Gorgon's head tentacles. "And sorry for calling you Fish Bait. Just a slip of the tongue."

Gorgon peers down at him. "I understand completely. It's not often you see someone like me."

Jake waves a hand. "You can say that again."

Two of Gorgon's head tentacles expand in a flash and wrap snugly around our waists, lifting us a few inches off the ground with no apparent effort. Weird and yucky. Gorgon swings Jake to his other side, maybe to balance our weight.

"Okay, that's...uh...different." Jake keeps his hands away from Gorgon's tentacle, as if he's afraid to touch it.

I touch the tentacle with one finger. It's a little slimy, tough like rubber, and also feels like it has steel strength. Resigned, I rest my hands on it. I tell myself that it's not too creepy.

Jake sees me. "Ms. Touchy-feely can't resist, huh?"

"It's really not too bad." But my face must look like I'm being forced to swallow live spiders, because Jake nods knowingly at me.

Surprisingly Gorgon still doesn't move. He even seems relaxed as Mentore charges. The massive ape runs at us on all fours like a train coming full throttle.

A dozen paces from Gorgon, Mentore launches himself into the air with his strong arms held high, fangs bared. Gorgon still doesn't move. We're going to get smushed. Obviously Mentore's promise to protect us is secondary to his desire to take down Gorgon.

"Incoming, Fish Bait!" yells Jake.

I lift up my hands for protection.

A blur of movement strikes Mentore in midair, knocking him sideways. His angry expression twists to shock as Canaste hammers him with her snout. Mentore rolls away as the body of the massive snake falls to the ground in front of us. What amazes me is that Gorgon counted on Canaste to protect us.

He leaps over the five-foot-thick boa with ease, landing softly, and then quickly glides through the gully. Gorgon moves as fast as Lewella. I look down. Each of his feet have changed into three thick, short red tentacles, which bend back and slide over the ground.

"Okay, that's more than a little creepy." Jake is staring down at Gorgon's tentacles too. He glances at me and I shake my head.

Jake immediately adds, "Uh, no offense Gorgon. You know, it just took me by surprise is all."

"No offense taken, guardian." Gorgon sounds strangely happy. Like a kid in a candy store coming away with a bagful of goodies. That bothers me.

"What are you?" I ask. Gorgon ignores my question. Dad and Mom taught me everything they knew about wildlife, and their love of animals pushed me to learn more. For as long as I can remember I've read wildlife books and magazines, and watched YouTube videos and wildlife movies. Yet I have no idea what kind of creature Gorgon was before he left KiraKu.

In seconds Gorgon arrives at the distant tunnel entrance. Stopping there, he casually turns. I stare at the gully.

A hundred yards away the frilled-neck lizard stands beside the wolf. Both are bristling with their teeth bared, blocking Canaste and Lewella.

Canaste slithers forward, striking the lizard in the chest with her snout, knocking it backward. Lewella darts to the side of the giant wolf and slams it in the ribs with the soles of her feet, sending it tumbling.

Jake peers intently at the fight. "Alright!" Then he looks up, "Ah, sorry for your friends getting slammed, Gorgon buddy."

The wolf and lizard scramble upright and bolt toward us, while Canaste and Lewella chase them. Tom and Brandon run beside

Lewella. I silently cheer for my friends. I don't want to be alone with Gorgon, and say, "You said our friends could come with us."

Gorgon stares ahead. "They wouldn't have a nice reception among my followers, and I doubt you want to see them hurt."

"True. Thank you for being so considerate." I swallow.

Mentore roars, running behind Canaste and Lewella, flailing his thick arms. His Lessers and Originals flood into the gully. While we dangle from his tentacles, Gorgon doesn't move a muscle. My stomach lurches when I realize why. Everyone has forgotten something.

"Incoming!" I shout it loudly to warn our friends.

The Komodo flies along the center of the gully, opening his jaws and spewing fire along the length of the ravine. I stare in wonder. It's a reminder that Lessers are more than the animals they resemble.

Searing flames erupt ahead of the lizard, drying the air in front of us and warming my face. Canaste hisses and flings herself to the side before the firestorm hits. Lewella darts to the other side. Everyone scatters out of the ravine, including a screaming Mentore.

The Komodo flies through his fire and lands on the run, the flames in his jaws doused. The wolf and frilled lizard run down from the sides of the ravine and join the Komodo, racing beside it. Flames lick the air ten feet high in the gully, sending scorching heat in all directions.

Gorgon pivots and slides into the dark tunnel. I twist in his grasp as his companions run in after us. Shadowy figures move on all sides of the gully, and Mentore appears charging the tunnel entrance, growling, his face twisted.

Gorgon spurts ahead to a wooden lever that sticks out from the wall. One of his head tentacles wraps around it and pushes it down. An explosion rocks the passageway, leaving my ears ringing. The ceiling collapses, beginning at the entrance and filling the tunnel for a hundred yards behind us as we flee. No one will be coming after us.

Not wanting to watch the Komodo or his companions as they stare at me, I face forward.

Jake glances at me, his eyes dull, and then hangs his head. Gorgon has what he wanted, and I know in my heart that we have no way to defeat him.

SEVENTEEN

GORGON CARRIES US AT a steady pace along the slightly descending path. The tunnel walls go on for hours and he doesn't talk. Gliding. Endless gliding. The three Lessers follow silently. The stale air is warm.

Canaste's last stare haunts me. The boa wanted to avoid a war between Lessers and we put her in a position where she had to attack Mentore and the frilled lizard to protect us. Every major decision I've made since refusing to give the staff to the Komodo has hurt others.

The staff calls to me from Gorgon's fist and my hand twitches. My head hangs lower and I close my eyes. Dad. His face floats into my thoughts. He could be dead or close to it.

I search for something to give me hope. When I consider strategies, plans, and escape, nothing feels winnable. Especially since I don't know what we're up against. It takes a while, but I do find it. Gorgon has one weakness. From the way he acted outside it's obvious that he thinks he's smarter than everyone else. Maybe he is. But that also makes him arrogant. Eventually he'll make a mistake. We just have to wait him out.

My compass points north, toward *Love*, reminding me of Mom. There isn't a day that goes by that I don't remember her. I miss her, and understand what Jake might go through if his mother dies.

"We're here, guardians." Gorgon's tone is friendly.

I open my eyes, wary.

We're entering a huge, dark cavern with a smooth rock floor that looks polished from years, if not centuries, of use. Large stalactites hang from the high ceiling and beneath them tall stalagmites grow up from the cavern floor. It looks exotic and otherworldly.

In the northwest corner of the cavern a narrow waterfall exits the wall, feeding a stream that runs along the west wall until it empties into a large, glistening underground lake. All the rocks and walls of the cavern look damp and the air is slightly cooler. My hot skin welcomes the change from the stuffy heat of the tunnel.

Several thousand eyes watch us from the walls and ceiling. Lessers. Mostly lizards, like rock monitors, spotted salamanders, blue iguanas, rough-skinned newts, and geckos. A giant spotted skunk has a horn in the center of its head and a wild boar has four tusks. There's also a few monster snapping turtles and cane toads. All are twenty feet long or larger. They might be enemies, but I love seeing them.

Among them lie or sit men and women who are young like Tom and Brandon—dressed casually in various shirts with jeans or shorts. All barefoot with gold-tinged eyes. Originals.

I look farther ahead and blink several times. "Draconis occidentalis." I can't keep the awe out of my voice.

Two red-eyed, black-scaled dragons sit alone in the far perimeter of the cavern. They're fairy tale dragons with wings, scales, claws, and jaws big enough to crush a car. Huge Lessers. Their presence strengthens the claim that Lessers are actually the creatures mentioned in human mythology around the world. They make the Komodo look like a midget.

"Oh my gosh! Jake!"

"Yes, the twins are beauties, aren't they?" Gorgon sounds like he means it.

"Huh?" Jake lifts his head to peer at them. "They're freaking giants!" He glances at Gorgon. "Ah, nice bodyguards."

The twin dragons snort, smoke drifting from their nostrils. Otherworldly. Gorgon's complaint that Lessers have to hide in our world is accurate. If humans ever found dragons, they would kill or capture them.

Lowering their heads, the twins stare at us intently.

Gorgon carries us to a small arched door-like opening on the east side of the cavern and lowers us until we can stand. It's good to have solid ground beneath my feet again. I eye WhipEye. The sight of the staff in his hand makes mine twitch.

His tentacles gently nudge us through the entrance into a small dirt cave with two piles of large green leaves on the floor. "You're my guests and don't have anything to fear here. You need rest. We'll have the ceremony tomorrow morning."

Relief washes over me. I'm not ready to face him or try to retake WhipEye. I have no ideas or energy left. Jake's shoulders droop too.

I turn to Gorgon. "What ceremony? Are you going to keep your word and bring us home in time to save our parents?"

Jake yawns. "Your Komodo assassin promised if we bring the staff, you'd give us the antidote. So where is it?"

"Tomorrow." Gorgon spins and swiftly glides away, soon slipping into the lake across the cavern. The tentacles on his head writhe as he sinks beneath the surface with WhipEye.

I wonder if tomorrow's ceremony involves us. Hopefully it isn't a sacrifice. I also hope water doesn't harm the staff.

Jake mumbles sleepily, "Sam, those dragons were in my visions. Maybe a couple of the lizards too. One turtle. Maybe a frog. Talk soon." He walks to a pile of leaves, drops to his knees, and curls up on his side to sleep.

I'm just as tired and stagger to the other pile of bedding. Sitting down, I kick off my shoes and try to find a comfortable position. My eyes wander around the little cave, stopping when I see something running along the ceiling. Spiders. Great. I pretend they're not there. I'm asleep immediately.

Mom is smiling at me. Her youthful face and bright eyes make me feel warm inside. Her appearance begins to change and expand until she's the demon. Claws. Fangs. Red eyes. The creature is chasing me, claws reaching for my neck...then the demon changes to something even larger, massive, that I can't quite make out. It gives me chills and I try to run, but there's nowhere to go...

I wake up tense. Stupid demon. It's more stressful knowing that the demon is probably real—and that we're going to meet it. The leaves were nowhere near as soft as a mattress and the shoulder I slept on is sore.

Something hits my shoulder.

"Give me a minute, Jake." My back is facing the cave door and I sleepily stretch a little, wanting a few minutes to fully wake up. My mouth feels like I ate dry cake all night.

I'm tired, but relieved to be out of the nightmare. After another nudge on my shoulder, I roll over, a little annoyed.

Instead of Jake, a tentacle tip looking like a headless snake is hovering in front of my face in the dim light. I flinch, and then watch the limb retreat through the doorway.

Gorgon says from outside the cave, "It's time for the ceremony, guardians."

EIGHTEEN

GORGON SOUNDS CHEERFUL, MAKING his invite even scarier. "Come when you're ready, Samantha of the Green Clan and Jake of the Morris Clan. We will be waiting in the white crystal cavern."

"Something to look forward to." I'm glad I can't see him.

"Can't wait! Have the antidote ready." Jake is already sitting near wooden bowls of water, fruit, nuts, and flatbread.

In a stern tone, Gorgon adds, "Stay out of the lake."

Jake lifts a hand. "No problem. I can't swim anyway. Scared of water."

But a swim sounds great to me. Swimming is one physical activity I'm good at, and I feel grimy.

Sitting up, I check my limbs. No spider bites. But white webs with bugs stuck in them cover the ceiling. I try to ignore it.

I rub sleep from my eyes. Tension knots my stomach. My back feels okay and the pain of missing WhipEye has receded to a small ache.

I join Jake. He's staring at the butterfly scale resting on his left palm.

"Are you going to put on the armor?" His black hair is a mess, but he still looks handsome. Self-conscious, I run my fingers through my tangles. My shorts and top need a wash, like his.

He yawns. "I woke up early and couldn't get back to sleep, so I experimented with the armor to see what it can do."

"Anything that can help us?" Feeling hopeful, I slug water and chew on some bread.

He shrugs. "Nothing that's going to defeat an army of Lessers." He flicks out his fingers. "I really hope we don't have to fight the dragons. Do you think the ceremony is a sacrifice to his jungle god or something?"

"Gorgon thinks he's god."

"Yeah. I got that vibe too."

We eat and drink in silence. The food perks me up but the dim cave light doesn't wake me fully.

"What time is it?" Jake peers at my wrist.

I check my watch. "Eight a.m."

He nods, his lips twitching.

Saturday morning. That speeds my pulse. We have less than a day and a half to get the antidote to our parents. Tarath said Dad and Cynthia have two days at most. Maybe it's less.

I study Jake, wondering what he's thinking. I wonder if he would ever bring me flowers or ask me out on a date. I shake my head to focus.

"We have to return today, Jake. This morning. Gorgon has to give us the antidote, and then we have to trick him into giving the staff back." Just saying it gives me a headache. It feels impossible. Jake's silence increases the pounding in my head. "Do you have any ideas?"

He brushes back his hair, his dark eyes on mine. "Ask Gorgon to bring us home with the antidote. Even if he keeps WhipEye, he should be willing to do that. He's honor-bound to his word, so maybe we can force that at least."

I avoid his eyes. "Right."

He flicks a hand at me. "We can't sacrifice Mom and Bryon just to keep the staff, Sam."

"I can't argue with that." I did that once and don't want to repeat it.

"If we have each other's back, we can do this." He poses it almost as a question.

"I agree." Jake has to be wondering if my obsession with the staff will cause us to fail. Like it did with the Komodo. I fear the same thing. What if WhipEye controls me again, forcing me into something against my will? More than anything I want to save Dad.

I grab some berries. "Gorgon knows how to play people."

Jake already has a mouthful of berries, and he dribbles some berry juice on his yellow T-shirt but doesn't seem to notice. "Yeah, he played Mentore for a fool. That whole event was timed down to the second. He's like an evil supervillain."

I hold his gaze. "Look, we might not fully remember it, but we defeated the evil guardian and I think he was a badass too."

Jake leans forward, his voice earnest. "We just have to give Gorgon whatever he wants to save our parents. We can't worry about saving the world. Ditto KiraKu. Neither of us even want to be guardians."

"I agree. We have to keep it simple." I gesture to the cave door. "Why do you think he warned us to stay out of the lake?"

"What if it's healing water?" Jake sounds excited.

"I don't see how that helps us. Tarath said it won't heal our parents."

He nods. "But maybe it would give us a boost. I mean we've got night vision, and day visions, so what's the next step, right?"

That gets my blood pumping and I feel hopeful. "Great idea, genius. Love it!"

Jake waves a hand. "I can't wait to throw Fish Bait across the cavern."

"Okay, let's check it out."

We finish eating and I put on my shoes. When I stand, Jake opens his arms, his eyes questioning. It surprises me. He wouldn't have done this a day ago, and in the past it's always been me who initiated it. I step forward and we hold each other tightly. When I pull back from him, he looks worried.

"Partners." He says it with a little uncertainty.

"Five-stars. Always. Always. Always."

"Okay. I believe you, Sam."

I look at his dark eyes. For a moment he looks like he wants to say or do more. But then he turns and we walk into the cavern together.

The Lessers and Originals are gone. I'm glad we have it to ourselves. I need time to think.

The high ceiling has a few small holes that allow some light in, transforming the cave's appearance.

Layers of deep red, amber, brown, and burnt orange streak the walls. The distant lake is dark blue, and bright green moss and ferns grow near the center of the cavern and near the lake. Towering red and yellow stalagmites are scattered throughout the cavern. Green stalactites hang from the ceiling.

At the north end of the cavern another massive tunnel leads out. Faint voices drift in from the other cave.

"Come on, Sam. If Gorgon and his crew are waiting, we better do this pronto." Jake jogs toward the lake.

My body wakes up fast as I follow him. "If it's healing water, Gorgon must have smuggled it out of KiraKu like Rose did for Lewella and the brothers for thousands of years."

Jake flicks a hand. "Maybe we could report him to the crocodile in KiraKu, send him to naughty Lesser jail."

That makes me smile. "I'm all over that."

We weave around stalagmites and moss-covered boulders, and then cut through a large patch of knee-high ferns. In minutes we cross the cavern.

Jake stops at the rocky edge of the lake in front of six-foot-wide stairs cut into stone and leading down into the water. He stares out across the pool. The brook that feeds the lake gurgles along the far wall.

To the side of the stairs I kneel on a bed of moss among small ferns. The water is a foot below the rocky side and I lean over to cup a handful of it in a palm. Not frigid, just cool. It looks clear and clean in my hand. I sniff it. It has a nice scent but doesn't appear special in any way. I remember what the healing water smelled like in Jake's flask when he gave it to our parents. Sweet. Bright. Alive. This isn't that.

I'm disappointed. Thinking of bacteria and diseases in water, I hesitate to taste it, especially since Gorgon spends time in it. Ugh. "It's just water, Jake."

The lagoon has poor visibility due to the shadowy interior of the cavern. Jake takes a step down into an inch of water.

A quick bath would be appealing. I could clean my hair. "Are you going to clean off? I'm thinking of doing that too, but I'm nervous about going in."

Jake doesn't answer and takes another step down into calf-deep water.

I sit back on my heels. "Why don't you take your shoes off?" He still doesn't answer.

I straighten. "Look, maybe we shouldn't go in." I'm surprised he's thinking of it since he can't swim and is scared of water. Maybe he's planning on sitting on the lower steps to clean off.

He takes another step down. Then another. He's thigh-deep in water and still staring out over the lake. I bend forward to see his face.

His eyes look blank. I finally get it. He's having one of his visions. Kind of like sleepwalking. Hustling to my feet, I lean over and grab his left arm from the shoreline. He slaps my hand off without any effort and takes another step down and to the right. He's waist deep and I can't reach him now.

"Jake!" I hope the water will wake him up, but I quickly kick off my shoes to go in after him.

I stop for a moment when I spot a distant ripple out on the lake. It confirms the pool isn't empty. Maybe that's why Gorgon warned us to stay out of it.

"Snap out of it, Jake! Jake!" I splash down the steps. The water is refreshing on my legs. Another ripple erupts closer to us. Whatever is moving beneath the water is coming fast.

Jake leans forward. I grab his shoulders from behind and try to pull him back, but his momentum carries us both off the steps and into deep water. He splashes forward with a bad doggie paddle for a few seconds and I let go of him to keep myself afloat.

"Jake!"

He stops abruptly and starts to sink. Panicked, I kick and stroke forward, grab his armpits, and kick like crazy. When I get him onto his back, I reach an arm across his chest in a lifeguard carry, turn onto my side, and scissors kick and stroke hard to keep us above the surface. I've had senior lifesaving classes so it's not too difficult, and my shorts are making it easier to swim.

Coolness sweeps over my limbs as the water cleans off the last day's grime. I'd be happier if I was in a Minnesota lake filled with sunfish and crappie.

A ripple sweeps by as I keep us moving. Jake's eyes are still glassy. I look down. Something dark flashes just below my feet. Panic. I stop kicking and lift my knees. My throat is dry over the image of a tiger or great white shark chomping on my legs. That seems impossible, but a sharklike Lesser doesn't.

Jake starts to sink, taking me with him. Watching below my body, I begin kicking again, stroking hard with my free hand. Jake is heavy muscle weight, and his cargo shorts and tennis shoes don't help. We're almost there.

Jake swallows some water and sputters and blinks. Coughing, he looks around wide-eyed, and then twists out of my hold and grabs wildly for my shoulders. I struggle with him, kicking my legs to move us toward shore. When he tries to climb on top of me, I hold my breath and go under, stroking toward the side while dragging him with me.

My hand finds one of the lower submerged steps, and I grab the stone and pull myself up to the next one. Jake claws his way over my arm to the step, where he pulls himself up far enough to sit, still chest deep and coughing up water.

Spooked over whatever is in the lake, I climb several steps higher, also spitting out water.

A *swish* comes from the lagoon, but I don't see anything. I stand up in knee-deep water. "Get out, Jake!"

Continuing to cough, he pushes to his feet and turns.

From the center of the lake a foot-high wave speeds across the surface unnaturally fast.

"MOVE!" I yell.

Looking startled, he steps up, still thigh deep in the water with his back to the surge. He takes another step when the wave hits him. The water splashes up to my waist and out of the lake onto the surrounding ground. I lean back and grab at nearby rocks so the return flow doesn't carry me back down the steps.

Teetering, Jake's eyes widen as his arms fly out to the sides. With nothing to hang on to, the water is pulling him out. "Sam!"

"Grab my hand!" I splash down and reach for him, leaning back so he can't pull us both in again.

He flails an arm in my direction and our fingertips touch. I take another step down to grab him, but a vertical bulge of water rises beneath him, carrying him upward and away from me.

His eyes are wild with fear. "Sam!"

"Jake!" My heart races as I watch. I'm about to dive in after him when a massive dark blue tentacle sweeps out of the rising water, wrapping around him and lifting him ten feet above the lake.

Jake struggles furiously against the limb. "Sam! Sam!"

"Jake!" Gaping, I back up the steps, staring at the tentacle—wondering what it's attached to—while waiting for him to be dashed on the rocky side or eaten. The thought of him dying tears at me. *No no no.*

About to scream for help, I hesitate when the tentacle carries Jake toward me. I move out of the way as it gently deposits him on the moss and uncurls from him, rolling him free.

Jake flops to his stomach, gulping air.

Stepping over the retreating tentacle, I help him to a kneeling position, while keeping one eye on the water and the disappearing limb.

My chest heaves. "I thought I lost you," I murmur. Words rush out of my mouth. "I was thinking of Mom dying, Dad dying, Cynthia dying. You dying was just too much."

He sees the concern on my face. "When you came in after me, it's good I was kicking too to get us out."

I roll my eyes. "Yeah, that was a big help. So was climbing on top of me."

He gives me that goofy grin of his and runs his fingers through his hair. "I wish I had a comb."

"Dork." I shake my head.

There's another major splash in the lake and we both turn to look. A figure rises with water sheeting off it. A woman's head appears first, topped by the same writhing tentacles adorning Gorgon's crown, but hers are slender and bluish with a golden tint. Dazzling instead of repulsive.

Jake and I gape at the creature.

Her face is wild, exotic, and stunning. And her white skin has blue streaks running from her forehead to her neck, shoulders, and down her sleek torso, eventually blending into all blue tentacles where there should be legs and arms. From her lower body those larger tentacles extend into the water and keep her upright. Tentacles on the back of her head and neck give her an appearance of strength and majesty.

I help Jake to his feet, but he grips my arm to pull me back. "Step back, Sam!"

"No, it's okay, Jake." I don't move and he releases me, still looking like he's ready to bolt.

The creature studies me intently. I waver between finding her beautiful and worrying that her Medusa-like crown will change me into stone. But Gorgon's didn't so I let that go. "Who are you?"

"Heshia. I have many names. Mermaid. Medusa. Death Bringer. Awakener."

"I knew it!" Jake averts his eyes from her head.

Medusa. But unlike Jake, I can't take my eyes off her and her clear voice has a sweet ringing quality that leaves me wanting more. "She's safe, Jake."

He cautiously lifts his head and peeks at her. "Huh."

One of Heshia's tentacles snakes out of the water toward me.

"Sam!" Jake backs up a step, but again I don't move.

I'm a little wary until her tentacle tip pauses near the small dolphin on my bracelet. Next it traces the artistic dolphin on my shirt. "Kin to water."

"Yeah, I like it." That sounds stupid, even to me.

Her tentacle moves toward Jake and he stands rigidly while it traces the dragon tattoo on his arm. "And you, spirit of dragon."

"Ah, yeah, I guess so." Jake stares wide-eyed at her tentacle tip. As her limb slides back into the water, he hesitantly steps up beside me. "Ah, I guess we're safe, Sam."

I roll my eyes at him. "Ya think?"

Heshia says quietly, "Gorgon has WhipEye."

"Can you help us get it back?" I've never seen anything like her and wonder where she came from. Had to be KiraKu.

Jake coughs out more water and gestures weakly to her. "Can you get us an antidote to dragon's breath poison?"

"We'll take any help you can give," I add.

"We're desperate." Jake sounds like it, and I feel it inside too.

Heshia leans forward, her face dazzlingly bright, chiseled with smaller features than Gorgon's. "Gorgon assumes it's finished, but it isn't." Her blue eyes and tender voice mesmerize me, keeping me immobile. But it's my choice, not a spell. Her head tentacles keep moving.

She floats sideways so she's in front of Jake. "Your visions are accurate for one so young, but they're not everything. They only prepare you for what may lie ahead. Remain patient and calm."

Jake lifts a hand a few inches. "Yeah, kind of hard to do that when Mom is dying."

She leans forward, quiet for a few moments as if she's assessing him. "It will take strength, but you have that."

Jake's eyebrows raise, but he doesn't respond.

Heshia faces me next, the softness of her skin and radiance of her eyes melting away all of my resistance. All I can do is stare, but I eventually manage to ask, "Who is Gorgon?"

"Gorgon is one of the oldest Great Ones. However the crocodile is older and more powerful, and defeated him, preventing him from ruling KiraKu. When the Originals were forced out of KiraKu, Gorgon saw it as an opportunity. He left with the other Great Ones. But he didn't come to help the Originals—he came to conquer your world. He overestimated his abilities and the Lessers in your world didn't follow him. Recently he came to the Amazon to try to gather followers. Many Lessers hide from humans here because the jungle reminds them of KiraKu."

She pauses. "Gorgon has petty charisma, and like me he has some unique and dangerous skills. Lessers would rather follow him than have no direction. He gives them hope for recreating KiraKu here. All a lie."

Jake gestures to the tunnel leading to the other cavern. "So he'll break his honor-bound word?"

Heshia says, "He has no honor and his word means nothing."

"What a loser." Jake sounds disgusted.

"What can we do?" I ask.

Heshia lowers her head toward me and her voice has a tinge of sadness. "Love is everything, Samantha. You understand that. Remember it."

I don't just hear her sadness, it reverberates in my chest and throat, as if it's mine. Unexpected tears burst from my eyes. Thoughts of Dad, Cynthia, and Jake, along with the ache of missing the staff, all roll into one big ball of misery.

I wipe my eyes. "Why are you here with Gorgon?"

"Shh." She raises an arm tentacle so the soft tip of it covers my lips for a few seconds.

I hesitantly lift my hand to touch her limb. Soft and velvety. She slowly pulls it away.

"You mustn't tell him we talked." Swaying back above the water, Heshia sinks beneath the surface.

I stand there, wanting her to rise again, wanting her clear sweet voice in my ears, wanting those endlessly radiant eyes on mine once more.

Heaving a breath, I sit down and pull off my socks to wring them out. Jake does the same thing, but first he empties the water out of his shoes. Finished, I slip on my shoes.

I study Jake. "Are you okay?"

"Yeah." He wipes water off his face and flips a hand at the pool. "It was like waking up out of a nightmare and realizing I was in a real one. I mean not you holding me, but you know, the whole me-in-a-lake-and-I-can't-swim thing."

"No worries. I needed a bath anyway. What did you see?" I push to my feet.

"This time I saw two Lesser armies ready to fight." Finished with his shoes, he stands. "And we're standing at the head of Gorgon's army."

I frown. "Are you positive we were with Gorgon's followers?"

"The Komodo was there, Sam. And the dragons. I saw everything more clearly this time." Tension fills his voice. "Mentore's army was across from us."

His vision is disturbing. "How can we fight Mentore? He's a better option than take-over-the-world Gorgon."

"Yeah, nothing fits."

"Are you sure it was your vision, and not Heshia's?" I doubt she's trying to deceive us, but I have to ask.

"It felt like it was mine. Heshia just lured me into the water, in my mind. I couldn't break her spell over me even when you grabbed my arm." He eyes me. "I guess that's how WhipEye feels to you, huh?"

"Kind of." I'm glad he understands, and I think of something else. "Did you see the demon in your vision?"

He shakes his head. "Lessers are immortals, Sam. We have no idea what they're capable of. What Gorgon is capable of. We have to be careful with all of them. We can't assume anything. I mean, look at Heshia's other names. Medusa and Death Bringer. Talk about a first date killer."

"Yeah." Jake's warning doesn't feel right to me. "I can't believe Heshia would kill us, and I wonder what her name *Awakener* means." I touch his arm. "Wasn't she stunning? I mean her voice, her eyes—I couldn't look away."

"You're going gaga over tentacle lady." Pulling his T-shirt over his head, he whips it into a thin rope to wring water from it.

My eyes waver on his chest, which is strong like the rest of him. "I trust her," I insist. "She pulled you out, and she betrayed Gorgon."

"You're too trusting, Sam."

I stare into his eyes. "I trust you."

"Well of course! We know each other." He pulls his T-shirt back on and raises an eyebrow. "I also saw Ms. Touchy-feely in action again."

"Hey, she put her tentacle over my lips so it's not like she wasn't touching me."

He raises a hand. "Hello! What if she gives you some kind of disease?"

"Thanks for that thought." I hadn't thought of that. Different species do have different bacteria and viruses. Ugh. Something else to worry about. "Besides her tentacle felt very nice."

"I can't imagine what I'm missing." Jake flicks a hand at me. "Remember, I had one of her tentacles wrapped around me." He pauses. "Okay, it wasn't bad, as far as monster tentacles go."

"Better than Gorgon's. Hers reminds me of a stingray's wing." I felt one years ago while snorkeling in the Caymans.

We walk across the cavern, soggy and dripping. Jake's shoes still *squish*. At least I'm clean.

Jake speaks softly. "I tried to talk to you about my visions for weeks, Sam, but you wouldn't listen."

"You're right. I should have listened. And asked questions." It seems selfish now. I glance at him. "I'm sorry."

Wheeling on me, he blurts, "Sorry? Mom might die and the best you can do is, *Sorry*?"

I brace myself. "I thought we were both just having creepy dreams, not visions that might come true. You didn't know they were visions either. And I'm blaming myself for Dad too. I'm not perfect, Jake."

Jake continues walking, his voice calmer. "Yeah, I get it. I'm just worried about Mom, that's all. Gorgon's the enemy."

I kick a stone. "Heshia said your visions aren't everything so things can change."

"If she's telling the truth." He squeezes the lower part of his shorts on one leg to wring water from it. "Let's hope so."

I take a deep breath. "Gorgon won't be happy if he learns we were in the lake or that Heshia talked to us."

"I wonder what his stupid ceremony is?" He wrings the other leg of his shorts.

A terrible idea pops into my head. "Maybe we're fighting his demon."

"Great. Something to look forward to."

As we walk through the cavern, Heshia's words come back to me. "Who do you think Heshia is? Gorgon's wife? If so, I feel sorry for her."

"Maybe Gorgon was a mail-order husband." Jake is silent a few moments. "It doesn't matter. That's another reason to be careful around her. We can't trust anyone."

"You're right." But Heshia seems like a friend. At least I want to believe that.

Assorted sounds drift through the tunnel ahead. Shouts. Shrieks. Roars. The crowd is impatient.

I feel like a Roman slave about to enter the Colosseum.

NINETEEN

THE LONG, DAMP TUNNEL arches thirty feet over our heads, stretching eighty feet wide. No plants grow in it and there's little light. The volume of animal and human voices increases from the other end.

A bright glow beckons us forward, making me curious about how they generate light. I doubt they have electricity. Maybe candles or torches. Jake hunches his shoulders.

A hundred paces later we stop and stare.

"You don't see that every day," I say.

"Like never." Jake's voice is filled with awe.

White crystals cover the ceiling of the cavern, but small openings allow sunlight in, directing it into the crystals, which amplify and scatter the light into sparkling rays, making everything warm and bright. The walls of this cave have the same beautiful colors as the lake cavern, but more ferns, moss, and exotic wild flowers grow on the floor in large patches, with paths running through all of it. An oasis that looks cared for. No stalactites or stalagmites grow here.

Easily as large as the other cavern, in its distant center rests a black stone thirty feet high and shaped like a minipyramid with the top cut off—serving as a platform for a stone throne. The side of the pyramid facing us has steps, and the area in front of it is free of vegetation. The Komodo dragon lies in front of the bottom step.

Gorgon sits on the throne, six-foot-four again, dressed in his red shirt and black jeans. His red and gold tentacles slowly writhe atop his head. Surrounded by his minions, he appears every bit the king he wants to be. Staring at us with their red eyes, the twin dragons sit on either side of the pyramid, towering over Gorgon, faint hues of gold shimmering across their dark green undersides.

Lessers lounge across the floor and walls, all the way up to the edges of the white crystal ceiling—but not on it. Maybe the footing isn't good on the crystals or it's forbidden to touch it.

Gorgon's army appears larger than Mentore's, but I haven't seen the ape's forces during daylight. I study the Lessers, not wanting to call them enemies and hoping they'll be allies. I know that's a bit optimistic. I'm happy I don't see the demon anywhere—but maybe Gorgon keeps her locked up.

Gorgon stands and smiles. He's holding WhipEye, which immediately puts me on edge. His chiseled features appear friendly as he beckons us forward. Every individual in the cavern quiets.

Large lizards, amphibians, snakes, and the horned skunk we saw yesterday part for us as we walk along paths that wind around them. Most Lessers have curious, friendly expressions, and the Originals standing among them nod or smile at us. I stare at them in wonder.

Jake whispers, "Let's remember that Rose is a prisoner here."

"And they're Gorgon's followers." The other thing I remember is that Mentore has a spy in Gorgon's camp. I wonder if he'll contact us. I look around but don't have a clue how to recognize Mentore's informant.

As we walk, I whisper, "Let's push him hard in front of his followers to keep his honor-bound word."

Jake nods. "Antidote and Rose before we do anything for the creep."

"And maybe you shouldn't call him Fish Bait today."

"I was looking forward to it." Jake nods. "Alright, agreed. Polite for now."

I fix my attention on WhipEye. I swear it's singing my name, calling to my hand and heart. I ache for it and will never leave it behind. My hand finds my compass. There's some comfort in that.

When we near the pyramid, the Komodo lifts his head off the dusty stone and hisses, sending chills along my arms and angry words into my head.

Growling, the lizard rises and steps toward me. I stop, my stomach tight. Jake stands beside me, his shoulder against mine. Together we're stronger and I think he gets that.

The Komodo stops in front of us, flicking out his tongue as he looks down at us. "Your elders, how are they?"

I want to shout in the lizard's face. "Get lost, errand boy."

"Shut up, leather face." Jake's voice is hard, his hands fists.

Lowering his head to face me, the Komodo opens his mouth, which sends the odor of decayed flesh into my nostrils. "Cheap insults, guardians."

The Komodo settles to the ground beside us, swishing his tail to the other side to allow us to pass.

My chest heaves and Jake tugs on my hand to get my feet started. We walk along the Komodo's bulky body, stopping ten feet from the bottom throne step. Even though Gorgon is atop the throne, it's the twin ebony dragons that capture my attention. They make Gorgon look like a midget. I wonder why they follow him. Neither of the dragons move as they stare down at us.

Gorgon's brow knits. "You've been in the lake."

I wave it off. "I splashed some water on myself to wake up." Never able to tell a lie very well, I do a good job with this one. Whatever Heshia's motives are, I don't want to betray her.

"Didn't want to show up for the ceremony smelling like crap." Jake loosens his fists.

Gorgon's smile returns. "Fine." He lifts WhipEye and turns in a circle. "These are the heroes who released the methuselah energy that saved us, who brought us WhipEye to save this world! Samantha of the Green Clan and Jake of the Morris Clan! Let's welcome them!"

A deafening cheer rises among the Lessers and Originals. My limbs relax when mostly grateful, acknowledging faces stare at us. The Komodo ignores us, but the twin dragons puff smoke from their nostrils and bow their heads.

Jake leans over and whispers, "Better than what we received from Mentore's crowd."

"Let's see how long it lasts. Mentore's group was like Jekyll and Hyde."

"Good point."

Gorgon lifts a palm and everyone quiets. "Some believe these are the true guardians, because they have the markings. But they must prove themselves first and unite all of KiraKu. And we are part of KiraKu, aren't we?"

Another loud roar soars up from the crowd, but I wonder about Gorgon's interpretation of the prophecy.

Gorgon quiets the crowd again and looks down at us. "We're gathered here for the ceremony. The twins and I will enter KiraKu to claim the Jewel of Origin and bring it here so we can rebuild this world in the image of KiraKu. This world will be ours to care for, not the Great Ones' kingdom to ignore or control."

Excited shouts and howls again rise throughout the cavern, and this time the twin dragons roar. I also hear hopefulness in their voices.

My stomach tightens as I listen to them. Mentore said if Gorgon takes the Jewel of Origin, it will destroy KiraKu. I shove that aside. We have to save our parents. We can't fight Gorgon and his army to save KiraKu. It's ridiculous.

When everyone quiets, Gorgon continues. "Samantha of the Green Clan and Jake of the Morris Clan, I want you both to witness the beginning of our new world, since it's because of you that it's possible."

His words annoy me, and I say, "You promised to give us the antidote to the poison you gave our parents."

"They're dying because you sent your assassin Komodo to kill them." Jake says it loudly and I hear his anger.

The Komodo growls behind us, but doesn't even lift his head.

I decide to push harder. "What kind of ruler murders helpless humans?"

The twin dragons twist their heads, staring at Gorgon. Murmurs run through the cavern. Gorgon hasn't told his followers everything he's done.

"Your parents will live, now that you brought us the staff, Samantha of the Green Clan and Jake of the Morris Clan." Gorgon holds his hands wide. "I regret using such force, but WhipEye does not belong in the hands of a young woman when it can improve the fate of all Lessers."

There are murmurs of agreement throughout the cavern, which surprises me. Even though they might not like his tactics, apparently Gorgon's followers support him. I wonder if his Lessers even care about humans. For that matter, I also wonder if Mentore's Lessers would care about us if we weren't the guardians their prophecy talks about.

"Where's the antidote?" asks Jake.

"And we want Rose freed." I stare up at him.

All eyes shift to Gorgon.

"A Lesser shouldn't break his honor-bound word," I add. "After all, who would follow a liar?"

More whispers drift through the crowd.

Gorgon's voice is cold. "Of course. The twins and I will retrieve the Jewel of Origin and then bring you home with the antidote and Rose."

I shake my head. "That will take too long. Our parents could die before you get back."

"Keep your word." Jake slashes the air in front of him. "You promised."

All eyes fix on Gorgon. His face is relaxed, but his mouth twitches at one corner. "I'll test the staff by going to the lake cavern. If all is well, I'll show you the antidote and then take you home with it to save your elders. With Rose. As promised."

Something bothers me at the edge of my thoughts, but another idea consumes my attention. Since Gorgon's followers didn't know he poisoned our parents, they might not be aware of other things either. "If you take the Jewel of Origin, KiraKu will be destroyed."

Gorgon shakes his head. "Mentore's propaganda. No, Samantha of the Green Clan, taking the Jewel means a few Great Ones will no longer have power over every living creature in KiraKu. It means the barrier dividing KiraKu and this world will dissolve and both worlds will become one. All of us will share in the bounty of the Jewel, not just the Great Ones in KiraKu."

Mentore was right. With one move—stealing the Jewel—Gorgon plans to not only take over this world, but KiraKu too. I wonder how much stronger the Jewel's energy will make Gorgon. We have no idea what kind of power he has now. I try to stall him so I can think. "Why not ask the Great Ones to dissolve the barrier?"

Gorgon's face turns somber. "It's a fair and good question. For countless centuries we have asked the Great Ones to do this. And they have refused, haven't they?" He shouts the last two words and the cavern erupts again with raucous calls.

I stare at Gorgon. The conflict between his Lessers and Great Ones is clear. Lessers live like outcasts, cheated of the beauty of KiraKu, and Gorgon has convinced his followers that everyone can share in KiraKu's riches.

Gorgon looks down at me. "Now, Samantha of the Green Clan, instruct me on how to use WhipEye."

The thing nagging at me earlier is suddenly front and center in my thoughts. Gorgon brought us here because he doesn't know how to use the staff. It isn't the easiest thing to figure out either. According to Tarath, Rose bonded me to WhipEye, and I bonded Jake to the staff. Gorgon isn't bonded to it so it won't work for him, even if I tell him what to do. And if I bond him to the staff, he'll use it to destroy KiraKu. I realize something else.

"You never sent the Komodo to take WhipEye. You sent him to poison our parents so we'd have to come to you. You needed us to bond you to the staff." I want to hurt him in the worst way.

"Make your choice, Samantha of the Green Clan."

My lips clamp shut. Heshia's words come back to me; *Love is everything*. My fingers curl around my compass. Dad's life or KiraKu. If I refuse Gorgon, Dad will die, but KiraKu will be spared. My head is pounding. I have to save Dad.

"Just do it, Sam," I whisper.

TWENTY

I GAZE UP AT Gorgon.

My compass needle points north, toward *Love*. Mom is in my thoughts. She would never want a whole world of wild animals and Great Ones destroyed. Neither would Dad. Both of them have always had a deep abiding love of all creatures. They would say, *Do the right thing, Sam*. My heart aches.

Jake steps forward, motioning to Gorgon. "WhipEye won't work for you unless you're bonded to it."

I touch his arm. "Don't, Jake. It's not worth it."

He avoids my eyes. "It is to me." He motions to Gorgon. "I'll bond you to the staff."

A huge impulse in my gut prompts me to step ahead of him. "I bonded first with WhipEye, Jake second. You should bond with the person who has the strongest attachment to it, which is me."

Gorgon regards Jake thoughtfully, and then me. "Then Samantha of the Green Clan, we will go to the lake cavern together."

Jake whispers behind me, "You have to do it, Sam. Please."

If I blow this, which I intend to do, our friendship will be over. I'll lose everything, and Gorgon will probably kill me. I wince when another idea comes to me. If I fail, Jake will bond Gorgon to WhipEye anyway. My sacrifice won't do anything. There's no way to win. I walk closer to the steps.

Gorgon motions me to come up, but I shake my head. "WhipEye has to strike the ground so the stone up there won't work." Huh. I'm surprised I remember that. And I think I remember how to bond him to WhipEye too.

As he comes down the steps, Gorgon's feet change to a half-dozen tentacles again, which I ignore. My attention focuses on WhipEye. My hands clench.

Stopping in front of me, he raises the staff between us and says quietly, "Guide me correctly, young Samantha of the Green Clan, if you wish to have your antidote, and if you wish to stay alive."

"Since you're asking so nicely, sure, I'll give it a try." I lick my lips. His thick fingers draw my attention. He's wearing a gold ring on the thumb of his right hand. It looks very much like the one in my pocket. The rings are connected to shadow monsters. I remember that. I wonder if his has the demon in it.

I grab WhipEye above his hand, my hands curling around the wood like two vices. Warmth seeps from the chestnut-colored wood into my grip. My eyes roam along the carved faces of the Great Ones on the staff as heat fills my chest and mind, calming me. The tension in my throat eases and the ache I've had ever since Gorgon took WhipEye from me melts away. So does my headache.

I don't want to share the staff with Gorgon or bond him to it. My stomach lurches. It would betray Tarath, the Great Ones, and KiraKu. Yet I don't want the responsibility of saving KiraKu. I shouldn't have to bear it. I just want to save Dad and Cynthia. My brain shouts, *I'm not a guardian! This isn't my fight!*

I glance at Jake and see vulnerability in his eyes, as if he's at my mercy. I know how he feels about saving his mother. A small voice inside screams that I'll do anything to save Dad too.

More warmth flows from the staff into my hands, rocking me back on my heels. Everyone watches in silence.

Abruptly my gut says do it. Bond Gorgon to WhipEye. Some thoughts rage against that, and I feel a little numb inside. "Hold the staff with both hands. Move it in three sideways figure eights in front of us, and repeat *Lake cavern* three times. Then strike the ground three times."

Gorgon nods solemnly.

I'm at war inside, my guilt and Heshia's words fighting some primal urge to bond him with WhipEye. I'm betraying everything I value. Except saving Dad. I can't stop anyway. I feel like a puppet following WhipEye's commands. I give in to it. It makes it easier.

We move the bottom of the staff in three sideways infinity symbols, repeating three times, "Lake cavern."

Then we lift the staff and smash it into the stone.

In that instant I'm aware of three simultaneous things. First, no *boom!* echoes through the cave from the staff's blow against the rock, but increased heat flows into my hands. Secondly, bright, golden lines crackle along WhipEye's surface from top to bottom, along with a blast like a lightning bolt, which resounds throughout the cavern. And thirdly, Gorgon shouts as he flies backward fifty feet from me, landing on the throne steps with a loud thud.

Silence.

I stand there, fatigued and leaning on the chestnut rod. WhipEye guided and protected me, and rejected Gorgon. It felt good to see that. Even if I don't understand everything about the staff, it's safe to let it have its way with me. Though I don't see how that fits the decision I made that allowed Dad and Cynthia to be poisoned.

The Komodo dragon rises on all fours and turns around to face me. Hissing, it lowers its head as if it's going to charge. Angry outbursts fill the cavern. When I glance at the crowd, I no longer see friendly faces. Gorgon lifts his head and glares at me.

Panic. I have to escape. Fly back to Mentore with the staff and get help. I lift WhipEye off the ground a few inches and move it in front of me in a sideways figure eight, but a hand grabs the staff, stopping me.

"No." Jake stands at my shoulder, his dark eyes wide. "You can't do this again, Sam."

I gape at him. "Come with me."

His voice is pleading. "We need the staff for the antidote. I can't let you take it."

Gorgon rises to his feet, somehow doing it without using his hands or legs, his face contorted. I embarrassed him in front of all of his followers.

"Holy crap." Jake immediately brings out the butterfly scale and puts on his armor.

Gorgon is a few feet from me before I blink, and ten feet tall again. One of his red crown tentacles expands and wraps around my neck, lifting me off the ground in front of him. Then he squeezes, hard.

Jake runs between me and Gorgon, shouting, "It's not her fault!"

One of Gorgon's head tentacles punches him in the chest and he sails backward a dozen feet and slides over the ground another dozen. I can't worry about him, since I'm trying to stay alive.

Choking, I kick my legs, trying to find something solid to stand on as I hang from Gorgon's limb. Warmth flows from the staff into my arms, through my chest, and into my neck. Muscles I didn't know I had resist Gorgon's tentacle, but it's like a mouse trying to lift a lion's paw. I figure it buys me a few more seconds to live. I swipe the staff at his tentacle, but his limb lengthens and bends away so I miss.

"Traitors must die." Gorgon's usually smooth voice is raspy and harsh.

I glimpse him going through some kind of physical change, but I can't afford to watch. The Komodo is crawling toward me, his jaws wide. *I'm so dead.*

From my side, Jake shouts, "Use the staff, Sam." He grabs a baseball-sized rock and throws it at the lizard's head.

Without pausing the Komodo turns his head, snaps the rock from the air, and spits it out. Jake steps in front of me and faces the Komodo—I can't believe he's that brave—and the lizard uses his tail to hit him in the torso. Jake flies away. Twisting his head sideways, the Komodo lunges at my left leg, jaws gaping. The Komodo is going to rip my leg off.

I ram WhipEye into the lizard's mouth near his jaw hinge and hit a tooth on the opposite side. I cry out as his teeth puncture my leg. But the staff blocks the Komodo from closing his mouth. Expecting WhipEye to shatter, I'm relieved when it doesn't. Instead golden energy flows from it over the Lesser's skull, outlining his head in a web of crackling lines.

Grunting, the big lizard opens his mouth and steps back—I pull WhipEye to me. The energy around the Komodo's skull fades away and he wags his head side to side as if trying to shake off a bad headache. He growls at me but backs up in retreat. Exhausted from using the staff and from Gorgon's choking tentacle, I go limp. Blood streams down my leg.

I glimpse Jake stepping in front of me again, his hands making wild arcs as he faces Gorgon. "Sam didn't lie! That's how I would bond you to the staff too!"

Blood rushes into my ears. All strength leaves my body, but my hands won't release WhipEye. My thigh burns where the Komodo bit me.

"Gorgon." A resonant female voice, powerful and authoritative, cuts through all the chatter in the cavern.

Dizziness blurs my eyes. The tentacle's grip on my neck loosens and I fall hard to my feet, cry out with pain, collapse to all fours, cry out again, and fall to my right side, coughing and holding WhipEye. At least I fell on moss and not stone.

"Oh, Sam. You're like a magnet for teeth and claws." Jake rests a hand on my shoulder as he kneels beside me. I'm too weak to lift my head. "Breathe," he says softly.

That's about all I can do.

"She betrayed me," snarls Gorgon.

Thick, massive, red and white tentacles writhe everywhere around us, slapping against the stone. I'm facing Gorgon and I tilt my head to see all of him. He's the opposite of Heshia in every respect.

Fifty feet tall, with a bulbous white torso streaked in red, his body is a distorted cross between a squid and octopus. He has tentacles for arms and his rounded shoulders lead to a thick neck. A wicked set of pointy teeth are set in his red, primitive-looking head. Bulgy eyes, lumpy cheeks, a pointy jaw, and a head topped with short tentacles. His lower body is all tentacles too, like Heshia, only his are six feet thick near his torso, tapering to two feet thick near their ends. The last three feet taper to a blunt tip. Sixty-foot whips.

I finally get it. I'm surprised I didn't see it with Heshia, but her body was mesmerizing, not freakish.

"Kraken," I whisper.

"Kraken?" Jake is wide-eyed. "He looks like a squid-octopus combo on steroids."

My voice is hoarse. "Kraken were legendary monsters in Norse and Icelandic tales that terrorized ships at sea." I wonder how many sailors Gorgon killed.

"Yeah, definitely a ship sinker." Jake continues to stare at the monster.

One of the twin dragons faces Gorgon. If the two fought I'd have to bet on the kraken. He smells like dead fish. His need for water must be why he spends his evenings in the cavern lake. And he must be the massive monster of my last nightmare.

The dragon speaks calmly. "The young man speaks the truth about bonding with WhipEye, as does the young woman. Killing her is not the answer, nor our way."

I immediately love the Lesser, who continues talking. "Perhaps only those chosen by the staff are able to use it."

"Yes." The other twin has her face near my head—her large ruby eyes lined in gold—staring first at me, then Jake. Lowering her head farther, the dragon sniffs WhipEye. "They forged it that way."

Jake's eyes are saucers and for once he doesn't speak.

I didn't hear the dragon move, but my hoarse breathing fills my ears. The Lesser's feet end in massive bronze claws inscribed with beautiful patterns of curling lines. The tip of her tail lies over her forefeet. I roll slightly onto my back and look up to take in the rest of her.

Orange gums surround curved teeth as big as rhino horns, some larger than elephant tusks, and she has a slender, long tongue. Her breath is sweet. The scent of orchids. Mom grew orchids and I've always loved them. Thick, black scales cover the Lesser and puffs of smoke leave her nostrils, drifting over our heads. It smells like burnt charcoal.

The dragon speaks calmly. "Let an Original try."

Words of agreement fly through the cavern.

Gorgon twists to a nearby Original. "You. Try it."

Jake stands and steps in front of me, his voice desperate. "I'll bond him to the staff. Sam's injured."

I stare at his back, hoping he's doing this for me and not trying to find a way to bond Gorgon to WhipEye.

"She'll do it!" snaps Gorgon.

Jake hesitates, and then gently helps me to my feet. I lean on him. It helps to see worry in his eyes. I barely have enough energy to stand on my right leg, while trying to favor my burning left thigh. Three large puncture wounds from the Komodo's teeth dot my skin on both sides of my leg. One of the wounds is just above the knee, an ugly tear that's already turning purple.

I'm not sure if a bite from a Komodo Lesser is venomous. Oddly I'm not numb or overly weak, given the wounds, but I'm already fatigued from using WhipEye so it's difficult to tell what the injuries are doing to me. The bleeding has already slowed to a trickle. Maybe the staff is protecting me from the bite, as it did when Gorgon's tentacle squeezed my neck.

The Original is a beefy man wearing jeans and a tee. He reminds me of Brandon, although he looks worried as he walks up to me.

The dragon withdraws her head a few yards.

Licking his lips, the Original grips WhipEye with two hands and eyes me.

Looking concerned, Jake steps away from me, leaving me wobbling on one good foot. I repeat the ritual with the Original. Hot energy sends him flying farther than Gorgon and he lands with a thud amid some ferns. He tries to sit up, moans, and drops back to the ground. I feel sorry for the guy, but at least the staff didn't kill him. I slump against WhipEye, too tired to use it anymore.

Jake hurries to my side, placing an arm around my waist to keep me upright. "Good job, Sam," he whispers.

"Yeah, wonderful." I'm not sure why he's congratulating me, when I'm just trying to stay on my feet.

"They die now." The last twenty feet of one of the kraken's lower tentacles loosely snakes around our legs.

"It's not our fault!" Jake glares at Gorgon.

The dragon facing Gorgon says, "Let the guardians go to KiraKu."

Silence engulfs the cavern, except for Gorgon's restless tentacles slithering and slapping against stone.

The other dragon bends down in front of me, puffs of smoke rising above my head. "Yes, let the young guardians prove themselves and complete the task." Her gentle voice has strength in it, quieting everyone.

"Impossible," growls Gorgon.

The other dragon speaks; "They defeated the evil guardian. That was also impossible."

"They have only hours before their elders die." Gorgon's words are bitter. "Not enough time to prepare them for entering KiraKu and stealing the Jewel. They'll flee home to be with their dying elders." He smirks, jagged teeth sticking past his thin lips. "But I could send one of them and hold the other here as hostage."

I don't want to go without Jake, and blurt, "We have a day and a half."

"Liar." Gorgon's tentacle remains loosely curled around our feet. "Who brought healing water to you?"

Jake gives a limp wave. "I had some from our first visit to KiraKu."

The dragon nearest us lowers her head, her eye first inspecting the dolphin on my wrist bracelet and tank top, then moving to study Jake's forearm tattoo. "Water and dragon signs, and they bear the battle scars of the prophecy." Her nostrils are inches from ours. "I like them. They have strength. Together, with training, they might succeed."

Straightening, the dragon steps away smoothly with her twin until they sit on either side of the throne pyramid again. All in silence. Unbelievable.

Gorgon's tentacle uncurls and slithers away from our bodies with the rest of his limbs. In moments he stands in front of us, mostly human again and at his usual height.

His chiseled face and eyes are cold. "To save your elders and Rose, you'll get the Jewel of Origin for us or die in the process. And if you escape to your elders, we'll slow the effects of the poison so they will die a horrible, painful death over many months or years, while you watch helplessly. Then we'll kill you."

TWENTY-ONE

ONE OF GORGON'S HEAD tentacles yanks WhipEye from my hands. It hurts even more this time. Although if he had asked for it, I would have refused.

I glare at him. "You need some manners, jerk." My hand curls into a fist.

Jake gestures to Gorgon. "Yeah, Fish Bait, you really should learn how to say *Please* and *Thank you*."

I think Jake is trying to take some of the heat for my comment, because he grips my wrist and gives a small shake of his head.

Gorgon's eyes narrow.

I stand there, trembling and yearning for the staff. Given that I've just been strangled, bit by the Komodo, and Dad is dying, my desire for WhipEye seems over-the-top crazy, but it's too powerful for me to subdue it. Jake is right—the staff owns me.

"Ah, by the way, do you have any healing water?" I should have asked this before insulting the monster.

Gorgon smirks. "Healing water is in short supply here."

"Sam can't go like this!" Jake places his hip against mine when I wobble. "When do we go? She won't have time to heal."

"Stay here." Gorgon spins and leaves, gliding through the parting crowd and heading toward the lake cavern. No one follows him, but Lessers and Originals drift away from us. I'm too tired to move. Wiped out. I hope Heshia is safe. The real Gorgon is vicious enough to do anything.

Jake keeps his hand on me, his hip against mine. His voice is soft, "You're right, Sam. Gorgon needs help with social skills."

"He needs a makeover too. Talk about butt-ugly." My leg is burning and I bite my lip.

Jake motions feebly to my leg. "That looks horrible. I mean your back was worse, but still..." He grimaces at my wounds.

"You didn't have to stop me from leaving." My voice has an edge to it.

"It didn't feel right to let you leave." He straightens. "Like you're always saying, I didn't have a choice."

I want to yell at him. Anyone. Instead I take a deep breath. "Okay, I can't say leaving was the best option, but it would have saved me a Komodo bite."

"Going back to Mentore would have just put us back to square one, Sam." Jake looks at me innocently.

I scowl. "So I had to take one for the team?"

He nods slowly. "Yeah. You know, that's not a bad way to see it. Kind of like when I got Tasered. And I took a few more for the team trying to protect you."

"Glad I could be of service."

"I never wanted you hurt, Sam."

I believe him and wish we could talk, but not where Lessers can hear us. And even though he almost got me killed, it's hard to be upset with him. He did try to protect me from Gorgon and the Komodo.

Something big enters the cavern from another tunnel. The vampire bat.

"What's the bloodsucker doing here?" Jake frowns.

I expect alarmed shouts from the Lessers and Originals, but they don't even seem to notice the visitor. The bat flaps across the cavern and lands next to Gorgon. They exchange words, and then the bat takes off again, flying toward us.

One thing falls into place. The golden eyes I observed high in the jungle while climbing Mentore's tree belonged to the bat. It spied on our meeting with Mentore and fed the information to Gorgon. "Gorgon's spy," I mutter. "I wonder where Mentore's spy is?"

Jake frowns. "Maybe he knows we betrayed Mentore and won't help us."

That tanks my hopes.

The Lesser vampire bat lands in front of us. In a blur the giant bat shifts to a tall, thin man wearing jeans and a suit, both brown like his hair and indistinguishable from his skin. He looks about thirty and has a dark complexion. East Indian. No fangs push past his lips. I want to ask him what he eats. Lessers are more than the animals they represent, but this man's eyes are like ice. The stories about vampires might not be nonsense.

"I'm Vesio." His voice is cold too.

The vampire probably never wanted to stop us from running away from Mentore. He wanted WhipEye for Gorgon. I shudder when I imagine him ripping my arms off to get it.

"Traitor," I mutter.

He bends lower, his eyes piercing mine. "Careful, little guardian."

Jake gestures to him. "Gorgon's Lessers will tear you apart if you hurt their only chance to bring KiraKu to their world."

Vesio straightens, glares at Jake, and then gestures curtly for us to follow him. "This way." He walks toward the tunnel he arrived from minutes ago.

I take a step and gasp in pain. My leg gives out and I lean forward off balance. Jake steadies me, and then drapes my arm over his shoulders so he can hold my wrist. Keeping his other arm around my waist, he doesn't complain when I hop in small steps, most of my weight carried by his legs. The effort still brings tears to my eyes and if not for his help I'd lie down. After a dozen steps I stop. The pain is making me nauseous.

"Do you want me to carry you, Sam?" Jake's voice is tender.

I look up at him. "Would you mind? My leg is killing me."

In a smooth motion he picks me up and I gasp. My leg pain is still intense, but at least my weight is off it. Jake holds me tightly. I'd find it more romantic if I didn't feel like puking.

Leading us around ferns and flowers, Vesio eventually walks into the large tunnel. The walls and floor are stone and they stretch far into the distance. As far as I can tell it's the only other opening into the crystal cavern so it has to lead to the surface. Another point of entry into Gorgon's stronghold. My compass shows west.

Three oversized iron doors are set into the tunnel's walls, two on the south side and one in the north wall. Twenty feet high and fifteen feet wide, they look big enough for a small dragon to duck through. The vampire takes us to the single door on the north side.

An iron crossbar twenty feet in length, a foot wide, and six inches thick blocks the door. The crossbar must weigh a thousand pounds, yet Vesio lifts it with one hand as if it were balsa wood. He pulls open the massive iron door, which creaks with its weight.

"In," he orders.

Jake hesitates. "Why?"

"You want to see Rose, don't you?" He nods sharply at the entrance.

Jake carries me in and the door slams shut behind us.

"Stupid vampire," mutters Jake.

Gently he lowers me onto my good leg near the wall. Wincing, I sag against the cool stone, trying to come up with some way to begin a conversation that won't anger either of us. "You're a great uberbabe."

"That's German for superior babe, right?" He looks hopeful.

I wince over my pain. "I was thinking superior taxi babe."

"That's what partners are for." Stepping back, he studies the cave.

A few white crystals on the ceiling provide light for the center of the small cave. The walls are rock, but the floor is dirt. Shadows hide the sides and far wall.

I clear my throat. "I like bats. Brown bats can eat a thousand mosquitoes in an hour and fly forty miles per hour."

"Huh." He flips a hand. "Where's Rose?"

"Maybe Vesio is bringing her." My nerves rattle like loose electrical wires. We're running out of time and I have no idea when we're leaving for KiraKu. And I'm barely able to walk.

Jake gestures to me, his voice in control. "You nearly cost us everything, Sam."

"You think you're the only one who cares? I want to save Dad and Cynthia as much as you do." The image of Dad dying a slow, horrible death over months or years is unbearable. I can't do that to him or Cynthia.

Jake's eyes soften. "Look, Mentore and Gorgon could both be lying to us. If we go to KiraKu we can talk to Tarath, learn the truth, and then decide." His hands whirl. "We can't throw away Mom's and Bryon's only chance to live without understanding the facts." He hesitates. "I can't believe you were going to leave me here. I thought we were in this together. I thought we were partners..."

"You're right. That was a bad choice." I shake my head. "But Tarath said if we go to KiraKu the crocodile will try to kill us and take WhipEye."

He flips a hand. "We can't attack Gorgon. You saw how his army reacted to him getting tossed. He'd squeeze us to death in seconds anyway."

"Okay, so we go to KiraKu and find Tarath. She must have friends that will help us."

"I can live with that." Jake looks at me. "How did you figure out how to make the staff reject Gorgon and the Original?"

I shake my head. "The staff did it. It wasn't me."

"How stupid do you think I am, Sam?" He shakes his head. "WhipEye just decided to toss Gorgon and the Original? You keep blaming the staff for your choices." He sounds disappointed. "I don't know you anymore."

An acid *whatever* is on the tip of my tongue, but I'm interrupted by soft words from the shadows.

"Yes, you do."

I peer at the far corner of the wall I'm leaning against, my eyes piercing the dim light—a figure is slumped on the dirt floor.

"Rose?" Jake hurries away from me.

"Hey, little help here," I mutter. I hop behind him, mostly sliding along the wall, trying not to fall over. My throbbing leg is making me dizzy.

By the time I reach her, Jake is kneeling at her side. Rose is wearing tennis shoes, jeans, and a white blouse, but her clothing is torn and dirty, her long, brown hair matted and tangled on her shoulders, and her eyes pale. It feels horrible to see her like this, but I'm not sure how I should feel about her otherwise. I mainly remember her as the old lady who rented Dad's cabin.

She bonded me to the staff so I guess I owe her, but really, what did that do for me? I've nearly been killed three times and had demon nightmares. And for what? The staff drew Gorgon and his Komodo assassin to me, which resulted in Dad and Cynthia being poisoned. It's hard to cheer about all that misery.

I painfully lower myself on the other side of Rose. She has her legs curled beneath her and she leans her head on my shoulder. That feels a little awkward but I don't object. Her face, dirty and smudged, has deep wrinkles.

She looks about fifty, not in her seventies like before. Maybe she was given healing water, but that makes no sense because she doesn't look well. I feel sorry for her. Gorgon is a cold-blooded monster in every sense of the word. A gush of emotion bubbles up into my throat. I surprise myself when I blurt, "I've missed you, Rose."

"I've missed you too, Samantha and Jake." She coughs weakly.

"Are you okay?" asks Jake.

She clears her throat. "I'm just worn out. I'll be better after I rest."

"Why did you risk coming here?" I ask.

She smiles weakly. "I used to be a guardian, remember?"

I'm starting to. Flashes of memories sweep through me occasionally, but they don't lessen the stress of wanting to save Dad, and also don't provide help for doing that.

Rose continues. "I heard that Gorgon's and Mentore's forces were gathering here and I tried to head off a war by talking to Gorgon. By the time I understood that he had no interest in compromise he took me prisoner and sent the Komodo to take the staff from you." Her eyes brighten. "How brave of you to come here."

"The Komodo dragon poisoned our parents with dragon's breath poison." Jake motions to the door. "Gorgon won't give us the antidote to save them unless we bring him the Jewel of Origin."

"Tarath said she would look for an antidote in KiraKu," I add.

Jake flicks his eyes at me. "Gorgon tried to bond to WhipEye, but Sam made sure it didn't work."

"No." Rose shakes her head. "No one else can bond to WhipEye unless you both want them to. You two would have to agree to this in heart and mind—similar to when you use the staff. It's a safeguard in having you both as guardians. I had WhipEye for thousands of years and still didn't master everything about it. But the staff ultimately decides who can use it. I told you long ago that WhipEye has a mind of its own. Remember?"

"Now do you believe me?" I shoot Jake an *I told you so* look.

He stiffens a little. "Alright, Sam. I was wrong."

"It's okay. Like you said, it's complicated." His shoulders sag when I say that. I turn back to Rose. "I only know how to do a few things with WhipEye. Not enough to defeat Gorgon."

Rose smiles. "Experiment with it. Bind your heart and mind to it."

I take that in, and say, "Six months ago Tarath erased our memories of KiraKu. She restored them yesterday and we're getting back bits and pieces."

Lifting both of her hands, Rose touches the center of our chests. "Trust your hearts. They won't fail you, no matter what you've forgotten."

I want confirmation on something. "Mentore said taking the Jewel of Origin will destroy KiraKu, but Gorgon said it will expand KiraKu's greatness to our world." I glance at Jake, wanting him to hear Rose's answer.

Rose coughs. "Gorgon is only after power. He's ruthless and willing to destroy a world to get what he wants."

Jake continues to frown but remains silent.

I touch Rose's shoulder. "What about Heshia? How is she related to Gorgon?"

"I've never heard of her, but trust no one in Gorgon's camp." Rose shivers.

Jake raises his eyebrows at me. He thinks he's right about Heshia, but I don't want to believe either of them.

"Gorgon has a ring like mine." I shove my hand in my pocket and bring it out. It gleams in the dim light.

"You got that after the battle with the evil guardian." Rose closes my fingers around it. "You mustn't let Gorgon get it. The evil guardian turned the methuselahs into shadow monsters and enslaved them in his rings. Gorgon was in league with him, and he can use that ring to enslave an individual of power. I'm certain Gorgon's ring has a shadow monster in it."

I was right about the rings. "Great, I'm carrying around a weapon for Gorgon. Should I hide it here?"

Rose shakes her head. "No, he may find it. Keep it with you. When you go home it will be far from him."

Nodding, I put it back into my pocket.

Jake pales. "The shadow monster in Gorgon's ring wouldn't by any chance be a giant two-headed cobra?"

"Or a demon?" I ask.

"The snake is more likely," says Rose.

"Wonderful." Jake winces. "What were the methuselahs?"

"The Great Ones sent ten methuselah animals into your world to gather healing energy over centuries and then release it. They hoped the released energy would end human destructive behavior toward nature. But the evil guardian trapped the methuselahs in rings and turned them into shadow monsters. His slaves. You freed most of them in Sequoia National Park."

Rose holds our hands, her grip weak. "Even if Gorgon has a shadow monster in his ring, the gold in your eyes will allow you to see it."

Jake flicks his hand. "Like that's supposed to make us feel better?"

"Yeah, what a bonus." My palms sweat over Rose's words. Tarath told us the same thing, but at the time we had other worries on our minds. I don't want to see any more monsters, especially the demon.

Rose adds, "Whoever holds a ring controls the shadow monster in it, so you need to get the ring from Gorgon if you can."

"Yeah, no problem." Jake shakes his head. "He's a freaking monster."

"We're no match for him, Rose." I can't believe she's suggesting this.

She says with confidence, "The opportunity will present itself, just be ready for it."

"We'll take you with us when we leave, Rose." Jake holds her hand with both of his.

Rose coughs. "I'll be fine. Go to KiraKu and contact Tarath. She'll help you. And she might be able to find an antidote." She places a frail hand on my arm. "Samantha, have Faith in your heart."

Faith. My mother's name. I get it. The four words on my compass echo inside me: *Trust Love. Trust Mom.*

"Your leg." Rose stares at my bloody thigh.

My leg still aches fiercely. "The Komodo bit me, but I haven't had any of the numbness or poisoning that usually follows a Komodo bite."

Rose pats my thigh. "WhipEye gives the bearer some strength. KiraKu's water or Tarath can heal you."

"What does the Jewel of Origin look like?" Jake combs back his hair with his fingers.

I don't like his interest in the Jewel, but I'm curious about it too.

Rose's hand trembles. "It's the energy source of KiraKu, but I never saw it. Nor have most Great Ones. I doubt the Jewel should be removed from KiraKu or that the crocodile would ever allow it. But if Tarath agrees, and you do bring it out, Gorgon must never get it."

"Why not?" Jake sounds surprised.

I stare at him. "How can you ask that?"

He shrugs. "Someone has to."

"I doubt the Jewel's energy can cover KiraKu and your world," says Rose. "And Gorgon wants it for himself. He'll become a thousand times more powerful with the Jewel's energy and take control of both worlds."

"A thousand times?" Crap.

Jake flashes a hand. "Aren't the Great Ones controlling their world? The crocodile kicked out the Originals and won't let Lessers return."

Rose nods. "The crocodile ensures that KiraKu remains healthy and safe for all who live there. The biggest decision Great Ones made involving power over others was forcing the Originals to leave millennia ago, which caused some Great Ones to leave with them. That decision might come back to haunt them now."

Hearing her caution about removing the Jewel from KiraKu feeds a deep fear that Dad is going to die horribly and that I won't be able to save him.

The door creaks open and Gorgon appears, his chiseled features neutral. The writhing slugs on his head remind me of his real appearance. Yuck.

He lifts his chin. "So much for the reunion with your beloved Rose. She's alive and well, and now the training begins."

The sarcasm in his voice turns my hands into fists.

When we don't move, he shrugs. "Your parents are dying. It's your time to waste." He slides out of view and Vesio appears.

I grasp Rose's hand. "We'll come back for you, Rose. I promise. No matter what happens."

"We won't leave you here." Jake holds her other hand.

Her eyes flicker with gold. "Take care of each other, Samantha and Jake."

"We'll be back in no time." Jake's tone is optimistic, but his eyes show otherwise.

He stands and I reach up to him. Gripping my hand, he helps me to my feet. I groan in pain.

"Do you want the uberbabe taxi again?" He frowns at my leg.

I shake my head. "Let's see if I can hop out of here on my own."

He loops an arm around my waist and places my arm over his shoulders. "Ready?"

"Time to meet the sadistic jerk." My stomach sinks as we leave Rose alone in the shadows. I want to slug Gorgon. When we reach the tunnel, the monster is gone. Vesio bars the door and leads us back through the tunnel. Jake helps me limp along. My leg throbs on every step.

"It's horrible that we're leaving Rose," I whisper.

"I'm dead sick about it too, Sam."

I think he's as angry at Gorgon as I am. Rose, Cynthia, Dad, Brandon, and Colonel Macy's soldiers were all hurt because Gorgon wants power. I understand Colonel Macy's interest in destroying at least one Lesser. Gorgon is a threat to humanity.

Mentore has to be frantic to find a way into Gorgon's stronghold, and Canaste and Lewella will search too. I wish they were here now, but the dragons are massive. Combined with Gorgon's strength, I doubt Mentore's army would have any chance to defeat them.

Jake was probably right to stop me from leaving. But he has to accept that we can't save our parents by giving Gorgon the Jewel of Origin. Rose supported what Mentore said. It's not just KiraKu that's at risk, but our world too. We have to trick Gorgon into giving us the antidote.

I peek at Jake. His head is lowered, his face strained. I need time to talk to him alone. He has good ideas, but he's focused on one goal: saving his mother.

I clench my jaw over the pain in my leg. When we reach the cavern, Gorgon is waiting. The glint in his eyes tells me he's kept something from us. And it's going to hurt.

TWENTY-TWO

VESIO STRIDES A SHORT distance away from us, shifts into a large bat, and flies toward the lake cavern. Gorgon is waiting for us, fifty yards from the tunnel entrance. With Jake's help I hobble toward him.

When we stand in front of Gorgon, Jake helps me maintain balance with his arm around my waist, my arm still draped over his shoulders. Gorgon holds WhipEye in one hand, regarding us with an impassive face. Seeing the chestnut rod brings a deep longing to my chest.

Jake speaks first. "We could take you and the dragons to KiraKu. You don't have to hold the staff." He shrugs. "You and the twins are a little stronger than us."

Instantly upset, I stare at Jake.

Jake glances at me. "I just thought of it. Sam."

I stuff a comment. I don't want to argue in front of Gorgon.

"Interesting idea." Gorgon scrutinizes Jake. "And while the twins and I fight our way through Great Ones and steal the Jewel of Origin, you could leave with WhipEye and we would be stranded in KiraKu."

Jake slashes the air. "We wouldn't—"

Gorgon holds up a hand. "I don't trust you, Jake of the Morris Clan."

Heshia said the crocodile defeated Gorgon so I think that's the real explanation he won't go back to KiraKu. He'll get his ass kicked. I don't say anything because I don't want to betray Heshia, and it won't change things. But if Gorgon is afraid of the crocodile, it makes me hopeful that maybe we can get the croc on our side.

Gorgon speaks coolly. "If you plan to betray me, there's no reason to go to KiraKu."

I stare at him, my hand twitching.

Jake's free hand flutters. "We'll get the Jewel of Origin."

Something about the way Jake says it, along with the desperation in his eyes, worries me.

"You don't believe Rose?" Gorgon's eyebrows arch. "She doesn't support my having the Jewel. I wanted you to hear her because she shares the Great Ones' point of view that they are the only ones who should have it."

Jake motions. "The Great Ones use the Jewel for power over others. Why should they control it?" It doesn't seem like he's bluffing.

Gorgon studies him carefully, and then turns to me. "And you, Samantha of the Green Clan. You've shown no interest in helping me so you should remain here."

His words shock me. I can't bear the thought of not holding WhipEye again or letting Jake decide the fate of our world and KiraKu. I shuffle through reasons to convince Gorgon to allow me to go. All I have is the truth. "I didn't know the staff would reject you when I tried to bond you to it, and I want to save my dad."

Gorgon regards me with neutral eyes, his silence making my heart pound. "Very well. You'll train the rest of today, which will leave less than a day to enter KiraKu, get the Jewel of Origin, and bring it back. If you are successful, I'll give you the antidote and Rose."

Jake says firmly, "Why should we believe you? I mean, no offense, but you seem to lie nonstop. Or at least you keep coming up with excuses to not keep your word."

"I'm honor-bound to the truth." Gorgon appears sincere and his smooth voice sounds honest.

I'm sure he's lying, but I'm also certain he'll take revenge on us if we fail.

Gorgon quickly reinforces that idea. "If you fail or commit an act of treachery—"

"Yeah, yeah, our parents will die horribly, Rose will die horribly, we'll all die horribly." I glare at Gorgon. "Did I leave anything out?"

Gorgon bows slightly. "That's a perfect summary."

"Hey, that's positive motivation, right Sam?" Jake raises an eyebrow.

I keep my gaze on Gorgon. "We're wasting time talking."

Jake bites his lip. "Why do we need training?"

Gorgon smirks. "Do you expect Great Ones to allow you to take the Jewel of Origin without a fight? With the twin dragons the three of us had an excellent chance to get it. I doubt you can, but I have faith in the twins' judgment."

Gorgon's words chill me. I have no interest in fighting, much less hurting, Great Ones. More likely they'll eat me for a snack anyway.

Jake says with impatience, "Look, I already have a black belt in kung fu, but that took five years of intense daily training. One day of training won't turn me or Sam into gladiators." He glances at me for confirmation.

I raise my hand in agreement. "Yeah, I'm not going to learn enough in one day to even beat a bunny to death. Not that I want to. Besides, how am I supposed to train when I'm injured?"

Gorgon smirks again but doesn't reply.

Frustrated, I ask, "Where's the antidote?"

Jake lifts his chin. "If we can't see it now, we're done."

Gorgon smiles. "You already have seen it. As you probably know, the poison is from a rare plant in KiraKu called dragon's breath. I brought it to this world, and the cure for it is the bite of a dragon. Their saliva is the antidote."

Mentore conveniently didn't mention the dragons to us. Nor that Gorgon was a kraken. No one did. Getting dragons from a kraken to save our parents would have felt impossible. I wonder if Tarath knows any dragons in KiraKu. My hopes plummet. We'll never be able to force a dragon to come with us.

I scowl. "Our parents would die from a dragon bite."

"Not if the dragons are in their human form. If you succeed, the twins can fly to your parents in less than an hour and save them. You have my honor-bound word."

I stare at Gorgon with dull eyes, not believing him.

He continues. "But if you flee to your home without bringing the Jewel of Origin to me, the twins will give a tiny amount of saliva to your parents to slow the effects of the poison, so they'll die horribly over a long period of time. Ask the twins. They'll be your trainers."

Jake's eyes narrow. My gaze slides from Gorgon's smile to the staff in his hand. I want to smash it into his face.

Gorgon gives a small wave to the dragons.

From beside the throne the twins spread their folded black wings, casually flapping them to take to the air. In flight they're magnificent black-winged gems with red, fiery eyes, snorting smoke from their nostrils. I wish they weren't on Gorgon's side.

When they near us, the dragons spread their claws, their shapes dissolving and shrinking, all in quiet. By the time they land thirty yards away they've melted into two young women of average height, dressed in dark red clothing resembling a form-fitting ninja's wardrobe. Their outfits end at their necks, wrists, and ankles, and appear to be part of their bodies too.

"Ninja dragon ladies!" Jake's hand whirls. "I gotta say, that is one cool party trick!"

"Wow!" I stare in wonder. "Never would have seen that coming."

Jake whispers, "Better watch the touchy-feely stuff, Sam."

"I'll try."

The twins have bronze skin, with straight, long black hair and red eyes, and move smoothly, as if they're floating. Their hands and feet are miniature bronze dragon claws that have beautiful patterns of lines on them. Unlike Gorgon, they're both smiling.

Stopping in front of us, they bow. I can't tell them apart. Both have identical sharp-featured faces and the scent of orchids fills the air again. They're beautiful.

"I'm Rella," says the twin in front of me.

"Happy to meet you." I spot one difference between the twins. Rella's claws have wavy lines, while the other twin has curling lines on hers.

The sister facing Jake sweeps a claw over her head, leaving a small white streak in the left part of her hair. "I'm Issa. We've heard much about the young guardians who sent the methuselah energy to us. We wanted to thank you in person."

The twins' voices are light and beautiful, like their movements, and their warmth seems genuine. It's hard to believe they're giant Lessers, harder yet to believe they support Gorgon.

That annoys and puzzles me. "Thanks for taking time out of your busy day."

Jake nods. "Really nice of you. Just sitting all day by Gorgon's throne must wear you out." He gives Gorgon a quick glance, but the monster doesn't react.

"And it's true," says Issa. "Our saliva can heal your parents. A small bite delivers it into the blood stream more effectively. It's also true that our saliva can prolong the dying process."

Jake's calm face shifts to a glare.

Rella raises a claw. "Of course, it's not our wish to make others suffer."

Gorgon still shows no reaction.

I study the dragons, unnerved they heard everything from as far away as the throne. Or else Gorgon planned all of this. Rella appears sympathetic, but is she just pretending to care?

She steps forward and places her claw on the compass on my chest. "Exquisite."

"Is it special?" Gorgon arches an eyebrow.

I grasp the compass, suddenly fighting back tears. "It's from my mom, you can't have it."

"Why care about human workmanship?" Issa lifts a claw to the side.

"Why, indeed." Rella steps back.

Gorgon regards the twins, and then his eyes harden on us. "Before I leave you to your training, there's one more condition. A contest. Tomorrow you'll fight each other. Whoever wins goes to KiraKu. The other stays here—if they survive the fight. If the one going to KiraKu doesn't return or fails, the one here will be killed."

Jake gapes at him, and it takes a few moments for me to get words past my clenched lips. "We both go or the deal's off. We're your only chance to get the Jewel of Origin."

"You can say that again!" Jake looks like he wants to pummel Gorgon.

"This is nonnegotiable." Gorgon's eyes shine. "Take more time to decide if you wish, Samantha of the Green Clan, but I think Jake of the Morris Clan will cooperate." He glides away, leaving us with the twins.

I glance at Jake, feeling surprised. "We can't agree to it, Jake."

"We have no choice, Sam," he mutters. "For now."

I wonder if Gorgon is just playing us against each other, or if he actually detected that Jake will go along with his contest. Either way it's horrible.

"Please step away." Rella motions to Jake. "I won't hurt her."

Looking uncertain, Jake allows his hand to fall from my waist and moves sideways. My arm slides off his shoulders and I'm left to teeter on one foot. I gasp when I put weight on my injured leg. Deeply fatigued, I barely remain upright.

Rella steps forward and smoothly scoops me up in her arms. I groan in pain as she lifts me. Her face doesn't show any strain carrying me. Her strength, and how tightly she holds me, makes me feel like a child in her arms. Something about that, being held by a dragon in human form, is somewhat unnerving and intoxicating at the same time. The scent of orchids is comforting. My hand is on her shoulder; her ninja outfit feels more like skin when I stroke it.

Rella turns her head to me and winks. My hand freezes on her shoulder and I give her a strained smile and quickly look away.

Jake is staring at me and he rolls his eyes, while mouthing, *"Ms. Touchy-feely."* He strokes his shoulder a few times while giving me a dreamy face to drive the point home. I stick out my tongue.

"Come." Issa leads us farther back in the cavern to a large area of bare stone. I notice that each of the twins have an empty tubular sheath on their back.

Rella carefully eases me down on my good foot near a boulder, which I lean against. I want to ask her questions but decide to wait.

"I appreciate the lift," I say.

"Of course." She gives a small bow.

Issa smiles. "Watch closely, Samantha and Jake."

From their back sheaths the twins pull hidden three-foot bronze staffs, which they elongate to six feet by pulling on one end. Each staff has the same engraved lines that mark their claws. The lines on Issa's staff curl more, and those on Rella's are wavier.

They face each other, bow, and then bend their knees in a sideways stance, resting the ends of their staffs on the ground between them, the rods at forty-five-degree slants. Nearby Lessers and Originals walk and crawl closer to watch.

"Hah!" Rella attacks, jabbing her staff at Issa's midsection. Issa jumps back to avoid it, swinging her weapon at Rella's feet. Rella leaps over it. Whirling, striking, thrusting, and slashing, they follow a dancelike pattern. No blows land, they both fight hard, and both seem equally capable. They don't even break a sweat.

Their speed increases with the difficulty of their movements, which become more acrobatic. Flexible as yoga masters, they squat, leap, roll, and twirl, their staffs flashing through the air. Yet they never hit each other. Their staffs collide and ring through the cavern, while they quickly become blurs of motion that my eyes can't track.

After a few minutes they stop, bow, and face us again. The spectators move off.

"Okay, ninja dragon ladies, that was the best show ever!" Jake's hands whirl. "But we can't learn to fight like that in a day. Maybe in ten years."

I grunt. "I just jab and swing, and I'm a klutz."

The twins look at each other and speak simultaneously. "They assume we don't know what we're doing."

Issa laughs. "Your eyes have recently changed to gold, correct?"

Jake flicks his hair back. "Two weeks ago."

Issa nods. "Have you noticed increased speed and strength?"

Jake and I exchange glances.

Jake slowly nods. "I've felt faster a few times."

I remember fighting Colonel Macy's soldiers. "Maybe a little stronger and faster."

Issa continues. "Everything in your bodies is changing. You'll learn much easier than in the past."

"How did we get gold in our eyes?" Tarath already answered this, but I want to see what the dragons say.

Rella steps closer, peering directly into my eyes. "KiraKu's energy." She winks. "That's how everyone gets it."

"Huh." Jake bites his lip.

Another memory floats back to me. "I don't remember everything about KiraKu, but I remember that the healing water and air there have a lot of energy."

Issa's voice is wistful. "KiraKu is impossible to forget."

"What if we don't fight?" I hope the twins might offer another solution.

Rella regards me. "If you don't train and fight, Gorgon won't give WhipEye to either of you, and neither of you will go to KiraKu."

She doesn't have to finish. We all die horribly. I don't see any way out of it. Jake shrugs when I glance at him.

"What can a staff do to a Great One anyway?" Jake eyes Issa's staff. "We're puny and weak compared to them."

"Yeah, and I'm weaker than Jake," I add.

"Are you?" Issa eyes me with curiosity.

Her comment surprises me. I don't know what to say to her.

Using both claws, Rella twists the middle of her staff in opposite directions. A thick triangular spear blade snaps out of one end. She twists the staff again, and a sharp prong clicks out of each side of the main blade, the three blades forming a V-shaped weapon that resembles a claw.

"Dragon claw," she says.

Walking up to a rock as high as her waist, she sweeps the blades at the stone, leaving three deep gouges in it. One more twist retracts all three blades back into the staff.

Issa walks over to the same rock, crouches, and jabs the blunt end of her staff into it. The rock shatters, crumbling to the ground.

Jake's eyes brighten, but my mouth is dry. I can't bring a weapon like that into KiraKu. I've never harmed anything, at least not on purpose. And I don't want to fight or hurt Great Ones. Everything about going to KiraKu seems darker and more revolting.

Issa takes several quick strides and sweeps her staff at Jake's ankles, knocking him off his feet. He lands on his butt and stares up at her with wide eyes. When he gets to his feet, his hands are fists. "Cheater."

Issa nods. "Good, you're ready to fight."

Rella approaches me. Fearful she'll sweep me off my good leg, I raise a hand. "I'm not very fast on one leg."

"Of course not." She kneels in front of me, laying her staff on the ground. Raising a claw, she spits on it. Carefully she smears her saliva across the Komodo's ugly puncture wounds, which still drip blood and look gross.

I cringe, expecting the pressure of her claw to hurt, but instead a soothing, cool sensation spreads through my leg. The circular jagged holes in my muscles grow together like stitched seams until all that remains is dried blood on my legs. My fatigue also vanishes—I have energy again.

Gingerly I rest all my weight on my foot. No pain. Just muscle tension. "Wow, you can be my doctor any day." I want to hug her.

Rella retrieves her staff, rises, and gives a small bow. "Anytime."

"You can't, uh, get rid of scars with your saliva, can you?" I look at her hopefully, thinking of my back.

"Once a scar has formed, our saliva won't change it."

"No swimsuit modeling for me, I guess." It burns me that Gorgon didn't have the twins heal me earlier. I think he wanted to punish me for WhipEye rejecting him. The sadistic monster.

Jake stares at my leg. I see the excitement in his eyes, matching my own. Like me, he didn't quite believe Gorgon, but this proves the dragons can save our parents. And all we need is their saliva, not the whole dragon. Everything becomes possible again.

"Dragons are revered among Lessers and Great Ones for healing." Rella sounds earnest. "We're not killers."

"If you're not killers, then why won't you heal our parents?" I look from Rella to Issa. "One of you could do it during the night when Gorgon is in his lake."

"We won't tell him," Jake says softly, his eyes and voice hopeful. "Please."

"I am sorry, Samantha and Jake." Rella bows to both of us. "If your parents were here, we would heal them."

Issa studies her sister, and then faces us. "Gorgon has some unusual abilities, and one of them is the skill to track us at all times. Regrettably we cannot do what you ask." She straightens. "Enough questions. Now you two fight until one of you lands a strike." She holds her staff out to Jake.

He slowly grasps it, his eyes uncertain.

Rella extends her staff to me. Just as reluctantly, I take it. For some reason the cool staff repulses me. It feels solid, but doesn't weigh much. It's not metal; something else.

"Bow to each other first," says Issa.

I step out and face Jake. Since he's a black belt in kung fu I expect him to take it easy on me. Even the way he holds Issa's staff looks practiced. Plus he's taller, stronger, and has a longer reach.

We imitate the dragons by placing the tips of our staffs on the ground between us. Then we bow to each other slightly.

Jake's weapon rises in a blur and strikes my forearm hard.

I yelp and glare at him. "Jerk."

He shrugs, his words matter-of-fact. "We have to practice, Sam."

"Good," says Rella.

I glare at her too.

Issa gestures curtly. "Start again."

The next time I'm faster and jump back to avoid Jake's strike. I smirk at him.

"Again," says Rella.

We face each other a third time, staffs lowered. Jake's lips press tight. This time I block his blow with an upward motion. On the fifth attempt, I drop to a knee and sweep his legs from under him, surprising both of us.

When he gets up frowning, I say, "We have to practice, Jake."

By the tenth effort we parry each other's strikes with some speed.

Oddly, when I relax, the staff seems to move my hands, pulling them where they need to be and moving my body with it. I shouldn't be able to fight like this, even doing basic blocks and strikes. I've never used a weapon except for performing simple jabs with WhipEye.

More astonishing to me is that, outside of swimming, I've never been coordinated at anything. It's exhilarating to learn how to fight. It's as if my body is foreign, something I have to learn how to use all over again. Sweat soon covers my skin.

Jake works hard, always a fraction faster than me. I don't care, except when he gets through my defenses and hits me. But the blows hurt less and less too. I soon forget why we're training, completely absorbed in learning how to defend myself. For the first time in my life I enjoy not being a klutz.

"Enough." Issa moves in front of me and faces Jake. "Now you practice with me."

Rella motions me away from them. Taking me a short distance aside, she patiently shows me blocks, strikes, and other movements like rolls, twists, and turns. All of it appears impossible when she demonstrates it, but the staff seems to guide my hands and body. The first time I do each movement, I'm slow and awkward. However the second time I'm faster and have more balance and precision. By the fourth or fifth repetition, I own the move.

My confidence in my body's abilities grows. I also believe the twins' staffs are somehow helping us.

After a while Rella holds up a palm. "Now we spar." From the sheath on her back she pulls out another identical hidden staff and drops one end of it on the ground between us.

I follow suit, a surge of fearlessness in my head. I notice that the middle digit of each of her feet is missing a claw. Lost in fighting? The twins are likely ancient and I wonder if they were in battles with humans or other dragons in KiraKu. Animals often have mock fights for dominance, and maybe their middle claws are easier to break off.

"I see a question in your eyes." Rella looks at me knowingly.

"Well, uh, you won't be upset if I hit you with the staff, will you? I mean not that I can, but just in case it happens."

"Of course not, Samantha."

"Good to know." I decide not to use full strength. Just in case. I don't want her getting angry at me. We bow to each other, and Rella immediately plunges forward with a strike, hitting my stomach. I never even lifted my staff off the ground.

"Umph!" The blow sends me flying twenty feet where I land on my back with a thump, the air knocked out of me. Gasping, desperate for oxygen, I roll to my belly and push up to my knees. The image of the rock shattering under Issa's strike sends my hand to my stomach. No injury. Amazed, after gulping air I shakily get up, my hair trailing across my face. Rella hasn't moved, but my eagerness for fighting evaporates. I don't think I have to worry about hitting her.

"Again." She places the tip of her staff on the ground, waiting, her black hair framing her perfect face.

As I walk toward her, Jake takes a blow from Issa on the arm and yelps. Another strike to his legs sends him to his knees. Maybe there's a chance I can beat him in a fight.

Standing in front of Rella, I nervously grip the staff and stare at her, trying to anticipate her first move so I can jump backward. She scares me and I don't mind admitting it.

"Imagine there's a tight oval line around my body," she says. "When any part of my body breaks it, move."

I visualize it, trying to see her whole body. The next strike hits my shoulder, but I start to back out of the way. After a few more attempts I'm able to anticipate and avoid her blows, but I'm never fast enough to attack her. And I know she's holding back with me as it is.

We progress from simple blocks and strikes to series of movements, primitive compared to what the twins demonstrated earlier, but exciting for me.

After several hours Vesio walks across the cavern with a tray of water and food bowls. Wordlessly he sets it down, shifts to a bat, and flies away.

The four of us sit.

"I worked up an appetite." Jake starts grabbing food, but he glances at the twins. "That was incredible! You're both fantastic ninja dragon staff warriors!"

"And teachers!" I add in a more somber tone, "Even if it's for a life or death mission."

The twins nod to us, and Rella says, "You are good students and it is our pleasure."

Jake and I slug water, and then devour nuts, bread, and fruit. Rella and Issa take small sips and bites. Maybe they already ate as dragons—I wonder what they eat. I want to talk to Jake, but there's no privacy and he seems preoccupied with shoving food into his mouth.

"This bean paste has cinnamon!" he says with a full mouth. "Perfect."

I gesture to the twins. "Why are you with Gorgon? You're healers and he's a killer."

They glance at each other, but don't answer. Jake is staring at them.

I try again. "How can healers hurt others? It doesn't fit."

Rella lifts a claw. "Sometimes you have no choice in what you do."

I nod. "That's how it was when I couldn't give up WhipEye."

Jake glances at me, his eyebrows raised. Maybe he can understand me better, hearing those words from someone else.

Issa nibbles on bread. "We're more complicated than you think, Samantha."

I keep pushing. "Why did you leave KiraKu? Do you want it destroyed?"

Giving a wan smile, Issa says, "KiraKu is beautiful and we want no harm to come to it."

Rella adds, "Coming here was also not a choice."

I'm not sure what she means by that, but they both rise and move a few yards away, obviously not wanting to answer any more questions. And they're still too close for me to talk to Jake privately.

Drowsiness hits me. I close my eyes. Seconds or minutes go by before a claw resting on my shoulder brings me alert.

"Time to continue." Issa motions me to my feet.

"Yay me." I get up, trying to look calm. Jake took some hard strikes from Issa so I'm not eager to trade her for Rella. I follow her. When Jake faces off with Rella, I hear a click.

Rella is holding a spear. Jake backs away from her, wariness in his eyes. Reaching into his pocket, he pulls out his swallowtail butterfly scale.

"Beautiful scale." Rella lifts a claw. "But no armor."

"Why not? I mean, you're a little better than me with the staff." Jake looks disappointed, but he puts the scale away.

Another *click* turns my attention to Issa. Her staff is also a spear, her voice sharp. "You have to experience what it's like to face claws. Prepare yourself."

I glance at Jake, glad that he looks as worried as I am. "Can we skip this part?"

Issa doesn't respond so I twist my staff, snapping out the blade. I wonder how far the twins will take our training. They can't seriously wound us or we won't be of any use to Gorgon.

I place the sharp point of the spear on the ground between us. Like Rella, the middle claws of Issa's feet are also missing. Maybe all dragons lose their middle claws when they fight. I wonder if they grow back.

In a flash Issa cuts my tank top, leaving a thin line of blood on my side. The wound burns.

"Hey, this is my favorite top!" I try to look confident, but I'm trembling inside.

Repeatedly Issa attacks, leaving tiny lines of blood on my skin after each blow. I don't want to get hurt, but I also can't imagine cutting her. Each time we face off, dread paralyzes me. After a dozen blows, which leave bloody lines all over my arms and legs, I shudder due to nerves and pain. My skin is on fire.

Issa retracts her blade, shaking her head. Walking up to me, she spits on her claws and gently massages saliva across all my cuts, healing them. “You have a gentle heart, Samantha. I hope it’s strong enough for what’s ahead. We’ll train with only the staff after this.”

“Well, if you insist. Yay.” My shoulders relax. Jake has a few small cuts, but he’s able to counter some of Rella’s attacks. There’s no way I can beat him in a fight with blades.

The other thing I’ve seen all day is that, like me, he seems to be growing in confidence. His movements, posture, and eyes all shine with it. I’m glad for him, but wonder what that means for the two of us and Gorgon’s statement that we have to fight each other.

I continue training with Issa.

Outside of a break for dinner, we practice the whole day, late into the evening until Jake and I can barely shuffle our feet. My body aches from strikes, sore muscles, and weariness. The twins don’t seem tired, their eyes bright and their movements still crisp.

When we stop, Rella heals Jake’s cuts, and then the twins take our staffs and escort us through the dark crystal cavern. Lessers and Originals are asleep on moss beds amid the ferns and flowers. Filtered moonlight barely lights the cave. We’re led through the tunnel and across the lake cavern until we’re standing in front of the small cave where we spent the first night.

“Sleep well.” Rella gives a small bow to us at the cave entrance. “You did well today and are ready.”

Issa eyes me thoughtfully. “Ready enough.”

The twins quickly shift into massive black dragons, take to the air, and fly through the tunnel leading to the throne cavern.

We enter our sleeping quarters.

Dead on my feet, I still manage to say, “Jake, you’re not seriously planning to fight me tomorrow, right?”

He sits on his bedding and takes off his shoes in silence.

I add, “You’re the protector. You said you’d never let me get hurt.”

“No worries. Talk in the morning, angel,” he mumbles. He lies down and in seconds he’s asleep.

I fall into my fresh bedding and close my eyes. I have no energy left to think about anything. I'm sure that's how Gorgon planned it. Jake mumbles something, and then sleep claims me.

The demon is chasing me. I run and run and run until I'm barely dragging my feet. Jake waits for me with his spear. Happy to see him, I smile—and he slashes my arm. I yelp and jump back from him. The demon appears behind Jake, its claws reaching for my opposite shoulder, and then something larger looms over me...

It takes a few shoves against my shoulder before I open my eyes. The jumble of images from the nightmare fades and reality hits. Sunday. That brings panic to my thoughts.

Gorgon's tentacle nudges my shoulder again. "We're waiting for you in the crystal cavern." He sounds eager as his tentacle slithers away. "It's time to fight."

TWENTY-THREE

BOWLS OF FOOD AND water wait for us in the dim light.

I sit across from Jake. Head bowed, he mechanically chews a piece of bread. His black hair is a mess, his cargo shorts and yellow shirt dirty, and his face smudged. I can't look any better.

Famished and thirsty, I push hair out of my face and grab some nuts and sip water. My thoughts swirl over what's coming. Fighting Jake, and separation from him. Both options put me on edge.

If he wins our fight, he might take the Jewel of Origin, no matter what the cost to our world or KiraKu. Or he might die there. The idea of being apart from WhipEye if Jake has it brings fire to my belly. But if I go to KiraKu and fail, it will guilt me for a lifetime if Gorgon kills Jake and gives our parents a slow, horrible death.

I rub the jade dolphin on my bracelet. "Remember when you gave this to me?"

His eyes flick up no higher than my hands, then return to his food. "A few days after your sixteenth birthday."

"We can't do this." I stare at him, waiting.

He doesn't reply and continues eating. His face is scrunched up, so I know he's worried. But I would know that anyway.

I say softly, "Gorgon is playing us against each other. Talk to me."

"It's horrible, Sam." He looks up.

Then he leans forward to peer more closely at me.

"What? Do I have something on my lips?" I swipe my mouth with my hand.

"No, but the corner of your lips is doing that little tick thing."

"Well of course I'm worried! We're supposed to fight each other! Our parents could die! We could die!" I calm down. "Any ideas?"

He looks at the dirt. "I've thought about it, but I can't see any way out of it." He glances up at me, looking bewildered. "I want to protect you, not hurt you."

"I don't want to hurt you!" Memory fragments have floated back to me from a year ago, when we both saved each other's life and fought together. Not completely clear, but at least they show we risked everything for each other. But our parents weren't dying.

"We're better than this." I eye him. "We were when we went up against the evil guardian."

"I agree, Sam." He nods knowingly. "I've remembered things too." He heaves a sigh. "I've been thinking of something."

"What?"

He flicks a finger. "I know I already mentioned this."

"It's okay. What is it?"

"I don't want to sound like a whiner."

"Jake."

He sighs. "Yesterday you were going to leave me here." He looks at me, his expression making him look like a sad puppy. "I'd never leave you, Sam. That kind of still bothers me."

"I panicked. I wasn't thinking straight. I planned to come back. I knew Gorgon and the Komodo were going to attack me." I reach over to touch his arm. "You matter the world to me, Jake. I would never abandon you. I'd do anything for you. You know that!"

He flicks his fingers. "Okay, so how do we get out of this?"

"We don't have to fight," I say excitedly. "Let's tell Gorgon we won't fight and we'll both go to KiraKu."

"What if he refuses?" His forearms rest on his knees, his eyes on mine as he talks. "I can't let Mom die."

My heart aches thinking of Dad dying too. "Gorgon is bluffing, Jake. He needs us. This is all about getting the Jewel. Nothing else matters to him."

"Maybe. But you're guessing on how far he'll push us." Jake stares at the food bowls. "Let's try it your way, Sam. But if he doesn't go for it, then we're back to where we started. You can't beat me so you would have to bow out of the contest."

I'm silent. He's right. He's a better fighter. Even so I can't bring myself to concede the fight.

He talks earnestly. "I'm the best fighter and I would have the best chance in KiraKu. I mean that training was superstar quality! I feel like a real badass warrior! Let me go." He pauses. "I know you care about KiraKu and the animals. I care about animals too, you know that. And if there's some way to help our parents instead of bringing the Jewel, I'll do it. I promise."

I swallow. "What if I go to KiraKu and you stay back?"

He hems and haws and can't seem to get the words out. Finally he straightens. "That's not fair, Sam. You got us into this and I'm not letting you decide if Mom dies."

I can't argue with his logic. I'd say the same thing if our positions were reversed.

After a few moments of silence, he lifts his chin. "If Gorgon makes us fight, and you don't want to get hurt, you should withdraw, because I'm going to KiraKu, with or without you. I'm going to save my mother." He rises and leaves.

I drop the nuts in my hand and sit there, staring after him. I'm numb, and half-expect him to come back. Frustration wells up inside me. I'm not a guardian. I just want to save Dad. Not the world. Not KiraKu. I get Jake. He's keeping it simple. Save Cynthia at all costs.

I hold the compass, remembering Mom's love. I don't know what to do with it though. I head out. Jake's nearly across the cavern, weaving around stalagmites in an easy run. Obviously he wants to avoid any more conversation. That hurts.

Needing time to think, I slowly shuffle through the cavern. Halfway across, a splash comes from the lake. I study the lagoon and see a ripple moving across the water. I jog toward the lake. Even though I'm uncertain what Heshia might want or if I should confide in her, my gut tells me to go to her.

When I arrive at the shore, she erupts in a fountain of water, writhing blue and gold tentacles atop her head. Her swirling blue tentacles beneath the surface keep her slender torso aloft.

Again I'm mesmerized by her wild, exotic appearance. Her blue and white gentle face eases the tension in my shoulders, and her bright blue eyes ringed with gold meet mine, their radiance relaxing me further.

"Who are you, Samantha Green?" Her voice is soft, but demanding.

"I...I don't understand what you mean."

"Don't lie to yourself. How much do you care? Are you willing to make sacrifices?" She lowers herself closer to me. "I have made sacrifices for so very long, but they were needed. Will you do what is required by love? If not, you should leave now."

I don't want to leave her, and I don't understand what she's asking. "What can I do? Gorgon is too powerful."

She rises higher. "He is a fool. There is no power in that. Love is the most powerful weapon, but it will demand everything from you." Her blue tentacles gently swish the water. "Are you ready to give everything?"

She reminds me of Mom, who always encouraged me to do the right thing, no matter what. So did Dad.

My voice is a murmur. "Dad's dying because of me. I can't lose him."

"Gorgon poisoned him, not you. But the true guardian cannot betray love, even to save an elder."

I gaze up at her, tears in my eyes. "Mom died for me."

Heshia lowers herself closer, her voice full of empathy. "We are much alike, Samantha. I lost my elders long ago. Respect your mother's choice to save your life."

"You're asking me to abandon my father."

She straightens. "I'm asking you to believe in love."

I stare at her for a minute, panicked. "What if I'm wrong and Dad dies?"

"To be steady in kindness and love, one must have great courage. Especially for the truth. The bearer of WhipEye must have that or you will fail."

"What if I don't want to be a guardian? Don't want to fulfill a prophecy? I just want to save Dad."

"Then give Gorgon whatever he asks for."

I fumble in my head with ideas and thoughts.

Heshia bends toward me again. "Trusting Gorgon is a risk that has no honor, no love, and no strength. It will weaken you, and then if you fail to save your father you will never forgive yourself."

"If I fail, I'll never forgive myself no matter what I do." I shake my head. "I'm just a teenage girl with a staff. It's not enough. I mean I'm not strong enough. Physically. He's fifty feet high. Huge."

"One person can change a world. And you are not alone. Others will rise up beside you." She floats closer. "Never underestimate WhipEye. Even from here I can sense its power."

"I don't know how to use it." She's silent, waiting. I want to believe her, that I have a chance, but it's hard. I heave a deep breath, and whisper, "Okay, I'll try."

One of her arm tentacles reaches toward me, the tip wiping the tear that's running down my cheek. "You are loved, Samantha Green."

Her eyes hold mine and I can't look away. "How can I save Dad and stop Gorgon?"

A larger arm tentacle curls out of the lake, circling my waist. Gently she lifts me up in front of her face while her lower limbs churn the water. My hands rest on her tentacle—soft and velvety.

She speaks softly. "If you ask the twins, they'll help. They're the most independent of Gorgon's followers."

Her sweet, clear voice captivates me, cutting through my pain. "How?"

She brings me closer. "Do you trust me?"

"Yes." Even though I can't explain why, I've trusted her from the very first time we met.

"Then close your eyes, Samantha."

I do.

Her soft lips slowly caress my forehead, moving to both of my cheeks, and lastly my lips. It's not odd or strange to me. Or sexual. Instead it's hypnotic. Soft. Sweet. Warmth sweeps through me and I'm swaying, rocking in a comforting motion. The water is fresh, alive and invigorating, and the light above the lake shines. Heshia's tentacles are filled with unbelievable strength, sweeping beneath me in all directions. I'm sensing everything, aware of things in the distance too, like the crystal throne cavern, which vibrates with voices while the crystals give off warmth. Everything near and far surrounds me with warmth and safety. I don't want it to end.

"Wake up, Samantha."

I blink, and wobble. I'd fall over, except one of Heshia's tentacles is loosely wrapped around me. I'm standing in front of the lake amid ferns. Her limb slides away and she lowers herself into the pool to her shoulders, the water bubbling around her.

"Ask the twins for help." She sinks beneath the surface and disappears.

It takes a minute to regain my balance. Walking across the cavern, the foreign sensations stay with me, gradually evaporating and leaving me a little disoriented. The experience was so rich that my own senses seem barren by comparison. I remember Heshia's lips on my face, on my lips. Sensual. Warm. Loving. Awakening.

I felt what she felt. I wonder how I can talk to the twins. And why would they help me?

I ponder that as I walk through the tunnel leading to the throne cave. The noise increases when I enter the bright cavern and the crystal ceiling showers light on everyone. Bright ferns, colorful walls, pretty flowers. I focus on Gorgon, sitting on his throne in the distance.

It's eight-thirty a.m. Less than ten hours to get the antidote to our parents. Two dragons or their saliva. Panic nearly floods me, but I push it away. I have to save Dad. I want it as much as Jake wants to save Cynthia, and I'm still not certain how far I'll go to do it.

My promise to Heshia rings in my head. KiraKu might be destroyed on my watch and Gorgon might take over the world.

My shoulders hunch.

TWENTY-FOUR

MANY LESSERS CLING TO the cavern walls, all observing my entrance. The remaining Lessers and Originals form a large circle that includes Gorgon's throne in its far perimeter. Human shouts and animal cries quiet as I walk toward Jake. He's standing in front of the pyramid and Gorgon, who sits on his throne chair.

The Komodo lies across the lowest steps of the pyramid, occupying most of them and keeping one eye fixed on me, making me jittery. The lizard will probably never forgive me for hurting him.

In dragon form the twins look like carved stone on either side of Gorgon—black, gargantuan silent shapes.

Holding WhipEye in one hand, Gorgon scrutinizes me, his chiseled features relaxed. A deep red shirt and black jeans cover his strong frame. Vesio stands to the side of the bottom throne step, holding the dragon staffs we used in training. Rose isn't anywhere in sight, which lowers my spirits.

As soon as I stop beside Jake, I think, *Rella, Issa, please help me.* The dragons stare back without responding. What am I doing wrong? Or don't they care?

Jake stares forward, without glancing at me. What happened to *partners*?

Gorgon stands, his voice crisp. "Samantha of the Green Clan will fight Jake of the Morris Clan. The winner will retrieve the Jewel of Origin and the loser, if alive, will remain with us, safe unless the other fails. Any questions?"

I'm about to speak when Jake steps forward, his voice hard. "We've decided we're not fighting. We both go or no one goes. Take it or leave it. You'll lose more than we will if we don't go."

I'm relieved that he spoke up first and that he's directing his anger at Gorgon for a change. Gorgon's face tightens. Maybe we've pushed him into an impossible position, where he would rather save face with his followers than allow us both to go.

"I can't be sure that you will return." Gorgon's voice is calm.

"Why wouldn't we?" Jake arcs a hand. "We need the antidote and we want to free Rose."

I doubt Gorgon knows that Tarath is looking for an antidote for us in KiraKu, but he has to be considering that we might find another dragon to help us. Then we could ask Mentore or Great Ones to help free Rose. That would be my plan.

Gorgon's eyes narrow. "I'm sorry, but you might betray us. For now you both can join Rose. You have less than a half day left, and when that time is gone you three will suffer the same fate as your parents." He motions to some Originals near us, and they grab our arms and begin dragging us away.

"You can't do this!" My hands form fists. I want to hurt Gorgon in the worst way.

Jake struggles, flailing an arm. "Wait! Wait!"

Gorgon lifts a hand and the Originals stop. His voice is cold. "I'm listening, Jake of the Morris Clan. Make your decision."

Jake hangs his head. "I'll fight."

Gorgon looks at me. "Samantha of the Green Clan, will you fight or will you let Jake go?"

"No, Sam." Jake gives a little shake of his head.

I whisper, "I'll fight."

Jake looks at me wide-eyed. "Sam."

"So be it." Gorgon waves a hand, and the Originals release us and step away.

I glance at Rella and Issa again, and think about talking from my mind and my heart. Maybe not with words though. Instead I picture myself raising open arms to the twins, questions in my eyes. Nothing happens. I still have it wrong or they don't care.

When I face Jake, an image appears in my mind of me holding WhipEye. It takes a few seconds for me to interpret it. The dragons never move a hair.

I gesture to the two bronze staffs. "I want to pick my weapon."

Gorgon smiles coldly, his words dripping with sarcasm. "Your request is granted, but since Jake of the Morris Clan accepted the fight before you, he will make his selection first."

"Issa's staff." Jake points to it.

Gorgon gestures to Vesio. Vesio walks over with the two staffs and hands Issa's to Jake. He then extends Rella's to me.

I ignore him and look up at Gorgon. "I choose WhipEye for my weapon. I won't try to leave with it." Jake stares at me, but I ignore him. "And you already granted my request."

All eyes shift to Gorgon, whose calm exterior stiffens, his face red. His lips twist and his eyes begin to bulge. If he loses control the twins might not be able to stop him with words.

Rella stomps a clawed foot. "A fair request, and I trust Samantha's word."

"I agree." Issa also stomps the cavern floor.

Quiet fills the cave. I'm not the only one who grasps what's happening. Gorgon has been put into a box with his words, and the dragons are making sure he stays in it. Uncertain why the twins are helping or if it means they'll help in other ways, I'm still grateful.

Gorgon rocks back on his heels. Without moving his feet, he tosses the staff across the distance separating us. WhipEye sails vertically in a high arc toward me.

I shoot out my right hand, catching the chestnut-colored staff in front of me. The impact stings my palm, but warmth flows through the staff into my fingers and arm, comforting and calming me. Everything feels possible again. I want to shout in relief. I'll never let Jake have the staff, no matter what, and a small part of me says I'll kill Gorgon if he tries to take it from me again. I try to ignore that.

Tarath's carved face is level with my eyes. One slam into the stone, her name shouted, and she'll be here. And be destroyed by Gorgon and his followers. And I doubt the other Great Ones on the staff will come when I haven't even committed to being a guardian. In any case they wouldn't be enough to stop Gorgon's followers. I allow the wood to slide through my fingers until it softly touches the ground.

"Let the fight begin." Gorgon sits, gripping the arms of his chair.

We place our staffs in front of us and bow to each other.

Jake barely meets my eyes. "Please, back out, Sam."

"Can't." I'm still thinking I don't want to fight him when my feet fly off the ground. Tumbling hard to my back, I glimpse him raising Issa's staff to jam it into my stomach. I roll away and his weapon pounds rock.

Jake follows me, swinging his staff down hard in an overhead strike. I sweep WhipEye above my stomach to block Issa's staff. The bronze staff rings against wood. I fear WhipEye will crack, but it holds.

I roll farther, rise to my knees, and swing the staff in a circle aimed at Jake's waist. He blocks it, but I quickly withdraw my weapon before he can push it to the side. When he rushes me, I lean forward and jam WhipEye into his stomach.

He grunts, buckles over, and stumbles back several steps, holding his midsection. Wide-eyed, he gapes at me.

Surprised by my success, I stand, hoping it's over. I want to apologize, not continue.

Lessers and Originals watch us intently.

Wincing, Jake straightens, obviously hurt. A rib?

"Let's end it, Jake," I whisper.

"Then concede." He waits but I can't do it. Reaching into his pocket, he pulls out the swallowtail scale and holds it in his hand, closing his eyes. Yellow, orange, and red hues grow around his hand and in front of it, forming a round, two-foot-diameter shield. His experimenting paid off.

I glance up at Gorgon, expecting him to raise an objection. Instead he smiles.

Jake clamps his lips and twists his staff, snapping out the spear blade. His eyes fill with something desperate. Wild. Maybe he's just trying to scare me.

"Walk away, Sam," he whispers.

I shake my head.

His face tightens. "You have to."

"No."

Yelling, he charges.

Stunned, I step back and lower myself into a defensive posture, my staff facing Jake. He comes straight at me, twirling when he's close, blocking my weapon aside with his shield, which rings softly, while sweeping his blade tip upward. It catches my stomach, burning my skin. I lean away as the blade flashes past my face.

Flinging myself to the ground on my back, I roll to the side through ferns, quickly rising to my knees. Blood trickles down my stomach. I'm shocked, unsure how much Jake is willing to hurt me.

He rushes me, thrusting his spear at my torso. This time I easily block it to the side, then sweep my staff into his ankle. Falling to one knee, he grunts and jabs again, the spearhead sliding past my neck. He draws it back and thrusts it to the other side. I roll my head away from it, but my cheek burns as he scores it. My eyes water.

We thrust and parry from our knees half a dozen times, and then fling ourselves away by rolling. I'm already tired and bleeding, and my bare knees are sore from the hard ground.

Struggling to our feet, we warily stalk each other in a circle.

Jake gives another twist to his staff. Dragon claw. His eyes darken further.

WhipEye thrums in my hands, heat flowing along my arms and into my chest, keeping me alert. I hurt everywhere.

Holding up his shield, Jake runs at me. I thrust WhipEye at him, but he blocks it aside with the shield, followed by a downward strike that catches my wrist with the tip of his claw blade. My dolphin bracelet breaks and falls off.

I cry out and jump back, bleeding from another cut.

His eyes betray concern. "Sam," he whispers. "Please."

I shake my head and his forehead creases.

I can't compete with his conditioning, nor his shield, so I have to end this sooner rather than later. With his speed, going left or right will be dangerous. Backward, and he'll follow me, which leaves one direction. I charge.

WhipEye sings to me. Heat flows into my hands and arms and the wood moves me like a puppet. Anticipating his foot sweep, I leap on the run and flick the staff sideways against his unprotected forearm. I hear a *crack!* He shouts in pain and stumbles back, still hanging onto the dragon claw with his injured arm.

I land on my feet, drop to one knee, and sweep WhipEye into one of his raised ankles while he's still moving. He topples to his back.

I scramble up and jump again to get past his shield.

With his injured arm Jake lifts the claw, jamming the other end of it into the ground, while his shield melts away in an instant, flowing down his arm to cover his torso.

I've mistimed my leap and twist in the air when I see Issa's staff aimed at my side. *I'm so dead.*

My shirt tears when his blade rips into it, my side on fire, but I manage to land on my feet beside his head. I'm surprised I'm not impaled. I shove WhipEye against his throat, both of us gasping for air.

Either my will or the will of the staff exerts itself then, and lines of golden energy crackle and flow over the wood, stopping near his neck. He closes his eyes and drops his weapon, which clatters on the stone.

The energy crawling over WhipEye sinks back into the wood. Using the tip of my staff, I fling Issa's claw away, and then step back, my lungs heaving. Jake must have moved his staff before he skewered me. Even to save his mom he wasn't willing to give me a lethal wound. It's hard to cheer about it, but better than the alternative.

He sits up, pulls his knees to his chest, and buries his head in his arms. The cavern remains quiet.

Dizzy from the heat of WhipEye, and fatigued, I stagger in a circle, blood rolling down my cheek, wrist, and stomach, and trickling along my side. I ignore the wounds and muster all the strength I have. Lessers and Originals stare at me as I speak.

"If you want me to go to KiraKu, then Jake comes with me. I promise to return, no matter what. If you want us to have any chance of success for the new world you desire, let us both go."

Jake lifts his head, his eyes hopeful.

Am I lying or making a promise? The words flow past my lips without any effort on my part. I lean on the staff, glaring at Gorgon in defiance. “The guardians should never be split up. You would have to be a fool to miss the chance to send the two that defeated the evil guardian.”

Fear edges its way into my thoughts. Gorgon could erupt and kill us. But his face remains impassive.

“The guardians are stronger and wiser together.” Rella stomps the ground with a clawed foot, the thud echoing throughout the cavern. “I second the proposal.”

“As do I.” Issa also beats her foot against the ground, sending another reverberation into the cave. “I'll give Jake my staff to take to KiraKu. It's my gift.” She lifts one foreclaw. The middle of the five claws is missing. Issa's staff.

Gorgon rises, the tension in his body evident. Yet his face is calm. I remember how calm he was when Mentore believed he had him trapped. Gorgon might have planned and counted on all of this, perhaps even from the beginning assuming we had healing water or that Tarath would bring us some to extend our parents' lives. And maybe the twins are in on it. But I reject the idea of Heshia's radiant eyes and sweet voice composing lies too. At least I don't want to believe it.

Gorgon's voice rings through the cavern, strong and supportive. “Then go, Samantha of the Green Clan and Jake of the Morris Clan. Your parents' lives, your lives, and Rose's depend on you. Our world hangs in your hands.”

I exhale through pursed lips. Jake rises, his eyes showing hope—and something else—guilt? After recovering his staff with his good arm, he walks over to me, a subdued expression on his face. He wraps his good arm around me and gently leans his head against mine, his mouth near my ear. “I'm sorry for hurting you, Sam.”

“Me too.” I feel a little tingly with him so close, but I note his arm hanging limp at his side. I can't believe I did that to my best friend.

He pulls back, his eyes showing vulnerability. “Thanks for taking me.”

"Are you kidding? I'm not going to KiraKu to face Great Ones alone. Besides, that's what partners are for. To watch each other's back. I need my protector."

His eyes light up over that.

I glance at the cavern floor, unable to spot the jade dolphin and broken bracelet. That bothers me.

Issa and Rella walk forward, sending Lessers and Originals in front of them scampering to the sides. The two dragons melt into the red ninja twins. In moments they reach us. Using their saliva, they quickly heal our wounds with gentle strokes. Jake removes his armor. Soon I'm energized, and Jake flexes his arm and taps his ribs, which both appear good as new.

Rella hugs me and whispers in my ear, "Our spirit goes with you. We never wanted any of this." She betrays something in her eyes that I can't quite gauge. She's on our side or pretending to be.

Issa hugs Jake. Then the twins retreat a few steps.

"I owe you for the staff." Jake gestures to Issa.

She gives a small bow.

Jake looks at me. "Let's get out of here before Fish Bait changes his mind."

"Sure, partner."

He grasps WhipEye with his free hand, and I move it in a sideways figure eight three times in front of our feet, and then repeat three times, "The Jewel of Origin."

Lessers and Originals cheer us in a rising din, growing louder and louder as we slam the staff repeatedly into the ground, sending echoes resounding off the cavern walls.

Gorgon just stares at me, his face unreadable.

And then we're gone.

TWENTY-FIVE

A FIFTY-FOOT SALTWATER CROCODILE is walking directly toward us from a hundred yards to the west, his wide jaws opening. He's massive, probably weighing at least ten tons. Since he defeated Gorgon, he has to be mega-powerful. He looks it.

"The crocodile." I have a memory of him attacking us when we came here the first time, and later helping us. "I think Gorgon is afraid of him."

Jake bites his lip. "From what I remember, he's a control freak."

"Bigtime." Seeing Jake worried is better than seeing him angry.

I turn, my heart beating faster. Ringing us in a distant circle, a hundred Great Ones are approaching us, all in their massive enhanced state, twenty to forty feet long or tall. All staring at us with bright eyes. All ancient immortals.

Among the group are mostly mammals, some lizards, and a few raptors. All are ordinary animals in appearance, despite their size, without the oddities of Lessers in our world. All beautiful. Just seeing them makes me want to shout in happiness.

Dozens of Great Ones have their faces carved into WhipEye, but many of the Great Ones approaching us now are not on the staff. I'm not sure what that means. However the appearance of one of them eases the tension in my shoulders. "Tarath." My heart races. "Maybe she found an antidote."

"That would make my day." Jake stares at her too.

Tarath pads toward us from the north side, wedged between a wolverine and a white rhino. The caracal dips her head to me.

A silverback mountain gorilla, green iguana, and massive Kodiak bear are also here. Great Ones have come to help us. They might even have a way to defeat Gorgon. I wonder how they managed to anticipate our arrival point. And where's the Jewel of Origin?

We're standing under bright sunshine and blue skies on a plain of tall, sweet-scented, green grass waving in a light breeze. A large, pure blue lake sparkles to the west. North, a mile past the croc, hills grow into a low mountain range. Several miles to the east I see thick jungle, and behind us a quarter mile to the south flows a fast-moving river.

There's a sweet, bright scent in the air from the nearby water. The river has to be healing water. Lining the bank of the river are massive trees, three hundred feet tall and two to three dozen feet in diameter. The large trees have oaklike leaves and soft red bark similar to giant redwoods. I see them growing in all directions. Maybe they grow everywhere in KiraKu.

Just north of us are grazing herds of pronghorn, sable antelope, giraffe, elephants, and even a herd of llamas. Species don't seem to be separated here by continents like they are in our world. Memories from our first visit here fly through my brain, but my emotions are the same. The wildlife amazes and excites me.

Monarchs and giant swallowtail butterflies flit across the grass, a few with wingspans of thirty feet. I blink at those. They have to be Great Ones. Possibly with scales like Jake's that turn into armor. I'm delighted when a bluebird lands on Jake's shoulder and a yellow warbler lands on the tip of WhipEye. Their melodies comfort me. Like the Galapagos' animals in our world, animals in KiraKu have never been hunted and don't fear humans. KiraKu is paradise to me—as it was the first time. No wonder Mentore wants to return.

The air also feels alive and dazzles my nostrils, eases my lungs, and brightens my mind. My body hums with energy. All tension seeps from my bones. "I love it here, Jake."

Stiffening, he whispers, "We'll probably have to deal with the croc first."

"He might have come to help us, Jake."

"Maybe." His questioning eyes find mine. How much have things changed between us? I remember the croc from last time we were here. He's explosive, just like crocs in our world, and very territorial.

When the crocodile draws closer, he gives a deep bellow. Gray bumps cover his back and his belly is yellow. His green eyes turn gold. "I am Yakul. I'm in contact with WhipEye and knew where you would come through. I blocked your attempt to reach the Jewel of Origin and we're ready to stop you."

Jake pales and releases WhipEye. "Hang on, leather face, we're not the enemy."

My arms tense as the croc keeps coming. "Gorgon poisoned our parents and imprisoned Rose. We escaped with our lives and came for help."

With a quick step forward, the crocodile twists his head sideways and snaps his teeth at Issa's staff.

Jake pulls it away and rolls backward on the ground faster than I've ever seen him move before. Rising to his feet again, he faces the crocodile, his staff aimed at the reptile. He twists out the spear.

Tarath crouches and hisses. Other Great Ones roar and shriek or else I'm hearing the blood rushing to my ears. I lift WhipEye with both hands.

Yakul lunges at Jake.

Yelling wildly, I ram WhipEye into the side of the reptile.

Light flashes from the chestnut staff to Yakul, and he rockets sideways through the meadow, digging his claws into the dirt to stop his slide. Screeching Great Ones jump out of the way.

Fatigue hits me all over. All the Great Ones stare at me, and Jake is wide-eyed. I've pushed ten tons, the weight of five heavy cars, thirty feet through the grass. Again I'm in awe of the staff and wonder how I was able to do it.

Recovering from his astonishment, and apparently unhurt, Yakul twists his head toward me. "You dare strike a Great One?"

"You were attacking Jake." I step forward. "If you ever try to hurt him again, I'll kill you!" My words leave me shaking and I lean on the staff.

Jake hurries to my side.

Yakul's eyes widen, then narrow.

Tarath steps in front of us, blocking our view of the croc. "Now you know, Yakul. Your attempts to limit and control the guardians have always failed and you have only yourself to blame."

The croc bellows, and then his voice hardens. "I want to hear them speak. Then we will know if they are the true guardians of the prophecy."

Tarath walks past, dipping her head as she looks at us. She's telling us that we have no choice.

Yakul settles to the ground and eyes me. "The truth can't be hidden in your words. The young woman first."

All the Great Ones watch me.

My back stiffens. Any slips, anything even approaching a hint of possibility that we've come to take the Jewel, and I sense that our chances of getting help are finished. The croc stares into my eyes and I can't get started. He hasn't put me into a trance. It's just nerves. Jake's hand slips over mine on the staff, squeezing it. It's enough.

I clear my throat. "Gorgon wants the Jewel of Origin. He claims it will save our world, but he wants it for power. Mentore wants to stop Gorgon, but he also wants to return to KiraKu. Many Lessers want to come back. Many don't. Gorgon has the antidote to save our parents; the saliva of a dragon. The two twin dragons, Rella and Issa, helped us outwit Gorgon."

Jake gives me a sharp glance, but I continue. "We want any help you can give us."

Tarath walks along the inner edge of the circle. "We should help the guardians. They're heroes and should be treated as such." She lifts her jaw to the crocodile. "They haven't brought harm to KiraKu."

"It's good to see the guardians again." The female green iguana's voice is steady. "I trust them with my life."

I remember her from before and nod to the lizard. She bows slightly to me.

The Kodiak bear huffs. "I'm glad to meet the guardians again too. But they must accept that the Jewel of Origin cannot leave KiraKu.

Its removal could dissolve the barrier between KiraKu and their world, allowing human desires and technology to contaminate and destroy the purity of this land. It mustn't be allowed, even for their parents. I'm sorry, Samantha and Jake."

I sense that the bear is another past friend, and he makes a logical argument. Unable to wait any longer, I look at Tarath. "Did you find an antidote?"

She speaks softly; "I tried, Samantha and Jake, but the dragons and others that I approached had no interest in helping your parents."

Yakul turns his head to the caracal, obviously unaware that Tarath was looking for a cure.

"Is there another cure for dragon's breath?" Jake twists around to gaze at all the Great Ones.

Turning back to us, the croc says, "Deep in the mountains are old, wild creatures with the ability to heal that poison, but they won't help your cause. They care solely about their domains."

A red-tailed hawk standing eighteen feet tall screeches, and then cocks her head, her voice harsh. "The guardians have to leave."

I'm shocked and my back tenses. Especially since the hawk's face is carved into WhipEye.

The croc's eyes narrow. "Return to Gorgon and tell him you failed."

"That's the best you can do?" I make a fist.

"Gorgon will kill us, our parents, and Rose." Jake gestures to the Great Ones. "You have to help us."

I face Yakul. "We were told you defeated Gorgon before. We're on the same team, fighting the same enemy."

The croc hisses. "If he was here, we would fight him. But we won't go to your world to do that."

My voice has an edge. "You're quite the leader. You dump your problems in our world and let us clean up the mess."

"Why should leather face get to decide any of this?" Jake eyes the other Great Ones.

Yakul gives a low growl.

"I call for the full council to vote if and how we'll aid the guardians." Tarath continues to pad around the inside of the circle.

The crocodile ignores her. "The guardians must surrender their staffs, the ring of power I sense in the woman's pocket, and the butterfly scale the man has. All connections to KiraKu. Then we'll bring them home."

"We need WhipEye to rescue Rose." I'll never give up the staff. But something tells me even the ring is too important to lose or at least it doesn't belong with the crocodile. I also doubt Jake is going to give up Issa's staff or his swallowtail butterfly scale.

Heaving his belly four feet off the ground, Yakul hisses. "These are not the true guardians the prophecy speaks of. The woman hides her true wishes and the man desires the Jewel of Origin. I hear it in his words and see it in his eyes. Also the male has a dangerous weapon. Issa's claw cannot remain in his possession while he is in KiraKu."

"Issa's staff and the armor were gifts." Jake lifts the bronze rod off the ground. "And I don't want to use either of them against anyone in KiraKu."

Murmurs fly around the ring of Great Ones.

"Two dragons, a fire-breathing Komodo, and Gorgon forced us to come here." I take in all the Great Ones with my gaze. "Could any of you refuse a request from that foursome?"

The gorilla thumps his chest. "None of us could."

More voices chime in around the circle.

"We love our parents." Jake turns to view all the Great Ones. "We're asking for your help."

The rhino stomps his foot several times. "We should help them."

Yakul walks toward me. I tense, but note Tarath lowering her head, walking on an intercept course with the croc.

The crocodile walks to within a yard of me, stops, and opens his jaws rimmed with white, glistening teeth. "They tell lies and are dangerous, and should surrender what I asked for or die now."

"Forget it," snaps Jake. He steps away from me, gripping Issa's staff in both hands. His face is taut, his body stiff.

Yakul looks like he'll take my head off any second. The yellow tongue in the bottom of his mouth is larger than me.

The iguana hisses, extending the dewlap skin beneath her chin. "Killing is not our way."

The gorilla thumps his chest with a fist. "You lower yourself to human behavior if you do."

"Just do it, Sam," I whisper. Then louder, "Ruling with fear and threats sounds more like Gorgon than a Great One from KiraKu. That's why some Lessers don't want to return." My words astonish me. I didn't intend to lecture the croc; the sentences just flew out of my mouth.

I lean back as the croc inches forward, his snout a foot from my lips. His hot breath, scented with marshy muck, bathes my face. I swallow and wait.

Yakul spreads his jaws farther, but when Tarath hisses, he swings his head to her.

"If you attack them, you attack me." Tarath's voice is calm, but knife sharp. "I'll fight to the death to avenge them. I may die, but you most certainly will."

Grateful the cat is putting herself on the line for us, I also don't want her hurt.

The croc gives a low rumble. "You're siding with those who want to take the Jewel of Origin? You should leave with them."

Growling, Tarath pins back her ears. Stepping closer to the croc's midsection, she moves fluidly and with grace, forcing the big reptile to twist around more, away from me. "You don't speak for all of us, crocodile. For too long you've assumed a power never given to you. The full council should decide the fate of the guardians, not you."

Yakul gives a throaty roar that travels across the plain, making me shiver.

Tarath ignores the reptile, lifting her head calmly while inspecting the circle of Great Ones. "Speak now or forever bow to the crocodile. Speak now if you want all of us to have a voice. This is another reason why so many Great Ones left KiraKu with the Originals. Now many want to return. The council votes on that today too. The rule of the crocodile ends today for me."

"And for me." The iguana steps forward. "I bow to no ruler or self-made king, no matter how much he claims he wishes to protect us."

Others begin speaking all at once. Many step forward. Some don't. Yet Tarath wins a majority. I note that the Kodiak bear hasn't moved, his expression somber. Given that he was a past ally, it bothers me. Jake is still warily watching the croc.

The caracal ignores Yakul as she says, "It's settled. We'll let the full council decide."

Lifting his head nearly vertical, Yakul gives a deep bellow that echoes over the land in all directions.

Leaping forward, Tarath extends a single dagger-sized claw to the underside of the croc's neck, the razor point against the reptile's softer exposed yellow skin. "You've called for your allies, Yakul, but they won't arrive in time. Give us your word that we'll have full council, all with a vote, or I take your head off now."

Silence as deep as the blue sky rings us. I back away from the croc with Jake, wary of how much explosive power he has.

Without moving his head an inch, Yakul swivels his eyes to Tarath, his voice full of hate. "I give you my word, Tarath, but you will never be trusted again."

Tarath hisses. "Nor you, Yakul."

Retracting her claw, Tarath stands calmly beside Yakul as he lowers his head. I'm afraid for her. With one snap of his jaws the croc could take the caracal's legs, but the croc gave his word so he's honor-bound. And unlike Gorgon, maybe that means something to him.

The croc faces me and growls. "If you wish to live, say *I bond to you, Yakul.*"

Surprised, I ask, "Why?"

Yakul snarls, "I'll always know where you are in KiraKu. Humans have never had the council's permission to come here."

Tarath gives a slight nod so I comply.

The croc turns to Jake. "Now you."

Jake hesitates, but then repeats, "I bond to you, Yakul."

"One hour," hisses Yakul. "Then we'll find out how much support you have, caracal." Giving a throaty rumble, the croc turns away from us, his tail sliding away through the grass. Forty Great Ones leave with him. The Kodiak bear glances back with regret in his eyes, or maybe that's just what I want to see.

I slump to the ground on my knees, still exhausted from pushing the croc. Jake kneels beside me, his arms around me and his chin on my shoulder.

TWENTY-SIX

AFTER FOLLOWING THE CROC through the grass to the distant river, the Great Ones move east along its bank. Tarath watches them intently.

"I'm scared, Sam." Jake clings to me.

I drop WhipEye and wrap my arms around him. I know his fear—it's mine—that we can't save our parents. "It'll be okay." Lame. What's okay? But he doesn't challenge me. He wants to believe, as I do, that we have a chance.

"It was brave, what you did with leather face." His black hair brushes my cheek and his arms comfort me.

"Not bad for a carved stick, huh?" I heave a sigh, glad to have my friend back.

When he pulls away, his eyes show something different in how he regards me. His lips tremble and so do my nerves. His voice carries regret. "I never wanted to fight you."

"Ditto." I heave a sigh. "At least you didn't kill me."

"I tried to not stab you but still make it believable. I didn't do too bad, did I?"

"You cut me four times! And you put two more tears in my favorite top!"

"You cracked my rib and broke my forearm, Sam."

"True."

His dark eyes meet mine. "Gorgon's the one to blame."

We stare at each other and he leans forward, his lips finding mine. Surprised, I can't imagine him being this bold even a day ago.

All I can think of is everyone staring at us. Awkward. Still I notice how soft his lips are.

I gently push him back. Besides embarrassment, something else about kissing him doesn't feel right.

Jake releases me, his dark eyes questioning. "Okay, not the best of timing."

"I've seen worse." What? I must be an idiot. He just hurt me in a fight to the death! But I know the fight was as much my responsibility as his.

Jake tilts his head slightly. "I'm concerned about you, Sam."

"Why?"

"You didn't do your touchy-feely thing with the croc." He shrugs. "He might have enjoyed a little stroke along the jaw."

"Shut up." I rise with him, our hands entwined together. That feels yummy and he looks content too.

I'm concerned over the deep anger I felt toward the crocodile. Was that my emotion speaking or WhipEye? I don't want to kill anything and it's unnerving to think the staff might make me violent.

Tarath wheels to face us. "Yakul has been humiliated. He called Great Ones who support his views, hundreds of them, and when they arrive they'll attack. There won't be a council."

"But he's honor-bound," I say.

Jake throws a hand wide. "Really, doesn't anyone keep their word around here?"

Tarath hisses. "Yakul can justify breaking his word to us by saying we threaten the Jewel of Origin, to which he's also honor-bound to protect."

"What about the other Great Ones in KiraKu?" Jake gestures to the distant jungle. "Must be thousands, right?"

Tarath growls. "The majority of Great Ones don't back Yakul, but do nothing to stop him either. They haven't chosen sides so they won't help the crocodile or us."

Jake flicks a hand in frustration. "No one wants to get involved. Just like our world. It's always someone else's problem. Sheesh."

"Idiots. Their whole world's at stake." I had many discussions with Dad about why so many humans in our world are sitting around watching nature being destroyed. It's disappointing that Great Ones in KiraKu are just as passive about Yakul's power.

Tarath speaks to the circle of Great Ones. "We held our own council earlier and chose to act before the crocodile has all of us under his claws, but if any of you have changed your mind and wish to leave, do so now."

I'm grateful when none of the Great Ones move. "Tarath, what did you mean when you said the crocodile tried to control all the guardians?"

Tarath pads closer. "Ten thousand years ago, before methuselahs were sent to your world, the Jewel of Origin created WhipEye at the request of the crocodile. Yakul wanted the staff because he sensed the evil guardian was turning toward power. But the crocodile also wanted to control Rose. He thought bonding Great Ones to the staff would keep her connected to KiraKu.

"However WhipEye influenced Rose in other ways. She helped Lessers and Originals in your world by bringing them healing water, something that Yakul had forbidden. And a year ago Rose bonded you to WhipEye and brought you into KiraKu. All against the crocodile's wishes."

Jake and I exchange glances. I remember some of it. I can see from Jake's eyes that he does too.

Tarath continues. "By giving you the staff, Rose removed it further from the crocodile's influence. You couldn't hand WhipEye over when the Komodo dragon asked for it because the staff also decided it wouldn't be a good thing. But it can't force you to do something against your wishes. Your actions, Samantha, have been influenced by what created WhipEye—the Jewel of Origin."

Jake turns to me, raising a hand apologetically. "I'm sorry for ever blaming you, Sam."

"It's all right," I say softly. "I was blaming myself too." I remember what Rose said, about our heart and mind needing to be in agreement to bond someone to WhipEye. I never fully believed that I should hand the staff over to the Komodo. The staff isn't controlling me, but rather it's forcing me to make my heart's and mind's true choice. And after everything that's happened, I have to believe keeping the staff was the right thing to do.

I look at Tarath. "How can a Jewel determine what action is best for everyone? And from so far away?"

"Yeah, is it a talking diamond or emerald?" Jake raises an eyebrow.

"The Jewel of Origin is a living being." Tarath glances south, toward the river. "Few Great Ones have seen it. Yakul used his energy to prevent you from arriving closer to it with WhipEye."

A deep bellow comes from the southeast, followed by distant animal calls from all directions. My feet itch to run.

Tarath's ears flatten and she hisses. "Quickly, guardians, on my back. We run for our lives now."

"Well that's new." Jake shakes his head at me.

"I like riding Tarath." I smile, but see Tarath glance at me with what looks like a scowl. Worried she thinks I'm viewing her like a pony ride, which I am, I quickly add, "But of course only when it's necessary."

Jake rolls his eyes at me.

Tarath huffs and lies in the grass and this time I almost feel smooth getting onto her. I throw one leg over her and only half-fall onto her back before I straighten up. She still looks at me, I think with a frown. Cowboy Jake gets atop her smoothly. I hold Tarath's soft, thick red fur in one hand, WhipEye in the other, while Jake grips Issa's staff and wraps his free arm tightly around my waist. I like it there.

Having Jake *with me* again allows a small bit of happiness to lighten my spirit. "Where to, Tarath?"

"We need answers and only one being can give them now. The Jewel of Origin."

"Could we use WhipEye to get closer to the Jewel?" Jake bites his lip.

"Yakul would block you again." Tarath turns her head slightly. "I agreed with Yakul on that. I didn't want you closer either. It's not safe."

"We just can't catch a break," mutters Jake. "Chase, attack, bite, chase, attack, bite."

I smile at him. "We're together though."

"Good point, beautiful." He winks at me, and I face forward, my smile widening.

Tarath's legs bunch and she leaps forward, racing east like a stiff wind, faster and faster until the grass blurs into solid green.

The other Great Ones run, hop, and fly silently on both sides of her, keeping pace. Ahead of us, herds of Cape buffalos and hippos part to let us through, and we sail around a troop of Gelada baboons, recognizable by their hourglass faces and thick crowns of hair. When I check my compass, the needle remains on north, on *Love*, in the direction we're headed. My heart agrees.

Something stirs behind us—like a breeze but with more force. Twisting around, I follow Jake's gaze. From the south, galloping after us like a tide of moving water, the crocodile leads hundreds of Great Ones. An invisible force carries our pursuers forward, their feet and claws not striking the ground.

Jake squints. "What the heck is that?"

"Whatever it is, they're going to catch us." I hope Tarath has a plan.

"They're riding the energy of KiraKu." Tarath barks once. "Yakul is ancient and powerful in many ways. And he knows where we're going."

The caracal leans forward, her legs stretching farther and flying faster until her paws lift off the ground too. Energy radiates like heat around us and I taste sweetness in the air as the energy of KiraKu surrounds us in a thick wave. It energizes my fatigued body. It also makes me wonder if Tarath is as old as the crocodile. Remaining to the sides of us, the other Great Ones ride the same energy wave as Tarath.

"Sweet!" I say softly.

"That's got a kick to it." Jake inhales deeply.

The grassland fades as we race up the foothills leading to the mountains. Stony, with scrub bushes and fewer trees, the hills offer no place to hide.

Jake pats my shoulder. "Sam!"

I check back. "Geez."

The crocodile is a hundred yards away.

I fear for our lives, and for Tarath and the other Great Ones helping us. We could all die here, and then Gorgon will take revenge on our parents and Rose. I search for anything resembling a jewel, anything sparkling or shiny ahead of us, but there's only the rising slope of the steel gray mountain.

A loud screech makes me flinch. Diving at us, the red-tailed hawk plummets like a missile at Tarath. I flatten over the caracal, holding the staff along the length of her back, while Jake presses into me, his armor again molded comfortably against my back.

Something broadsides the hawk in midair. A great horned owl. The two tumble end over end past us, giving loud cries until they crash into the ground.

Yakul's Great Ones leap over or run around the fighting birds, not pausing in their strides. And they've cut the distance to us in half. I can't believe Great Ones will kill each other. I don't want any of them harmed. The fight sickens me.

Yakul's wave seems to propel a large dingo forward into Tarath's line, where it pounces on a red fox. Snarling and yapping, they roll through our pursuers. A roan antelope goes after a ring-tailed lemur, a Brazilian horned frog attacks a beaver, and so it goes, with Yakul's Great Ones picking off our allies one by one.

The crocodile is close enough that I can see the anger in his eyes. I face forward, the wind making my eyes water, my hair trailing behind me.

Tarath flows up the last hill and onto the mountain slope, dodging boulders, swerving around trees, and jumping over logs and across a stream, all while our pursuers attack more and more of our friends. An Andean condor and harpy eagle clash in the sky above us, giving sharp cries in another battleground of which I only catch glimpses.

Our companions on the ground are quickly reduced to the mountain gorilla and wolverine running to the right of Tarath, and the green iguana and white rhino on her left.

Like wolves pursuing a deer, several times the crocodile's allies try to close on Tarath, but they're batted away by the ape's fists or tossed aside by the rhino's horn. The wolverine and iguana swat and butt away leftovers.

After several thousand feet of climbing, the slope levels and the sparse forest opens into a meadow filled with yellow blanket flowers and lemon-scented geraniums, their fragrant perfume scenting the air. In the distance looms a wide gorge with a narrow wooden bridge stretching across it, held up by ropes.

High in the sky, hovering over the bridge, a massive martial eagle holds a boulder in its claws. It drops the rock—it isn't the first. Large holes are visible in the footbridge. The boulder smashes into the far side of the bridge with a loud crash, snapping it in two, and the pieces fall away into the canyon.

We're trapped. Yakul has won. Our only chance to survive is to give him what he wants and beg for mercy. My stomach lurches over thinking I've failed Dad.

A peregrine falcon dives at the eagle and they tangle in talons and beaks, dropping into the chasm. Yakul gallops a dozen paces behind us now, his mouth opening as if he's eager to take us all in his toothy jaws.

Tarath spits out words in a strange language. Waves of energy with a golden tinge rise from the ground in front of us like fumes of heat, but they cool and energize my skin, making me giddy as I inhale them. But it isn't enough to stop my stomach from knotting.

"We can't jump!" I exclaim.

"I'm sure we're not going to. Right, Tarath?" When she doesn't answer, Jake tightens his hold around my waist. "Ah, just pretend it's a carnival ride."

"I hate roller coasters!" I'm unable to close my eyes as Tarath flies over the ground.

Three of Yakul's Great Ones—a gibbon, wombat, and crested porcupine—close on the caracal from the left. Horn lowered, the rhino veers into them, hooking the wombat and flinging it back into the crocodile's charge, which buries it. The rhino runs over the porcupine, but the gibbon trips the rhino, sending it sprawling on its side through the yellow flowers, sliding toward the canyon. Tarath leaps off the edge of the ravine as the rhino falls into the gorge.

"No!" I stare at our falling friend. But there's no fear in the rhino's eyes as he gazes up at me.

The iguana butts the gibbon, pushing it over the edge, and then runs impossibly fast down the side of the canyon wall, chasing after the disappearing rhino. I'm dizzy looking down and focus my gaze on Tarath's neck for a moment before looking behind us.

Yakul and his followers leap off the edge of the ravine without hesitation. To the right of us, a musk ox rams the mountain gorilla from behind, pushing it ahead of us where a diving raven bashes it from the side. All three tumble together, sinking in the wave of energy and losing altitude while their momentum carries them forward.

We float across the canyon in a thick wave of gold that shimmers, barely visible, arcing from one side of the chasm to the other like a rainbow. Behind us the wave dies, leaving no trail for others to use. I glimpse a vulture grabbing the wolverine, but lose sight of that fight.

I can't help myself and glance down again. The bottom of the chasm is just a faint streak of brown. I waver on Tarath.

Jake pulls me in tighter to steady me. "Focus, Sam."

"On what?" Sailing over emptiness terrifies me, but I glance back and only see wonder on his face. Annoying.

Impossibly the caracal keeps her height and speed until two thirds of the way across we begin to drop. Slowly at first, and then faster we plummet until the eastern wall ahead rises toward us.

"We're toast," I murmur. The wind blows my hair across my face.

I glance at our pursuers. We're somehow farther ahead of Yakul now. Thirty yards behind us, he's flying through the air with a dozen of his followers, a similar wave of energy enveloping them. Most of Yakul's Great Ones remain watching from the west side of the gorge, either incapable of the leap or the croc felt their help wasn't needed.

Tarath pins back her ears and yowls.

The far side is rushing up at us too fast. Shivers run along my arms. "I can't look!"

Jake shouts, "Ahhh!"

To the right of us the mountain gorilla slams into the canyon wall ahead of us with the musk ox and raven, twenty feet below the plateau. The ox bounces off and drops out of sight and the raven dives after it. With his fingertips, the ape clings to an inch-wide ledge. I hope he survives.

Tarath lands on four paws just past the edge. Bounding fifty yards twice, she stops in a slide and wheels, panting hard. The wolverine lands nearby, skidding across the rock.

The wave of energy carrying Yakul hits my face like a breeze of cool air and I drink it in, wild with excitement. Then reality takes hold. Two Great Ones and two teenagers pitted against a dozen Great Ones and Yakul. We don't stand a chance.

Landing on his feet, the crocodile slides a short distance, coming to an abrupt stop fifty feet in front of a snarling Tarath. The other Great Ones with Yakul also land, quickly forming a semicircle in front of the caracal and wolverine. The Kodiak bear, easily the largest Great One with Yakul, lowers his head as if ready to charge.

"How come you're not running, Tarath?" Jake releases me and grips his staff.

"Off guardians." Tarath crouches. "Find the path in the stone cliffs behind us and follow it."

We slip off Tarath's back to the smooth, black rock. I almost shout in relief over having something solid beneath my feet again.

"It's over, traitors," growls Yakul. "You will never take the Jewel of Origin and WhipEye will not be allowed to leave KiraKu again. I will block it. True guardians would never put KiraKu at risk. And no Great One would either."

Tarath hisses as she backs up.

A hundred yards east of us, rising ebony rock forms a jagged wall running parallel to the canyon we crossed. I run toward it with Jake, scanning the stone wall to find an opening.

When we get closer, I glimpse a path. Glancing back, I expect to see Tarath following us, but instead she's slowly retreating from Yakul's Great Ones. I hope she's not planning to sacrifice herself for our escape.

The turkey vulture drops toward us, claws outstretched. On the run, Jake stabs Issa's spear at the bird's extended feet. The blade cuts the vulture's tough skin, but it flaps away and circles to attack again.

Diving at me from the side, the vulture's claws are outstretched. I swing WhipEye overhead with both hands and hit one of the bird's legs. Crackling light runs along the chestnut wood and over the vulture's skin. Shrieking, the bird veers off and flies away.

I stop abruptly, worried for Tarath and the wolverine.

"You've lost, Tarath." The crocodile plants one foot after another. "Surrender and we'll show mercy in your death."

"Noble talk for a liar." Tarath steadily backs up. "How will your followers ever trust you again?"

From the side a spotted hyena runs at Tarath, but one slap from the wolverine's forepaw sends it rolling away.

"We have to fly, Sam." Jake yanks on my arm.

I dig my feet in. "We can't leave them."

Jake stares back at the Great Ones. "They're buying us time. We can't waste it."

My stomach sinking, I whirl and run with him the rest of the way to the rock wall. We find the path, twenty feet wide with black granite rising a hundred feet on both sides of it. Climbing steeply to the southeast a few hundred paces, the trail then angles sharply east out of sight.

As I whirl to watch Tarath, I want to shout over so many things. The Komodo poisoning our parents, Colonel Macy and Mentore playing us like pawns on a chessboard, Gorgon threatening us and imprisoning Rose, Yakul wanting to kill us, and that the only way to save Dad and Cynthia is to destroy KiraKu. I don't fight my anger, and instead let it build. All of it triggers a reaction in WhipEye, sending heat flowing into my hands, arms, and chest. My fingers hold the wood like small vises until they burn.

Behind Yakul a dark shape climbs up over the edge of the canyon. Faint voices call from the other side of the gorge, but the crocodile probably takes them as encouragement and doesn't turn around. Quietly the mountain gorilla runs forward on all fours.

Tarath stops. "All right, Yakul, I'll bargain."

Her words are enough to halt the advance of the crocodile and his followers.

Yakul growls. "Tell the guardians to surrender and we'll send them back to their world unharmed. Otherwise they die with you."

Jake jumps up and down to distract the croc. "Forget you, you oversized suitcase!"

The crocodile stares at him for a moment, but then jerks his head to the side to look over his shoulder. Standing upright, the silverback gorilla grips the crocodile's tail. Leaning back, he swings the croc sideways over the smooth rock surface, toward the cliff edge.

Yakul bellows, his feet scraping over rock. His allies turn in surprise, and then rush the gorilla, who releases the croc. The croc digs his claws into the stone, cutting deep gouges and slowing his skid until he stops with his head hanging over the lip of the canyon.

Tarath and the wolverine pivot and bolt toward us, but I watch the ape. The Kodiak bear rises on two feet, towering over the gorilla, and swings a massive paw.

Ducking the blow, the gorilla scampers past the bear and leaps high over the line of Great Ones rushing him. Landing sixty yards away from Yakul, the ape runs at us full tilt.

"Run, Sam!" shouts Jake.

I spin and race up the path with him. Tarath and the wolverine are quickly behind us. My legs move smoothly and I'm keeping pace with Jake.

Fifty yards in an idea comes to me. "Jake!" I stop next to the rock wall, my head buzzing with energy. "Go," I yell to the others.

Tarath and the wolverine brake to a halt just past me.

"Samantha!" snaps Tarath.

Jake stands opposite me on the other side of the path, clicking the blades closed on Issa's staff and nodding to me.

Imagining what I want, and allowing my heart and mind to explode with that desire, I slam WhipEye into the wall. All my frustration bursts like a waterfall from my head into my arms and the staff. Golden electricity crackles along the wood, striking the black stone and sending an echo along the path.

Another loud reverberation occurs from the opposite wall when Jake smashes Issa's staff into it. Cracks run along the granite, deep fissures that surprise me. My weary shoulders sag, but I raise the staff again. Twice more Jake and I strike the walls until lines run sideways and to the top like strands in a spider web.

The mountain gorilla runs past us in a blur when the first small stones fall from the wall, some landing near my feet. More falling rock crashes into the path and I jump back, wishing I had Jake's armor, and still uncertain if I need to hit the wall a fourth time.

Tarath barks, the wolverine growls, and the gorilla roars.

Large chunks of granite break off the cliff face. Movement pulls my attention to the trailhead. The crocodile is galloping along the path, coming so fast it frightens me. Great Ones crowd behind him.

Boulders rain down by the ton and we run for our lives.

TWENTY-SEVEN

EXHAUSTED, I STUMBLE TO Tarath. Jake is already on her and he pulls me up in front of him. I'm lying on my stomach and need his help to get upright. Tarath and the Great Ones leap away from falling rock, which follows us all the way to the first turn. There the cracks fade and the walls remain stable.

I glimpse a solid mass of stone blocking the path behind us, high enough that even Yakul won't find it an easy passage. I doubt the avalanche buried the crocodile, but it buys us some time.

We round the switchback, the steep path heading northeast. High above us the turkey vulture wheels, tracking our position.

"Sam, what you did with WhipEye, well—shocking, Einstein." Jake holds me tightly.

"Issa's staff wasn't half-bad either, Jake."

"I know, right?" Jake sounds excited. "Hey, gorilla, I'm sorry you didn't throw that piece of leather over the edge. Nice try, though."

"It was fun to see Yakul scared for once," I add.

"A brilliant effort." The wolverine is panting.

The ape smiles, if a gorilla can do so, and keeps running, his head hanging. We're all tired. I cling weakly to Tarath, and Jake holds my waist, Issa's staff resting across his thighs.

Bang!

It sounds like rock shattering on the path below. I have no idea what it means or what the croc is capable of doing. "Will it hold them?"

Tarath hisses. "Long enough." She runs, not assisted by KiraKu's energy anymore, but with the speed of a Great One. Numerous times the path switches directions on the mountainside, enclosed by high walls of black stone, always moving east. Trees line the top edges of the gorge.

We finally summit the rock trail onto a tiny grass field. Beyond the field lies forest. Tarath stops, panting, and pads back to the cliff edge, giving us a view of KiraKu.

Far to the west flows the river of healing water, appearing like a silver ribbon. Shimmering waves of energy cover KiraKu like a massive quilt, a slight hint of gold running through all of it. The land seems even more precious, innocent, and vulnerable from up here.

"Gorgeous," I murmur.

Jake rests his chin lightly on my shoulder. "Pretty enough for a postcard."

I wonder if he means me. "I understand why Yakul wants to keep us out. Humans do a poor job of taking care of our world, and they would ruin KiraKu." Who am I to threaten all of it? Dad would leave it alone. Those thoughts drive gloom into my heart, but I tell myself there has to be a way to save him and Cynthia, and still protect KiraKu from Gorgon.

Jake takes a deep breath. "We need more information, Sam."

I'm unsure what he means, but I remember the rhino falling in the canyon. "So many died, Tarath."

"None of it was our fault." Jake throws a hand wide. "Gorgon started this mess and now everyone is deciding what side they want to be on."

Tarath paws the ground, as if trying to detect something. "It's hard to destroy a Great One, Samantha. Those who fell in the canyon can use KiraKu's energy to break their fall." She pauses. "When Great Ones left with the Originals long ago, we lost many of our number. The crocodile would be foolish to risk losing more. We may fight for dominance, but I believe killing Great Ones out of revenge is beyond Yakul. Though he wants me dead." She pauses. "And Gorgon wouldn't hesitate to kill any of us."

Jake says quietly, "I want Gorgon to pay."

"I just want the antidote and Rose," I add. "And to give Gorgon a black eye."

The gorilla thumps his chest. "It's not over yet."

Tarath huffs. "Whatever you may believe about the crocodile, he sought to guide and protect KiraKu and all those who have lived here for millennia. Yakul has my respect for that. But over time he became afraid of what lies beyond KiraKu's borders. We became too isolated, too uncaring about what occurred in the human world, and too cold to the plight of the outcast Lessers and Originals. But I have no solution."

The wolverine gives a low growl. "No one does."

The gorilla is the first to turn away. "We need to go."

"What time is it, Sam?" asks Jake.

I check my watch. "Ten a.m. We have eight hours." I glance back at him, but there's no anger in his eyes, just worry.

"Okay," he says softly. "We can do it."

A bellow comes from below.

I take a deep breath. "Leather face doesn't sound happy."

Tarath enters the forest in an easy run, the wolverine and gorilla beside her. The vulture spies on us from above. We're bound to Yakul, so he doesn't need the vulture to locate us, but the bird might be waiting for a chance to grab WhipEye.

Jake makes that strange whistle again that sounds like an elk bugle call. I shake my head, smiling. In a minute we hear an elk bugle call coming from the woods.

Jake sits stiffly. "Hey, uh, Sam, uh, what will an elk do?"

"Probably just challenge you to a fight. I'm sure if you ask her, Tarath will stop for you to participate."

"No, I'm good."

Deciduous trees, saplings, sparse brush, and the massive trees of KiraKu grow in the forest. The fresh scent of leaves and forest litter fills the air. The caracal often swings her head from side to side, watchful of everything around her. Her caution prompts me to peer into the woods too. I remember the crocodile's words that ancient, wild creatures live in the mountains.

The vegetation eventually thickens, forcing the caracal to slow to a fast walk. Sensing many animals in the forest, I send out my emotion like tendrils of warmth to any creatures I can reach. It doesn't take long.

Songbirds land on our shoulders and on the wolverine and gorilla. A maroon warbler lands on Jake's thigh, singing to him, which brings a smile to his lips. When the density of the forest forces Tarath into a slower walk, a few blackbuck antelope approach us, walking beside the Great Ones. Small mammals like marmots and woodchucks join us. All of it lightens my spirit. I'm in love with KiraKu. It gives me another reason to not bring any harm to this land.

An elk walks out of the woods, and I glance back at Jake, who is wide-eyed. "No more elk calls. Unless you want to go meet it later for a date."

"I need to date someone." He gives me that goofy grin.

I roll my eyes at him.

Abruptly everything blurs, as if the forest is moving by fast. I see details such as ants on trees, buds on branches, and thin branches swaying. My view darts among the trees in a dizzying rush until I lose my balance on Tarath and lean sideways.

Jake grabs my arm, pulling me upright. "Sam! Hey! What are you doing?"

My eyes clear and the forest appears normal again. It takes a few seconds for me to reply. "It felt like I was flying with the birds."

"Are you hallucinating? Do you need some water?" Jake eyes me carefully.

I twist to him. "Heshia kissed me in the lake cavern before we fought, and I experienced her sensations. I think the same thing happened here, only it was as if I had the eyesight of nearby birds flying through the woods."

Jake raises an eyebrow. "Heshia kissed you? You mean like on the lips?"

"It wasn't like that."

"Huh. Was that your first kiss? With tentacle lady?"

"A woman never tells."

"Should I be jealous?"

"Probably."

As we continue, I keep checking behind for Yakul, but Tarath inspects only what lies ahead, as if searching for something. "What are you looking for, Tarath?"

The big cat ignores me, but the gorilla puts a finger over his lips. I'm not sure why they want silence, but I clamp my mouth shut. After another half-hour, more fallen trees block our way and vines and gnarled branches curve in and out of each other, creating a latticework of thickening growth.

All the ground animals with us retreat, as if unwilling to go farther, and soon the birds fly away too.

Slowing more, the caracal quickly picks her way around winding vines, fallen trees, and twisting limbs. Following single file, the wolverine and ape remain silent, often studying the shadows of the forest.

To see massive Great Ones nervous makes me jumpy. Jake holds Issa's staff in both hands behind me, his face drawn.

Not far ahead, the vegetation resembles what WhipEye is capable of when called to weave plants into a barricade. Impenetrable.

Tarath stops in front of a mass of tangled limbs that a mouse would have trouble squeezing through. The three Great Ones stand silently, shoulder to shoulder, waiting and studying the forest wall.

I lean over to the gorilla and whisper, "What are we waiting for?"

"An Old One lives here. A Great One with more power than most of us." The gorilla stares at the barrier, talking softly. "It might take an hour to get a response."

"An hour?" Jake exclaims loudly. "We don't have time for that!"

I glance back, keeping my voice soft. "I agree, Jake. But we don't know what kind of danger we're in."

He faces the woven forest and says, "Come on, open up! We're in a hurry! Life or death mission here!"

Tarath turns her head and hisses at Jake, but then she faces forward and speaks calmly. "We come in peace, Worlath. We seek an audience with the Jewel of Origin."

Rustling comes from behind the thick vegetation, but no reply follows.

"I've come here before." Tarath lowers her head, staring at the wall of green. "Long ago. Do you remember me?"

"Thousands of years." The female voice sounds sweet and lonely. The tone becomes harsher, but the loneliness remains. "A long time."

Tarath chuffs. "I'm sorry, Worlath."

"Come here only when you want something."

Tarath and the other Great Ones back up, glancing to the sides and ahead. A chill runs through me. Jake peers past my shoulder, his brow furrowed.

Worlath's voice hardens. "No need for Great Ones to leave, but humans shouldn't be here."

I grip WhipEye. "We're friends of Great Ones."

Tarath stops moving. "Samantha and Jake are guardians. Bearers of WhipEye. Their eyes have gold."

A loud snapping comes from behind the wall of greenery. The three Great Ones stiffen, as do I. Jake lifts Issa's staff.

Worlath's voice is stern. "Samantha wears a water sign. Gorgon's camp."

"Enough about the water signs already! It's just a ripped-up T-shirt! I like dolphins and I like to swim." Everyone glances at me, and I add sheepishly, "And I can't stand Gorgon."

"Maybe." The female voice drops an octave. "Jake holds a dragon's claw. The pattern tells me it belonged to Issa. Did he kill her?"

I'm not surprised that the curling lines on the staff identify Issa, since individuals of most species have unique markings. But I'm amazed Worlath recognizes Issa's pattern. Worlath must have known the dragon.

Jake's voice is firm as he sweeps a level hand. "Issa gave me the staff to use as a gift. She's still alive. She trained me to fight, and Rella trained Sam. We're not half bad."

"Humph. Rella and Issa. Humph. Should have stayed in KiraKu. Always wanting to fly somewhere new."

Slithering vines, branches, and narrow tree trunks part, leaving a small, dark tunnel in front of us. It's not large enough for the Great Ones to enter. I'm jittery, imagining a giant funnel-web spider.

Tarath doesn't move as she whispers, "Worlath controls the forest with old power. Something only the Jewel of Origin and a few other Old Ones can do."

"And WhipEye." I respect the staff even more.

"We've come to talk with the Jewel, Worlath." The ape lifts a hand. "Nothing more."

"We'll see." A bent, slender green limb slowly extends out of the tunnel and unfolds.

Please don't be a spider. I'm not sure what it is until it's closer. A tremor runs through my limbs. "Oh, geez."

Jake whispers, "What is it? Looks horrible already."

"*Mantis religiosa*, a.k.a. praying mantis. Able to kill prey three times their size. Like to eat their prey while it's still alive. Strikes faster than the blink of an eye and—"

"Okay, I get it. That's enough of the creep factor." Jake stares wide-eyed at the insect leg.

Instead of three inches long, this mantis must be a hundred times bigger. Even Tarath's speed might not match an attacking praying mantis. The darkened tunnel hides the rest of the creature.

When the tip of her leg reaches Tarath, Worlath gently taps the caracal's neck, just beneath my hand. I sit rigidly and the Great One doesn't flinch. The spikes on the mantid's jointed limb are long enough to pierce my torso. For a moment I consider touching the mantis' leg, but think better of it.

"The girl wants to touch me. Why?"

"No reason," I say hurriedly. "Just being friendly."

"Sheesh!" exclaims Jake. "She wants to touch every creature she meets. She's kind of crazy that way."

"Dork." I look in the direction of Worlath. "I love all creatures, that's all."

The mantis is quiet for a few moments. "Worlath remembers cat. You can come. Others stay."

Tarath purrs. "Yakul is chasing us, Worlath. The crocodile wants to hurt us. The others can't remain here. It's not safe."

Worlath starts to withdraw her leg, but halts in midair. "Why?"

Tarath watches the leg. "He's upset that we want to talk to the Jewel of Origin. He wants us to leave KiraKu because we won't follow him." She pauses. "He attacked the guardians and lied about a council vote. He has no honor anymore."

The foreleg folds and withdraws into the dark hole, accompanied by a series of clicks. "Crocodile has a temper. But he protects KiraKu. For a long time. He must have a reason."

I can't believe the mantis is siding with Yakul. "That big piece of leather will soon be telling you what to do, Worlath. Do you want that?"

"No. But Worlath respects Yakul."

"What can we give you so you'll let us through?" asks Tarath.

"Jake must tell me what he sees."

I glance over my shoulder. Jake is staring off to the side, glassy-eyed, his lips trembling. In moments he slumps, his eyelids twitching.

I wait, hoping he saw something positive for once.

Tarath turns her head. "Worlath wants to hear your vision, Jake." Very softly, she adds, "She'll know if you are lying."

Something flashes in Jake's eyes. Fear?

He straightens. "Samantha and I stand at the head of Gorgon's army, facing Mentore's army. We don't want to be there, but we are."

There's a long silence. Worlath might not like what Jake saw in his vision. I don't. It's the same vision he had before, which is disappointing.

Another series of clicks comes from the tangled growth. "All right. Pass through. But no tricks."

The forest tunnel expands enough to allow the Great Ones to enter with ease.

I'm surprised Worlath isn't upset about Jake's vision, but the praying mantis might not care about Mentore or perhaps never heard of him if she's been here for millennia. Tarath walks into the tunnel with tentative steps, glancing everywhere. Dimmed sunlight filters through the tightly woven roof.

A bellow floats in the distance. Yakul.

Tarath walks faster, while peering into the thick growth on both sides. The ape and wolverine do the same. Ahead of us the tunnel winds gently into the distance with no end in sight.

After a short stretch the greenery on both sides of the tunnel weaves together even tighter, making it impossible to see into the woods. Creepy. But so is a giant praying mantis.

"Jake saw more." Worlath's accusing voice comes from the north side, hidden somewhere behind the dense weave of plants.

I glance at Jake—his face turns ashen. Tarath's back tenses beneath my legs.

"But what he said is true." Tarath pauses in her stride. "He just didn't describe everything, Worlath."

"Worlath saw what he observed. The energy told me."

Everyone backs away from the north side of the tunnel.

Worlath continues. "Jake had the Jewel with him and he lied about the willingness. Gorgon is an enemy. You should wait here for Yakul."

Hearing that, I have to agree with the mantis. But I sense if we don't make it to the Jewel, Dad is as good as dead. Frustrated, I say, "If you want to save KiraKu, let us through, Worlath. If you can hear the truth, then you know I want to protect KiraKu."

"Maybe," says Worlath. "But Jake doesn't care."

Jake releases my waist to hold Issa's staff with both hands again.

Worlath's words put me on guard about Jake. He plans to take the Jewel to Gorgon and is willing to help him. The betrayal cuts deep. Is his friendship dishonest too? I feel numb inside, then clench my jaw. I'm not going to let him do it. I wonder what Tarath and the Great Ones think about Jake now.

I twist around as rustling branches and green vines weave together, closing the tunnel behind us.

"Run!" Tarath leaps forward.

Snaking vines curl around the gorilla's legs and one of his arms. Huffing loudly, he tears at the vegetation, but more of it wraps around him and drags him backward. "Go!" he yells.

When Tarath skids to a stop to look back, I slide my leg over her shoulder and jump to the ground. I land roughly and stumble a few steps. I'm weary, but I don't care what it takes. I won't allow another Great One to suffer for us. I'm surprised when Jake jumps down beside me, grimacing.

"I'm not leaving him," I say determinedly.

Jake nods. "Then neither am I."

I run, raising WhipEye with both hands like a pole-vaulter. Jake has Issa's claw raised. Tarath hisses behind us and the wolverine snarls.

Vines and branches coil around the struggling mountain gorilla, encasing the Great One faster than he can rip them off, quickly hiding him from view.

A wild, crazy burst of euphoria fills me as heat flows from the staff into my hands and limbs. Lifting WhipEye overhead, I jam it against the greenery.

Golden electricity streams over the chestnut wood, crackling along the vines and branches that hide the gorilla. I visualize the vegetation shrinking—and it recedes. Jake swings Issa's claw at the growth, cutting wide swaths in it, and Tarath and the wolverine bark and growl while they tear wildly at the vegetation with flashing claws.

Other vines keep growing like a mass of snakes trying to grab us, but by ducking, twisting, and stepping back, we're able to escape them.

I feverishly strike the wall of vegetation until it retreats enough so the ape comes into view again. Then I'm only able to lean on WhipEye, my lungs heaving.

Suspended vertically in the growth, his limbs outstretched, the gorilla's eyes widen when he sees us. Growling, he struggles with his living chains.

With blades, claws, and shouts the others rip and hack at the ape's bonds until he bursts free from the green shackles. Then we're all panting and staring at the vegetation, which retreats a few yards from us.

Quiet.

The gorilla places a hand on Jake's shoulder and mine. "I won't forget this, Samantha and Jake."

"Hey, I had nothing better to do." I heave a sigh. "You helped get us here."

Jake nods, his chest heaving. "We already owed you, big gorilla guy."

"On my back, guardians." Tarath crouches and we climb atop her. Backing away, all three Great Ones eye the woods.

"Liars. Liars. Liars." Worlath's voice comes from all around us. "All of you liars."

Tarath pivots and leaps away as spiked forelimbs stab out from the vegetation behind us. Worlath's limbs hit the ground like massive spears, spraying dirt at us. The caracal barely dodges the strike, while the gorilla jumps to one side of the tunnel and the wolverine leaps to the other.

I look back. From the tangled green growth, two large compound eyes glare at me. Those eyes burst through the foliage, revealing Worlath's large triangular head and mandibles—big enough to tear a Great One to pieces.

Worlath lunges forward several dozen yards, her forelegs striking down again, just missing Tarath and the dodging wolverine. "You can't escape Worlath."

"She's a monster." Jake's eyes are wide as he glances back.

"A beautiful one," I say.

If she wasn't so intent on ripping us to pieces, I'd love to see the mantis close up. Emerald green, her forelegs fold into the stance that earned praying mantids their name. Much larger than I thought, she cocks her head at us before the curving tunnel hides her.

The walls close in on us with writhing plant growth, forcing the Great Ones into single file as they run. Worlath doesn't have to catch us. She can come to us at her leisure after the forest traps us. Tarath flows like water through the winding pathway and everything blurs. Behind us the gorilla and wolverine are streaks of motion too.

“Liars liars liars.” The mantis’ words sound nearby, but the thick tunnel wall hides her.

The tunnel ceiling lowers until it’s only inches above Jake and me, forcing us to flatten on Tarath’s back. The Great Ones shrink to half their size.

“Help me, Jake!” I barely have enough strength to lift WhipEye, but he grabs it too, his strong arm thrusting it up. We hold it above our heads, letting the end of it slide across the vines behind us. Sparks fly where the chestnut rod scrapes against the living wall of green—I visualize the vegetation receding. It causes the tunnel roof to expand a little, enough for Tarath to run faster.

I pull the staff down and look ahead. Our path ends in a mass of vines and plants that block our way. Tarath lowers her head, murmuring strange words. I bury myself in her fur and Jake presses into me.

Without slowing, Tarath leaps at the woven wall with the gorilla and wolverine. Sticks and branches scrape my legs and arms, but we burst out of the forest, escaping the shrinking tunnel.

TWENTY-EIGHT

WE COME OUT UNDER blue skies and the early afternoon sun. The three Great Ones expand to their full height, skidding to a stop in a shower of dirt and stones, immediately wheeling to face the woods. I expect Worlath to fly out after us, but only her angry voice floats from the forest.

"Worlath won't let you leave. Ever."

Tarath growls, then turns and pads forward. "We'll have to find another way."

I remember Yakul saying he would block WhipEye. Maybe we won't be able to leave with it. I'm also spent. I can't use the staff again, which means handing it over to Jake. No way. I brush hair from my face.

"That was some show, Sam." Jake's whispered words are sincere. "Saving the gorilla."

"You saw the Jewel in your vision?" My cheeks warm and my words have an edge. "And you were helping Gorgon?"

His voice is defensive, his hand cutting the air. "It was different this time, and you were standing beside me. We didn't have a Jewel. Some woman was there, that's all."

I twist to see his eyes. I think he's being honest. It confuses me, because I won't help Gorgon for any reason.

His voice softens. "Maybe the woman is another Great One. Or someone just stopping by. It doesn't make sense."

"Yeah."

Tarath is silent. Maybe she doesn't understand it either. Too tired to argue or dwell on it, I study our surroundings.

High walls of granite rise up around us on three sides, running up to Worlath's forest in a giant U. In front of us is a large pond, maybe seventy yards in diameter. High on the rock wall across from us, thousands of cliff swallows dart in and out of gourd-shaped mud nests, their high-pitched chirping filling the air.

Suddenly I'm floating above the pool, looking down at the Great Ones and the forest, seeing all of it in detail. The sun's rays are bright to the west, the blue sky vivid.

A hiss from Tarath brings me back. I sway a bit, and then balance myself. "Weird," I mutter. "But very interesting."

Jake gives me a puzzled look, and I just say, "More birds."

Across the pool the rock face has a large opening where the air sparkles with gold. It looks like the mouth of a cave. Water blocks all access to it, unless we climb across sheer walls. There's a small area of level rock in front of the entrance, rising a few inches above the water.

Compared to leaping the canyon, this should be an easy jump for Tarath. Yet she's waiting for something.

"What's wrong?" I ask.

Tarath crouches. "Hang on, guardians. And be ready."

I grip her fur, and Jake holds me as the gorilla runs away from us on all fours along the south side of the lagoon. The wolverine remains at our side. Tarath waits briefly, and then runs at the water, leaping when she reaches its edge. The wolverine jumps beside her.

A geyser erupts on the far side of the pond. A yellow-and-brown eel, large as a school bus, flies out of the water, showing jaws lined with sharp teeth. It quickly sinks back into the pool.

"Freshwater moray," I murmur. "A.k.a. *Gymnothorax polyuranodon*. Aggressive. Carnivorous. Slightly toxic saliva."

"Another creepy monster." Jake sounds disgusted as he grips Issa's staff. "Does Ms. Touchy-feely want to touch it?"

"Maybe."

Tarath snarls and raises her paws.

I ready WhipEye, doubting I have enough energy to hurt the eel. Jake levels Issa's staff on the opposite side of Tarath.

When we're halfway across, the eel flies out of the water again, this time on a collision course with Tarath. It opens its mouth, a cavern of teeth. Tarath snarls.

I tense, ready to strike it. Jake hoists Issa's staff.

A black shape flies by in front of us. I have to blink before my brain registers the gorilla as he shoves his two feet into the back of the eel, knocking it down. Crashing into the lagoon, the monster sends up a spray of water that soaks our legs. The gorilla's momentum carries him to the far side of the pool, where he grabs tiny handholds on the rockface.

Landing together on the flat rock, Tarath and the wolverine stop abruptly. The gorilla is already swinging down behind us.

I study the sparkling gold in front of us. The points of light change continually but give the impression that they reach across the whole width and height of the cave mouth.

Tarath huffs. "Great Jewel, we seek entrance."

Nothing happens.

The caracal turns to me. "I had hoped your presence would stir the Jewel to allow us in. Yakul said the cave has been shielded like this ever since he spoke to Jewel about erasing your memories six months ago."

Jake raises a hand. "Come on, Jewel, open up already!"

I lean forward. "Let us down, Tarath."

The caracal shrinks smaller, and Jake and I slide off and walk up to the golden shield. I can't see anything beyond glittering gold. Cautiously I touch it, but it feels like a brick wall that sparkles wherever my fingers press against it.

"We need your help, Jewel." I wait, but there's no response.

"You have got to be kidding! We came all this way for nothing?" Jake's eyes show desperation. "Our parents are dying!" With a fist he pounds against the sparkling barrier, with no results. His hand drops to his side and he looks at me, his lips trembling. "Now what? We lose?"

I feel the same bitter disappointment, but something occurs to me. I softly hum Mom's song. Nothing happens, so I say the words of the song.

Still nothing.

"Why the song?" Jake frowns. "Your mom had nothing to do with KiraKu, right?"

"Mom gave me the compass and it always guides me." I pause. "And Mom said the song would have great power to help me in times of need. I don't know. Somehow I thought it was worth a try."

Jake throws a hand wide. "Well, we're all feeling desperate."

Tarath swings her head to me. "It's a song, Samantha, so it must be sung."

"Do you know it?" I ask.

Tarath chuffs. "Sing and we will see what happens."

I face the cave again, clear my throat, and hum a few bars.

Jake looks at me like I'm nuts. "What are you doing, Sam? A monster crocodile is coming for us and you're practicing humming?"

"Quit hurrying me. I'm just trying to get in tune. Maybe it matters." Not wanting to sing too off-key in front of the Great Ones, I sing softly; *"I'm waiting for my true love, the one who always knows, true friendship is the rock, that true love always sows, for love I'll make my stand, the only true power to command."*

For the first time the words of the song resonate inside me differently. I get it. It was what Heshia talked about, and what Mom believed. It gives me strength.

The glittering air in front of us begins to shimmer brightly in waves, and then it fades and disappears altogether. I step forward and extend my hand, but the barrier is gone.

"Way to go, Sherlock!" Jake throws an arm around my shoulders and squeezes me. "We're in!"

"Someone wanted us in," I murmur. Questions swirl through me, but I'm too happy to care.

Our eyes full of wonder, we walk in together, the Great Ones behind us.

Beyond the cave entrance is a thirty-foot tunnel. We stop at the end of it, facing a circular cavern a half-mile wide and a quarter-mile high, holding me in awe. Sparkling black and white jewels glitter on its walls. A large, round opening in the rock ceiling narrows like a funnel, allowing sunshine to brighten the cavern. The ebony stone floor glitters.

In the center of the cave, on top of a large mound of black rock, rests the Jewel of Origin.

TWENTY-NINE

SHAPED IN AN OVAL fifty-feet-wide and twice as tall, the towering Jewel seems attached to the rock it sits on. The large, multifaceted black jewel glitters like a starry night, but much brighter, as if each sparkle represents a star twinkling directly into our eyes.

I raise a hand, allowing my eyes to adjust to the brightness. When I peek, I still can't look at it for long.

"It's massive." Instinctively I realize that placing my hand on the gem and trying to move it back to our world with WhipEye won't tear it from the stone. And I don't want to try. Relief and sadness sweep through me. There's no way to bring the Jewel of Origin to Gorgon, no decision to make. But that means Dad and Cynthia will die. My heart sinks.

"Can't shove that into a pocket," whispers Jake, his face downcast.

Tarath growls. "We came only for information, Jake."

Jake's comment means he was still hoping to take the Jewel back to Gorgon. It makes it easier on me that he can't. I don't see how his recent vision can come true either. "Maybe the Jewel can help us in some way we don't understand, Jake."

"Yeah."

Waves of bright golden energy run off the Jewel onto the cavern floor, creating a layer that flows over the stone and pools around the Great Ones' feet. From the ground this energy drifts into the air as golden mist, streaming up and out the cavern's open ceiling. KiraKu's energy source.

Seventy-five yards from the Jewel the energy shimmers strongly in the air, creating a circular wall that rises vertically from the floor, eventually arching to form a high dome over the gem. This transparent shield is several feet thick and looks stronger than the one that blocked the cave mouth.

The Jewel's radiant light subdues enough so that we're able to lower our arms. Tarath pads forward, increasing in size. She stops a dozen feet from the energy wall and lies down. The caracal is silent, joined by the wolverine and ape on one side of her, Jake and me on the other.

Tarath's voice is respectful when she speaks. "We come for answers, Greatest One."

"My name is Jewel." The voice is gentle and the black gem sparkles as it talks.

I like her immediately. It's strange to think of the Jewel as *her*, but she sounds like a young woman.

She continues talking. "The energy of KiraKu runs through you, through all things, and allows your hearts to be visible. The guardians want to save their parents, Yakul wants to protect KiraKu, Lessers want to return to KiraKu, Mentore wants to stop Gorgon, and Gorgon wants enough power to rule two worlds."

Jake flicks out a hand impatiently. "What do you want?"

"To save your parents, stop Gorgon, bring the Lessers and Originals back, and save the world beyond KiraKu, which humans are destroying. What all of you want, of course. They're all good things to try for." She pauses. "I closed myself off to visitors and waited all this time to hear the song from the true guardians." She pauses. "But you still have to choose that."

"Can we save our parents?" Hope rises in my throat. "Without hurting KiraKu?"

"You say without hurting KiraKu, but Jake will do anything to save his mother. I can't help you, Jake."

"But you said you wanted to help us." Jake slashes the air with a hand, his voice desperate. "You have to." When Jewel doesn't respond, he adds, "Worlath said you were in my vision."

"I'm trapped inside this rock. If you break me free, I could leave with you, go to Gorgon, and perhaps he'll save your mother. But KiraKu will be no more."

Jake stares at the wall. "Sing the song, Sam."

I don't hesitate. "No."

He swings to me, pleading, "Please, Sam. Or I will."

I worry that he can sing the song and gain entrance, but that concern vanishes when Jewel says, "The song won't dissolve this barrier, Jake. It was only bonded to the cave entrance."

Jake's face scrunches up, but he steps forward and extends a finger, which slides into the golden barrier. His eyes widen. Pulling his finger back, he returns to me and wraps his free arm around my shoulders. Holding me close, he whispers in my ear, "I'm sorry, Sam. You're the best friend I've ever had."

"Five-stars." I wrap my arms around him. "I'm sorry too."

His hand slides off me. When I pull back, he gives my shoulder a hard shove. Gasping, I fall clumsily against Tarath's shoulder.

Jake runs forward and leaps at the thick wall of energy. I'm startled when he passes through unharmed. It must surprise him too, because he hesitates after he lands, and then he charges the stone.

I regain my feet, shouting, "Jake!"

Tarath rises, hissing, her ears flattened. "No farther, Jake. I won't allow it." The cat stomps the ground with her paw. The gorilla stands and crouches as if to jump, and the wolverine's fur bristles as she steps forward.

Already a fourth of the way to Jewel, Jake stops and turns. He twists Issa's staff twice, bringing out the dragon claw.

I lift a hand to him. "Jake, let's talk." He can't really believe he can defeat three Great Ones. They're going to stop him, no matter what. KiraKu is at stake and, though they defied Yakul, they won't allow their world to be destroyed to save Cynthia.

Jake backs toward Jewel, his face twisted. He glances over his shoulder, as if debating whether he can reach the stone before the Great Ones can stop him. No way. Even if he frees Jewel from the gem, Tarath and the others will never let him leave. Unless he's gambling that they'll have no reason to stop him if Jewel is already free. But I have WhipEye, and I'll never let him use it to take Jewel to Gorgon.

Jake takes another step back. The Great Ones roar and leap. Jake plants his feet and raises his staff, his face taut.

All three Great Ones hit the thickened energy wall and bounce back a score of paces, sliding across the stone with force and speed.

I gape. The energy shield is obviously designed to protect Jewel against intruders, including Great Ones. So how did Jake get through? His armor?

Tarath lifts her head as she slides. "Samantha, stop him!"

Without hesitating I run, wincing when I hit the energy barrier. But I pass through the shimmering wall as easily as Jake did. On the other side there's a heightened glow, as if I'm standing in a sparkling fishbowl of bright lights. It would be glorious if I wasn't focused on stopping Jake.

Jake recovers from his surprise, wheels, and runs.

I'm exhausted and can't catch his flying feet, so I stop and fling the chestnut staff as hard as I can. WhipEye spins through the air into his legs, tripping him. Falling hard onto his armor, he bounces off the cavern floor and slides to a stop. He quickly pushes to his knees.

I'm already running forward, and I bend over and grab my staff. From his knees, Jake swings Issa's claw at my legs. I somersault over it and roll past him, rising quickly to face him, my back to Jewel.

Standing, Jake twists the staff to retract the claw, and points it at me, his voice flat. "Out of the way, Sam. It's a stone."

"Dad and Cynthia wouldn't want it." I doubt he'll be able to hear anything I say.

"Shut. Up. You're putting animals ahead of our parents." He lunges.

I parry his strike, knocking it to the side. He backhands Issa's staff at my head and I duck—the bronze rod brushes my hair, making my skin tingle.

I back up to maintain my position between him and Jewel, aiming my staff at him. "Dad and Cynthia spent their lives helping animals and caring about the planet."

His lips twist.

I try again. "How will Cynthia feel if you destroy a world to save her?"

His voice is sharp. "We can't save the whole world."

My voice softens. "We can try."

He comes at me with a rapid flurry of strikes, forcing me to back up off balance. With another flurry he gets past my guard and jabs my ribs with the side of the staff. Sharp pain runs through my torso and I groan, lowering my arms. I shuffle back farther.

Tarath hisses, the ape roars, and the wolverine growls.

I purposefully remain bent over so that when Jake rushes me, I sidestep and jab WhipEye into his thigh, just below his armor. I could have aimed for his neck or head, but couldn't bring myself to do it. It's his turn to gasp and falter as golden energy crackles over his leg.

I hustle in front of him again before he recovers. He yells and charges. I try to block his staff to the side, but he rolls to the ground past me, rises to his knees, and swats the back of my knees with his staff.

"Ah!" I let go of WhipEye with my right hand so I can break my fall with my palm, while my left knuckles smash into rock, my bare knees banging hard. Rolling right, I avoid Issa's staff, which hits the ground near my shoulder.

I push to my knees, but he's already swinging his staff down and batters the back of my left hand. My grip on WhipEye loosens and I cry out as a tremendous tug yanks the chestnut-colored staff from my fingers. The pain of loss runs through me, a longing that sears my limbs and chest worse than any time before.

I glance over my shoulder. Jake has both staffs in his hands.

"Jake," I say hoarsely. "We can find another way."

Turning away from me, he hurries toward Jewel. Panicked, I scramble low over the stone and slide on my hip so I can kick his calves, tripping him. With his hands full he falls harder this time.

I'm already pushing to my feet and dash past him, bending over to grab WhipEye. But he yanks it away from my grasping hands. Stopping ten feet past him, I whirl to face him again.

He stands, his face taut. Dropping WhipEye behind his feet, he grips Issa's staff with both hands.

I hold my palms up at shoulder height. If he doesn't reason with me, I'll push him and go for WhipEye. "Jake. Please."

"I promised Mom I would save her and that's what I'm going to do." He lifts Issa's staff, aiming it at my chest.

Part of me wants to let him strike the black rock to free Jewel, to save Cynthia and Dad. But something deeper rejects that. I'm also angry. "You don't care about anything except your stupid, selfish little world."

His lips twist. "You don't know anything."

"The animals here will be hunted, killed, and poisoned just like in our world. Humans will destroy all of it. And Gorgon will control both worlds. The Great Ones will be finished. And all because of you."

He steps closer, glaring at me, his voice crazed with desperation. "You heard Jewel! She said she would come with us to Gorgon if she were free. She wants to be free!"

Weariness softens my words. "I want to save Dad as much as you want to save Cynthia." Pain rips through me. I can't face life without Dad any more than he can without Cynthia. "But I love all of it, Jake. That's my problem. I love everything, and I can't sacrifice all of it for Dad. Maybe you love Cynthia more. Maybe I don't understand anything about love."

He raises the staff high in both hands, his eyes on mine, his face locked into a grimace.

Tears are in my eyes and I lower my hands. "Do it. Go save Cynthia and Dad. But you'll have to go through me."

Jake shouts and thrusts the staff.

THIRTY

STONE SHATTERS AS ISSA'S staff strikes the ground in front of my feet.

Jake slumps to his knees. The bronze staff falls out of his hands, clattering on the rock. I slowly kneel and wrap my arms around him. He rests his head on my shoulder and slides his arms around me.

Silence. Tarath and the others sit and wait.

After a minute, Tarath rises and lopes to the cave entrance. She quickly returns. "Guardians, Yakul is close."

A distant bellow drifts into the cavern. Worlath must be allowing the crocodile through her forest.

Jake whispers, "I'm sorry, Sam. I couldn't help it. Kind of freaked out."

"I've been there." I squeeze him.

He pulls back from me to look at the others. "Now what?"

I lift my head to look at the Great Ones, uncertain what we can do.

Tarath growls. "I'll help you fight Gorgon to save your parents."

"As will I." The gorilla thumps his chest.

"And I," says the wolverine, clawing the ground.

Their loyalty makes my throat catch.

"I won't forget this." Jake wipes his eyes.

"Neither will I," I add.

"Guardians." Jewel's voice is tender.

We rise together, squinting at Jewel's brightness.

"I'm sorry. That was a necessary test of character, Jake, and you passed." The Jewel sparkles brighter, and then calms again.

"You let us through the barrier?" I ask.

"Bonding to WhipEye—and to me since I created it—allowed you to cross through it."

Jake's hand spins. "I couldn't break you out?"

"Maybe you could have, and KiraKu's boundaries might have dissolved. Sometimes tests have to involve real consequences, don't they?" Jewel quiets for a few seconds. "I'll go with you to Gorgon."

"No." Jake shakes his head. "I...I don't want you to. I don't want to hurt KiraKu." His voice lowers. "No matter what it costs."

"I'll send a small part of myself. Gorgon never visited me. He might believe I'm small or that he could have ripped me from the cavern and transported me back to your world. Perhaps with the twin dragons he could have. But now he'll only know what I tell him."

"It won't hurt KiraKu?" I ask.

"No." Jewel talks calmly. "The barriers between KiraKu and your world will remain intact. I won't risk humans coming here. Humans have great imagination and can see what *might* be. That's why Yakul fears them. The Great Ones and animals of KiraKu, no matter how old or wise, can't invent things in their minds the way humans do. They're attuned to nature and only see what *is*. Humans often are not satisfied with nature as it is. That's because they don't *see* it. But your eyes have gold and you pose no threat to KiraKu."

The rock glimmers with a million points of light, making us shield our eyes.

Jewel continues. "Long, long ago in the beginning, before all great beings existed, I was hardly conscious—just a blanket of energy formed by the planet over millennia, covering everything and running through everything. Life grew, taking some of this energy and using it. In some places small amounts of the energy gathered, collecting in pools. Eventually in this cavern it coalesced, forming this Jewel on this rock."

I'm lost in the beauty and energy of Jewel's voice more than the story she's telling us. It reminds me of listening to Heshia and I don't want her to stop.

"Over eons life continued erupting all over the planet. The Great Ones evolved and something amazing began to happen. I changed. I could talk to myself, hear myself, and experience myself. Slowly I spread my consciousness into the world, and eventually into every living thing. At far distances my abilities lessened, and in time these became the current borders of KiraKu."

The lower side of the Jewel facing us begins to throb in pulses, becoming less opaque. Something is moving inside it, a form that remains vague no matter how much I squint against the light.

Jewel continues. "I contacted the Great Ones and Yakul came. And Tarath and a few others. I limited my contact, preferring to experience everything firsthand through the energy bonding me to the world. Sometime later Yakul returned. I agreed with his plan to close off KiraKu to your world, where a few Originals had traveled beyond the borders of my perception. It was the right decision.

"Later Yakul became fearful when some Originals pursued technology in KiraKu. He feared they would destroy the natural world. Thus many thousands of years ago he ordered all remaining Originals to leave. Many Great Ones left with them. That was sorrowful for me."

I shiver when I hear a louder bellow outside. The Great Ones glance toward the cave entrance.

The figure moving inside the Jewel comes closer to the outer surface, still vague in outline. Eyes blink open. "And now things are out of balance in KiraKu and in your world. I must investigate, but I won't risk KiraKu, Samantha and Jake."

Those last words calm me as the shape inside begins to take on definition. A golden foot and leg push out of the Jewel, then an arm, and then the figure of a petite, young woman. She's still connected to the gem along her outline. Separating from the oval stone completely, she floats to the ground, landing quietly on bare feet, her knees bent.

Jewel wears a gold blouse, with golden pants that end below her knees. Just as with Issa and Rella, I can't tell where her skin ends and the clothing begins. She straightens, her eyes, long fine hair, and skin all different shades of gold. Her sharp-featured face is calm.

She smiles. "Guardians, so good of you to come."

I step toward her. She hugs me, and warmth from her body and eyes fills me. Mom used to give me hugs like this, and of late Cynthia and Dad. I want to bathe in it and don't move. As I hold her, a tiny tingling of warmth fills my hands, as if her skin is humming with energy.

She withdraws her arms and hugs Jake next. He looks brighter when she pulls back.

One question is eating away at me. "You created the song?"

Jewel's eyes shine. "So only you could enter. Long ago I gave the song to your mother, Faith Summers—"

"Who was an Original," I finish for her. "That's why she gave me the compass, loved big trees, always looked so young, and was so magical with wild animals. It also explains why Rose bonded me to the staff."

"Brilliant, Sherlock!" Jake is wide-eyed. "Is your Dad an Original too?"

"No. I've put more gray hairs on his head." I smile over that. "I'm only half-Original." I wonder if it was harder for Dad and me to let go of Mom when she died because she was an Original.

Jewel grasps my hand. "Faith was widely known and loved in KiraKu."

That makes me feel good—even excited—and curious. I want to learn more about her. It also means KiraKu is part of my heritage, and I have another reason to protect it.

Jewel's hand floats to the compass on my chest. Her finger points to each of the four words on it: *Trust Love Trust Mom*. "This holds so much love. I hope it has helped you, Samantha."

"It has." I remember all the times the compass guided me, and reminded me of Mom's love.

She continues. "Hold the compass level and whisper over it, *Jewel loves all.*"

Holding it level, I repeat the three words. The round compass face opens on a hidden inside hinge. Sparkling gold liquid fills a small depression inside the compass, shimmering as if it's alive.

"It's my energy, Samantha. And part of the reason you obsessed so much about the staff, and why, when the timing's right, WhipEye will call to you again."

Jake studies it. "Wow. I thought it was alive! No wonder it could guide her. Does it do anything else? Sing and dance?"

"Maybe." Jewel smiles. "Close it now, Samantha."

I carefully snap the lid shut. "Issa and Rella sensed your energy in the compass, and it's also why I didn't want to take it off, isn't it?"

Jewel gestures to the cavern floor. "Your staffs, guardians."

I step next to WhipEye, but glance at Jake.

He flicks a hand. "It's yours. I always knew it was." He picks up Issa's staff.

I grab the staff, the wood sending warmth and peace into my core. Every time I part from it, I'm more obsessed than ever about never letting it out of my hands again.

When I straighten, Jewel is beside me. She runs her fingers over the chestnut-colored wood, studying her handiwork. "Beautiful. Perfection. Carved from the WhipEye tree's roots. I've always admired the WhipEye tree's durability and strength of character. Like yours, Samantha. I was happy when Rose disobeyed Yakul and bonded you to the staff."

My cheeks warm over her praise. "Someday I'd like to see the WhipEye tree."

Jewel's eyes shine. "Your staff has some of my essence in its core. That's why WhipEye has power, strength, and the ability to call Great Ones."

I also wonder if that's why I can't bear to be away from it. "It's an honor to have it."

Jewel smiles. "How do you move WhipEye to travel somewhere, Samantha?"

"A sideways figure eight. The infinity symbol." As soon as I say it, I realize what she means. "Interesting."

"What am I missing?" Jake comes closer.

I look at Jewel. "You're saying the staff's power has no limits."

Jewel nods. "It's connected to me, to KiraKu's energy, so WhipEye's limits are only those of the bearer." She looks at Jake. "You both have powerful weapons now to fight for love."

Jake bites his lip. "Can you heal our parents?"

I wait, my pulse thumping. The energy source of KiraKu should be able to handle something as small as dragon's breath poison.

"Energy alone won't heal your parents." Jewel strokes his forearm. "Otherwise Tarath could have healed them. Gorgon planned for that."

Disappointment thickens my throat.

Jake's eyes lower. "I saw us holding our parents' hands when they die."

Jewel gently lifts his chin with her hand. "The future is never fixed by visions. They only give you one strong possibility. Live from your heart. Then anything is possible."

Jake's eyes brighten.

Jewel says cheerfully, "I agreed with your memory loss because I never doubted that WhipEye would call to you again." She looks at us, a playful tone to her words. "Did you really need your memories to guide your choices in this journey?"

I think about it, and shake my head. "No."

"Are you kidding?" Jake whirls a hand. "You know, I gotta say it might have made things like a hundred times easier."

Jewel beams. "And we'll find a way to heal your parents. Now let's go talk to Yakul."

I trade looks with Jake, and gesture to the cave entrance. "Yakul is a little upset right now."

Jake throws a hand wide. "More like raging crazy."

Jewel laughs. Lightness and happiness fill her eyes and her optimism brightens my mood. "Run!"

She sprints toward the energy barrier and we follow her. When we cross through, Jewel leaps atop a surprised Tarath, flying with a grace and speed that no human could match.

"I'm honored to be in your presence, Jewel." Tarath bows her head formally.

"As I am." The Gorilla nods.

The wolverine lowers her head. "And I."

"And I'm honored to be with all of you." Jewel giggles and bows with her arms spread wide.

The caracal crouches, and Jake and I climb up behind Jewel.

Jewel says, "I'm glad you were able to use your wonderful training from Issa and Rella, guardians. But we're all on the same team now. All for one and one for all?"

"Yes." Jake and I say it simultaneously.

The gorilla thumps his chest. "All for one and one for all."

Tarath and the wolverine growl.

I remember Worlath. "Shouldn't we use WhipEye to leave?"

"This cave is shielded by my energy so the staff won't work here." Oddly, Jewel sounds happy over that.

No wonder Worlath didn't care about us going into the cavern. The praying mantis must have known we couldn't escape with WhipEye from inside the cave.

Jewel pats Tarath on the head. "Fly, kitty-cat."

"I'm not a kitty-cat." But Tarath lopes out of the cavern.

I clutch the staff, expecting to use it immediately.

Tarath stops on the stone in front of the water. The sun is lower in the sky, painfully reminding me of Dad and Cynthia.

On the far side of the pool lies the crocodile, flanked by a half-dozen Great Ones, including a cheetah, Gila monster, and the Kodiak bear. The turkey vulture circles in the sky, and directly above us the cliff swallows are chirping.

The thin figure next to Yakul draws my attention. Standing upright, forty feet in length, Worlath stares at us. She twists her head one-hundred-eighty degrees, inspecting us from all angles. Monstrous. Beautiful. A green killing machine if she chooses to be.

I want to run back into the cave.

THIRTY-ONE

STANDING ON FOUR LEGS, Worlath lifts her forelegs and folds them in the traditional prayer pose. Next she spreads her arms in warning. It's impressive.

I clear my throat. "Mantids can twist their heads three hundred and sixty degrees, but they can't fly fast." I add quickly, "Of course a Great One mantis may be able to fly faster."

"Nice," mutters Jake. "Like a horror movie."

"We should use WhipEye." Tarath growls. "Even if Yakul tries to block it, you have enough energy to overpower him, don't you, Jewel?"

"Great idea!" I'm ready to slide off the cat.

"Love it!" Jake looks ready to bolt too.

Jewel lifts a hand. "Not yet."

"Chase, attack, bite," grumbles Jake.

"You can't pass." Worlath's confident voice carries over the water. "If you try to use WhipEye, I'll stop you."

Worlath must be very fast. Maybe Jewel has been too isolated and is ignorant of what the world is really like.

A grumble escapes Yakul's teeth. "Give up, Tarath. You're trapped."

Jewel's voice is bright. "Yakul, I go willingly. Let us pass, Worlath!"

Worlath's large eyes move, her head shifting side to side. "Jewel can't leave."

"Just to help friends, to put things right," sings Jewel. "Let us go, old friend who has guarded me so well for so long."

The crocodile roars. "You've tricked Jewel with your lies."

"No one tricked me, Yakul." Jewel raises her hands. "You've been a great protector of KiraKu for a long time. Now trust me once more. This is a small part of me, and I'm still your friend. Let us pass."

The crocodile hisses. "You'll never take Jewel out of KiraKu, Tarath. You've imprisoned her, confused her."

"Worlath," pleads Jewel.

"Worlath, stop them!" Yakul does the impossible. He stands upright on his two hind legs, balanced on his thick tail. His jaws open, revealing swordlike teeth.

"That's a lot of teeth." Jake clutches my waist.

"Sixty-four," I say. "Crocs lose them and go through about three thousand in a lifetime. Did you know they have the strongest bite of any animal alive?"

"That makes me feel better already!"

My worries fly to the cliff swallows above us. A thick flock of birds leaves the nests. Motioning to them, I send my wishes. Thousands of swallows split into two separate streams, arcing toward the Great Ones loyal to Yakul.

"Fly, Tarath, fly!" cries Jewel.

Near the opposite shore the giant eel leaps partially out of the water. It dives beneath the surface, headed in our direction.

Jake readies Issa's staff. I grip WhipEye.

"We're never going to make it," I whisper.

"Ya think?" Jake sits stiffly behind me.

Tarath's muscles bunch beneath us and she leaps, aiming for the crocodile. The gorilla and wolverine jump with her.

My thighs tighten on the caracal. I'm ready to swing the staff, which is suddenly hot in my hands.

Worlath takes all of my attention. The mantis flies at us in a blur, moving faster than any Great One I've seen thus far, except for Lewella and Gorgon. Her compound eyes stare at us, her wings and body a green streak. She'll cut us to ribbons in midair and leave the parts for the eel.

We're so dead.

Jewel squeals as if she's delighted.

That seems crazy to me. Maybe Jewel is half-mad after sitting in a cave for millennia.

Tarath growls.

The eel erupts out of the water, blocking my view of Worlath, its jagged teeth aimed at Tarath's head. Abruptly the eel moves impossibly sideways.

Worlath appears holding the creature between her two forelegs. Veering away, she flings the beast to the far side of the pool, where it splashes, sending a wave of water over the side.

We float toward the opposite shore, while Worlath flits back in a blur behind Yakul. Grabbing the giant croc's torso between her two forelegs, she throws him sideways. Rolling end over end, the roaring reptile tumbles into Great Ones to his left.

We land on solid ground.

Jewel raises both arms, giving an enthusiastic, "Wonderful, Worlath!"

Simultaneously the Kodiak bear charges the cheetah and Gila monster, butting them with his head. Other Great Ones face Worlath. I worry she'll kill them if they attack her. But the cliff swallows fly at their faces.

I don't want any of the birds hurt, but I'm right in assuming Great Ones don't either. They care about the animals as much as I do, and duck the assault, waiting for the swallows to stop.

Worlath blurs into the woods, leaving a tunnel for us. Tarath bounds toward it, the gorilla, wolverine, and Kodiak bear behind us.

Before we enter the forest, the swallows soar back into the sky in two thick ribbons, chirping loudly. Uncertain what they perceive, I wave and send them my silent thanks.

Running into the woods, Tarath follows the winding tunnel, which closes behind the Kodiak bear.

"Well that wasn't stressful at all." Jake wipes his brow.

"Piece of cake," I mutter.

"Worlath loves Jewel." The happy voice comes from the forest to the right of us. The mantis isn't hiding this time and flies with her gaze on Jewel. I can't take my eyes off her emerald body.

"And Jewel loves Worlath." Jewel is practically singing. "We'll return. Let the crocodile through as soon as we pass. Don't let them harm the forest, Worlath, and don't harm them."

"Worlath promises. Jewel will come back?"

"I'll come back!" cries Jewel.

"Good. Or Worlath will come for Jewel."

Jewel smiles at the mantid. "Thank you, dear friend."

When we leave the thick forest, Worlath stops and watches us. I wave goodbye and she raises a leg to me. A cleared narrow path through the forest appears ahead of us—the mantid is helping our escape.

After weaving single file through gradually thinning forest, in a half-hour the Great Ones are able to run four abreast, their legs blurs of motion. My spirit is lighter, and Jake's arm is wrapped around my waist. Everything is brighter. Possible. For the first time I really believe we can save Dad and Cynthia.

Tarath barks at the Kodiak bear. "You helped us."

The bear huffs. "I trust Jewel more than Yakul."

"I knew you would!" Jewel says with exuberance.

The bear growls. "When the crocodile didn't keep his word to hold council, I lost respect for him."

The ape glances at him. "I didn't think you put much effort into hitting me when I dragged Yakul toward the canyon."

"I had doubts even then." The Kodiak turns his head. "It's good to run beside you again, guardians."

I'm glad the bear is with us. "We need you, friend."

Jake gives the bear a thumbs-up. "Glad you came to your senses, fur head."

"Humph." The bear snorts.

It takes an hour to run back to the ledge above the rocky cliffs. There Jewel yells, "Stop!"

Tarath pads to the edge, giving us a wide view of KiraKu. High above us the turkey vulture tracks our position.

Jewel is motionless, staring.

I see why. A midafternoon sun shines over the land. The beauty of it me makes me want to cry, laugh, and sing. I soak it in. Hues of every color of green, brown, and blue spatter the horizon and everything in-between, vivid, all covered in a layer of gold.

"No wonder Lessers and Originals want to come back," I say.

Jewel raises her arms, her face shining. "I had to see it before we left, to reaffirm why it has to be protected, and why it's so precious."

"It doesn't get any sweeter." Jake sounds mesmerized.

I squeeze his hand on my waist. I want to believe everything will be all right. It has to be. We have Jewel.

A distant bellow comes from the forest.

"Time to end the lovefest." I don't want to face Yakul and his crew again, even with Jewel.

Tarath lowers herself and the three of us slide off. We form a circle. Jake grabs WhipEye. Jewel takes the gorilla's hand, who rests his free hand on Tarath, who rests her shoulder against the Kodiak bear, who presses into the wolverine, who rests a paw lightly on Jake's foot.

"Should we join Mentore?" Jake stares at me.

"Yeah, if we go back to Gorgon we might be DOA." Everyone regards me. Even though it seems stupid, risky, and dangerous, that's what I want to do.

Jewel slides her hand over mine on the staff. "If you wield WhipEye, it increases your deep convictions of right and wrong, of what you must do. It will seem as if there is no other way. All of us have this capacity to accept the true path we should take at any moment in life, but often our fears and confusion hide our own truth. The energy in the staff brings your path into stronger focus, if you allow it. It helps connect your true spirit and intelligence to all energy, the whole planet and all of life. The sense of what's right is so powerful that the wielder of WhipEye sometimes can't bear to be parted from it. Truth is powerful. So is love."

Her words amaze me, as does WhipEye. I glance at Jake, wondering how he feels about all this.

"I trust you, Sam." He shrugs. "Gorgon should never have WhipEye, no matter what, so let's do whatever gives us the best chance to kick his butt."

I nod. "I'd love to."

Jewel's eyes are bright. "Bringing me to Gorgon poses risks, but not bringing me may pose more risk."

"Sam and I had visions of fighting Gorgon and his monsters." Jake pauses. "And dying."

Jewel smiles. "One possible outcome."

Jake's eyes widen. "Like one of two outcomes? You know, fifty–percent chance of dying? Seventy–five percent?"

Jewel keeps smiling.

I close my eyes. Gorgon wants Jewel. He wants WhipEye. He wants power. I gave my word that I would return, but under his threats. It's risky bringing Jewel or WhipEye anywhere near Gorgon, but my gut tells me to do it. I have to trust it. I hold the compass on my chest. Mom would be proud and that gives me strength.

I look at Jake. "I don't want to land in the middle of Gorgon's followers."

"We might end up at the bottom of a Lesser doggie pile." His eyes are determined. "The lake cavern."

Three times we draw the infinity symbol at our feet, while we repeat, "Lake cavern."

We bang the staff three times into the ground. *Boom! Boom! Boom!* The echoes stretch into the distance as another bellow comes from the forest, much closer this time.

I have a fleeting glimpse of Yakul galloping into the meadow before it all fades.

THIRTY-TWO

THE LAKE CAVERN IS empty when we arrive at its center. The holes above only allow dim light. Stalagmites surround us and we're standing in a bed of ferns. After visiting KiraKu, it looks ancient and primitive.

I should be falling over from fatigue, but Jewel held WhipEye too, so it didn't drain Jake and me as it might have otherwise. I also assume she overrode any attempt by Yakul to block WhipEye from leaving.

The gorilla, Kodiak bear, wolverine, and Tarath spread out in front of us, facing the tunnel leading to the throne cavern.

However Jewel releases WhipEye and skips away from us toward the lake like a little girl on a fun outing. Something about her happiness puts me at ease, giving me confidence. We run after her.

"What time is it?" Jake's face is strained.

"Two-thirty." We have three and a half hours to save Dad and Cynthia. Plenty of time. Or maybe they're already dead. My gut says no. I cling to that for sanity.

We stop beside Jewel at the side of the lake, which gives off a fresh scent.

The water boils in front of us and Heshia rises, her blue and gold tentacles writhing atop her head, her larger blue tentacles keeping her upright. Exotic and wild, her gentle face calms me, especially when her blue eyes find mine.

"Great Queen of the Merpeople, it is an honor to finally see you again." Jewel bows to her. "You are ever beautiful and charming."

"It is an honor to meet even a fraction of the love of Jewel." Heshia bows to her too.

I'm surprised Heshia sees immediately that this isn't the full Jewel of Origin, and I worry Gorgon will too. I also wonder who the merpeople are and if Heshia is truly their queen.

Heshia glances at me and confirms my fears. "Gorgon will know this is only a part of Jewel." She turns back to Jewel. "You made a mistake coming here."

Despite her warning, Heshia's voice mesmerizes me. Sweet and clear. I want to listen to it forever. I stare into her eyes.

Jewel sounds happy. "Some things must be risked to gain something greater."

"I live the same way." Heshia is quiet then, the water swishing below her as she looks down at Jewel. Leaning closer, she says, "If you doubt everything my brother says or does, you will know his true intentions."

"Brother," I murmur, glancing at Jake.

His hand slices the air. "A.k.a. cold-blooded killer freak."

I'm surprised Heshia is related to the ugly loser. She must have suffered having him in the family. Maybe Gorgon was a wannabe king.

"We've missed your kind spirit." Jewel stretches her arms up. "You should return to KiraKu."

Tears spill from Heshia's eyes. "I would love to. I have been away for so long that the sweetness of KiraKu is a distant memory that only carries the pain of loss. To see you here brings those memories back in full."

Heshia's pain adds sadness to my own heart.

Jewel raises her arms. "I honor you for your great courage, and your love of KiraKu and this world, Heshia. You live like the noble queen that you are, and risk everything for everyone. You are truly my sister in heart and mind."

"I hope we meet again, Jewel. But you know the darkness that is coming." Heshia slowly sinks. "Beware." Before she disappears, she turns to me. "You may doubt yourself at times, Samantha, but never doubt your heart." And then she's gone.

I stare at the water, moved by Heshia's tears, her pain deep in my marrow. I sense Gorgon is responsible for it, and I want to make him pay for that and so many other things.

Tarath hisses from nearby. "Jewel, guardians, we must go. Gorgon and the others are aware of our presence."

We hustle after Jewel as she skips back to Tarath. Chills run along my spine as Heshia's caution echoes through me. My hand sweats on WhipEye and Jake clenches Issa's staff. I'm so glad he's at my side again that I want to hug him.

"We kept our word, Sam. Gorgon can't do anything to us in front of the other Lessers." Jake sounds confident.

"I hope so." But his words don't slow my racing pulse.

Tarath leads all of us. The other three Great Ones form a V around Jewel. Jake and I follow them. Concerns fly through me: rescuing Rose, saving Dad and Cynthia, and returning Jewel to KiraKu. My tennis shoes clap against the stone floor.

We walk through the tunnel, the light at the end of it growing brighter until we enter the throne cavern. I forgot how beautiful it is. The multicolored walls, emerald ferns, bright flowers, and white crystals are glorious.

Tarath doesn't slow her gait as we pass through hundreds of standing Lessers and Originals. Lizards cover the walls all the way to the white crystals, where the light from the holes in the ceiling bathes all of us in a warm glow.

The silence makes me jittery.

All eyes race from the Great Ones leading us to the golden, lightly-stepping young woman ahead of me. They might not recognize her, but everyone must instinctively understand she's Jewel because Lessers bow to her and Originals kneel as she passes. All of them have hope in their eyes, and some have tears. She beams at all of them.

I smile crookedly at Jake and he returns a cautious smile.

One thing confuses me. Lessers worship Jewel so she should be able to convince everyone to follow her. So why would Gorgon bring her here?

Ahead of us the Komodo dragon lies at the bottom of the stairs. My eyes follow those stairs up to the throne chair, to Gorgon's gleaming eyes. His chiseled features and broad shoulders give him a kingly appearance. As usual he wears black jeans and a long-sleeved, red silk shirt, his feet bare. The tentacles on his head wave like headless slugs.

Towering over him, Issa and Rella stand on either side of the throne, quiet and motionless. I want to communicate with them, but wait to see what Jewel will do. I'm not certain I trust the dragons. They helped me once, but they might have been serving Gorgon.

The Komodo raises his head and growls at Tarath. The caracal responds with a hiss, her ears pinned back.

Gorgon stands. "There will be no fighting in this cavern."

Swinging his head around, the Komodo looks at Gorgon, and then takes a few steps to the side and drops heavily to the stone floor.

Tarath stops at the bottom step and sits, the black tufts of fur on her ears straight, her reddish fur shining in the light. The other Great Ones stop beside her. None of them appear happy to see Gorgon.

Giving a low growl, the Kodiak sits beside the Komodo, forcing the lizard to move his tail. Seeing the two together, I bet the Kodiak could take the Komodo. The massive bear might even be able to hold off one of the dragons. Lounging on the lower steps, the gorilla and wolverine face the crowd.

Jewel runs past Tarath, up five steps where she whirls, her back to Gorgon. Her rich voice holds everyone's attention. "I'm the essence of the Jewel of Origin and I've come to help Lessers and Originals, to bring balance to KiraKu. I'm honored to be here."

Gorgon holds his hands high, a triumphant smile on his face. His smooth voice radiates power. "Let's welcome Jewel to our world!"

Jewel keeps her back to Gorgon as the cavern erupts with cheers, roars, and hisses of celebration. It continues until Gorgon raises both palms once more. When everyone is silent, he adds, "And let's thank the guardians, Samantha of the Green Clan and Jake of the Morris Clan!"

More shouts and excited cries fill the cave, boosting our chances to force Gorgon to honor his promises. I wonder if he expected Jewel to be an energy source without intelligence that he could use at his whim. But he doesn't betray any surprise over her appearance or words. According to Heshia, he knows this isn't the whole Jewel, yet he shows no disappointment.

If he doesn't learn that Jewel has come here to stop him, I believe we have a shot of doing just that.

Jake climbs the steps with me, stopping beside Jewel and facing Gorgon. "We want the twins to leave now to heal our parents." He cuts the air with a stiff hand. "No more lies." Everyone in the cavern quiets as he speaks. "And we want Rose released. No more delays, excuses, or crap."

My tone is harsh. "We've done what you asked, now it's time for you to keep your honor-bound word and give us the antidote."

Silence. All eyes rest on Gorgon.

He gives a magnanimous gesture. "You've earned it. But everyone in this cavern, even Jewel, I'm sure, recognizes that time is precious. Mentore and his allies have discovered our tunnel entrance to the outside, and if we don't go to him, he'll enter and trap us here. We wish to avoid a fight."

"You're stalling." Distrust fills me over another delay. I look at Jewel.

She whispers, "We'll have time to save your parents, Samantha and Jake." She faces the crowd, her voice light and full of confidence. "I will talk to Mentore for all of you. We'll be able to have peace and avoid a battle. KiraKu has never had war, and Lessers and Originals should never fight each other, especially over me."

Supporting cries rise throughout the cavern.

Gorgon silences them once more by raising his hands, his voice somber. "But we must first meet Mentore. The twins can't leave to heal your elders until this conflict is resolved, Jake of the Morris Clan and Samantha of the Green Clan."

Jake's eyes darken, but he remains silent.

Frustrated, I motion stiffly. "We want Rose released now."

"A fair request. I'll take you to her myself." He sweeps a hand to the Lessers and Originals in the cavern. "The rest of you prepare to go to the surface."

Many voices echo satisfaction, and Issa and Rella stomp their feet. Everyone shows excitement. I remember Mentore's anger against Gorgon, but Gorgon isn't a threat if he doesn't have control of Jewel or WhipEye. Regardless of what Jewel might propose, we have to be ready to flee. And we need the twins or their saliva with us.

Jake walks down the stairs with me. "Fish Bait is faking it," he murmurs. "I don't believe anything he says."

"Never," I whisper. "He's planned for this. But maybe Jewel can outsmart him." We stop at the bottom of the steps.

While Gorgon descends the steps, I decide to take a risk. I create a clear image in my mind of the twin dragons flying, arriving outside the hospital and going into our parents' room to heal them. No image returns, but they both bow their heads to me. I push further and create an image of Gorgon in his ugly kraken body, fighting and throwing Mentore and Lessers around. An image comes to me of the twins breathing fire at Gorgon. It feels sincere. Relief fills me. The twins won't allow Gorgon to ruin Jewel's attempt for peace.

When Gorgon stops beside Jewel, Tarath and the other Great Ones growl at him. He ignores them and stares down at me intently, a glint in his eyes. "We have little time," he says calmly. "Mentore is close."

"You don't seem worried," I say.

He smiles, but there's no warmth in it. "I'm overjoyed with your success."

"Enough with the nonsense." I glare at him. "Take us to Rose. Free her like you promised."

"Everything is fine." Jewel's voice remains steady. "We have time, and Rose will come with us."

"As you wish." Gorgon gives a slight nod to Jewel, his eyes shining.

That frays my nerves, and Heshia's warning rings in my head. Gorgon kept Rose prisoner for some reason, and I have to assume he's planning to go back on his word with us. I gaze up at the twin dragons. "Issa and Rella, will you walk with us?"

Gorgon appears startled as the two dragons step forward, shrinking to smiling women who stride toward us in red ninja outfits. Issa still has the white streak in her long, dark hair and her left middle toe lacks a claw. The dragons move as smoothly as Jewel.

Tarath and the other Great Ones eye the twins intently as they approach us.

Rella stops in front of me, her eyes shining. “Brave guardians, we salute you.” Her dragon claws wrap around me and Issa hugs Jake. The perfume of orchids fills the air. It comforts me.

Issa pulls back, smiling. “I hope my claw helped you, Jake.”

Jake’s eyes brighten. “I, uh, love it. But it’s yours.” He holds the claw staff out to her, but she pushes his hand back and gives a slight twitch of her head.

“You might need it,” she says very softly.

Jake nods to her, and then glances at me. I see the same confidence in his eyes that I feel; the twins will help us. I glance at Gorgon to see if he noticed, but he’s staring at Jewel.

Jewel ignores him and skips down the steps to us.

Issa takes Jewel’s hands in her claws. “We have memories of you in KiraKu, Jewel. We greet you and honor you.”

Issa’s words startle me. If the twins remember Jewel, wouldn’t they also remember her true appearance as a massive jewel? And be surprised now by her appearance? But maybe they just remember Jewel’s essence covering the land.

Jewel’s eyes sparkle. “KiraKu’s favorite sisters. Everyone misses your whole family.” One at a time she warmly embraces the twins.

Rella is misty-eyed. Issa places a claw on her sister’s shoulder as if to comfort her. I’m not sure what to make of it.

A shadow passes over us. The giant vampire bat circles around, flapping its wings. It lands nearby, blurring from a bat to Vesio. The tall, brown man flashes his golden eyes at Jewel, but he hangs back, seeming more reserved in her presence.

From the steps Gorgon speaks to everyone. “We’ll free Rose and then meet Mentore and his followers and try for peace.”

Jake gives me a sideways glance, obvious distrust in his expression.

I blurt, “Less talking and more action.”

“Come.” Gorgon glides down the steps, following Vesio who is striding for the tunnel.

Jewel follows Gorgon, with Rella and Issa beside her. Tarath and the Kodiak bear trail Jewel. Jake and I hustle after them. The Komodo dragon rises to his feet and crawls after us, hissing. With warning growls, the wolverine and gorilla take positions on either side of Jake and me.

A large procession of Lessers and Originals crawl, walk, and slither behind the Komodo. Over a thousand. Maybe a fight can be avoided. Gorgon won't have a chance to pull any tricks in front of everyone. Adrenaline races through my limbs.

Once in the tunnel, Vesio lifts the heavy crossbar and pushes open Rose's prison door. I rush into the cave with Jake. Rose lies slumped in the shadows in the same corner, her head hanging.

In moments I'm kneeling beside her. I gently shake her shoulder, but get no response.

"Rose." Jake touches her arm.

She looks worse than this morning, her wrinkled face pale and gaunt, and her limbs thin. What happened in the few hours we were gone?

"Sam." Jake swings his gaze to me. "I remember. Before we lost our memories, Rose looked young. Like in her twenties."

I look at her again, and a sliver of a memory flashes back, of her sitting on a bench, smiling at us. "I remember too," I murmur. "Gorgon did something to her." When I turn, Gorgon is standing at the door, expressionless. I stand, my free hand a fist. "You coward. What's the matter, afraid to fight someone your own size?" His eyes narrow, but I don't care.

"What did you do to her, Fish Bait?" Jake also rises and glares at him.

We start walking toward him, staffs up. WhipEye is hot in my hands. Jake twists out the spear. Gorgon's head tentacles writhe faster. I don't care. I want to hurt him.

Tarath pokes her head in the entrance, alarm in her eyes. "Guardians."

Rella walks past the caracal and in front of Gorgon, her sister Issa beside her. They step forward and effectively block us from Gorgon, so smooth in their movements that they cover a score of yards as if they're floating.

I stop and bring my staff vertical, as does Jake. I've never hated anything or anyone in my entire life, but a simmering fury is building in me toward Gorgon.

Rella places her claw on my shoulder. Issa does the same to Jake.

"It's good to protect the weak." Rella bows to me.

"But never let your emotions rule a fight." Issa bows to Jake.

Vesio walks through the door and strides forward until he stands to the side of me. I'm not sure what he wants, but Gorgon frowns so he didn't order it.

Vesio's wrinkled brow seems to betray genuine concern, and he bows. "It would be an honor to carry Rose."

Jake shrugs when I look at him. I nod to Vesio. "Thank you."

He walks behind us and scoops Rose into his arms and carries her through the cave. When he strides ahead of us, we follow, staffs ready. Jake's face remains taut. He looks like he wants to go after Gorgon as much as I do, but I force down angry words I want to hurl at the monster.

Rella and Issa are right. Our parents' lives depend on everything going smoothly now. We can't afford to give Gorgon a reason to break his promise. Besides he would obliterate us if we attacked him.

At the doorway Jewel blocks Vesio, her face and body brightening like a small star. I shield my eyes with my arm as she touches a shining finger to Rose's forehead. When the light dims, I look at Rose. The wrinkles on her face have faded and her skin glows. Still unconscious, she appears as a woman in her twenties. I'm astonished and relieved.

Jewel's eyes sparkle. "Rose will be fine. Everything will be perfect."

Her confidence buoys me and the change in Rose lifts my hopes further. Gorgon's frown deepens, but he slides out of the cave, following Vesio.

"Thank you, Jewel." I touch her hand.

"Don't worry, Samantha." She winks, pivots, and strides into the tunnel.

The twins both give small bows and quickly leave to follow the others. I want to trust them completely. I tell myself everything is going to work out. Gorgon is smug, but outnumbered. His arrogance is blinding him to the defeat waiting for him.

In the tunnel my compass needle swings west, but then returns to north, and *Love*. I remember Mom, Dad, and Cynthia. Their love fills me and carries me forward. I don't want hate in my life. I don't want to be like Gorgon.

We change direction several times, walking south and north, but always returning west. The dark tunnel has a slight, steady incline and remains large enough for Great Ones and Lessers. Perhaps worried about Mentore, the whole procession moves over the stone without even a whisper of sound. I quiet my slapping tennis shoes too.

Often I exchange glances with Jake, both of us giving nervous smiles. Several times his hand strays to mine—squeezing it.

After two hours we round a bend and light streaks into the tunnel. The exit appears ahead, covered by a thin growth of vines. Jewel squeals and skips forward in impossibly long strides. Tarath and the Kodiak bear have to lope to keep up with her and the running twins.

I want to stand in the sunshine too, to be out of the dark tunnel. Even the crystal cavern, as bright as it is, isn't the same as the sun in a blue sky.

Hurrying forward, I push aside green leafy vines and step onto the top of a hill. Jake walks beside me as we cross fifty feet of grass and stop between Tarath and Jewel. Rella and Issa stand on the other side of Jewel, between her and Gorgon—I'm glad he's not next to Jewel.

The hill slopes down a half-mile to a large grassy valley. Beyond that is another long sloping incline leading up to a tree line. The surrounding jungle is startling in its brilliance of green and brown hues, and the scent of forest vegetation fills the air. A flock of noisy scarlet macaws flit among nearby trees, their red, yellow, and blue colors vivid. I take it all in, while sunshine and jungle heat warm me.

Everything appears more dazzling than I remember. As if I'm seeing all of it for the first time; not this particular area, but the colors, glow, and complexity of the land. I'm pleasantly lost in it. Jake's eyes shine too.

"Outstanding." He nudges my shoulder. "It's different somehow. How did that happen?"

"I don't know." I heave a deep breath. "But it makes me happy."

Jewel smiles at us. "Once you recognize the beauty of KiraKu, you begin to notice that deeper energy everywhere. Nothing will ever be the same again."

The rest of the Lessers and Originals pour from the cave, forming a line that faces west. My attention is pulled to the opposite hill, where a long line of Lessers and Originals step out from behind trees and onto the ridge, as if they've been waiting for us.

Mentore stands at their center. I doubt he'll allow himself to be defeated by Gorgon again. Canaste is coiled beside him. I'm relieved she didn't suffer consequences for helping us escape. I respect Mentore even more for that.

There's no sign of Lewella, Tom, or Brandon. That's confusing. I don't believe they would leave without us.

Not far to the south thunder rumbles and dark clouds race across the sky toward us. I smell rain approaching. Jake's vision has come true. We stand willingly with Gorgon, with Jewel beside us, facing Mentore. But Jake never said he actually saw a battle. Yet his taut face echoes my concern.

Jewel steps forward, smiling brightly and gazing across the valley at Mentore's Lessers and Originals. She lifts her arms, but drops them when a deep bellow issues from behind the opposing line.

Lessers part near Mentore, and through the opening crawls a crocodile. A big one.

Yakul.

THIRTY-THREE

YAKUL'S PRESENCE STIFFENS EVERY fiber in my body. Jake makes a fist at his side. Five p.m. One hour to save our parents. I want to scream.

I remember the croc's reluctance to come to our world, and thus I hadn't expected him to follow us, nor bond with Mentore. I look up at Tarath. "Can all Great Ones come here from KiraKu without using WhipEye?"

Tarath's gaze is fixed on Yakul. "Some Great Ones, the oldest of us, have enough energy to move between KiraKu and your world at will. We can bring others with us if we have to. I'm among that number, but it takes more energy than moving with WhipEye. All Lessers, including Gorgon, have lost this ability."

"Forced exile by the croc," I mutter.

Jake flings a hand to the side. "That big piece of stretched leather. He and Fish Bait should be on a small island together with a volleyball. They deserve each other." He glances at Gorgon, who ignores him.

I wonder if Jewel can also go to KiraKu on her own without WhipEye. I want to ask her, but not in front of Gorgon.

Gorgon calmly stares across the valley. For once he doesn't look eager to speak. Clouds roll over the grass between the two lines of Lessers, darkening the valley.

Yakul's voice booms. "All Lessers who abide by my commands will be allowed to return to KiraKu. The Jewel of Origin has been split, and her partial presence here is a threat to KiraKu's existence, and yet not enough to change this world. Bring her to me, and any who wish can come home. Mentore and his companions have already agreed to this."

There's no reaction from Gorgon. Even when many of his Lessers and Originals turn to him, his face remains expressionless.

Jewel raises her arms, her voice singing across the land, bright, clear, and comforting. "Lessers and Originals, I'll help all of you go back to KiraKu, if you wish to do so, but not under Yakul's rule. Any Lessers or Originals choosing to stay here will also be allowed access to KiraKu's healing water."

Gorgon still betrays no emotion, but Yakul growls. With a few words Jewel has reduced both of them to insignificance. She's rallying everyone to her, sidestepping both Gorgon and the croc. I want to cheer her on.

Jewel continues, her voice merry. "I bear no ill will for Yakul or Gorgon, but we must not give power to a few. All who want to join me in a new order of cooperation, love, and mutual help, which is what KiraKu has always stood for, step forward now to the center of the valley. All Lessers and Originals who wish to can return to KiraKu."

"It's a trick," roars Yakul. "Lies."

"Yakul invites only Lessers to join him," calls Jewel. "He wants the old order to continue, to exclude Originals."

"Don't believe Gorgon," Mentore says harshly. "He's controlling Jewel and will never let her escape."

Gorgon raises his arms, his voice kingly. "I won't harm Jewel. Her request is genuine and I'll abide by it." He motions left and right to his followers. "I release all of you to do as you wish."

Those words astonish me, but Gorgon's face appears sincere. I don't trust him, but he can't fight everyone here.

From the other side of Jewel, Issa leans forward and nods to us.

A smile spreads over Jake's face. I grin back. We're going home with the twins to save our parents.

Jewel skips in thirty-yard chunks down the gently sloping hill, a smiling, shining young woman of gold. The twin dragons, Tarath, and the three Great Ones bolt after her. Jake and I start walking down too, as several thousand Lessers and Originals rapidly walk, crawl, slither, or fly toward the center of the valley. On the opposite hill Canaste crawls among those going down to meet Jewel. Others on both hills hold back at first, but soon join those moving toward Jewel, their eyes changing from doubtful to bright.

For a minute Mentore doesn't budge. But when everyone leaves his side and Gorgon's, the big gorilla takes hesitant steps down the hill. The Komodo remains behind with Gorgon, loyal to the end.

Yakul doesn't move.

Heshia and Jewel were right. Jake's vision of a potential war didn't show everything. I continue walking, eager to join the celebration. I look at Jake—his eyes shine.

Gorgon doesn't follow us, and he's soon far enough behind that I no longer feel threatened. Gnawing doubt tells me it's all been too easy. But Jewel outplayed Gorgon. And he couldn't have guessed that Yakul would be here—and the croc already defeated him once.

Chatter from excited Originals fills the air, along with grunts and roars of happiness from giant Lessers. Jewel sweeps into the center of the valley, surrounded by Lessers and Originals. If we weren't on a time crunch, I'd love to socialize with all of them for days.

Another slap of thunder sends lightning across the clouds and the sky shifts darker as the first few raindrops hit my face. Something slides into my pocket and I twist around.

Gorgon is just behind us, wearing my gold ring on one of his head tentacles. He takes the gold ring off his thumb and places it on another head tentacle.

Both rings send a chill into me and I aim WhipEye at him. "Jake."

Jake whips around and raises Issa's staff. I watch Gorgon's head tentacles, remembering how fast he can move them. Even with our training, we're no match for his speed.

Gorgon's eyes glitter and a slight breeze ruffles his red shirt. "I sensed the spare ring when I first met you, Samantha. It's mine, so you shouldn't mind me taking it back. I gave the rings to the evil guardian. He was a fool who thought at the end he could defeat me so I abandoned him to defeat."

His words send a jolt through me. His confidence means he planned everything today, so things have unfolded exactly how he wanted them to. My stomach does another flip as things fall into place. "The twins lied about helping us."

"I knew of your communication with Rella and Issa before you left for KiraKu, and when you returned. They knew I heard them." He chuckles. "Did you really think the twins were on your side? Samantha, that's so naive."

Jake grimaces and I swallow hard. Without the dragons' help our parents will die.

Gorgon sighs. "You probably also thought I wasn't aware that Heshia tried to help you. Everyone keeps underestimating me."

Lessers and Originals are celebrating in the center of the valley, surrounding Jewel as if nothing is wrong. I hear the macaws still chattering in nearby trees.

Gorgon's head tentacles slowly writhe, while Jake and I edge to the sides of him.

"You knew all along you couldn't bring Jewel out of KiraKu, didn't you?" It amazes me how long and how deep his plans have been, and how good an actor he is. "You needed us to do it for you." Saying it leaves a sour taste on my tongue.

Gorgon continues. "I needed someone who could command WhipEye. A hero. Someone who had already defeated a powerful opponent. It was too dangerous for me to return to KiraKu, and since I learned long ago that I couldn't wield WhipEye, I needed you, Samantha."

"And you used me to push her." Jake's eyes narrow.

Gorgon regards him. "I needed you, Jake, to provide the fire to bring Jewel back, given your obsession with saving your mother at all costs. Even forcing you two to fight was just a way to focus you on each other instead of me."

Jake winces.

"Don't listen to him, Jake." But my stomach sinks when I remember how easily Gorgon outmaneuvered Mentore when we first met him.

"So what?" Jake lifts Issa's staff. "We knew you were an egomaniac, Fish Bait."

Gorgon eyes me. "I hoped you might succeed fully, Samantha, but bringing part of Jewel to me is better than nothing. I'll have to take what I can get."

I don't know where Gorgon is going with his admissions, but the Lessers in the valley will massacre him if he tries to take Jewel. Wanting to understand what he's planning, I try to stall him. "You can't win a fight against all the Lessers and Originals here."

"I don't have to," he says calmly.

The Great Ones have superb hearing so why haven't they responded? I risk a glance down the hill. Jewel's brightness shines from the center of the valley, but next to her, Tarath has her head lowered and her ears pinned back as she glares at Issa and Rella. The mountain gorilla, wolverine, and Kodiak bear are also bristling as they face the twins. Both dragons are in their ninja forms and holding dragon claws, blocking the Great Ones from coming up the hill to us.

Desperation hits me. Tarath can't get past the dragons or doesn't want to leave Jewel with them. Yakul remains apart from everyone, viewing us from the opposite hill. Fifty yards to the side of us, Vesio lays Rose on the grass and stares our way.

Jake twists Issa's staff twice, snapping out the dragon claw. "The others will attack you if you try to harm Jewel. So will I. Give me a reason, Gorgon."

Jake's boldness surprises me, but maybe his shining armor gives him confidence. "We already have enough reasons to hurt him, Jake."

Gorgon sounds confident. "Jewel may only be a fraction of her true self, but that is all I need. After I consume her energy, I'll be able to travel to KiraKu on my own and absorb the rest of her. You both know what happens then."

Something else falls into place. "You drained Rose." My neck is hot, my hands fists on the staff.

Gorgon nods. "And I'll do it again. I can drain anyone's energy with a kiss. It's a gift I have, like Heshia, who uses her death kiss far too little. As I expected, Rose chose not to tell you what I had done to her the first time. She didn't want to worry her little heroes. After you left for KiraKu, I took more of her energy. I feel exceptional."

"You sicko. Nothing but an overgrown leech." Jake looks ready to attack him.

I glance to the side, where Vesio still stands beside Rose, watching us. It makes me sick to my stomach that I allowed the vampire to carry her.

"Jake, let's go." I take a backward step down the hill, relieved when he follows.

"Ah, guardians." Gorgon looks beyond us. "I've made certain we'll have a little excitement coming our way. Don't you want to see what it is?"

I stop, glancing everywhere for anything suspicious, but nothing alarms me. The spiked wolf and frilled lizard, which helped Gorgon when we first met him, are among the others below, but the monster might have other followers like the Komodo who plan to disrupt things.

Helicopter blades sound in the distance.

My stomach lurches.

Gorgon gestures to the valley. "Some of us have unique skills. Heshia's is communication, allowing someone to share what she or others observe. Mine is creating images, like a mirage, to hide things. It cost me a lot of energy, but it was worth it. An hour ago I sent Colonel Macy a message that I was a traitor and gave him the coordinates of this valley. I had Vesio tell Mentore the location of this tunnel entrance."

He smirks. "I win. You lose. And I'm sorry about your elders."

I don't see how Gorgon plans to capture Jewel, but one thing is obvious; he's been in control from the beginning. That scares me more than anything. My hands are rigid on WhipEye.

"You won't get away with it," I snap. Then I yell, "Tarath!"

The caracal hisses from below.

Gorgon smirks. "You're like an amateur chess player, Samantha, going up against a grand master. Did you really think you could outsmart me?"

"You're not the only one good at chess," scoffs Jake. "You think you and the dragons can defeat all these Lessers? Whatever you planned, you've lost."

Gorgon gives a dismissive flick of his hand. "We'll see."

"Everyone in the valley, lie down and don't move!"

THIRTY-FOUR

SILENCE CUTS LIKE A cleaver through the celebration. All movement stops. Stepping farther away from Gorgon to view the valley bottom, I still keep an eye on the monster.

To the north the air bends and shifts like an evaporating mirage until Colonel Macy's blunt, hard face appears. He's standing on some kind of high-tech hovercraft floating a few feet off the ground. Shaped like a slender triangle with twenty-foot sides, the ship has mounted Tasers, a flamethrower, and a small missile launcher. Macy is wearing green camouflage body armor, as do the half-dozen VIPER soldiers with him. The colonel gazes across the valley, then up the hill until his eyes lock on mine.

In stunned silence everyone in the valley faces Colonel Macy. The mirage keeps fading, the air looking as if it's melting away, revealing a thousand VIPER soldiers walking out of the jungle beside Macy; just as many appear on the south side of the valley, along with three more hovercraft and several tanks.

Mentore thumps his chest from the middle of the opposite hill. "Gorgon betrayed all of us!"

Gorgon raises his arms. "It's Yakul, trying to steal power! Any who wish a new world, come to my side."

"Any Lesser who wishes to return to KiraKu, come to me!" Yakul's eyes flare gold.

Bright light erupts in the center of the valley. In the growing dark of the coming storm, Jewel raises her arms, shining like a star. Facing Colonel Macy, her voice is sweet and calm, with too much power for someone her size. "We wish you no harm. Talk with us and we'll solve this peacefully."

"Lie down now or we'll put you down." Macy's glare holds no reason. All he sees is another weird alien threatening his world.

I want to shout at Jewel to run. Tarath and the Great Ones circle her protectively as her light diminishes.

Lessers and Originals look to Gorgon and Yakul, many with worried expressions. Jewel gazes up at us, her face still bright. Issa and Rella don't budge.

Two Blackhawk helicopters appear out of nowhere above the center of the valley, the chop of their blades much louder now. Gorgon hid them too.

Lightning arcs out of the clouds down to the jungle in multiple places.

In a flash Gorgon grows to ten feet tall, still appearing almost human. Several of his head tentacles elongate and grab a nearby twenty-foot-tall tree, ripping it from the ground. I'm in awe over the strength it must take to do that. I've underestimated even that aspect of him.

Those below stare up at him.

Taking three blurred steps, Jewel sweeps past Tarath and the twins, covering a thousand yards in a flash. She arrives at Gorgon's side, her hand on his wrist.

"No, Jewel!" I yell.

"Step back, Jewel!" yells Jake.

Thunder booms and rain drizzles on my face.

Bright golden energy flows like molten liquid down Gorgon's arm to Jewel's hand. She's draining him, and the surprise in his widened eyes is satisfying to witness. My throat is dry as I watch. I hope she sucks him dry.

Gorgon's tentacles release the tree, letting it fall to the soil. Grimacing, his brow wrinkles until the energy flow to Jewel slows, stops, and then reverses, rapidly streaming back over his arm. He clutches Jewel's forearm.

"Jewel!" I thrust WhipEye at Gorgon.

Simultaneously Jake stabs Issa's claw at him.

In a blink Gorgon slides back a dozen feet, out of our reach, his gaze still focused on Jewel. "You underestimated me, little one. The methuselah energy along with Rose's has done wonders for me."

His arrogance enrages me and I rush him with Jake, but Gorgon backs up another fifty feet in a flash. I sprint after the monster, as does Jake.

Two of Gorgon's head tentacles flash out, hitting both of us in the chest. We fly downhill and land on our backs, sliding down the slope.

My chest aches. Pushing to my feet, I watch, feeling helpless. Jake stands beside me, his eyes on Gorgon, Issa's claw in his hands.

Jewel's eyes look vulnerable and innocent, as if she's as surprised as we are. She doesn't speak, but her body suddenly sags as if she might faint.

One of Gorgon's head tentacles whips around Jewel's waist and lifts her off the ground, holding her above his head.

I scramble closer to the monster with Jake, trying to think of some way to attack Gorgon. We need help. There's no way we can defeat the kraken.

This time Gorgon doesn't move. "Stay back or she'll be hurt." He says it loudly, so all Originals, Lessers, and Great Ones watching from the valley hear him. Tarath looks at Gorgon intently.

I glance down the hill, still keeping my eye on Gorgon. Issa and Rella are backing up toward us, still blocking Tarath and the others. The twins' loyalty is painfully clear now, which adds to my confusion. Why would they help Gorgon?

With flashing tentacles, Gorgon grabs the dropped tree and throws it at one of the helicopters. The tree sails up and grinds into the helicopter's revolving blades—which screech to a stop. The Blackhawk falters, and then falls toward the center of the valley. On the way down its blades hit the other helicopter in the side, causing it to veer over the jungle where it crashes into trees.

Everyone stares as a giant ground sloth extends its arms to catch the remaining falling helicopter—I doubt Macy views the Lesser as friendly. Meanwhile the twins shift into dragons and blow fire at

Tarath and the others, before taking to the sky, quickly disappearing in the clouds.

Originals sprint from the valley up the sides of the hills, running in streaks.

"Don't, Macy!" I cry.

"Stop!" shouts Jake.

Colonel Macy slashes the air with an arm. "Fire!"

Tasers send a thousand darts into Lessers, Great Ones, and Originals. A number of them hit the sloth. Falling heavily, the Lesser and helicopter crash to the ground. Flamethrowers spew lances of fire across the crowded valley.

An explosion of movement occurs. One moment the valley is full of giant Lessers, and the next it's an empty meadow with a few bodies and the helicopter wreckage. But it's not a chaotic retreat. Half the Lessers and Originals attack Macy's soldiers head-on in a blur of perfect formations.

Some Lessers charge Macy's troops at a slight angle, moving in flashes up the hills a short distance before racing at the soldiers in weaving patterns. Originals race up the sides of the hills in even more indirect routes, then circle toward the soldiers, their legs flashing pistons.

Hundreds of Lessers flee toward Yakul—they want his offer to return to KiraKu. Other Lessers and Originals scatter across both hills, many toward Gorgon, further blocking the path of Tarath and our friends who are racing up the hill.

Gorgon flashes toward us, and I twist reflexively, striking out with WhipEye. Jake is already swinging Issa's staff. Our speed can't match the kraken's. Two of his head tentacles push our staffs to the sides, and in that same instant he's between us.

"Sam!" cries Jake.

My chest is squeezed tightly and I'm lifted by Gorgon, as is Jake, our arms pinned to our sides by one of his tentacles. We're both on opposite sides of his head.

A tremendous pull yanks WhipEye from my grip. *No.* Pain rips through me like an electric shock. Dazed, I watch the chestnut staff lifted farther away from me by another of Gorgon's head tentacles.

Another tentacle already holds Issa's staff. Jewel is silent, her eyes glassy. I see the rings on Gorgon's head tentacles, but they're too far away to grab them.

"No closer!" shouts Gorgon. "Or Jewel and the guardians will be killed."

"Come anyway!" shouts Jake.

"Do it!" I gasp.

But Gorgon lifts all three of us higher as a warning, and Tarath and our friends stop abruptly halfway up the hill. I wonder if Gorgon wants us, or is just using us for protection. Strangely he doesn't retreat further and instead looks confident and relaxed. I send my emotions to the macaws.

Hovering above us in the air, the Komodo unleashes a torrent of fire at startled Lessers fleeing up the hill, creating more confusion when they try to escape the flames. Many turn downhill, further blocking our friends.

I lose sight of Tarath and the Great Ones, hidden by the mass of bodies on the hill, but across the valley Mentore roars and runs toward us. My eyes barely follow the snippets of large bodies in fast motion, while screams and alarmed cries from Lessers and Originals fill the air.

A collared lizard whips its tail into a hovercraft, sending it crashing into a tree. An ocelot swipes at a tank, sending it tumbling through the air. Leaping aboard a hovercraft, a Tasmanian devil and orangutan tear it apart.

Tasered Originals fall to the ground and Lessers carry them off the battlefield.

A layer of gold covers Yakul—he glows like a massive light bulb. One after another a long stream of Lessers race to touch the crocodile—and vanish. Yakul is keeping his word, and building his forces in KiraKu. When no more Lessers approach Yakul, he bellows at the fighting below. The croc's eyes briefly meet mine before he disappears in a flash of light.

Two more helicopters appear flying over the middle of the valley, coming toward us and targeting Gorgon. But he still doesn't move.

The twin dragons drop out of the clouds, blowing puffs of smoke, their ruby eyes rimmed with gold. Flying upside down beneath the Blackhawks, they grip the landing skids with massive talons, then right themselves, holding both helicopters beneath them. Swinging their legs, they toss the gunships toward the trees where I lose sight of them in the rain.

Most of Colonel Macy's soldiers retreat under the onslaught of the Lessers and Originals, but the colonel's hovercraft accelerates toward a giant black-footed ferret. Other Lessers block my view of what happens to him.

Gorgon finally slides backward with dazzling speed. "Sorry, guardians, but I want to control WhipEye from here on out, which means you'll have to come with me."

I glimpse Tarath below. She still hasn't moved; probably worried Gorgon will kill us and Jewel if she attacks.

"Get him, Tarath," I call weakly. Gorgon's tentacle squeezes air from my lungs until I can't speak.

"Attack him, Tarath!" Jake's voice is steady. Even against Gorgon's strength, his armor is protecting his chest.

"Vesio!" yells Gorgon. "Bring Rose!"

My mouth dry, I roll my head to the right and glimpse Rose still lying unconscious on her back. Vesio isn't anywhere near her.

Gorgon moves faster toward the tunnel entrance. Déjà vu. I remember how he used explosives to block Mentore from following him the first time we met. We've lost.

The Komodo dragon lands and runs alongside us, stopping once to send another belch of fire down the hill. Lessers scatter, some into the path of Tarath and the others. The caracal yowls.

Issa and Rella hover just above the ground halfway up the hill, unleashing fire and forcing Tarath to run to the side, buying Gorgon more time.

Gorgon stops as if he hit a steel wall. My head jerks with the impact. Stunned, I glance behind him.

Vesio is a dozen feet tall and has his arms wrapped around Gorgon's neck. The vampire speaks with ferocity into the monster's ear. "I was always Mentore's spy. We fed you the information we wanted you to have. And I've disabled your explosives in the tunnel. You're finished. You'll never touch Rose again."

I want to shout in victory, but I can't fill my lungs to do it. I'm glad to see Gorgon's eyes widen in surprise. Vesio played his double agent role with excellence.

Jake yells, "Bite him, Vesio!"

"Now," I croak.

Vesio opens his mouth and sinks two large fangs into Gorgon's neck. I'm rooting for the vampire.

Gorgon grows a few feet taller and his neck expands to two feet in diameter, stretching Vesio's jaws, while some of his head tentacles elongate and grip the vampire's arms, trying to pry them off his neck.

Vesio's eyes widen when his jaw stretches farther. He's forced to withdraw his fangs from Gorgon's flesh. More tentacles fly at him, but Vesio releases Gorgon's neck and grabs two of the tentacles. He jams a foot into Gorgon's lower back and pulls the monster backward until Gorgon's eyes bulge. Shifting partially into his bat form, Vesio sprouts wings and beats them against the sides of Gorgon's body.

Gorgon punches two head tentacles into Vesio's skull and the vampire stumbles back, looking dazed. Slipping another tentacle around Vesio's waist, Gorgon lifts and throws the vampire down the hill, where I lose sight of him in the melee of bodies. Gorgon whirls and races for the cave.

I send my desires and unleash my friends. The blue and yellow macaws hit Gorgon's face with extended claws, reaching for his eyes.

Gorgon grabs a bird with a head tentacle and holds it in front of my face. "Samantha."

I stare at the helpless macaw, fragile in the monster's grip, its eyes wide. Gorgon will kill all of them. I close my eyes and reach out to the birds, sending them away. Gorgon releases the macaw he caught and it escapes with the others. I don't have any more tricks and the thought that I've failed Dad is frozen in my mind.

Gorgon flees for the tunnel.

A green-eyed, golden-haired figure with eight-foot golden wings drops down from above, blocking the entrance. Lewella. Her presence sparks hope in my heart.

Tom and Brandon run up on either side of her. Tom's face is strained, but Brandon's stocky frame appears relaxed, his expression steady. Lewella's eyes shine, her lips pressed tight.

Jake shouts, "Stop him! He has Jewel!"

Without slowing, Gorgon spins like a top, his head tentacles elongating, whipping us at Lewella and the two Originals. I'm dizzy as I twirl with Gorgon. Jake gasps.

Tom and Brandon are flung aside by Gorgon's flying limbs, but Lewella darts upward to safety. The rainfall turns heavy.

"Help Rose." I doubt anyone hears my murmur.

Gorgon flies through the vines and into the tunnel, moving faster. I catch one last glimpse of the Komodo flying after us, with Issa and Rella flying low behind the Lesser. The three of them block my view of anything else on the hill.

Gorgon rounds a corner and darkness and silence surround us.

THIRTY-FIVE

GORGON GLIDES OVER THE stone, the walls flashing by in a blur. His tentacle squeezes tighter until my chest hurts.

We took two hours to walk through the tunnel, but the kraken speeds through it in minutes to the crystal cavern, its light dimmed by the clouded sky outside.

Jewel is silent, her bright face marred by a twisted expression, as if she's struggling with an inner conflict.

"Are you okay, Sam?" whispers Jake.

I manage a small nod to him. His pressed lips shout that, given the chance, he's going after Gorgon.

Gorgon flies through the garden paths until we reach the tunnel leading to the lake cavern. There he pauses to look back. From the west tunnel flies the Komodo dragon, beating his wings hard. The twins soar behind the Komodo, and a small army chases them. It kindles a fire inside me. Vesio's help bought my friends a little time, and means something.

Issa and Rella circle and swoop at Tarath and the others, spewing flames.

The mountain gorilla and other Great Ones veer off and race in flashing strides along the nearest cavern wall, away from the fire, but Tarath roars and bounds through the dragons' flames. I worry what the effort is costing her.

Gorgon whirls and speeds through the tunnel and into the more dimly lit lake cavern, where he streaks around stalagmites toward the lagoon. He must have a secret exit in the pool. He never leaves anything to chance. It's over.

With his tentacle squeezing me, I won't be able to hold my breath underwater. Maybe he doesn't care.

We're halfway across the cavern when water splashes upward in the lake.

Heshia.

She's magnificent. Water cascades off her blue and white skin, her blue eyes bright. Immediately her large tentacles pull her from the water and across the stone until she stops sixty yards from the lagoon. Thirty feet high, her gentle face turns hard.

The tentacles atop her head writhe and her blue, gold-ringed eyes meet mine for a moment. She glares at Gorgon, her sweet, clear voice firm. "I won't allow you to take the guardians. Release them, Jewel, and WhipEye, and I'll let you pass to save your pathetic self."

While speeding toward her, Gorgon changes to a white and red bulbous kraken, enlarging quickly to fifty feet in height and carrying us alongside his freakish, bumpy head. Massive white and red tentacles replace Gorgon's legs, but don't slow him down. I lose sight of Jake; he's now on the other side of Gorgon's skull.

Stopping a score of yards in front of Heshia, the monster's lipless mouth opens, revealing pointy teeth. "Out of my way, sister, if you wish to live." Anger fills his raspy voice.

I want to tell Heshia to let him pass—I don't want her killed—but I can barely breathe. Worse, I'm nauseous over the height. The stony cavern floor looks very far away and I'm hanging out over it with no way down.

Heshia's voice turns cold. "Why do you think I came with you to this world? Do you really believe I wanted to leave KiraKu? That you coaxed me with your petty charms? I left KiraKu to ensure you failed here. You're not the only one who plans things far in advance, little brother."

Gorgon gapes. Along with Vesio, Heshia outmaneuvered him. I'm hoping she has a secret power to stop her brother because her height and slender body are no match for his.

Gorgon whips his head around.

The Komodo and the two dragons are lined up in front of the tunnel entrance, all blowing flames into it. I don't see our friends, so the lizard and dragons are holding them off for now.

Gorgon presses the gold ring he took from me against Jewel's head. Her brow furrows and her light fades as Gorgon captures her essence in the ring.

I try to cry out, but can only manage a whisper; "Jewel."

"You sick leech!" cries Jake.

Heshia slides across the stone and slams into Gorgon. Two of her large arm tentacles wrap around Gorgon's head tentacles that hold WhipEye and Issa's claw, sliding along the smaller tentacles and slowly forcing them open while moving the staffs closer to Jake and me. Her other tentacles try to pry us free.

Snarling, Gorgon whips his two white and red arm tentacles around Heshia's neck and body, bending her backward while squeezing her.

Jewel pales and her head hangs, a white mannequin without life. Gorgon removes the ring from her head and Jewel's body disintegrates to powder which drifts to the cavern floor. The ring holding her essence now sparkles.

My stomach sinks over seeing bright, beautiful, innocent Jewel destroyed. My heart and hands yearn to hold the chestnut wood, but this time it's because I want to fight. I glimpse the cavern floor again, instantly dizzy with the height, and close my eyes.

"Samantha!"

Heshia's voice is stern and I blink my eyes open again, focusing on Gorgon's body so I don't lose my lunch.

Heshia's eyes find mine. Her tentacles loosen Gorgon's hold on me enough so that I'm able to jerk an arm free. At the same time, with a shuddering effort she uncurls Gorgon's head tentacle, forcing the kraken to release WhipEye. The staff tumbles free and I desperately reach for it. When the chestnut wood falls into my palm, heat sweeps along my arm and into my chest.

Gorgon's head tentacles writhe toward me, but Heshia's larger blue limbs catch his red limbs in midair and overpower them. Roaring, the kraken wraps two of his larger tentacles around

Heshia's upper body and neck, choking her. She tries to pry him off with her head tentacles, but he bends her back farther.

Seeing Heshia close to death drives panic into my chest and I allow that emotion to blossom and flow through my heart and mind to the staff. Using one arm, I slam WhipEye into the side of Gorgon's head. Golden energy crackles along the staff and over the side of his fleshy skull. He shrieks, his eyes widening—I think in shock. Quivering, his head tentacle releases me.

"Ahhh!" I fall against his bulbous torso—it's like hitting a tough rubber wall—and then slide and bounce my way down onto one of his massive limbs, landing with a *thump!* Yelling, I slide on my butt down the writhing tentacle, my legs spread as if I'm riding a horse. My eyes widen. I'm on a bizarre roller coaster and the slightest teetering to the left or right and I'll take a dive to the ground. I lean forward so more of my body is on his slimy tentacle. As gross as that is, at least it's safer.

Near the last third of the tentacle, still six feet above the ground, I lose my balance and fall off with a yelp. I roll in the air and land hard on moss and ferns on my back. I think I'm still in one piece. Scrambling to my feet, I run, trying to put distance between myself and Gorgon's flapping limbs.

Several times one of his tentacles curls toward me, only to be stopped by one of Heshia's. She's buying my escape. Gorgon wraps more tentacles around his sister.

I run around a patch of tall stalagmites to avoid Gorgon's flailing limbs. One of his tentacles smashes through several of the stalagmites and I duck beneath it. Gorgon's limb passes over my back, ruffling my tank top. Without hesitating, I run toward Heshia.

She eyes me, and in my mind I hear, *"Run away, Samantha."*

Instead I run closer and jam WhipEye into one of Gorgon's massive tentacles that is curled around her. Shining energy flows from the staff into Gorgon's limb, outlining it in crackling gold until it drops off Heshia and flops onto the ground. On the other side of Heshia I glimpse Jake, his iridescent armor shining in the dim light. One side of his face is black and blue. He slashes at another of Gorgon's limbs with the dragon claw.

Giving a rasping cry, the kraken releases his arm tentacles from Heshia and flings them at us. I lift WhipEye to block the blow, which sends me tumbling across the cavern floor as if I've been hit by a truck. Ending up on my stomach, I'm groggy and need a few seconds to recover. I roll to my side and rise to my knees.

I hear a loud *snap!* and murmur, "Heshia."

Her head rolls to one side, her torso limp. Gorgon drops her, and she falls onto the mossy stone, her eyes glassy and her tentacles slapping against the cavern floor like dead weight.

"Heshia!" I choke on her name. Her sweet clear voice, her warm heart, her love, all gone forever.

Strangely I'm aware of the whole cavern, the Great Ones fighting the dragons, the light above, the coolness of the water in the pool, and the hardness of the stone underfoot.

Heshia's voice is in my mind; *"We'll meet again, Samantha."*

I pull myself to my feet and lean on the staff, wanting to cry and yell. My ribs and hip hurt. Between writhing limbs, I glimpse Jake's bright armor on the other side of Gorgon.

I expect Gorgon to flee, to slide into the pool and escape, but he squints at me with one eye. He still wants WhipEye, and me.

A roar sounds. Tarath. The caracal runs out of the tunnel and through the dragons' flames. Issa, Rella, and the Komodo rise in the air to avoid her charge. Behind Tarath race the rest of our friends.

Gorgon turns to face the Great Ones, his limbs spreading out like a dozen whips in front of him. The monster gives a raspy, throaty roar. "Come on! All of you. This is what I've been waiting for!"

As monstrous as he is, he's not a match for the Great Ones, but he has two dragons and the Komodo fighting with him. I don't think our side has a chance.

The Komodo dragon lands in front of me, folding his wings on his back. We glare at each other, and I weakly raise the staff with both hands. The lizard swings his head away from me though.

Growling, the Kodiak bear runs in a blur north of the dragons in a direct line toward the Komodo.

The lizard hisses and turns his head to me. "You're next, guardian."

I try to sound tough. "I'll be waiting, leather face."

The Kodiak bear charges, his massive paws pounding on the stone. Running hard, the Komodo smashes into the Great One with a *thump!* that echoes in the cavern. Jaws gnashing, they roll away with grunts and snarls.

Uncertain if I've earned enough cred with the Great Ones, I decide to find out. I slam WhipEye into the ground and shout out three names of faces carved into the staff, "Iguana, hawk, wolf!"

WhipEye spins in my hand and the iguana's face hisses. The staff spins again and light shoots out of the staff twenty feet from me where the thirty-foot green iguana appears.

She speaks immediately. "Great Ones that pledged to WhipEye are under attack from Yakul, and the crocodile is also blocking the staff's power with his own."

Yakul is still trying to get at us any way he can. "Stupid crocodile."

Stepping forward, the iguana bends her head down to me. "But I am always happy to answer the guardian's call." She turns and runs to help the Kodiak bear.

Gathering my strength, I spot Jake beyond Heshia's body. His taut face matches his rigid stance. We have to free Jewel and get saliva from Issa or Rella. I won't fail Dad. I don't want to look at my watch.

I'm about to take another swing at Gorgon, when he rubs the two rings against his head tentacles. A shadowy form slithers from each ring. From one ring comes the fifty-foot, two-headed king cobra of Jake's nightmares. Floating in the air, the shadow snake coils and looks as if it's assessing the battlefield.

From the sparkling ring comes a thirty-foot-tall creature; Jewel's bright energy has been transformed into a red-eyed, stringy-haired woman with bony cheekbones, fangs, and claws. A tattered black cloak hangs from her floating body. The demon of our nightmares. She's just as scary in person. Worse, I brought the ring that created her.

Floating in front of Gorgon, the cobra's two heads whip left and right. "You'll sssoon be my ssslavesss, guardians." Gorgon's fury burns in the cobra's eyes. One of the cobra's heads swings to Jake, and the snake flies toward him. The demon turns to me.

"Jake!" I cry.

Jake jabs Issa's spear at the cobra heads as they bob and weave around him. One head strikes down at him and he rolls away. The other head dives at him, and he slashes the spear at it. Both heads rear up and I lose sight of him.

Screeching, the demon flies horizontally over Gorgon's tentacles, arms outstretched. I see Gorgon's hate in the creature's eyes. A sliver of fear enters my gut.

When the demon reaches me, I drop to a knee and jab WhipEye straight up into the monster's torso. Golden energy blasts from the staff, pushing the demon upward fifty feet, where she stops her flight. Her red eyes fix on mine. Looking uninjured, she dives straight down at me.

A golden blur slams into the demon, sending the shrieking shadow monster sailing across the lake and thudding into the distant wall.

"Yeah!" I lift my staff in a cheer as Lewella blurs back and kicks one of the cobra heads from behind. Hissing, the snake's head twists to face her, fangs bared. It strikes, but Lewella flits away from it. She's forcing the snake to abandon its pursuit of Jake.

Canaste appears, speeding across the cavern floor toward the cobra with her side fins undulating. The boa rears up and the two hissing serpents ram each other, their swaying heads facing off fifteen feet above the ground.

The shadow Jewel shrieks as she flies across the water toward me. Even without injuries I wouldn't be able to run fast enough to escape her. But I don't want to.

The fury burning inside me moves my feet toward Gorgon. Lifting the staff high, I slam it into his nearest tentacle, this time visualizing what I want to happen. It's like hitting a thick rubber tire, sending a jolt into my shoulders. But energy pours from my arms into the staff, sending bright golden light flowing into the kraken's flesh, crackling along his limb all the way to his body. His white and red torso quivers and his tentacle tip is charred flesh.

Gorgon roars.

It energizes me that he never saw this coming—WhipEye's power, and my ability to harness it.

I look up. The demon is floating horizontally above me again, her claws reaching for WhipEye. I'm too tired to move.

Snarling, Gorgon flips his injured tentacle into my side, sending me rolling beyond the demon's grasping claws. Landing on my back in ferns, I groan. My ribs are on fire. I'm unable to move.

When my eyes focus, the thirty-foot demon is hovering horizontally three feet above my body. Gorgon's hatred fills her red eyes as her claws reach for me. The stench is like a rotting corpse. I gag as I hold WhipEye against my body with weak hands.

"Sam!"

I hear Jake but can't respond. It sounds like he's nearby.

The demon turns its head sideways, and I roll mine. Jake is leaping through the air, his armor shining, his dragon claw aimed at the shadow creature. He stabs Issa's claw into the demon's side, but the blades only sink an inch into her flesh. Shrieking, the demon wraps a hand around Jake's neck and flies forward, thrusting him into a nearby stalagmite that breaks in half. Jake stabs the claw at her.

"Ugh." My ribs grate as I struggle to my knees, still hugging the staff. Worried for Jake, I want to help him, but I can barely move without intense pain. One of Gorgon's tentacles whips toward me. There's no way I can escape.

Loud shouts. Tom and Brandon are running at Gorgon. Gorgon's tentacle pauses in midair on its way to me, and then flies toward the twins. The demon drops Jake and also races toward the brothers. Jake falls onto his back, but is up quickly.

Remembering Rose's words—that whoever holds the ring controls the shadow monsters—I shout, "We need to bring him down to get the rings!"

He gives me a thumbs up, and runs back toward the other side of Gorgon. Smart. We can attack the monster with more success from two sides, and it makes it harder for Gorgon to attack both of us.

I watch Tom and Brandon charge the kraken. I've never witnessed anything so brave in all my life. Both wield long knives and run nimbly amid the kraken's limbs until they leap up twenty feet and stab Gorgon's puffy white torso. Gorgon shrieks, twisting one way and then the other.

Brandon ducks, somersaults, and runs out, avoiding Gorgon's fleshy limbs. Tom swings from one tentacle to another to escape, but one of the kraken's head tentacles catches him around the waist, lifting him high. Soaring to the Original, the demon places her hands on either side of Tom's head. Tom screams and drops his knives to grab the demon's arms. His face pales and his back arches. Lewella streaks toward him.

Brandon reverses course and runs back. "Brother!"

The wolverine stomps a paw on one of Gorgon's limbs and bites it.

Gorgon howls, pulls Tom's body away from the demon, and throws him high into the cavern. Lewella chases after him. Tom crashes into several stalactites, which break off and fall with him toward the ground.

"Oh, Tom," I murmur.

Lewella weaves through the falling debris and catches him. Carrying him a safe distance away, she lays him on the cavern floor. Brandon runs to his brother.

I swallow hard. My side burns as if a hot coal is against it. A whine fills the air. Flying toward us, Colonel Macy stands on his hovership. His craft stops amid a clump of stalagmites near the center of the cavern. Even to the colonel's twisted mind the biggest threat has to be obvious.

I lick my lips in anticipation. Gorgon is going to pay.

Jake stands, nodding to me.

Gathering what strength I have left, I brace myself for pain and pull myself up along WhipEye. Warm energy flows through the wood into my hands, giving me a small boost. I stumble toward Gorgon.

A missile launches from Macy's ship, streaming at the kraken.

THIRTY-SIX

THE DEMON FLOATS IN front of Gorgon, waiting. Without showing much effort, she catches the missile with both hands, which pushes her back a dozen yards. My hopes sink as I watch her spin in a circle and whip the missile back at Colonel Macy in a tumbling flight. The hovercraft turns to avoid it, but not fast enough.

Colonel Macy and his soldiers jump off the ship before the bomb hits. The explosion rocks the cavern, sending the hovercraft spinning into the tunnel connecting both caves, resulting in another deafening explosion. Tons of falling rock bury the only way out.

Gorgon eyes Jake and me as we attack him. He wants to capture us, but I don't care. I want the rings, and him dead. I think I have a chance, since his demon is occupied with fighting a charging wolverine.

Ducking one swinging tentacle and somehow jumping over another, I look for the two head tentacles carrying the rings. They're fifty feet up and hard to see amid his waving sluglike appendages. Halfway to his body I realize I'll never get close enough to hit his torso directly. I'm too tired and his limbs are too thick and slap more wildly near his body.

Gorgon glares down at me.

Quicker and more agile, Jake runs in close and throws Issa's spear into Gorgon's right eye. For a moment I think it will kill the monster. But Gorgon roars and yanks the shaft out with a head tentacle. His eye closes to a slit, blood dripping from it, but he shows no sign of falling. He throws the spear at Jake.

Jake turns to flee, but the spear hits him in the back and he cries out.

Writhing tentacles hide him from view, and I shout, "Jake!"

The anger building inside me for days erupts into my chest and arms, flowing into the staff. Burning heat builds in my hands and arms. I embrace it, channel it, and allow it to flow into the staff until I find enough strength for one more effort. I slam WhipEye into the nearest tentacle, again visualizing what I want to happen.

Crackling light flows along his limb to his torso, outlining all of his bulbous mass and a third of his tentacles. Gorgon teeters.

I wobble away, hoping he's hurt enough to topple, and to allow me to escape. In my mind I keep seeing Issa's spear hitting Jake. I glance back. Tarath races in among Gorgon's tentacles, her size doubling. I stare at another mystery, aware of how little I know about Great Ones.

Gorgon's good eye widens and he shouts, "Jewel!"

Tarath leaps, her claws raking down Gorgon's face and torso. The monster shrieks as the caracal's weight sends him teetering backward. Deep gashes mark the kraken's head and body. He might be finished, but I can't run to get the rings, and I'm unsure Jake is even standing.

One of Gorgon's large tentacles wraps around a shrinking Tarath and tosses her a hundred feet away, and then the kraken slowly falls. The demon immediately grabs one of Gorgon's larger tentacles and drags him toward the lake.

In that moment a yellow blur flashes toward Gorgon's head. It's Lewella, but a smaller version of her that's one foot tall. She grabs one of the rings from Gorgon's waving head tentacles while the monster is still falling. Darting toward the other ring, she's knocked away by another of Gorgon's sluglike tentacles.

"Lewella," I murmur.

She recovers in midair fifty feet away from Gorgon and faces him. As she does the cobra shadow fades and streaks into the ring she stole. Gorgon slaps one of his large tentacles at her, and she flits backward. The demon also glares at Lewella—there's no way she'll be able to get the other ring.

The bright faerie flies toward me, slowing above me just enough to drop the ring. I catch it in my palm and pocket it. Then she flits back to the brothers. At least one shadow monster is out of Gorgon's control.

I hope others can get the second ring, but Gorgon still looks alert, his large tentacles flailing wildly at the other Great Ones that try to get closer to him.

I drop to my knees, woozy.

Tarath races up and grabs one of Gorgon's writhing limbs with her jaws. With rattling breaths, the kraken uses his tentacles to pull himself like an injured slug across the rock, dragging Tarath until he can grab the lip of the lake. He rests there on his side, staring at me with one eye. The odor of dead fish is strong.

The mountain gorilla grabs another of Gorgon's limbs.

One of the dragons tries to block Mentore, but the ape dances away from the dragon's claws and manages to grab another of Gorgon's tentacles. Backing away from the Kodiak bear and iguana, the other twin takes to the air with her sister. Roaring and snorting smoke, the dragons fly high into the cavern.

Growling, the Kodiak bear runs forward and stomps a massive paw onto another of Gorgon's tentacles. Lewella grips one too, and the wolverine clamps her jaws onto another. So does the iguana. It's a monster tug of war.

My chest heaves when I finally spot Jake. Resting on his knees on the other side of Gorgon, he's holding Issa's staff.

Even against the combined strength of Great Ones and Lessers, Gorgon keeps crawling. The demon is saving Gorgon. Her shadow form floats just above the water as she pulls him. The water seems to energize the kraken and he hauls himself farther into the lagoon, dragging the Great Ones across the cavern floor.

At the water's edge the two gorillas and Tarath have to let go of Gorgon or go in themselves. I doubt they want to be in the water with a kraken. The Kodiak bear swipes his claw through the tentacle he holds, cutting off a third of it.

Gorgon howls.

I can't bear what's coming next.

Gorgon's head remains above the surface of the lake as he swims to its center, his one good eye still gazing at me. The shadow of Jewel flies into the ring on his head tentacle, and then the kraken sinks below the swirling water and disappears.

Roars from the dragons fill the cavern.

From the center of the cavern the Komodo dragon soars toward the lagoon. Fire streams from his mouth and the Great Ones jump out of his way. The lizard hits the lake with a loud *thump!* that sends water cascading over the sides and slapping against the far wall. Disappearing beneath the water, the Komodo escapes too.

The Great Ones move farther into the cavern, toward the twins.

Everything rushes into my head. What's at stake. Using the staff, I gasp as I rise to my feet. Somehow I find the strength to run on shaky legs toward the lake.

Jake heads in the same direction. I stop thirty feet from the water, shoulder to shoulder with him. Sweat and dirt streak his bruised face and one of his forearms has a massive welt. He grips Issa's staff and I lift WhipEye.

"The ninja dragon ladies are not leaving." Jake twists his spear once to bring out the dragon claw.

"It's us or them," I say.

The two dragons fly one last circle, and then float low across the cavern floor, spewing fire ahead and to the sides of their flight, sending the gathered Great Ones scrambling out of their path.

Tarath shouts, "Samantha and Jake, move!"

Rella and Issa land, running quietly as dragons, daring anyone to stop them while they blow fire everywhere, scattering the Great Ones. Even Tarath avoids their flames, probably too exhausted to endure them now.

The dragons race faster, becoming blurs. They're going to run right over us.

But they shift into twin ninjas. Maybe they think it's a game. Even without weapons they show no fear.

I yell and charge with Jake at my side.

Barely slowing their strides, the twins use their arms to block our staffs inward, while twirling like fast ballerinas around the outside of us.

Jake and I twist to follow them, dropping to our knees, flowing with each other's movements and mustering enough speed to swing our staffs at their ankles. The sisters do handsprings over the staffs.

We rise, running for the lake, swinging and thrusting our staffs at the twins' heads. They duck and roll to the outside. Managing to get ahead of the twins, we turn to block them.

Great Ones stream in our direction. Moments.

The twins stand motionless in front of us. Rella meets my eyes, her voice calm. "You will see us again for hurting Gorgon."

"Soon." Issa's voice is also calm.

"So what." Jake's voice is acid.

"Whatever." I'm too tired to fear either of them. I stab WhipEye at Rella and Jake shoves his claw at Issa. Simultaneously the twins leap impossibly high over us.

We both whirl and shout, "No!"

The sisters dive into the middle of the lake. While we stare, waves lap against the edges until glassy water remains.

THIRTY-SEVEN

SILENCE.

I stare at the lagoon, a dull ache inside. It wasn't supposed to end like this. No antidote. No cure. Our parents dead. I'm ready to slam WhipEye into the ground and go to Dad.

"What time is it, Sam?" Jake glances at my wrist, his mouth and eyes wide.

Numb, I check my watch. "Six p.m." My throat chokes. *Too late. Too late. Too late.*

"We have to go." Jake says it without any urgency, his voice flat. "I want to say goodbye to Mom, even if..." He doesn't finish.

"I do too," I murmur. It's unbearable to see the sadness in his eyes. Guilt fills my thoughts over his mother, over Dad. "Okay, let's go."

"Not yet, guardians." Tarath pads toward us as a caracal, transforming into a red-haired woman wearing jeans, a white blouse, and a jean jacket. She looks fatigued, her forehead creased. "The Great Ones have to return to KiraKu, and we're exhausted. We need help from WhipEye."

I look at her, my voice cracking, "We failed, Tarath. I failed Dad and Cynthia." Tears escape my eyes.

"You did your best, Samantha." Tarath embraces me, and then Jake—tears streak his face too.

"The twins were always suspect," murmurs the Great One. "But I hoped I was wrong."

She waits, and I look at Jake.

He makes a limp gesture. "We have to help them."

I swallow and say to Tarath, "A few minutes."

"That's enough." Her right palm is suddenly glowing as she places it near my ribs. Warmth soaks my skin as broken bones shift inside me. She continues healing my wounds until the worst of the pain fades. I'm still fatigued and sore.

Next Tarath places her palm over the bruise on Jake's cheek, and then his injured arm. When she finishes, she says, "I'm spent so I can't restore your energy. Sleep and food will help that. Come." She strides across the cavern and we follow her, but on every step I want to flee home.

We stop beside Heshia. Her serene face rests on moss. Her words *Love is everything* echo inside me. Her death adds to the aches all over my body and in my mind. I kneel and gently caress her blue and white face, half-expecting her eyes to open again.

Jake says softly, "She sacrificed herself for us."

It's painful to hear. "She loved us and KiraKu."

"Losing the Queen of the Merpeople hurts all of us." Tarath moves on.

We follow her. I check my watch. A sob almost escapes my lips.

Near a stalagmite, Colonel Macy lies with a leg bent at an odd angle. His eyes widen when he sees Tarath. Five soldiers lie nearby, three groaning with injuries and two unconscious.

I don't feel any satisfaction over it.

Colonel Macy lifts a trembling hand. "We thought you were a threat." His voice breaks. "I was protecting my country. I'm one of the good guys."

Tarath kneels, one finger changing to a claw that she places against the colonel's neck, drawing a little trickle of blood.

"Please." Colonel Macy's face pales. "Anything."

"The guardians saved your world again and you will leave them alone." The caracal's voice is steel. "Your word on it. I'll know if you intend to break it."

Colonel Macy's eyes shift from her to us, and then back to her. "My word."

She says quietly, "If you ever break your oath, I'll come to you, wherever you are, and end you."

"Understood," he gasps.

I spot a nearby hand radio and place it in his hand. He looks grateful. It should get a signal through the holes in the top of the cavern. We leave him there and I don't look back.

In the middle of the cavern Lewella is kneeling beside Tom, her golden hair hiding her lowered face. Brandon holds his brother's head on his lap, tears streaming down his cheeks. Rose lies nearby, as if in peaceful slumber. Lewella must have brought her.

Tom's eyes are closed and I assume the worst. "Is he?" It's horrible that all I want to do is leave, especially when Tom risked his life for us.

Misty-eyed, Lewella looks up at me. "Jewel's shadow took too much of his energy, and his back is broken. I gave him what energy his body can handle. He'll wake up, but he might be a cripple."

Tom's eyes crack half-open. I doubt he sees us. "KiraKu," he murmurs. "Please."

Brandon says with emotion, "No, brother, we'll take care of you."

Lewella reaches a hand to Brandon's shoulder. "He should go with them. They can give him healing water daily in KiraKu."

Brandon hangs his head, stroking his brother's face. Tom's eyes close. I can't be sure, but it looks as if there's a trace of a smile on his lips.

Great Ones gather around us, sagging like Jake and me.

Tarath says, "We have friends, and KiraKu has places where we can hide from Yakul. Possibly with Worlath. We'll take Rose with us too, so she can heal. The crocodile has no reason to harm her."

I'm glad for Rose, and say, "She'll be happy to go home. Thank all of you," I manage.

Jake lifts a hand. "Yeah, we had no chance without you."

"It was the right thing to do." The Kodiak bear turns to each of us. "No regrets."

"You stopped a war, guardians." Tarath regards everyone. "We stopped Gorgon."

The wolverine growls lowly. "Another time and he'll be finished."

"I call all of you friends." Mentore motions tiredly. "We'll need each other again."

"And we'll come." The mountain gorilla lifts his hand to Mentore. "You would be welcome in KiraKu."

Mentore grunts, his tail flicking behind him. "Days ago I would have said yes, but the crocodile reminded me why I left. I'll remain here to make sure Gorgon fails and to protect my home here."

"Sooner or later all Great Ones and Lessers will have to choose sides," says Tarath.

The iguana says, "I was glad to help."

"So much sadness." Canaste lies coiled nearby. "But I'm glad the guardians survived."

"I'm happy you weren't hurt, Canaste," I say. The urgency to leave is choking my throat.

Jake is fidgeting and appears ready to bolt.

Lewella motions to Tarath. "Tom always wanted to return to his homeland. Take care of him, my friend."

Tarath bows slightly. "I will, old friend. If there's a way to heal him, I'll find it."

Brandon's head remains lowered, his boisterous voice silent.

Tarath steps closer to Jake and me. "I'm sorry for your parents. You sacrificed their lives to stop Gorgon and I honor you for that."

All I can think of is Dad. I hug her again, as does Jake.

She shifts into the large caracal. "Samantha, smash the cobra ring on a rock with WhipEye."

I give a limp wave. "Will do."

Jake gestures to Tarath. "Say hello to leather face for me."

Tarath adds, "Be careful from here on out. Gorgon and his allies will want revenge. And Gorgon will desire to possess WhipEye even more now after seeing its power." She streams into WhipEye.

The mountain gorilla cradles Rose and Tom in his arms and leaves next, followed by the wolverine, iguana, and Kodiak bear.

The rest of us form a circle, and Jake and I use WhipEye to transport everyone to the hill outside the tunnel. The grass is wet and the ground soggy, but the rain has stopped. With the sky still overcast, daylight is fading fast.

In the valley below, a few small groups of Lessers attend fallen Originals, but most have left. Even the sloth that grabbed the helicopter is gone. The remnants of Colonel Macy's soldiers have disappeared too. I expect the colonel will get help, but more importantly I wonder how many Lessers or Originals died today.

Lewella gestures to us. "I want to help anyone who might need it." She walks down the hill with Brandon.

My weary limbs hang like stones, but it's not over. The others gather around us as I place the cobra ring on a nearby rock. Déjà vu again. Jake and I lift the staff with tired arms and slam it down. Golden light bursts from the bottom of WhipEye, shattering the ring. Ten feet above us floats the two-headed cobra shadow, which quickly reshapes into the true form of a real single-headed king cobra snake.

Dissolving, the cobra methuselah sends blinding light streaking to the horizon in all directions, forcing us to turn away. The last trapped methuselah is free. I like to think that the cobra's released energy will heal any nearby injured Originals and Lessers.

"Good riddance to snake face." Jake flicks a hand at the air.

Mentore studies us, his features sagging. "Gorgon suffered a huge loss. He's broken and won't venture forth anytime soon. Others will be slow to follow him again. They learned something from this." He pauses. "We all have."

I give a small pat to the ape's arm. "You're a hero."

Jake nods to him. "You did what's right."

"All of us did." Mentore regards Jake and me. "I believe now that you are the true guardians."

Neither of us respond, and he leaves then, walking down the hill on all fours, toward Lessers huddled near the northern edge of the valley.

Jake and I head for the valley bottom, walking fast. I dread what's coming.

Canaste crawls beside me. "Some died." The giant boa's fins undulate. "And Gorgon has part of Jewel. It's all terrible, but I'm still your friend, Samantha and Jake."

"I'm sorry you had to fight," I say. "I'll always consider you a friend."

"I used to hate snakes." Jake gives a wan smile. "But now I'm going to miss one."

I stroke the boa's neck once and she departs, crawling away into the jungle.

We hurry to join Lewella, and find her staring north at departing Lessers and Originals.

"Did you find Vesio?" I ask.

She shakes her head. "He either left on his own or was carried off. Vampires are great self-healers though."

Brandon sits silently nearby. Lewella touches his shoulder and he stands. We form a final circle, Jake's hand on Brandon's shoulder, Brandon's on Lewella's—and hers on mine. Their faces are all weary, saddened by loss. Mine must look the same. I'm numb. Before I move the staff, my chest heaves. I work hard to hold it together.

Using WhipEye, I take them home to the forest behind our house. It's early evening, the woods silent.

Lewella and Brandon look at us, their eyes sad. Tom lived with them for thousands of years and seemed the least interested in helping us. Perhaps he best understood the price that might be paid.

With gentle fingers Lewella pushes my wet tangled hair to the side of my face. "There's something I need to tell you, Samantha. We were asked long ago to watch over the next bearer of WhipEye. It was predicted Rose would someday pass it on to one of the true guardians."

"By who?" I'm surprised.

"Jewel. She invited me to her cavern shortly before the Originals were forced out by Yakul, and asked me to go into your world. She said a time would come when the true guardians of WhipEye would need help."

The Lesser rests her hand on my shoulder, her green eyes full of sadness. "Brandon, Tom, their parents, and I agreed to do this for you. It was difficult for Tom to believe you were the one Jewel intended for us to help. Also his parents had already died, leaving him great sorrow. But in the end he risked everything for you."

"I'm sorry." I feel even worse about Tom's sacrifice, and look over Lewella's shoulder at Brandon. There's no anger or blame in his eyes.

"He was a hero." Jake gestures to Brandon. "He gave more than any of us."

Except Heshia. I keep that to myself. "I'm glad he's home in KiraKu."

Brandon barely nods.

"We'll come again, if need be." Lewella gives a small bow. "This isn't over. There is a greater evil than Gorgon threatening KiraKu."

I wrap my arms around her, and then Brandon, as does Jake. They leave quietly, walking into the woods. I watch Lewella's golden hair fade among the trees until I can't see her anymore.

THIRTY-EIGHT

WE HURRIEDLY BURY OUR staffs in the dirt, covering them with pine needles. Surprisingly, separation from WhipEye leaves me calm this time.

I notice a small indentation in the back of Jake's armor. My voice is dull. "Issa's spear couldn't pierce it."

Jake says quietly, "Spectacular, isn't it?" He places his palm on his chest and the armor shrinks into the swallowtail scale, which he pockets.

My chest heaves as he wraps his arms around me.

"We failed, Sam."

My voice is a whisper as I hold him tightly. "I'm sorry. I always thought..." I don't know what I believe anymore. Intuition failed me.

"We did our best," murmurs Jake.

"How can we be the true guardians and save two worlds, and yet fail our own parents?" He doesn't answer, maybe unsure as I am that he wants to be one of the true guardians. I'm unable to say anything else. But I remember Heshia said love had to come before saving Dad. Somehow I believed I could do it all.

We hustle into the backyard to check on the cats, deer, and birds. It soothes me when I see all the animals are healthy. Since the cars are wrecks, we grab our bikes and ride into town. We're both silent.

When we reach the hospital and walk in the front door, I'm suddenly numb again. I'll never forgive myself.

The hospital is quiet. Nearly empty. Sunday night in a small town.

When we approach the front desk, Dr. Paul sees us and grasps our shoulders. "I'm sorry, Samantha and Jake. We did what we could for them."

Jake's eyes betray sadness and I hang my head.

Dr. Paul walks us to our parents' room. He glances at our torn shirts. His eyes reveal he has questions for us, but he doesn't ask them.

Once we're inside the room, he closes the door and leaves us alone. We stand together, facing our parents' beds. Respirators push air into their lungs.

The clock on the wall reads five-fifty-five p.m. I'm confused until I realize it's Central Standard Time. My watch is still set for the Eastern time zone. They have another five minutes. It's almost harder this way. Jake's vision will come true.

Jake walks to his mother's side, and I walk to Dad's. Purple lines from the poison cover every inch of exposed skin on their arms, faces, and necks.

Dr. Paul quickly returns with the bags we packed when Macy first arrested us, quietly setting them near our feet. After he leaves, I find the torn family photo inside mine. Someone taped the pieces together. Probably Dr. Paul. Mom's face stares at me from the photo, triggering more tears in my eyes.

Sitting quietly on chairs between the beds, we spend the last minutes holding our parents' hands as they slowly die. The monitors connected to Dad and Cynthia show their slowing heartbeats. It won't be long now. Their faces are pale, their skin stiff like cardboard.

Jake wipes his eyes. I feel darkness inside, reminding me of when Mom died.

"It's my fault," I murmur.

"No." Jake grabs my free hand. "We both made the choice, Sam."

The door opens. We turn.

Two figures stride in, wearing red hooded cloaks, their hands hidden in sleeves. When they pull back their hoods, the scent of orchids fills the room. Red eyes blaze at us. Bronze claws and skin. Black hair, and one white streak.

Jake jumps up and goes into a martial arts stance, his face livid. "Lying ninja dragon sisters."

I stand, my jaw clenched. "You betrayed us."

"Gorgon imprisoned our younger sister." Bitterness fills Rella's words. "Thus we serve him."

That fits everything that's happened, but I don't care. "You lied to me in the cavern with the image you sent to me of you two fighting Gorgon."

Issa shakes her head. "We never lie. We gave you an image from our hearts, which we couldn't follow."

"What has your master told you to do?" asks Jake.

Rella takes a small step forward. "To kill you slowly."

"And to prolong your parents' suffering." Issa moves beside her sister. "And to get WhipEye."

"You'll never find it." I inch back, glancing at the respirator and the IV in Dad's arm. If I pull both, he'll die immediately.

Jake steps back too, eyeing his mother.

"Young warriors with so much strength." Issa glances at Rella. "We trained them well. You won't freely give us the staff?"

Jake's expression hardens. "Gorgon will never get it."

I want to hug him.

Rella lifts a claw. "Even if we heal your parents?"

"Get lost," I say harshly.

"Never." Jake glares at them.

Issa lifts her chin. "Good. Because the only way Gorgon will be defeated is if WhipEye remains in your hands."

I gape at the twins. Jake's hands waver.

Rella moves closer to Dad's bed. "The words I spoke in the cave, *You will see us again for hurting Gorgon,* was for his benefit, in case he was still listening. His mind abilities are uncanny."

Issa moves closer to Cynthia's bed. "Gorgon will hear from us that your army imprisoned you and that the staffs are in their possession."

Wild hope bubbles up inside me. "You're here to help us?"

"Dragons are healers." Rella steps next to Dad's bed. "Do you have any idea how much we want to tear Gorgon to pieces? When you two fought each other, we had instructions on how to behave. And if Gorgon had died today, we would never find our sister."

Jake's hands drop, his eyes wide. "Can you save Mom?"

Rella lowers herself over Dad's arm and bites into his flesh with two fangs. Issa does the same to Cynthia. The monitors show stronger heartbeats almost immediately. Next the dragons wipe their saliva on the thigh wounds of our parents. The cuts heal and the purple lines on Dad's and Cynthia's legs recede, followed by receding poison lines all over their bodies.

My eyes fill with tears. Jake's teary eyes brighten. We hold our parents' hands, but Dad's eyes don't open, and neither do Cynthia's. I look at Rella.

"They need sleep to fully heal." She gestures to them. "In a day or two they will be fine."

I fling myself into her arms with tears flowing down my face, unable to say anything, my faith restored in life, in my heart, in everything.

Jake hugs Issa just as fiercely.

Rella pulls back and takes some of her saliva, gently applying it to my forehead. All of my weariness evaporates. Issa does the same for Jake.

Afterward a deep breath escapes my lips. "Thank you, Rella." It sounds lame after what she did.

"Thanks, Issa." Jake flashes a hand. "For everything."

They both give a small bow and say together, "Of course."

Rella moves fast, her claw grasping and holding my compass level. "Your compass is stunning, Samantha."

I don't want to give it away, but they saved our parents. I start to take it off my neck. "You can have it."

Issa says sharply, "It's Samantha's."

"I'm just admiring." Rella smiles, allowing it to slide off her palm. "I could never take it from you, Samantha."

I'm relieved when the compass rests against my chest again. "You're risking a lot to help us."

"The true guardians risked everything for KiraKu." Rella bows to us.

"We owe you," I say. "How can we help?"

Jake motions. "Whatever you need."

"Anything," I say.

"Don't lose my dragon claw." Issa nods to Jake.

"No way. I love it. It's the best superhero thing I own." Jake pauses. "Well, I like the armor too."

"Free our sister." Rella's eyes are moist.

"Free us." Issa takes Rella's claw in hers.

"We will," I say.

"Whatever it takes." Jake slashes a hand emphatically.

We embrace them once more.

THIRTY-NINE

OUR PARENTS RETURN TO us not remembering what happened, but glad to be alive. Dr. Paul told us the strange poison and coma might affect their memory for a short time or forever. He said it's best to allow their memories to return on their own.

Amnesia. Dad's and Cynthia's memory loss reminds Jake and me of our own erased memories. I wonder if it's as difficult for Dad and Cynthia to cope with it.

It's easier for all of us this way. When Cynthia and Dad ask about the house and car damage and their injuries, we tell them a storm hit our home. They don't question us further.

Dad begins rebuilding, fixing the staircase and hallway wall, and sheeting over my bedroom wall so I have a large plastic window. We paint the outside of the house, fix tilted shutters, and go camping once. I treasure every moment with him.

Sometimes Jake and I hang out reading; me animal books, Jake comic books. He's teaching me ping pong and how to cook. I even try some of his new recipes. Sometimes we swap reading material or play a game of chess—I defend my pawns.

We spend time daily practicing our fighting skills in the woods. Preparing. We're always armed when we're in the forest.

Sometimes we just walk and sit, with birds landing on our shoulders and other animals coming close to us. Everything is vivid and beautiful, helping to heal our loss over Heshia, Jewel, Tom, Vesio, Rose, and the others that were injured or killed. Without each other, we would be lost. We never talk about what happened. It's too painful.

The rest of our memories return; the evil guardian, fights, battles, chases, Rose, new friends, and KiraKu. We talk a little about it, but it doesn't seem to matter. What does matter is that we saved each other's lives, and became best friends. And we stopped a madman with nine shadow monsters in his rings.

Dad and Cynthia don't seem to remember their engagement and spend little time together. They're more subdued around each other and don't smile or laugh as often as they used to. Jake and I feel responsible for that and neither of us is happy about it.

On the last day of summer vacation Jake sits on my bed and shows me a new tattoo on his right forearm which resembles Heshia. It gives me a pang of sadness, but I like that he honored her. His black hair is long, but trimmed, his face bright. His dark eyes shine lately.

"I could teach you how to swim." I smile. "Then you won't need me to rescue you."

"Woohoo." He twirls a finger and cocks his head at me. "And I could teach you how to overcome your fear of heights, angel."

"Snakes."

"Spiders."

He matches my smile, and then becomes serious. "When you didn't give the staff to the Komodo, I knew it was the right thing to do." He shrugs. "I was freaked out."

I stare at him in surprise. "So was I, Jake." I study him. "Any more visions?"

"No." He reaches into his pocket, his face turning a little pink as he extends his hand. A woven leather wrist bracelet dangles from his fingers. The jade dolphin hangs from a short piece of leather woven into the wrist weave.

"You had it!" I beam and take it from him, wrapping my arms around him. He holds me tightly. When I pull back, I try it on. "Perfect. Did you do this?"

"Are you kidding?" His hands make small circles. "I had to find a leather worker in town." His hands go still. "I felt bad when I broke it."

"Me too. I mean, not about you breaking it, well that too, but..."

“Yeah.” He clears his throat.

“That shield you made with the swallowtail scale was pretty cool, genius.” I glance at his hair, wondering how it would feel to run my fingers through it.

His eyes shine. “I’ve made other things with it too.”

“You’ll have to show me.” I get up, open a dresser drawer, and pull out a small cardboard box, which I hand to him. “We never really celebrated your birthday. I guess it was almost as fun as mine last year.”

He chuckles and exaggerates rolling his eyes. “No. Mine was way funner.” He opens the box and pulls out a thin silver necklace with a silver dragon hanging from it. “Love it, Sam.”

“I thought it would match the dragon tattoo.” I plop down while he puts it on.

When he turns to me, we stare at each other. I know he won’t do anything about it. He already tried once. I make another choice and lean in. When our lips meet, I’m tingly all over and warm inside. Our arms wrap around each other tightly. Yummy. It seems to go on for seconds or minutes. I can't tell because it feels so good, and right.

When we pull apart, our hands find each other.

“Much better timing.” He gives a soft smile.

“I liked it both times,” I say.

We sit in silence. But it’s nice, not awkward, like everything is whole between us again.

“I never thought I’d like a painting of a snake.” He lifts his chin to my latest work, a picture of Canaste in the jungle.

He releases my hand and leans back on his palms. “I’ve been thinking about our world, how we’re treating it, how we treat each other. The choices everyone makes every day.” He pauses. “The question I keep coming up with is, *Where’s the love?*”

“It’s a good question, Jake.”

“So.” He looks at me. “Jewel said we’d have to choose.”

My heart races a little. “Have you?”

He considers that, looking thoughtful. “What are you thinking?”

I know my choice, but I say, "I don't want to do it without my partner. But it has to be your choice."

"I'm in a hundred percent if you are, babe."

I'm relieved and happy to hear him formally say it. "I'm in all the way, Jake." I also realize my life will never be normal again. But I can live with that.

"True guardians it is then." Abruptly his face scrunches up as if he's really worried.

"What's wrong, Jake?"

"I need help with a problem."

"Sure. What is it?"

"Do you know anyone who might like to go to a Halloween party with Horsefly-Man this year?" He gives me that goofy grin of his.

"Maybe." I frown. "I think I know a superhero who's not too picky. She's dressing up as a ninja dragon lady this year."

We both grin over that.

There's a knock on my door.

"It's open," I say.

Cynthia enters, barefoot and dressed in red shorts and a lavender tee. Dad is having an influence on her, despite their spending less time together. He's behind her and wearing jean shorts and a white tee. They both appear healthy and fresh. Sadness strikes me that they're not together anymore.

"Hey you two." Cynthia smiles at both of us.

"Can we talk?" Dad is smiling too.

"Sure, Bryon." Jake steps away from the bed and pulls out my desk chair to sit on. I quickly stand up and lean against the wall, which leaves the bed mattress.

Dad ruffles his sandy hair, and then settles his lean frame at the head of the bed, near my dresser. Cynthia sits near the foot of the bed, far away from Dad. Maybe they're shy in front of us.

Dad looks at us, his eyes calm. "Sam and Jake, we have something to say to you."

"And we want you to be completely honest with us." Cynthia brushes her black hair off her forehead, her voice suddenly serious.

Jake flips a hand and winks at me. “You can count on me. I won’t hold back. No way.”

“Totally,” I exchange smiles with Jake. Our parents are together again! Although I abruptly wonder if that will make my relationship with Jake weird.

Dad glances at Cynthia and then takes a deep breath. “Good. We talked to Dr. Paul. That helped quite a bit.” He straightens. “We want you to tell us who the forty-foot Komodo dragon is that tore apart our house and nearly killed us.”

“And after you explain *everything* you know,” Cynthia turns to Jake, “we want to hear why you’ve been lying to us.”

Jake’s face scrunches up.

This time I can feel the tick at the corner of my mouth.

We are so dead, a.k.a. crap.

Don't miss the exciting thriller,
Magical Beasts, Book Two,
Guardian, The Quest!

The guardians are blackmailed: Jake has a magical weapon placed on his arm, and Sam and Jake have one day to capture the magical golden dragon Drasine—or Jake dies. Can Sam save Jake? Will Jake sacrifice himself to save Sam? Can Sam and Jake stop the Evil One?

***

AUTHOR'S NOTE

Thank you so much for reading my fantasy thriller, *Guardian, The Choice*. I hope you enjoyed it! I really enjoyed creating the character of Samantha—and that she is a wildlife expert. Sam is learning to trust her choices, gaining strength, and developing her relationship with Jake. Besides Sam and Jake, Jewel was one of my favorite characters in this book. If you have a favorite character in this story, I'd love to hear from you.

Reviews help me keep writing, and encourage other readers to take a chance on a new author they haven't read before. So if you enjoyed the book, please leave a review. Every review, even a few words, helps!

Thank you! ~ Geoff

Excerpt from MAGICAL BEASTS Book Two
GUARDIAN: THE QUEST

ONE

I SCAN THE FOREST, knowing an attack could come at any moment.

I want it to happen. I'm ready for it.

I grip WhipEye in my right hand, sweat covering my arms. I'm breathing easily, but the six-foot chestnut-colored staff is slowing me down. Jake is running fluidly next to me, holding his three-foot bronze staff—formed from the middle claw of Issa's dragon foot.

Jake is going to leave me. The words pop into my mind. That intuition has been gnawing at me for the last month. My mouth turns dry as I weave around a pine tree. I have a sick sensation in my gut that Jake doesn't like me anymore, at least not as much as I like him, and that we're going to be separated.

But we're a team now, so that doesn't make sense. Maybe he wants to break up the team. Maybe he's tired of it. My worry feels childish at times, but it also makes me want to cry. He's my best friend, actually much more than that, and I'd miss him terribly if he left me. We've never really spelled out what our relationship is, and I've never said to him *I love you*, but we both *know*. At least I thought we did. But when I think about it, it seems like all we do is train together.

The other thing I feel is stuck. It's not that I'm bored. But I'm ready for something different besides feeding the animals at Dad's wild animal shelter and the endless training every evening after school and every weekend. I'm also sick of waiting for Gorgon or his allies to come after us. I know Jake feels the same way. It's been two months since we fought Gorgon, but it feels like two years.

He's dressed in all black today—sleeveless T-shirt, running shorts, tennis shoes, and socks. My attention trails from his long black hair to his strong shoulders and arms. The summer turned his light brown skin darker, and the warm Fall has kept it dark. A six-foot American mutt, he's a blend of eight ethnicities, including German, Native American, Spanish, and Guatemalan. He has a dragon tattoo on his left forearm, a tattoo of Heshia on his right, and he's wearing the silver necklace with a dragon pendant that I gave him.

On my wrist the jade dolphin hangs from the leather bracelet he gave me over a year ago on my sixteenth birthday. I wonder if he would give me something personal like that now.

He notices my gawking and gives the same crooked smile I've seen for a month. Plus his face is scrunched up. The dead giveaway. Something is bothering him and I'm suddenly certain that it's me. My stomach drops with that realization.

Questions whirl through me. Like who usually initiates our time together, and if it's always me, and will he do it if I don't? I love his humor, loyalty, and bravery—I suddenly wonder if there's anything he likes about me.

"You're doing that tick thing with the corner of your lips, Sam. What's bothering you?"

Jake notices details, and I scramble for an excuse. "Nothing, I'm just hungry. Anything bothering you?" I glance at him. "Your face is scrunched up."

He hesitates. "No. I'm just tired."

I babble, "I'm starving. What did Cynthia make for lunch?" Cynthia is Jake's mother. At one point she was engaged to Dad. Now they're just good friends. They're waiting ahead of us at the bridge for a picnic.

Jake gives me that goofy grin that I fell for long ago. "Rraugh rraugh rraugh."

"Really?" I roll my eyes. Lately he's been making these silly sounds that remind me of a sick seal. It means something is false. Acting annoyed, I play along. "Okay, what's not true?"

"Rraugh rraugh rraugh."

"Dork." I forgot. He won't answer unless I mimic him. Really annoying. "All right. Rraugh rraugh rraugh."

He grins. "*I* made the lunch, not Mom. Avocado wraps with all kinds of good stuff inside."

"Yum yum. You can be my slave cook." He wants to be a chef and none of us mind being his guinea pigs. His food is great. I haven't settled on a career yet, but it has to involve wild animals. Maybe a wildlife biologist or vet. I'd get a PhD.

"I already am your slave cook." Jake chuckles and pulls away from me.

I blurt, "How about a superhero movie after dinner?" My voice cracks and my cheeks burn.

He drops back beside me. "That's the best offer I've had in five years. But I'm training again tonight."

His pupils flash gold. We both have that oddity due to our time in the parallel world of KiraKu. It gives us great night vision.

"All work and no play makes Jake a dull boy." I flash him a smile.

"Am I really dull?" He frowns.

"No, that's not what I meant, I—"

"Because I could catch a firefly for you if you want excitement. Or wrestle a bear. Maybe just hop down to the pond and catch a frog." He eyes me. "Are you still sworn off frog legs?"

"Dork." I give it another shot. "I should run with you. I need to increase my speed."

"Sloooow Sammy." He rolls his eyes this time, because I'm faster than any other teenager my age—except him.

I smile as he speeds up again. "So what time are you running?"

"I'll be sprinting tonight, Sam."

Which means he doesn't want a slower runner along. "I'm working on a new painting. You'll love it, if you want to drop by after."

"Let me guess." He swerves left around a birch tree. "You're drawing me?" He raises his eyebrows several times fast. Then he lifts his right bicep and flexes it. "Do you need me to pose, honey?"

"I don't do stick figures."

"Okay, I give up. What are you drawing tonight?"

"Black panther. I don't know why. I just started drawing it for some reason."

"Normally I would wuv to come over. But not tonight, Sammy."

He began saying *wuv* lately because one of our close friends does. The gnawing feeling that he's leaving me keeps pushing me to pester him. It feels as if I'm trying to hang onto him with an appointment, which is kind of pathetic given that I'm with him nearly every day. But for some reason I can't help myself, and ask, "How about tomorrow night?"

"Sure." His tone is mechanical. "Now boy must run. See you at the bridge."

I say lightly, "Orders are to stay together. Must obey."

"Scream if you get attacked by a rogue horsefly." Without any effort he pulls ahead, leaving me behind.

He always runs as if we're in a race. All out. I want to yell that he's not being a good training partner, but I shove down those words. I work to keep his black tee in sight, yet after a minute he fades among the trees.

"Loser," I mutter. My reaction feels childish. We've only been an item for a few months. But I'm still annoyed. And I wonder if WhipEye is amplifying my emotions again—it has in the past.

Pine scent fills the air and the ground is spongy beneath my blue tennis shoes. The early October afternoon sun is warm. Indian summer. Fir and spruce trees glisten in the sunlight, the colors vivid and dazzling—another byproduct of our visits to KiraKu

Cardinals and gray catbirds sing in the distance. Superior National Forest in northern Minnesota is one of my favorite places, and normally the beauty and bird songs soothe my worries. But the nagging concern about Jake won't leave me.

Ahead, a three-foot-diameter red pine log blocks my path. I consider going around it, but I'm sure Jake didn't. KiraKu's golden energy made us faster and stronger than normal, so I adjust my stride and leap.

As I clear the log, a blur of white rushes me from the right. Thick arms circle me like iron bars, pulling me in close. I gasp, watching the forest canopy above slide by as I rotate in a circle.

We hit the ground rolling, those strong arms quickly tossing me away. Pine needles and dirt fill my mouth as I slide across the ground. I dig my tennis shoes into the soil, my shoulder and hip scraping dirt too, and manage to stop just before I slam into a tree.

Scrambling to my feet, my fingers curl around WhipEye. The forest has gone quiet. I spit out soil and swipe my forearm across my mouth. My sleeveless peach top and blue running shorts are dirty and my calves have scratches. I ignore all of it.

Without looking west, I shout, "Jake!"

Brushing strands of my long brown hair off my face, I make a three-sixty, peering through the forest. Nothing. My attacker vanished. Had to be Uncle Biggie. Like all Originals—one of the first humans from KiraKu—Biggie moves in silence.

We first met him when battling the evil guardian. We helped each other and became close friends. Biggie turned up at our house a month ago and we began training together. I recently learned that Mom was an Original, which makes me half-Original—so I'm even more fond of Biggie.

I glance at the staff, the most beautiful thing I own, scanning the intricate animal head carvings on it until I find Tarath's. I won't call the Great One, but it's part of the training—to be ready. I send my wishes out like emotional tendrils for any nearby animals, but no responses come back. Any wildlife that might help me is too far away.

Frustrated I didn't see the attack coming, I'm determined to avoid a second mistake. I crouch, aware of Jake sprinting back toward me, with Issa's staff now extended to six feet. He's still fifty yards away.

A large creature materializes out of thin air a few yards to the side of me. Shocked, my arms tense.

Ten feet tall at the shoulder, the animal has sandy fur, black spots, and gold eyes. An animal nerd, I've spent thousands of hours researching wildlife and recognize the creature immediately. "*Crocuta crocuta,* a.k.a. spotted hyena," I murmur.

The hyena has to be a Great One from KiraKu; Great Ones that live in our world are called Lessers, and often have mutations and can't teleport.

I find the hyena beautiful, but I don't know if it's on our side or Gorgon's—the power-hungry Lesser that we defeated a few months ago. One thing is certain; Gorgon wants revenge. I'm able to pick up emotions from animals, but the hyena gives no reaction as it studies me.

Great Ones and Lessers can put you in a light trance just by staring at you, so I avoid looking directly in its eyes. "Are you a friend of Tarath's?"

The hyena gives a short high-pitched laugh. I sense it's nervous, but it leaps at me.

I roll to the side beneath its slashing jaws. Rising, I stab WhipEye into the animal's hip. Golden energy crackles down the staff and into the hyena's body—its hindquarters whip away from me with the jolt. I roll away again when the hyena snaps its powerful jaws at the tip of WhipEye.

When I rise, the hyena jumps high at me, ten feet off the ground. I jab WhipEye at its chest. Twisting in midair, the hyena again tries to bite the staff. I pull it back and punch it into the animal's lower jaw when it lands.

The beast absorbs the blow and crackling energy, clenches WhipEye between its teeth, and savagely jerks it out of my hands. I back up, instantly upset with myself for losing the staff, and desperate to get it back. It's exactly the kind of thing I'm training *not* to do—get caught by surprise.

"Don't!" I flinch as the animal wags its head, trying to break WhipEye. Hyenas exert one of the most powerful bite pressures of any land animal, but WhipEye is made from the strongest wood in KiraKu. Failing, the hyena tosses the staff to the side, growls, and stalks me.

"What's this about?" I pick up a stick and hold it in front of me. Pathetic.

"Hey, dog face!" Jake charges from the opposite side, thrusting Issa's staff at the hyena's side. Shimmering yellow, orange, and red butterfly armor covers his torso.

The hyena rises on its two back legs, and Jake's staff misses, sliding beneath the animal's belly. Hopping backward, the beast ducks its head, trying to grab the end of Jake's staff.

Jake kneels and sweeps the staff at the hyena's back legs. The creature jumps to the side. I dart to WhipEye, bending over and grabbing it on the run. Slowly I circle back toward Jake as the creature turns and glares at me. Standing, Jake twists Issa's staff to bring out the spear.

The hyena whoops in a low-pitched wail. "The famous hero, disarmed and helpless in seconds." The hyena's cocky voice is young and male.

"We're not finished." Jake sounds angry.

"Want to go another round?" I ask.

The crocle-lion—a chimera with a crocodile head on the neck of a large lioness body—dashes from the woods, growling and nipping at the hyena's rear legs. The crocle-lion is a runt compared to the giant hyena.

Surprised, the hyena pivots and bares its teeth at the chimera, which hurriedly retreats.

"Leave wittle guardians alone!" The melodious singsong voice comes from above.

The hyena arches its neck to look up.

I glance up too, relieved. No wonder I couldn't find Biggie before.

Uncle Biggie plummets down feet first from sixty feet up a birch tree. Powerfully built, and eight-feet-tall, his arms are longer than his legs. The big guy wears a white tee, long ragged jean cut-offs that end at his calves, and is barefoot. A chain and leather leash is wound around his waist. It doubles as a weapon and a leash for the crocle-lion.

Landing quietly beside the startled hyena, Uncle Biggie grips the beast's torso and tosses the howling animal. The beast tumbles into a tree and yelps. Originals are strong, but Biggie's strength always astonishes me.

The hyena recovers, snarls, and charges him.

"Run wittle guardians!" Uncle Biggie waves us away. "Go!"

"No way." I would never abandon him, and neither would Jake.

"Sam, incoming!" Jake's eyes widen as he stares past me.

A woman is racing around a tree, attacking us from the side.

TWO

I DROP TO MY knees and swing WhipEye at the woman's legs. She leaps over the staff, and Jake thrusts Issa's spear at her torso. It's a move Jake and I have practiced often in tandem fighting.

In midair the woman twists to avoid Jake's strike, and grabs for his staff, but Jake pulls it back.

The woman lands and charges me.

I rise and swipe the end of WhipEye at her head, while Jake jabs at her stomach. She lifts a hand to block Jake's spearhead and takes my blow with a grunt. WhipEye cracks against her skull, but no energy comes from the staff when I use it for side blows. I still assume we'll have her on the defensive, but she tumbles to the ground in a roll, rises fast, and grabs one of my knees and shoulders on the way up, immediately lifting me over her head.

Her strength shocks me, and I cry, "Jake!"

She slams me down onto my back.

"Umph." The air is knocked out of me and my hand flies open; WhipEye rolls away. Dizzy and choking on empty lungs, my eyes water.

"Sam!" Jake tries to stab the woman, but she twists away, grabs my arm, and runs, dragging me over the ground away from him. Choking for air, I bounce over the dirt.

Jake sprints to cut her off.

"Leave wittle Jake and Sam alone!" From twenty feet away, Uncle Biggie snaps his leash at the woman.

The leather tip cuts her upper arm, drawing blood.

She stops, seizes the tip of Biggie's whip with lightning speed, and jerks it down so she can wrap it around my shoulder.

"No!" shouts Uncle Biggie. He's forced to drop the chain end of the leash and face the whooping hyena that's charging him again.

My lungs are starving and I inhale hoarsely. I try to roll over onto my side, but the woman jams a knee against my chest, pressing me into the ground. I punch at her face, but she knocks my hand away.

Appearing eighteen, tall and lithe, she has red and black streaks in her yellow hair. Rich brown skin. Barefoot, she's wearing jeans and a white tee. A thin gold chain circles her neck.

Jake swipes his spear at her head. She ducks, so he follows with a downward strike at her shoulder. The woman twists sideways and he misses again. She grabs Issa's staff with one hand and jams it at him to loosen his grip, and then jerks it out of his hands and tosses it.

A black belt in kung fu, Jake kicks at her side. She blocks his foot with her forearm. He slides in and chops at her neck.

With little effort she absorbs the hand blow with her arm, grabs his forearm, and jerks him down on top of me. Kneeling on his back, she keeps us immobile.

Her arm is already healing from Biggie's whip, so like the hyena she's a Lesser or Great One too. Originals don't heal like that. That also explains her speed and strength. She and the hyena have to be working for Gorgon.

My vision blurs. I'm suffocating. From ground level I glimpse Biggie shoving the hyena sideways into a tree.

Jake's face is red, but unlike me he can breathe. A Great One butterfly in KiraKu gave him the swallowtail butterfly scale armor. It has a mysterious cushioned interior that protects him from outside blows and pressure.

The woman cries out as thin spikes grow out of Jake's back armor. She lifts her pricked knee, revealing red dots of blood on her jeans, and grabs the back of Jake's neck. "Do anything cute with the armor again and I'll break something." She has a slight Hispanic accent.

"Got it," gasps Jake. The spikes recede into his armor.

From behind her, the woman pulls out a thick silver band and slaps it onto Jake's left wrist. She leans over him to stare at me, her slender face hard. "If you don't find and deliver Drasine to the smugglers by tomorrow night, the silver band will explode and kill your boyfriend. Go to the Smuggler's Oasis. Kert will tell you what to do."

Stunned, now I know she's working with Gorgon. "Forget you." I punch at her face, but she grabs my wrist. Her eyes harden, and then she looks up.

Somehow the hyena got past Uncle Biggie and it's charging us. The animal must be working with the woman. Her ride out of here.

The woman releases my wrist.

I croak, "You can't do this." I grab at her but her head is rising and my fingers curl around her swinging gold necklace. It breaks off in my hand as she morphs into a huge cheetah.

Her spotted yellow coat shines, and the red and black streaks in the woman's hair make sense now, matching a cheetah's coloration.

I cringe as the hyena flies over me. Jake covers his head with his arms.

The hyena shocks me when it knocks the cheetah backward. Rolling over the ground, the two giants yowl furiously.

Jake awkwardly pulls himself off me, staring at the silver band on his wrist. I roll onto my side, sucking air, while the two animals fight. Uncle Biggie and the crocle-lion run up beside us.

Snarling, the cheetah and hyena leap to their feet and face off. In the wild, hyenas dominate cheetahs, but among Great Ones and Lessers normal animal rules don't apply.

The hyena circles the cat cautiously. Darting forward, the cheetah slaps the hyena's shoulder with a paw, sending him flying.

Glancing at me, the cheetah hisses. "The clock is ticking. Go to the Smuggler's Oasis and Kert." She streaks away into the forest.

I struggle to my knees as the giant cat fades into the trees. Uncle Biggie gently unwinds his whip from my shoulder and helps me up, handing me WhipEye.

Jake's eyes meet mine, his voice strained, "Are you okay, Sam?"

Oddly he seems more concerned about me than the time bomb on his wrist. My stomach tumbles. Whining to myself about movies and hanging out with him suddenly feels stupid and selfish. And I finally understand the separation from Jake that I've been feeling over the last month. I now know what's coming.

His death.

Read all four of the *MAGICAL BEASTS* books!

And read *Wyshea Shadows*, Book 1 of the *Divided Dragons* series.

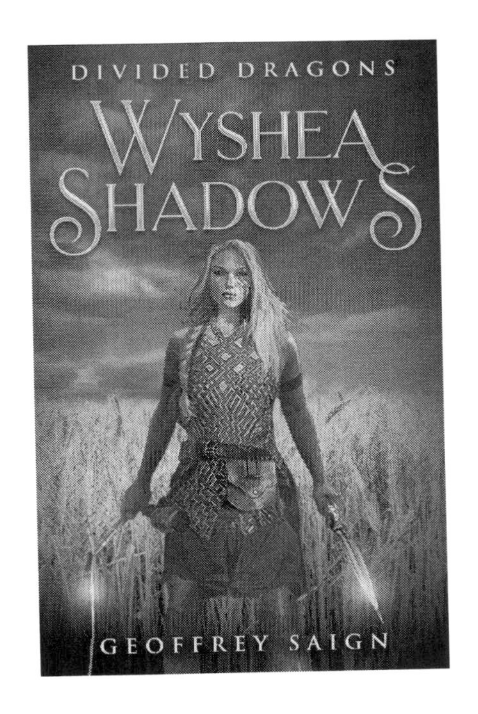

A hundred-year-war that won't end...

Three young women sworn to kill each other...

A hidden enemy that wants all three of them dead.

Famere fights to save her people with mythical beasts called shadows, while her pledged love is held prisoner.

Jennelle fights for her Northerners' survival using brilliant strategies, yet is unable to express her love for her second in command.

And Camette, an ancient divided dragon, searches for another evil divided dragon who kidnapped her lover...

Famere, Jennelle, and Camette must discover who is friend or enemy, who is responsible for the hundred-year darkened sky and death mists, and if the men they adore can return their love.

Welcome to the dangerous Wild Lands of Pangaea, where silver sahr leads to power, weapons, a goddess, magic, and war.

Acknowledgments

WRITING IS A JOY for me, and I'm lucky to have support, interest, and encouragement from my students, co-workers, friends, relatives, family, and all my readers on this journey. I know it wouldn't be as much fun without them. I especially thank Mom and Dad for their constant support, help, and feedback. Therese, Emma V., Emma O., Kathy, and Dennis all gave valuable advice. Claire gave invaluable feedback on a later draft. Thanks to all of their efforts, I have a much better book.

GEOFFREY SAIGN'S LOVE OF wildlife led him to write *Wyshea Shadows*, Book 1 of the *Divided Dragons* series, and the award-winning fantasy series, *Magical Beasts*. He often experiences the magic of nature and wildlife while hiking and swimming. He has a degree in biology and has assisted in field research on hummingbirds and humpback whales. Geoff loves to sail big boats, hike, and cook—and he infuses all of his writing with his passion for nature. As a swimmer he considers himself fortunate to live in the Land of 10,000 Lakes, Minnesota.

For email updates from Geoffrey Saign go to
www.geoffreysaign.net/magical-beasts

Made in the USA
Las Vegas, NV
20 December 2021